D0341529

HomeSpun

HomeSpun

NILITA VACHANI

A Novel

OTHER PRESS · NEW YORK

Copyright © 2008 Nilita Vachani

First published by Penguin Books India 2005.

"The months have ends the years a knot" by Emily Dickinson reprinted by permission of the publishers and the Trustees of Amherst College from *The Poems of Emily Dickinson*, Thomas H. Johnson, ed., Cambridge, Mass.: The Belknap Press of Harvard University, copyright © 1951, 1955, 1979, 1983 by the President and Fellows of Harvard College.

Excerpts from Malcolm X's speech to the London School of Economics, from *Malcolm X Talks to Young People*, reprinted by permission of Pathfinder Press. Copyright © 1965, 1970, 1991, 2002 by Betty Shabbazz and Pathfinder Press.

"Change of Garb" by J. Reynolds, "The Shirted and the Shirtless" by J.C. Hill, and "Our weapons are different, Mr. Gandhi, but one of us must finally win" from *Gandhi in Cartoons*, compiled by Durga Das, published by Navajivan Publishing House, 1970. Reprinted by permission of Navajivan Trust, Ahmedabad, India.

Production Editor: Yvonne E. Cárdenas
Text design: Jeremy Diamond
This book was set in 10.8 pt Adobe Caslon by Alpha Graphics of Pittsfield, NH.

10 9 8 7 6 5 4 3 2 1

All rights reserved. No part of this publication may be reproduced or transmitted in any form or by any means, electronic or mechanical, including photocopying, recording, or by any information storage and retrieval system, without written permission from Other Press LLC, except in the case of brief quotations in reviews for inclusion in a magazine, newspaper, or broadcast. Printed in the United States of America on acid-free paper. For information write to Other Press LLC, 2 Park Avenue, 24th Floor, New York, NY 10016. Or visit our Web site: www.otherpress.com.

Library of Congress Cataloging-in-Publication Data

Vachani, Nilita.
    HomeSpun / Nilita Vachani.
      p. cm.
    ISBN 978-1-59051-285-2 (acid-free paper) 1. Family life–India–Fiction.
2. India–Fiction. I. Title.
    PR9499.4.V33H66 2008
    823'.92–dc22

                                                    2007035425

Publisher's Note: This is a work of fiction. Names, characters, places, and incidents either are the product of the author's imagination or are used fictitiously, and any resemblance to actual persons, living or dead, events, or locales is entirely coincidental.

EC
MCHANI

In memory of Siddhartha Gautam (1964–1992),
a life that shone brightly.

TO SPEAK THE NAMES OF THE DEAD
IS TO MAKE THEM LIVE
AGAIN AND AGAIN.

—An inscription on the tomb of Tutankhamen

HomeSpun

PROLOGUE

It is confirmed. It is Nanaji's corpse they hold at the morgue. The Colonel breaks the news matter-of-factly. He lacks a bedside manner. The Colonel has seen many corpses in his time and it's all in the day's work for him, even if this one's a relative. Hari's eyes are red with weeping and the moment they return from the morgue, I see his eyes and I know. The Colonel makes his pronouncement. It has a prolonged effect: a wailing sets in that hangs in the air like a shroud. The women beat their breasts. Naneeji moans; the shroud lengthens and tightens. Hari leads Ratna away, screaming, into the kitchen. Bari Nanee, usually unruffled by emotion, closes her eyes. Mummy's fingers clench my shoulder. I feel the sharp edge of a newly manicured nail. Then Arun slips on the floor that Ratna has washed and polished only this morning and sets up a dreadful howling. He drowns everybody out.

Mummy lets go of my arm, runs to him.

I am relieved by the distraction. I wonder if the brat has fallen deliberately. Some atavistic instinct tells him that I am a threat to his mother's utter devotion. He has been trying to wrest her away from the moment they arrived. Mummy's crying is unsettling.

There are wells that have dried up inside us, and the news about Nanaji's death drills unwanted holes. I follow the senseless chatter in my head.

It's best if we don't get into tears, Mum. Tears come easily to me too. I cry in every Rajesh Khanna movie I see and I have seen them all, many times. I cry when he dies, I cry even more when his elephant does. I cry when he cannot marry his love, I cry when she becomes impregnated by the villain. I cry, but my tears only mean, Mum, that I love myself awash with emotion. Not here. Not now. I could easily slip into a role witnessed in a hundred movies and purge myself with crying. But Nanaji is dead. I will not cry.

I will have to skip the new Rajesh Khanna movie this Saturday, I tell myself. It will not be appropriate this soon.

The Colonel takes matters into his own hands as the women seem incapable of action. Naneeji announces that Nanaji's body cannot be brought into the house. Otherwise, she says, his soul will reattach itself to things and never find peace. And so I don't get to see him again. Through a complicated set of maneuvers they ensure that Nanaji remains at the morgue while the arrangements are made for his cremation. He is then transported directly to the cremation grounds. The women of the house stay away. I hanker to go, but it is strictly forbidden. I am to be left with that last image of Nanaji. I need to replace it with something else, I need to consign that too to the flames.

Like Osiris, I seek to rise from the dead.

—⚬⚬—

Nanaji's stories were the strangest. Stories are meant to put you to sleep but his would keep me up for hours. He'd come into my room and sit on the corner of my bed. I'd wait for him to turn off the lamp until only the night light glowed. I'd watch his silhouette, the glint of his glasses, his slow, sad face. Nanaji acted as though the weight of his stories pulled him down. I don't know if he knew these stories or made them up as he went along, but sometimes they made me restless; they kept me up all night.

There once lived a girl who had a story and a song locked up inside her. She was born without a tongue so no one knew of her secret wealth. Though she did not utter a word, she remained a perfectly happy child. The story and the song, however, were frustrated in their captivity. No one could hear them. They were unsure whether they existed at all. Only the girl knew she contained them and that made her happy. One day, she tripped on a stone and fell. The prisoners fell out of her. How did she know that they fell out, I asked Nanaji. She let out a cry, he said, a cry for the very first time. A bard was passing by. He picked up the story and took it away with him on his travels. The song flew into the throat of a bird. The world began to resound with music and literature.

And the girl, I asked. What happened to her? The girl became empty, Nanaji said. She now had a voice but nothing to say.

Nanaji tucked the covers around me and kissed me goodnight. I must have been nine or ten then and I stayed up all night.

Part One

A Marriage Made in Heaven

When Nanaji was shown Naneeji's photograph, he looked at it for a long time. His parents stood fidgeting before him. Accompanying them was his uncle, the bearer of the photograph. Nanaji had said "no" so many times that it was surprising when he looked up and said "yes" just like that. They were married a month later. Nanaji was twenty, Naneeji, seventeen.

According to my grandmother, she was only shown Nanaji's photograph after the marriage had been arranged. Her father had brought out Nanaji's picture and said this was the boy she was to marry. He had chosen him carefully, Babaji said, from over a dozen young men expressly met for that purpose. Babaji prided himself in reading souls like books and Nanaji's soul, he said, had shone out at him like a flashlight.

"What did you think of his picture?" I asked her.

"He was very handsome . . ." Naneeji said, blushing.

"But what if you hadn't liked him?"

"I did."

—⁂—

In my family album I have that very photograph of Naneeji, the one that Nanaji fell for. It has a matte finish; it has yellowed over time. There are brown stains on its edges that could be coffee or blood. Gold sleeves tack it onto a thick black page, the kind they don't make anymore. I, like Nanaji, have stared at the photograph for a long time.

She looks beautiful in it and not without reason. Naneeji was a beautiful woman. I do not think, however, that my grandfather would fall for just a pretty face.

I stare at Naneeji's picture and try to see her as he must have. She is strong, and her jaw, almost square, sits determinedly on her face. There is nothing coy or apologetic about her. Her gaze holds no pretext or falseness; she has settled neither lips nor hair. She is unadorned except for her *bindi* and a string of jasmine flowers that ties back her hair with severity yet softness. Her eyebrows are unplucked, mannish. And her eyes, they do not look at you. Instead, they look upward and outward as if she had been searching for something that day and had found it on the wall of a photographer's studio. Knowing Nanaji as well as I think I do, I believe this is the look he fell for. He must have stared at her and said, here is my life companion, my Aruna, my Kasturba, my Sarojini. Her name is Kaushalya and she will be my bride.

In all the years that I lived with them, I never saw the face in the photograph. Perhaps Naneeji was older then, and life had battered her illusions. Perhaps it was the photograph that bore the false testimony. A moment, fleeting in time, had frozen, crystallizing her fate.

—⟋⟋⟍—

Mummy always maintained that her childhood had been a happy one. Once or twice I tried to tell her that things had been miserable between Nanaji and Naneeji and I hated living with them, but Mummy shut her ears and said that I suffered from an overly vivid imagination. It's not nice, she said, to make up stories that are simply not true.

The skirmishes between my grandparents began in their first month of marriage, the very day, in fact, that they returned newly glowing from a honeymoon in the valley of Kashmir.

It was the summer of 1935. Nanaji returned to his job as head clerk in the Directorate of Public Instruction and while he was away in the office, Naneeji turned their one room habitation upside down. She opened every drawer and file and took stock of Nanaji's possessions. She counted two sets of kurta-pajamas, two shirts, two pairs of pants, a shawl, Gandhi cap, and five pairs of underwear, all manufactured from homespun *khadi*. She rifled through his files and examined every paper to his name. She came to the unfortunate conclusion that she had married an ill-clothed man with no property, no assets, and a total sum of 800 rupees in the Imperial Bank of India. The room was bare except for a bed, a desk, a chair, a kerosene stove, a kettle, two pots, and three spoons.

Naneeji was not surprised by the paucity of these possessions. In her father's view, material objects were encumbrances that cast shadows on the soul's light. Nanaji had scored highly on account of his impoverishment. Naturally, he had refused to entertain the subject of dowry. Which meant, thought Naneeji bitterly, neither had she inherited anything from her own family. Except for the honeymoon, which was Babaji's only gift to the young couple, there was little to look forward to.

Naneeji was a practical woman and she recovered from her disappointment. She appraised the situation and decided there was a lot to be thankful for. Nanaji was a good man, he was endowed with a fine education, and he held a government job. That was more, she told herself, than could be said of most young men of her acquaintance. Naturally ambitious, Naneeji was confident that under her tutelage they would break through the temporary poverty of their circumstances. For the moment though, she would have to make some purchases. She drew up a list of furniture and clothing appropriate for a man headed for a promotion: a chest of drawers, a pair of trousers, and a dinner jacket. Naneeji's jaw set resolutely, her face lifted, and for a second she resembled the girl in the photograph.

The chest of drawers arrived, and Naneeji began unpacking her trunks. Given the scarcity of Nanaji's clothing, there was plenty of room in the drawers to accommodate her things. Yet Nanaji made the mistake of asking my grandmother to jettison her silks.

I imagine how he must have said it, all gentleness and sincerity.

"My dear, you are so beautiful already. What need have you for silk, a symbol of our country's subjugation?"

Naneeji drew herself up to her full height, which was far from considerable. With unwavering firmness she said that she would NOT burn her silks, NO. Nor would she donate them to charities. Nanaji fell silent, disappointed by her attitude.

A little later, he ventured again, "Sericulture is a violent process, deeply destructive of the silkworm." Naneeji wore a look in her eyes that Nanaji did not wish to contend with. "Well, my dear, wear silk if you must. As long as it's *Swadeshi*," he ended lamely.

— ∞ —

This is the way it started between them, the Battle of Textile. Were it not for this singular dispute, my grandparents might, in fact, have gone along quite nicely. Naneeji could have bandaged her marital wounds in soothing silks, Nanaji in cantankerous khadi, and none would have been the worse for it. But when it came to Textile, each interfered infuriatingly with the other. Never again did Nanaji volunteer to ignite Naneeji's silks but he did continue his attack in subtler ways. When she wore a drab cotton saree, he made it a point to praise her beauty. When she dressed for an evening out and simply blazed in her silk and makeup, he never paid her a compliment. While Nanaji's friends ate Naneeji up with their eyes, he seemed not to notice her at all.

Naneeji retaliated by wresting complete control of Nanaji's wardrobe. Disobeying his orders, she bought him not just the trousers and the dinner jacket but a taffeta shirt and waistcoat as well. They could scarcely afford such luxuries and Naneeji was, by all accounts, an extremely tight-fisted woman. Such expenditure on her part can only be viewed as an act of rebellion.

Some twenty-five years later, Nanaji's "English" wardrobe, as it came to be called, still wrapped in tailor's sheaths, with original tags proclaiming it to be the proud handiwork of "Messrs. Tilakram and Sons estd. 1833," was handed down and divided up between my father and my uncle Monty. By then the clothes were quite out of fashion and I never did see Daddy wear them, though out of deference to Naneeji, Mummy preserved them carefully.

I first came to live with Nanaji and Naneeji in 1963 when I started kindergarten in Mount Mary School in Delhi. Daddy was transferred so often that it was decided I should live with my grandparents in order to receive a sound, uninterrupted convent education. Even though I was only five years old, I always chose my own clothes while Nanaji had everything laid out for him: undervest, underpants, shirt, trousers, socks, tie. In those days I thought Nanaji was lazy and Naneeji worked herself to the bone. It took a while before I began to understand the complex inversions of their relationship. The fact that Nanaji displayed no initiative in matters of clothing was a sign of his utter capitulation, I realized, and of Naneeji's decisive victory. It was only with his death, fourteen years later, that Nanaji had the last word and condemned Naneeji to wearing white for the rest of her days. Not khadi, God forbid, for even sorrow wouldn't take my grandmother that far, but white chiffons and organzas.

The early successes, however, were all hers. One day, while going through Nanaji's pockets, she came across a piece of uneven cloth, one and a half feet by two feet, loosely woven, edges undone. She hemmed up the piece and put it to use in the kitchen.

About a week later, Nanaji was rummaging about in his drawer and inquired whether she had seen that piece of fabric. Naneeji pointed in the direction of a black and stinking object that lay coiled around the kettle. Nanaji fossilized into one of those human statues that tourists stop to stare at in major European cities. No sound, no motion. Imagine then that a passing tourist adroitly flicks the statue's earnings. The statue bursts to life, electrified. Nanaji did just that.

"What have you done?" He stammered and shook.

Naneeji looked baffled. Nanaji's anger subsided. He was a most reasonable man. It was an accident after all, his fault for not telling her.

"Gandhiji made this. Gandhiji wove this himself," Nanaji said, cradling the filthy cloth.

"He'll be pleased to know it's been put to some use."

Nanaji and Naneeji had diametrically opposite opinions on the national contributions of Mahatma Gandhi. It was not the kind of thing you could say in public, at least in those days, but

Naneeji would not mince her words. Gandhiji was a lunatic, she declared. If he had his way, all India's able-bodied men would be sitting at home spinning yarn. India would become the world's largest exporter of kitchen *jharans*. Naneeji had a decided preference for Jawaharlal Nehru. He was handsome, she said, and had sense in his head. If Jawaharlal chose to dress like a *nanga fakir*, she added, adopting the insulting tones of a cigar-puffing statesman, I cannot say I would mind. She giggled. Naneeji was fearless when it came to expressing her political views to her husband. She never dared voice these sentiments in front of Babaji.

In his diary dated August 14, 1936, Nanaji describes the unfortunate incident in the following words:

Today is a day of sadness and disillusion. I no longer have the cherished cloth woven by Gandhiji, acquired through the tireless efforts of Kishen Chand Dhameja. The fault is entirely mine. I carelessly threw the cloth into my drawer instead of giving it the consideration that such an acquisition warrants. I had intended to hand it down to my children so it may pass from generation to generation, a relic of the Mahatma himself. This was not meant to be. Kaushalya mistook it for a kitchen cloth and it has met a wretched end. To rescue it in its present condition would be to dishonor the Mahatma further. With great sadness I have let it go. It will be disposed of in the compound with the rest of the debris.

The Mahatma's homespun was tossed into the garbage. The ragpicker, who salvaged most things, turned up his nose at the shredded bit of rag. It met its end in a feisty bonfire in the colony dump. Nanaji and Naneeji's marriage survived the incident. They had two daughters born to them and stayed married all their lives.

IN THE BEGINNING

The course of history would have been quite different if the Bombay movie producer B.L. Ahuja hadn't tasted one of Mrs. Mohini Kalra's *pakoras*. Or if all those years later, a young girl by the name of Anu, had. Or indeed, if B.L. Ahuja had suffered severe indigestion after that first bite and had stayed away. Or if Anu had buckled down and said, all right, just this once, Auntie, I'll have one to make you happy. But Anu had refused (politely, of course), saying she did not eat fried foods. And Ahuja had warmed to the fritters like a moth to a flame without burning his insides. And so it all happened as it did. Mohini Kalra's son, Ronu, became a movie star. He never married his true love. Instead, he married a lovely and docile woman who took the bite and asked his mother for the recipe. Great and tragic events spring from the unlikeliest of beginnings.

—ᨆ—

B.L. Ahuja first met Sub-Inspector and Mrs. Kalra at the residence of Shri N.M. Saxena, a member of the Legislative Assembly, whom he had assiduously cultivated on important occasions with large boxes of dried fruits and nuts. It was *Diwali*, and Ahuja turned up with just such a large box, his business card conspicuous in a corner. Mohini Kalra, who happened to be a cousin of the MLA's wife, was there bearing sweets and a platter of thinly crusted delicacies. Mrs. Saxena embraced her cousin warmly, and in a swift exchange, divested her of the pakoras while handing her Ahuja's box of dried fruits and nuts. She did glance briefly at his business card before removing it to the table. Perhaps it was this unceremonial transference of offering that emboldened Ahuja to step forward and rightfully reach for a pakora. He followed this with several rapid samplings. At this point, Mrs. Kalra thanked her cousin and said they had to continue on their way as there were several homes to visit. Ahuja rose to his feet and made his declaration:

"Madam, your pakoras," he said hoarsely, "are the best this side of Rae Bareli, and that is God's honest truth."

He retrieved his business card from the coffee table and handed it to Sub-Inspector Kalra.

"I am Bhagwan Lal Ahuja from Lucknow proper," he said. "Pleased to make your acquaintance."

Sub-Inspector Kalra returned the courtesy. He wrote down his address on a slip of paper and politely invited Ahuja to visit them when he was next in town. "For more pakoras," he said affably. Naturally, he never expected to see the fellow again. But less than two months later, there stood Ahuja on the Sub-Inspector's doorstep, intent on forging that improbable relationship.

Soon Ahuja's visits had become a regular feature. Whenever his business interests brought him to Delhi, he proceeded without demur to the house of delights. Under normal circumstances, and without the incentive of pakoras, Ahuja would have been happy to befriend a sub-inspector. The success of his business ventures depended variously upon the participation of petty government officials. He had, in fact, offered the Sub Inspector a bribe or two through intermediaries but Jagdish Kishore Kalra was the sort of cop who wouldn't smell a bribe if it was clamped on his nose doused in cologne. Reluctantly, Ahuja had dismissed what could have been a most useful partnership. Nevertheless, he continued to suffer the Sub-Inspector's sanctimonious earnestness for the sake of Mrs. Kalra's culinary perfections.

It was in May 1941 during one such unannounced visit that B.L. Ahuja noticed Ronu, the Kalras' four-year-old son. Ahuja sank his bulk into the constabulary's deeply sagging sofa that had received no padding from out-of-line payments. He waited with happy impatience for the goods to arrive. The war had driven essential commodities underground. Wheat, coal, or pulses, if indeed they could be found, were being sold at four times the price. Ahuja had taken no chances. He had come prepared, bearing a sackful of *besan* in his hired *tonga*.

Mrs. Kalra had left for the kitchen, deputing Radhika and Ronu to keep Ahuja company as the Sub-Inspector was still at work.

Radhika yawned and inspected her nails. She had reached the tiresome age of twelve when girls make it their vocation to be unequivocally sullen. Ahuja, in any case, was not the kind of man who could be expected to hold truck with children. He turned his attention to the single copy of the *National Geographic*, dating back to 1936, which rested upon the coffee table. Ahuja knew the magazine well from previous visits. Without further delay, he turned to page 32. Out popped the breasts of a grass-skirted native, lapping at her navel in happy profusion. Ahuja frowned and studied the picture, the anticipation of Mrs. Kalra's wares filling his taste buds.

Ronu, meanwhile, was intent on flying a paper plane around the room. "Vroom vroom," he said in a fatefully loud voice. Ahuja raised his eyes in irritation and remained transfixed. Something in the boy's deportation proved more arresting than the resplendent breasts and Ahuja allowed the magazine to slip from his hands. He stared into what may well have been the longest, unruliest of eyelashes.

"Vroom vroom," chimed Ronu unsuspectingly. "Vroom vroom."

"*Suno, beta*," said B.L. Ahuja finally. "What is your good name?"

"Ronu," said Ronu.

"What do you want to be when you grow up?"

"Fighter pilot," said Ronu. "Vroom. VROOOM! CRAASH!"

Ahuja clicked his tongue. There was little originality in children these days. They were all drawn from the same stamp, the differences between them mere imperfections in the ink. Now when *he* was little and had been asked the same question, he had given the most unusual of replies.

"Cloth merchant," little B.L. is reputed to have said.

And indeed, he had lived up to that promise, winning the franchise to a most lucrative chain of stores that sold Manchester cloth in India. He had amassed a minor fortune in retail until his voracious appetites had led him to more ambitious pursuits, the most recent being movie production.

"Yes, that is passing phase. Every boy wants to be fighter pilot but how many fighter pilots can a country have? India, especially, where the Angrez want *gora* boys to fly their planes . . ."

B.L. Ahuja rarely spoke to children and can be excused for his less-than-age-appropriate tone.

"You have to be practical," Ahuja continued.

"Vroom vroom," said Ronu.

"What about acting?"

The doorbell rang.

"Radhika!" yelled Mrs. Kalra from the kitchen.

"I'm busy," said Radhika, engrossed with her nails. B.L. Ahuja gave her a look of intense dislike but made no effort to hoist himself from the sofa. The doorbell rang again and Mrs. Kalra ran out of the kitchen bearing a ladle. She opened the door, then rushed back to her frying.

"*Namaskar, namaskar*. Ahujaji, *aaeeye, aaeeye*," said the Sub Inspector redundantly, since his visitor was already very much there.

"Welcome! Please do not get up." He waved Ahuja's creaking bulk back into the sofa.

"What brings you to Delhi?"

The Sub-Inspector's chatty conviviality soon subsided. A question such as this always elicited in his guest the most evasive of replies, making Kalra wish he had not asked. Frankly, he was flattered but more than a little dismayed that such a rich and powerful man should seek him out. It had not occurred to the Sub-Inspector or his Mrs. that culinary delights, pure and votive, lay at the heart of B.L. Ahuja's enterprise. Kalra remained in a state of orange alert during these meetings lest his visitor, unbeknownst to him, solicit and procure some compromising favor. He had to admit, however, that Ahuja had behaved in an exemplary fashion so far, keeping his wallet firmly out of sight.

Mohini Kalra entered the drawing room bearing a tray with a deliciously wafting smell. Forgetting her nails for the moment, Radhika jumped up to make room at the coffee table. Ronu's plane crash-landed in excitement. On account of the war shortage, it had been several months since pakoras had been served at the Kalra residence and the family appeared to share Ahuja's weakness. The Sub-Inspector looked rightfully stupefied and Mrs. Kalra said by way of explanation, "*Aap dekhiye na.* He is coming to our house after so many months and that too with hands full. Five maunds of besan he is bringing! As if we could not afford to make four, five pakoras for our Ahujaji . . ."

She was being altogether untruthful since there hadn't been a vestige of chickpea flour in the house prior to their guest's arrival.

"*Bhai saab*, thank you for thinking about us, but there is no need . . . ," began the Sub-Inspector, hit by the uncomfortable realization that a bribe had not only been accepted, it had been cooked, and was rapidly being ingested.

Ahuja, meanwhile, continued to stare at Ronu.

"This is too much, Ahuja saab. We must pay you for the flour," said the Sub-Inspector dully, wondering how he would cough up enough money for five maunds. And then, wouldn't he be playing straight into the hands of the blackmarketeers whose operations he had vowed to bust?

Ahuja sighed with vexation. "Not to worry. I have arranged it from one of the chaps."

Kalra looked stricken.

"*Suniye.* If you don't want to eat, don't eat; that is okay. Let the others enjoy. If nobody wants, that is also okay. I will eat when I come." He reached for another pakora. Mrs. Kalra looked meaningfully at her husband, forbidding further argument.

"Madam, these are delicious," Ahuja said, shaking his head reverentially. Then, he changed the subject. "My latest venture is Hindi fillum. Your boy must play hero's son. It is very good role, first class."

His pronouncement was lost on the Kalras so he ate another pakora and repeated his request. Ronu, who did not know what

SIMMS LIBRARY
ALBUQUERQUE ACADEMY

19

a fillum was, gave Ahuja a sweet and unthinking smile and continued to fly his plane around the room. It now balanced a pakora on each wing.

"I have been observing your boy carefully. He will make very good actor. He is sweet, fair, good-looking, cute. He will be instant hit. I will give him chance."

The dim room had visibly brightened with the knowledge that it accommodated a movie producer. Radhika sat tall and intently fixed her hair.

"But . . ." said Mrs. Kalra. "*Mera matlab hai . . .*"

Ahuja waved aside her buts with a flying pakora.

"There is nothing to acting," he said reassuringly. "Anyone can act. You. Me." Radhika smiled winningly at the producer. "Him," continued Ahuja, pointing at Ronu. "The boy has to smile, that is all. He has to look sweet, *bus.* He is sweet, so sweet. In one scene he will cry but not to worry, makeup artist will give glycerin, tears will come. Havaldaar saab, your son has a bright future."

"That is also Ronu," ventured Mrs. Kalra pointing to a calendar on the wall. The year was 1938, and a chubby, chortling baby held a can of Glaxo milk powder between his legs.

"So sweet," assented Ahuja.

"But Ahuja saab . . ." The Sub-Inspector looked alarmed at the turn the conversation was taking. "What about his studies?"

"Studies can continue," Ahuja said airily. "No harm in that. Shoot will take two weeks. He can take sick leave. Madam, you and the boy will come to Bombay, all expense paid, train, hotel-shotel, food, plus axellent remuneration."

Ahuja turned his bulk to face the Sub-Inspector. "*Achha, aap bataaiye, havaldaar saab.* What is your good income? No need to feel shy. Seventy to 80 rupees? Your five-year-old son can earn

100 rupees per fillum, tax free! Now tell me, can you refuse my good awffer? In these days when wheat is selling for 17 rupees a maund?"

He looked meaningfully at the fast-diminishing plate of pakoras.

"And *besan* too," said Mrs. Kalra, falling into the trap.

"There is nothing illegal in this, bhai. You are always worrying about illegalities. This is a job like any other. You do job, you get paid, that is all. There is nothing objectionable about this fillum: it is a good, patriotic Hindi fillum. Your wife will be there throughout to keep check. *Chalo*, matter closed."

"Vroom vroom," Ronu agreed.

A Star Is Born

Eight months passed and there was no sign of B.L. Ahuja. Sub-Inspector and Mrs. Kalra decided that the "awffer" was nothing more than a passing whim. Then the following telegram arrived.

MASTER BUNTY REQUIRED IN BOMBAY TENTH INSTANT
STOP REPLY WITH RAIL DETAILS STOP PASSAGE AND
EXPENSE PAID FOR BUNTY AND MOTHER ONLY STOP
CARRY RECEIPTS STOP KANDEKAR PA

Bedlam ensued in the otherwise torpid household. Radhika pointed out, unnecessarily shrilly, that there was no person by the name of Master Bunty living in their midst, and neither did they know a Kandekar Pa. Hence the telegram was obviously misdirected. Sub Inspector and Mrs. Kalra pooh-poohed the suggestion. B.L. Ahuja was a most important man. Could he be expected to remember a child's name? Could he be expected to draft telegrams personally? Naturally, he had entrusted the task to an underling.

Mohini Kalra took Ronu shopping. She bought him his first pair of long pants and bush shirt and shiny black patent leather shoes. She took him to a beauty parlor and had his hair cut in the latest style. "Totally idiotic," was his sister's verdict when she saw him. Radhika, they had decided, would stay with the Sub-Inspector's sister while Mrs. Kalra accompanied Ronu to Bombay. Radhika relieved her sullenness with a raging tantrum. Finally the Sub-Inspector gave in and said she could travel with him when he went to Bombay to collect Ronu after the shoot. She had to be content with this less-than-perfect scenario. Mrs. Kalra packed, unpacked, and repacked their suitcase every day until it was time to board the train.

The Sub-Inspector clutched his forehead and sat down to compose a letter to Ronu's school. *"Ranjit has been confined to bed with a case of the measles,"* he wrote. *"Until the three-week quarantine period is over, he cannot attend school. His absence may kindly be excused."*

Never before had the redoubtable Sub-Inspector Jagdish Kishore Kalra been the perpetrator of a lie. Lies, he knew, begat lies. Were he to ask the neighborhood physician for a doctor's certificate, the fellow would be only too happy to comply. There was the matter of the unauthorized wing he was adding to his dispensary. The Sub-Inspector sighed and bowed his head in shame. No, he would have to ask Ahuja to arrange the medical certificate. There was no fear of currying favor at *that* end, he decided. He was allowing his boy to act. That was favor enough.

Ronu and his mother alighted at Victoria Terminus and were instantly lost in the swirling crowd. An imperious young coolie made a grab for their luggage and made off at a rapid pace. "*Roko!*" screamed Mrs. Kalra charging after him, dragging Ronu off his feet. She tried to keep her eyes peeled on their bobbing fortunes but it was impossible in the push and shove of the crowd. Soon they had lost all sight of the man.

She burst into tears. "Police!" she screamed, "Help!"

It was most inconsiderate of her husband not to have accompanied them to Bombay. She had argued furiously against traveling alone for the very first time in her life. The Sub-Inspector had patiently explained that there was no question of getting leave at such a time what with all the civil disobedience and the anti-war protests and arrests. Either you go alone, he said, or Ronu does not take up the awffer.

Mrs. Kalra's tears were being observed with some interest by a young man carrying a placard. He alternated his curiosity between mother and son, and finding the woman completely consumed with misery, thrust the placard in Ronu's face. "MASTER BUNTY" it said, in thick, black letters. Ronu did not respond, not because he could not read, but because he had rightly concluded that the words had little to do with him. The placard, when she noticed it, had an extraordinary effect on Mrs. Kalra. She clasped the stranger's hand, wrung it excitedly and said, *yes, indeed,* they *were* Master Bunty and would he please call the police and recover their luggage at once? The stranger extricated himself from her grasp and announced that he was Kandekar, Personal Assistant to Producer B.L. Ahuja. His orders were to take them directly to Ahujaji's office. "No point worrying about your luggage," he said. "If it is gone, it is gone. The police can do nothing. These coolies are all thieves and it is well known that the police share in the loot." Mrs. Kalra burst into tears but allowed herself to be led out of the station.

"Mummy, Mummy, look, look, *there!*" said Ronu, grabbing his mother's arm. Resting against a grand arch of the station was their suitcase and bedding roll. Their coolie sat astride the bedding, smoking a *beedi*. He spat out a spool of phlegm and castigated them loudly for taking up his whole day. Kandekar instructed him to carry the luggage to the parking lot.

"Madam, why did you bring bedding? Didn't you receive telegram? Full hotel accommodation is provided. No need to worry about your luggage as I said. Bombay is safe, civilized city, not like your Dilli."

The coolie loaded a white Humber trussed up with curtains. Kandekar handed him a coin and after a round of heated haggling, parted with another which the coolie accepted with sublime disinterest, his attention now diverted by the arrival of a rickshaw. Ignoring the protests of its passengers, he lifted their heavy trunk onto his head and charged into the station, chased by a frantic head of household.

"Poor man," said Kandekar kindly, "has to make a living. Very difficult in Bombay these days."

The Humber whisked them to B.L. Ahuja's office.

At the sight of Mrs. Kalra's matronly figure, Ahuja found himself thinking longingly of pakoras. Film production was more work than he had bargained for. It confined him to Bombay where the pakoras were too oily for his taste. It occurred to Ahuja that he was being overly generous in allowing Mrs. Kalra free board and lodging in the city. After all, it would not hurt to allow her to earn her keep. His P.A. could be deputed to make a little arrangement whereby a freshly fried batch of pakoras arrived at his office once a day. "Hahn," said B.L. Ahuja, pleased with the thought. Then he turned to look at the boy.

"Madam," he said despondently. "Why haircut, Madam, why?"

"I thought . . . *mera matlab hai . . .*" began Mrs. Kalra.

"Madam, you will not think, you will ask. Kandekar! Always tell Madam what to do. Such natural, bootiful, curling hair and you cut it off? Now I have to get wig."

Ahuja, in the habit of producers, hated making unnecessary additions to his budget. His tongue hit the roof of his mouth in loud irritation, the unexpected profit from the pakoras disappearing from his consideration.

"Kandekar will take you to your accommodation. He will explain the meal arrangement and tomorrow he will pick Bunty up for rehearsal. We will also sign contract tomorrow."

"*Ji*, his name is not Bunty," said Mrs. Kalra.

"What is it?" said Ahuja, scowling at the boy even though the haircut was hardly his fault.

"Ronu," said Ronu.

"Ronu," repeated B.L. Ahuja. "Master Ronu. Yes, that is fine also, but it is too late." He waved toward the wall.

Ronu and his mother turned to look at a large, grizzly poster that advertised a film called *Soldier*.

THE CRADLE ROCKS
THE MIGHTY ARE UNDONE
AND BLOOD FLOWS
THICKER THAN WATER

Ashok Kumar, dressed in soldier's uniform, waved a rifle in his left hand while his right hand clutched at his abdomen. Blood gushed from his insides and flowed into a river of red.

Kandekar walked to the poster and rapped his knuckles at the bottom right where a pink, red-lipped boy with long, curling hair (who looked nothing at all like Ronu) saluted the giant figure of Ashok Kumar tottering above his head.

AHUJA ENTERPRISES PRESENTS

SOLDIER

STARRING ASHOK KUMAR, SANDHYA, VICTOR ALLEN,

V. BHASKAR, GEOFFREY, JAGMOHAN,

AND INTRODUCING TO THE SILVER SCREEN

MASTER BUNTY

"You are seeing," said B.L. Ahuja, "it is too late."

EPISTLES FROM THE APOSTLE OF PEACE

While a small, dimpled schoolboy took his first unsteady steps toward stardom, Nanaji fell further and further under the Mahatma's spell. He purchased a crude version of the *dhanush takli* and spent half an hour spinning every morning before he left for work. His older daughter, Neena, who was four at the time, liked nothing better than to sit by his side and take a turn at the wheel. Naneeji was, needless to say, considerably irritated by these proceedings.

When I inherited the diary that Nanaji kept in those years, I found that every one of his entries began with a quotation from Mahatma Gandhi. Occasionally, entire essays from *The Harijan* were cut and pasted onto its pages. Naturally, it was only a matter of time before I became a devout Gandhian myself. I would look longingly at pictures of Gandhi's grand-nieces Abha and Manu, and lament the fact that I was not born half a century earlier so that it was on my shoulder that his great hand rested. I valiantly banished nonvegetarianism, lying, and masturbation from my life for longer than I could bear and also took the vow of chastity, which at the time was tolerable enough since I hadn't a boyfriend in sight.

Two letters in Nanaji's diary caught my interest. The first was the text of a letter that Mahatma Gandhi sent to Adolf Hitler encouraging him to renounce his violent ways. It occurred to me then how similar Nanaji and his mentor were. Like my grandfather in his confrontations with my grandmother, Gandhi had ended his letter with a whimper.

> Friends have been urging me to write to you for the sake of humanity. Will you listen to the appeal of one who has deliberately shunned the method of war, not without considerable success? However, if you consider this letter an impertinence, I seek forgiveness.

Nanaji had left sufficient space after the letter as though he had expected Hitler to reply. I imagined the following response from Adolf Hitler to Mohandas Karamchand Gandhi:

Dear Mr. Gandhi,
    I do consider your suggestion an impertinence. You are advised to mind your own business.

Regards,
Adolf Hitler

Had Nanaji been alive I would have engaged him in a vital discussion. Had Gandhi really believed that he could dissuade Hitler with such a letter? Had he believed no such thing but felt compelled to write it anyway? Had Hitler not bothered to reply, or did a letter, such as the one I had envisioned, lie crumpled somewhere in the trash bin of history?

Also in Nanaji's diary, copied in his own hand, was a more

rousing letter by Gandhi addressed to the British press. It was written in July 1940 when France had fallen to the Axis and Britain stood next in line for an invasion. I read the letter several times and went searching for it in *The Complete Works of Mahatma Gandhi* before I convinced myself of its authenticity. It was indeed an unbelievable injunction.

> I appeal to every Briton, wherever he may be to accept the method of nonviolence instead of that of war for the adjustment of relations between nations. Your soldiers are doing the same work of destruction as the Germans. The only difference is that perhaps yours are not as thorough as the Germans.

> I hope you do not wish to enter into such an undignified competition with the Nazis. I venture to present you with a nobler and braver way, worthy of the bravest soldier. I want you to fight Nazism without arms, or, if I am to retain the military terminology, with nonviolent arms.

> You will invite Herr Hitler and Signor Mussolini to take what they want of the countries you call your possessions. Let them take possession of your beautiful island, with your many beautiful buildings. You will give all these but neither your souls nor your minds. If these gentlemen choose to occupy your homes, you will vacate them. If they do not give you free passage out, you will allow yourself, man, woman and child, to be slaughtered.

Nanaji had underlined the following sentence in red. "You will give all these but neither your souls nor your minds." I read the letter several times and it had the extraordinary effect of temporarily shifting the weight of my allegiance away from Nanaji, firmly in the direction of Naneeji. My self-appointed pacifism had its bounds, I decided. I couldn't help applauding the British public and my grandmother. It wouldn't do at all to simply stand by and watch them burn up your silks.

On Wednesday nights Naneeji made her odious black-eye beans. There was *bhindi* and *dal* as well so I left the *lobhia* untouched on my plate. I waited for her to harangue me about the importance of eating pulses. She did.

"I've finished my dal. That's protein too."

Every Wednesday night we had the same conversation.

"I don't like to see food wasted."

"Then don't give me lobhia. I don't like it."

"Your mother was never so difficult with food."

"I'm not my mother."

She turned her vexation on Nanaji and spooned my beans onto his plate. Sometimes he protested but usually gave in at the end. For the sake of his peace of mind, he would subject himself to the discourtesy of the discarded black-eye beans.

"Courtesy" and "discourtesy" were words that Nanaji used a lot. One day I asked him what the greatest courtesy was that he remembered receiving. I used the word pointedly but he did not seem to realize that I was laughing at him.

"The first time on a public bus that a young man rose and gave me his seat. . . . It confused me. I thanked him for his gesture and realized I had grown old."

"And the greatest 'discourtesy'?"

For a moment I thought he hadn't heard me. It was a while before he replied.

"I was whipped."

"Whipped?"

"Yes. Once, when I was imprisoned by the British. They flogged me publicly, twenty-four times on the bare buttocks. The wound healed but I have never forgotten the indignity."

It was the only time Nanaji spoke to me about his life as a revolutionary. I was too young then to ask the right questions. Later, looking at his diaries, I deduced that the discourtesy would have occurred between 1941 and 1943 when Nanaji was in and out of prison. He has not written about the incident, however, which led me, illogically, to question its veracity. The thought of anyone flogging my stately grandfather is too absurd to win credence.

SATYAGRAHA

When Mahatma Gandhi launched the individual *satyagraha* movement in October 1940, his basic tenets were three: oppose England's participation in World War II and her use of India's men, money, and arms; break the law peacefully while lodging protest; bear the consequences of disobedience cheerfully. Among the first luminaries selected to offer satyagraha were Vinoba Bhave and Naneeji's favorite, Jawaharlal Nehru. There was also an ordinary villager by the name of Brahma Dutt Sharma. Nanaji, it seems, became completely fired up by the symbolic use of a commoner in India's opposition to England. It convinced him that the time was ripe to throw in his lot with the national struggle. He expressed his conviction to the Delhi Congress Committee. He even wrote to the Mahatma. A veteran Congress leader by the name of Ramsitayya advised my grandfather to desist. "You have a good job," he said. "Stick with it. Nothing will come of this satyagraha nonsense. Because Gandhiji protests, will the British Empire pull out of the war? Besides, do we want them to pull out and lose to the Fascists? Do we want an India ruled by the Nazis?"

Nanaji was undeterred. He increased his spinning to one hour a day and maintained a log of every action that could constitute a good deed in his Mahatma's dictum. All of a sudden, his diary is full of self-congratulatory notations:

Feb 12: Harijan boy claims unfair practice in school selection board. I call for an inquiry.

Feb 21: I spend an additional half-hour spinning in the afternoon bringing the day's spinning to an hour and a half.

Feb 24: I serve dal and roti in the samiti's feed-the-poor drive.

Feb 26: Man tries to alight bus, slips and falls. I get off at the next stop and walk back to him. I offer all possible assistance. He assures me that hospitalization is unnecessary. I board the next bus and help him off at his destination. I am an hour late for work and O'Reilly is not pleased.

These entries in Nanaji's diary are unusual and I can only surmise that he compiled the list for outside readership. Perhaps he had hoped that Gandhiji would read this. It was well known that while local congress committees compiled names of volunteers for civil disobedience, it was Gandhi himself who made the final selections, based on the volunteers' records.

One day, Nanaji's dream came true. He writes in huge letters filling an entire page of his diary, the exultant words, **APRIL 16, 1941!** He had received that much-awaited letter: permission for satyagraha with a time, date, and venue, and the required words of the proclamation that he already knew by heart.

By accepting Nanaji as his satyagrahi, Mohandas Karamchand Gandhi dislodged the final screw that held my grandparents' happiness, however tenuous, in place. It was as if he knew what Naneeji had done to his homespun and was determined to pay her back.

—⟋⟍—

Two days before the appointed date, Nanaji tendered his resignation to the home secretary, citing "personal reasons" for his decision to leave the Directorate of Public Instruction. As he was required to do, he dropped off a letter to the district magistrate, intimating the date, time, and place of his planned protest. Then to avoid arrest, he disappeared.

Nanaji was someone who used his diary sparingly, not given to seductive turns of phrase or lengthy reminiscences. Nevertheless, he writes feelingly of his state of mind in those crucial hours:

Here is the moment I have been waiting for. Now that it is upon me, I do not know where to go, what to do with myself.

I think of Babaji but decide not to seek him out. While Babaji will be an inspiration, Kaushalya will certainly come looking for me there. I think of going home to Cawnpore but it does not make sense to undertake the long journey when I have to return in less than 48 hours. Besides, father will not take kindly to my resignation and I cannot tolerate conflict in my present mood.

I decide to take a walk in the great peace of the Lodhi Gardens. I rehearse my anti-war speech amidst the quiet witness of the tombs. I can almost hear the rumble of India's freedom, distant but distinct, like the sound of an approaching storm. I am calm.

I board a bus for Chandni Chowk. I might as well acquaint myself with the crowded marketplace, get some lodgings for the night.

Another two days and I will fulfill my life's purpose.

Surely anticipating arrest, Nanaji would not have carried his notebook with him. He must have written the account several months after the fact, having had the occasion to replay the events again and again in his head. His writing is more dramatic here than anywhere else in his diary.

Whether the day is hot or this is only a consequence of my untold nervousness, it is impossible for me to say. I am sweating profusely. It is market day in Meena Bazaar and the narrow lanes are even more crowded than usual, with people and rickshaws jostling, calling, festive, restless. There are scattered policemen everywhere, and I feel they watch me closely as I stand in my neatly pressed kurta and pajama, clearly the outsider in that din and uproar.

It seems impossible that I should stand there and make my speech in the midst of such upheaval to souls who are deaf to all but the immediacy of the bargain at hand. What can I hope to achieve? I feel overcome with shame and lack of courage.

I remind myself of the unique opportunity that history has afforded me. I remind myself that I have nothing to lose. I am now unemployed, a free citizen of an unfree nation. I think once again of Brahma Dutt Sharma, the illiterate villager, who had the courage to speak out against the power of the Raj. I think of Aruna Asaf Ali: dear, strong Aruna, who only months ago delivered a powerful anti-war speech and courted arrest, a woman accustomed to much luxury, willing to toss it away.

I close my eyes and pray to an unknown god. Then I plunge into the middle of the crowd and begin to shout the words,

"It is wrong to help the British war effort with men and money. The only worthy effort is to resist all wars with nonviolent resistance. We cannot allow a foreign power to dictate the terms of our humanity ... !"

The police surround me. I shout in Hindi,

"Fauj mein bharti hona haraam hai."

Someone clamps a hand around my mouth. I am handcuffed and led

away. A brave voice shouts after me, "Police ki naukri haraam hai!"

I struggle and shout back,

"The war tax is a sin. To join the Force will be our ruin."

The fact that a voice, a single voice, has picked up my words is

all the encouragement I need. In that moment I am born anew. All

revolutions begin with small steps. Mine began on the 16th of

April, 1941.

The next day, Nanaji was sentenced to one year's simple imprisonment (SI) and a fine of seventy-five rupees for his prejudicial act under Rule 38 of the Defense of India Rules. The British were known to collect in whatever way they could, annexing property and personal effects if cash was not readily available. Gandhi advised his satyagrahis,

> "Punishment courted has to be joyfully suffered.
> Therefore when fines are imposed and the person
> fined is able to pay he must do so willingly. The
> result may naturally be that such a person will be
> fined again and again. If he persists in his resis-
> tance he may have no property left. As a matter
> of fact it is the essence of Civil Disobedience that
> the resistor becomes indifferent to whether the
> authorities take away all his property or not . . ."

Fortunately for my grandmother, there were sufficient savings in the bank account to cover the seventy-five-rupee fine. I cannot see her taking kindly to Gandhi's suggestion and parting with her chest of drawers and other personal effects. I put myself squarely in her shoes. Imagine that you have two daughters, aged four and two, and one day your husband does not return from work. You wait out the night, collect your girls, and board a bus for the Secretariat. You inquire patiently after your husband on every floor of the Directorate of Public Instruction but nobody has seen him for two days. You are directed to his superiors and even though you are a proud woman, you spend half the day on a hard bench with an exploding infant wrapped around your neck. The Section Officer finally concedes the time to see you. He looks at you with pity and some distaste, as by now your neatly groomed hair and face are speckled with the angry emissions of children.

"Mrs. May-tah, aren't you aware? Your husband has tendered his resignation. It reached my desk, I would say, at noon yesterday. We were surprised and rather disappointed, I might add. He was a dedicated worker, good prospects. Now why do you think he would do something like that, hmm?"

O'Reilly looked inquiringly at Naneeji. His stare seemed to suggest that in fact he was not at all surprised, that the native, even the more educated among him, is at heart an incomprehensible beast.

"I am afraid, Mrs. May-tah, I know nothing about your husband's whereabouts. You are advised to direct your inquiry to the police station. If there is any salary owed to him, it will be mailed to your address at the end of the month. As for Mr. May-tah's pension and benefits, these, as you understand, are forfeit."

I suspect that if I were wearing Naneeji's slippers that afternoon, I would not have been a woman in love.

April 1941 marked Naneeji's descent into a vicious embitterment. Aruna, Kasturba, or Sarojini, she was not, had never deigned to be, and no songs are sung of the unwilling wives of freedom fighters. All the freedom that Naneeji had ever wanted was the one afforded by the well-padded bank passbook, and it was the one that had been denied to her by the lofty men in her life—Nanaji, and Babaji before him.

At the end of the month, Naneeji did receive her husband's remaining salary. Along with the check was a letter stating herewith that the said property was in the ownership of the government of India, and by reason perforce that the present occupant was no longer in the service of the government of India, he was being informed forthwith to expeditiously vacate said property within two weeks of the receipt of the letter and no later than three weeks from the date of its issue, the signatory remaining truly and in service, et cetera.

The letter had arrived so late that Naneeji had no time to indulge in a justified state of shock. Wiping back angry tears, she packed up her silks and her daughters and returned to live in her father's house. She hired a tonga and the services of a gloating younger brother who had never much cared for her superior attitude. They spent the day ferrying forth the bed, chairs, stool, chest of drawers, stove, pots, pans, and now considerable spoons. In deliberate rage she left behind Nanaji's khadi wardrobe and dashed his spinning wheel to the ground.

Nanaji, unaware of my grandmother's mood, wrote her long and loving letters from prison, letters that were confiscated and handed to him at the end of his period of detention, neatly tied in government laces.

My grandmother never bothered to read those letters. Though each of the envelopes was torn open (presumably by the censor's hand), the entire package was held intact with a government seal. I was the first to crack open that seal and read the words that were meant for another's eyes. At the top right corner, Nanaji had written in his closed, neat handwriting,

Delhi District Jail, April 21, 1941

My dear wife,

Here is my confession. I performed individual satyagraha on the morning of the 16th instant, and am now imprisoned for shouting aloud six sentences that the Government does not want to hear.

(The next two sentences, presumably the words he had shouted, had been crossed out by the censor.)

I confess that I have dreamed of this for several months and have worked actively toward it. Two weeks prior to my satyagraha, I knew my dream was to be realized but I kept the information to myself.

Why did I not tell you, my wife, who shares my fate and my fortune? Believe me when I say that it was both bravery and cowardice on my part. I wanted to save you the anguish as long as I could. At the same time I was afraid that if I informed you of my intent, you would force me to change my mind.

I know you are deeply upset and angry with me. By now you know that I have lost my job. Dearest, you feel betrayed by my treachery. Forgive me for leaving you without word. As God is my witness, I have tried time and time again to impress upon you the importance of Gandhiji's call, to . . .

(the next few lines were blacked out)

. . . you never had ears for me. I had wanted to take you into confidence, share my doubts and my resolve. Remember the time two months ago, when Mrs. Asaf Ali shouted anti-war slogans and courted arrest? I told you then that I too had signed the satyagraha pledge. I tried to talk to you, to share with you the pain and responsibility of my position, to discuss with you the decisions with which I could not possibly agree, but you were unwilling to entertain my concerns, unwilling to grant me that courtesy.

Dearest, sometimes it is easier to be heard from a distance when we cannot speak in each other's presence. The world is at war and I cannot sit at my desk and watch India burn to pieces

The rest of the letter was censored.

THE MARK OF A SOLDIER

The tedium was beyond anything Ronu had encountered in school. He was expected to sit around for hours doing absolutely nothing. Then all of a sudden, they'd get into a tearing hurry and whisk him around like an eggbeater. By turn he would have to look demure, determined, desolate, destroyed, and all without reason. When the shift was over, Kandekar, who never spoke unless it was to give orders, dropped him off at the guesthouse, where he slept for twelve grateful hours. The next day brought more of the same. Every day he patiently inquired when his rest day was, when could they go to Chowpatty beach and run around and eat *bhel puri?* When could they return to Delhi? He would work hard, he promised, do all his homework, he would never complain again. Mummy said coaxingly, *bus hafte ki to baat hai,* one more week and we'll be home soon, promise. It will be your rest day soon, we will go to Chowpatty beach and eat bhel puri and ice cream, I will buy you a balloon, promise.

The war had produced acute shortages in all things, including cinematographic film. Despite being a first-time producer, B.L. Ahuja had managed to lay his hands on a fair quota. I will make a fillum, he had declared, that will rally the Indian masses, the intelligentsia, the landowners, the peasants, even the Congress, to the Empire's cause. With such promise, how could he be refused? Given that Ahuja's family wealth was firmly built on the sale of Manchester cloth in India, it had not been difficult to convince the Government of the essential concurrence of their interests.

Indeed, for the most part, the British are a kindly lot in *Soldier*. There is David Bloom, who treats natives with fairness and equality. There is David's son, Allen, who develops a strong friendship with Suresh, the carpenter's son. Allen is so thoroughly liberal that he falls in love with Suresh's beautiful fiancée, Rajni. With staunch magnanimity, Allen does not allow his emotions to stand in the way of his friend's happiness, and instead, manages his sorrow by downing double pegs at a rapid pace.

After a gap of a few years in which Allen receives military training in England and Suresh in India, the friends are united on the war front in Egypt. Suresh is a corporal, Allen, a commanding officer. In a dangerous encounter with a troop of evil-looking Nazis, Suresh intercepts an important message revealing that Allen's platoon is in serious danger. Throwing caution to the winds, Suresh sprints across a hundred yards of open fire to convey the message to Allen. He is mortally wounded and dies in Allen's arms, but not before the enemy's intended strategy has been exposed. With his dying breath, Suresh begs Allen to take care of his wife and son, which Allen is happy to do for more than one reason.

On his return to India, Allen recounts his friend's act of heroism, for which Suresh is posthumously awarded the Victoria Cross. After a suitable passage of time, Allen wins the trust of Rajni and her son, Raju (played by Master Bunty), offers his hand in marriage, and is rewarded by the widow's acceptance. At the end of the film, Master Bunty dons his father's cap and pledges undying loyalty to father and stepfather, to India and England.

This was all very well for the time it was written, but various production delays had pushed the shoot well into 1942. In the intervening months, the mood of the nation had swung from high to a dangerous low. Japan had conquered Burma and was moving steadily toward Assam. The Crown had exposed herself, stockpiling food for her soldiers while scorching the earth in the northeast, depriving not only the Japanese army of food but the country's inhabitants as well. In 1941 England stood poised for victory in North Africa but by 1942 these successes had been reversed. The Cripps Mission that promised imminent freedom for India failed to deliver. Anti-British feelings raged at an all-time high. Soldier Suresh, it would seem, was tossing away his life for all the wrong reasons.

Ahuja surveyed the changing national scene with dismay. There were only a few scenes left to shoot, less than 800 feet from his allotted quota of 11,000. He decided to change the film's ending. In the hostile climate of the day, it would not go down very well for a war widow to marry the Angrez officer on whose account her husband had lost his life. He summoned the screenwriter, an unctuous fellow, whose only professional qualification was a recently completed secretarial course from the Young Men's Christian Association. His greater qualification, it would appear, was his blood relationship with producer Ahuja. When Ahuja landed the film, his sister, who was constantly strapped for cash, had stepped in and procured employment for her son.

Mohandas Scriptwriter ran a nervous pencil through his slick, oily hair. Uncle Ahuja laid out the changes for the end:

"Allen returns fresh from battle. He relates to Rajniji details of Suresh's martyrdom. He falls at her feet and says he is in love with her, at last they are free to marry . . ."

"But sir, uncle," protested Mohandas. As is often the case with minions, he had developed an opinion, and felt compelled by the responsibility of his position to exercise it. Thus far, Ahuja had dictated all details of plot, action, and dialogue, and it had been left to the scriptwriter-nephew to take it all down in shorthand and type up the foolscap sheets afterwards, exactly as he had been trained to do. Nevertheless, the fellow was beginning to think he had talent. Screenwriting, he had decided, was his natural vocation.

"But uncle, sir," Mohandas continued, "that cannot be."

B.L. Ahuja, who was not in the habit of hearing his nephew speak, did not hear him speak.

"Rajniji is horrified. Proudly she refuses . . ."

"But sir, uncle, Allen is a decent man, sir. To behave like that would make him er . . . lecherous and opportunistic . . ."

"Exactly," said B.L. Ahuja. "You are getting the point."

The actor, Victor Allen, who played Allen, was outraged.

"It makes no sense," he said. "Allen has always behaved in the most upright manner with this family. This sudden blubbering at her feet is a betrayal of his friendship with Suresh. Besides, it is completely out of character." Schooled in the tradition of Stanislavski and method acting, Victor Allen seethed in rightful indignation. "You will lose your audience. They will not believe in the film."

"Love has made the man mad," said B.L. Ahuja firmly.

As he explained to Kandekar in private, Allen was a two-bit stage actor, Anglo-Indian at that. What he thought was of no consequence.

The director, Vinayak Rao, did not protest. He had signed a contract that he could be hanged, drawn, and quartered if he did not go along with the producer's wishes in their entirety. What did he care about this stupid film anyway? Let her marry him or not marry him; it made no difference. Vinayak Rao considered himself the natural heir of German expressionism. He felt Murnau's passion surging inside him, deep, dark, diabolical. He was writing his own screenplay on the side, a reworking of Marlowe's *Faust* as a contemporary tale of forbidden love. Real cinema it was too, unlike this rubbish, but his salary on this film was crucial to furthering his dream.

"Fine," said Vinayak Rao stoically when he encountered the new pages. "In fact, why doesn't Master Bunty turn his back on Uncle Allen and salute the portrait of his dead father? We'll hang a map of India next to Ashokji's face so it will seem like he is turning away from England and saluting Free India."

"Axellent!" said B.L. Ahuja. "You are not number one duffer after all."

—m—

Ahuja rushed through the editing. Despite the new ending there was plenty there to keep the British happy and to procure him a censor's certificate. In all fairness, the censor hadn't much liked the idea of a Britisher marrying one of the natives in the first place. Ahuja had argued that it happened all the time, and besides, in this instance was perfectly laudable, a discharge of responsibility, a reinstitution of England as protector and potentate. Now he would simply argue the opposite. The Widow Remarriage Act is all very well, he would say, but Indian customs remained discouraging of remarriage. How could a chaste Hindu housewife marry her husband's best friend and so soon after his demise? Besides, he had to agree, marriages between rulers and subjects led to nothing but a breed of confused, cream-colored children. Mounting public pressure had forced his hand, he would say. As for Allen's unfortunate character transformation, the fellow had returned from the front after all, having witnessed many a horror, including seeing his best friend die in his arms. He could hardly be expected to behave rationally.

"It is like this with all great works of art," explained B.L. Ahuja to P.A. Kandekar afterwards. "You see what you want to see. If you are nationalistic, you see a revolutionary fillum. If you are the gorement, you see a patriotic fillum. The artist provides the space, the audience fills it up."

Soldier may well have been one of those passable films that pleases both sides of the fence at once and sinks without a trace. Ronu might well have sidestepped the prophecy of the pakora. But Mohandas Karamchand Gandhi intervened. He forced the mantle of heroism upon them all.

SHOWDOWN

Nanaji was detained in Delhi District Jail for seven months, until a general amnesty secured his release before the end of the year. Naneeji laments that those were the worst years of her life.

"The time that Nanaji was in prison?" I asked.

"No," she said. "The time that he came out."

My grandfather, it seems, was unable to hold a steady job all the way up to Independence. He clung to his party work, his earnings were meager and irregular. Proud to the last, he refused his father-in-law's offer of a roof over their heads and rented a room instead in a *chawl* in Karol Bagh. It was, in fact, half a room. A partition ran across the middle, and the other half was rented out to a family of six.

Many years later, Naneeji maintained that she remembered the man on the other side of the partition even though she had never dared to look him in the face. He was loud and given to drunken outbursts. His wife berated him with a high-pitched drill of a voice that he alternately ignored and greeted with howls. I figured that they represented the opposite spectrum of Gandhiji's creed of nonviolence. Everything terrible, that cannot be named, that cannot be imagined, happened next door, said Naneeji. Nanaji was always out and didn't have to deal with the goings on, but it was she who stayed in with the girls and had to reassure them constantly that all those screams and punches were nothing really, they were nothing, nothing, really.

The toilet was outside in the corridor. It was shared by Nanaji, Naneeji, their two girls, the family of six next door, and another family of five who lived on the floor above. When Naneeji had first inspected these living arrangements, she had refused to move into the chawl. But her father had reproved her mildly, saying that her place was by her husband's side. And where is my husband's place, Naneeji retaliated. In jail with the petty criminals? Babaji grew stern and said that was no way to talk about a freedom fighter. Now that his son-in-law had returned, she was no longer welcome to stay in his house. Well, said Naneeji, I don't have a choice, do I? So she helped Nanaji hire a tonga and they transported their belongings to the chawl. They left behind the bed, the chairs, and the chest of drawers since there was no place in the half-room to accommodate these things. Naneeji also left behind her silks and carried only her handlooms. My grandfather won the Third Battle of Textile. Naneeji now dressed in her worst raggedy cottons, and like Kasturba, cleaned the public toilet once every three days.

"We shall either free India or die in the attempt; we shall not live to see the perpetuation of our slavery . . . let every man and woman live every moment of his or her life hereafter, in the consciousness that he or she eats or lives for achieving freedom and will die, if need be, to attain that goal."

On August 8, 1942, in the vicinity of Gowalia Tank, which was B.L. Ahuja's neighborhood, Mahatma Gandhi made his now-famous proclamation and dealt the producer a near-deathly blow. It landed Ahuja in the hospital with a severe attack of angina.

"Quit India," Gandhi told the British, "now or never. Do or die."

"*Hai Ram*," moaned B.L. Ahuja, as Gandhi would, less than six years later.

I quote from Nanaji's diary:

Finally! It is here. The scent of freedom. Heavy and unmistakable as the Queen of the Night that flowers after dusk, bringing its scent to this most dreadful of slums. I feel India's freedom with every breath I take. There is chaos and fury everywhere and there is no doubt that there will be a terrible flood before the waters recede.

For some time now I have found myself seduced by Jai Prakash's call. I have felt frustrated and helpless with the Mahatma's reticence. At last he gives us consent with his words! The time for spontaneous revolution is here. Rich, poor, city, village: we are united at last in a common voice! No, we do not beg for our freedom, we demand it. "Swaraj is my birthright and I will have it."

In response to Gandhi's unprecedented announcement, the government retaliated by arresting all members of the Congress Working Committee and imprisoning them at unknown locations. The people were left without leadership, with only the mandate that "*every Indian who desires freedom and strives for it, must be his own guide.*" Their own guides they did become, and Gandhi, locked in custody, was unable to restrain the crowds. Rioting broke out all over the country, railway stations were burned, communication links destroyed, police stations picketed. Targets of British administration were decimated everywhere. Almost overnight, nonviolence had become a thing of the past.

One day, some rioters broke into the Karol Bagh *kotwali* and set it on fire. Fortunately, the station was largely unmanned and no one was hurt. Faced with the charred remains of his desk, Sub Inspector Jagdish Kishore Kalra turned his back on nationalism and swore allegiance to his badge. There was not much point in inheriting a country, he decided, that would end up looking like that desk.

—ᐯᐯ—

"*He' Bhagwan*," moaned Ahuja from his hospital bed. "My fillum! I am finished."

"Please be calm, sir," said the nurse, jumping to feel his pulse, but there was little for Ahuja to be calm about. He worried, not about the disruption of infrastructure and services, a signature of the times, which would naturally slow down his edit. He agonized over the fate of the film itself. *Soldier*, all said and done, was pro-British. If he should even attempt a release, the incensed hordes would burn down the theaters and heap financial ruin upon his head. Yet, it was not simply a matter of delaying a release. Ahuja knew there was no going back from that moment in history. In the smug words of the film's director, Vinayak Rao (spoken in confidence to an assistant but overheard by the omnipresent Kandekar P.A.), *Soldier*, not unlike a Sauropod, was headed surely for extinction.

"*He' Bhagwan*," moaned Ahuja, unusually religious this morning. His instincts told him that an action-packed, topical film it should be but topics change and masses are fickle. As for that Mohandas Karamchand, one day he sips tea with the viceroy and writes him a love letter, and the next day . . . Ahuja let out an anguished cry. The nurse pressed the buzzer in desperation.

"Please sir," she entreated. "Please, *please*."

"All the Angrezes are nice gentlemen in my fillum," Ahuja said feelingly.

"Yes, very good sir . . ."

"Not a single villain! And the hero, he is the Angrez's *chaprasi*, his private goat. He gives his *life* for him! So what if he does not give *wife*? Is that revolution, you tell me!"

"No, sir. Yes, sir," said the nurse despondently.

Ahuja started to yank the tubes that confined him to the bed.

"Please sir! I have to give sedative," decided the nurse, taking matters into her own hands as the buzzer went unheard and no doctor came to her rescue.

"That Karamchand! Always after me, I tell you. *Maine uska kya bigarha hai?* Tell me, how have I harmed that man? First he destroys my silk shops. Then he closes down my mills. Now, ruddy fellow is after my fillum!"

The injection worked and Ahuja passed out.

—∞—

With no regular income coming her way, Naneeji was forced to delve into her savings. Finally, one day, these ran dry and she went to her father for help. For all the years since her marriage, Naneeji had kept her woes strictly to herself, blaming no one but her fate and a photograph. Forced to borrow money for the first time in her life, she flew into a rage and screamed at her father for marrying her off to a lazy and impractical man. All men are selfish and self-serving, she said, and you, Babaji, are no exception. If you liked him so much, why didn't you marry him yourself? Her father opened his safe in shocked silence and gave her a wad of notes. Naneeji wept angrily and left saying she would return the money one day if she could. If not, well that was just too bad, wasn't it? Naneeji had hit the nadir of her existence.

Naneeji recounted to me the shame she felt borrowing money. It was only from your father, I reminded her. She shook her head vehemently. Once you leave your father's house, you are on your own, she said. Babaji asked me to leave, don't forget. After that, to come begging to him, ah such wretchedness! You cannot imagine the terrible times through which I have lived. Your grandfather was too proud to borrow, so I had to do it. Otherwise, your mother and your aunt would have starved. You would have never been born.

I looked at Naneeji with grateful eyes.

Now that the lid of her restraint had been lifted, there was no holding her back. Naneeji's lips curled into a permanent sneer, her eyebrows arched into mocking hillocks. Nanaji, on his part, withdrew completely into a secret life. He never told Naneeji where he was going or when he planned to return. Whenever he earned some money, doing whatever it was he did in those days, he handed her the notes and watched the hillocks climb a further notch up her forehead. That is also the way I remember them in the years that we lived together. Naneeji seemed to have grown bigger, to have taken up all the room there was, while Nanaji had slowly become invisible.

One day, Naneeji was headed back from the marketplace when she chanced upon Nanaji deep in conversation with a mullah some two blocks from the chawl. There was no doubting it. It was a maulvi all right with flowing beard and robe, his arm around Nanaji's shoulder. Naneeji felt sick to her stomach.

She had been raised in a staunchly Hindu household where Babaji's only Muslim friend was an erudite (and clean-shaven) member of the Congress. They had never mixed with the other kind. Babaji's professed secularism had received a jolt when the Muslim League launched a nationwide agitation for the partition of India along communal lines. Babaji had secretly thought that it was not such a bad thing after all, an India for the Hindus, but he didn't like the idea of parting with territory. I never did have the opportunity to meet my great-grandfather, Babaji, who appears to have been a most paradoxical man, and was most certainly a misogynist. Naneeji, Auntie Indira, and Mummy all vouch for the fact that he was the most modest of men, openly disdainful of material quest. Yet, his own landholdings were considerable. Mummy has said to me on more than one occasion that Babaji *inherited* his wealth and did not *earn* it, as though that settled the contradiction.

Naneeji imagined the worst that late December afternoon, watching the maulvi wrap his arm around Nanaji. He's lost his mind, he's lost his job, and now he's gone and lost his faith, she lamented. Even her Babaji would have no patience with *that*, she decided. She watched the maulvi pass Nanaji a parcel. Nanaji placed it under his arm and walked briskly in the direction of the chawl. There's no way, she vowed, setting up a rapid pace after him, no way I'm going to keep it in my house, no Quran, none of their inflammatory nonsense, no secret plans to cut up my country. That's where I draw the line.

That night, Nanaji put the girls to bed as usual and prepared to go out. The girls slept on a narrow *charpai*, its feet dipped in tins of water to keep out the cockroaches, which Naneeji insisted came from across the partition. Naneeji stopped him in the doorway. Her eyes glinted dangerously.

"What are you up to with maulvis?" Naneeji always had the habit of multiplying Nanaji's sins.

"Maulvis?" queried Nanaji blankly.

"Maulvis. Mullahs. Mussalmaans. Muezzins. Whatever you want to call them. I saw you this afternoon."

"Oh," said Nanaji unperturbed. "He's not a maulvi."

"Indeed? I suppose he's caste Hindu?" Naneeji said with supreme sarcasm.

"As a matter of fact, yes," said Nanaji. "Shaivite Brahmin to be precise."

Naneeji snorted so loud that little Indira yelped in her sleep.

"You may have lost your mind but I happen to be perfectly sane. Let me tell you one thing. If I find it in this room I will throw it in the gutter, that is all." Naneeji refused to speak the unspeakable word.

The next morning she searched high and low for the package but could not find it anywhere. He must have taken her threat seriously and removed it himself, she decided.

A week passed without incident. One day, Nanaji came home unexpectedly in the middle of the afternoon. "I need your help. For once, don't say no."

"What is it?" said Naneeji suspiciously.

"A friend needs a place for the night. He'll be no bother. We are working together, we'll come in late. He'll sleep in a corner and we'll be out of here before the crack of dawn. You and the girls won't be disturbed."

"Who is this? What work are you doing?"

"His name is Sharma. He's a professor. He may come dressed as a maulvi or a sardar but that's only a disguise."

"Have you gone mad?" Naneeji screamed.

"My god, the man is mad!" she said to the room in general.

The neighbors had also begun their daily communion. The wife called her husband a drunken, no-good bastard. There was a crash, followed by a moan.

"No!" Naneeji shouted. "This is it. I've had enough. Enough! Get out!"

Silence fell. Naneeji's scream seemed to have quieted the neighbors. Nanaji wrapped a shawl around him and stepped out. He did not return that night.

It was very quiet. Naneeji decided that the hairy beast next door had murdered his wife and children. She had run into him once in the landing and had quickly averted her eyes. His smell had been unmistakable though, a stale ugliness that had attached itself to her nostrils and followed her inside.

Early the next morning, Naneeji was awakened by a loud rapping on the door.

"Who is it?"

"Police."

So he *has* done them in, she thought calmly. The police were regular visitors to the Karol Bagh chawl and had on a couple of occasions questioned her about the neighbors. Naneeji had wisely maintained that she saw and heard nothing.

She opened the door, steeling herself for the worst. Two cops stood there. They were not the usual *havaldars* who combed the place at the slightest pretext. These were officers.

"Mehta saab hain?"

Naneeji said her husband was out. The officers exchanged a glance.

"He is not in town?"

Naneeji said she didn't know. The first officer hesitated, then said they would have to come in and search the premises.

"What for?" she said. "They live over there." She pointed to the adjacent room.

"Madam, I am entitled to search premises under Defense of India Rules 56 and 126," said the officer.

Naneeji let them in.

"Check *kar lo* carefully," the first officer told his subsidiary and waited by Naneeji's side, tapping his stick.

The other walked over to the open shelves and shook out her neatly folded clothes. He looked at the sleeping children, then reached for the trunk under the bed. The girls stirred but didn't wake up. He looked through the contents of the trunk. He then moved to the kitchen area and started upturning her pots and pans.

Naneeji half expected a severed hand or foot to turn up somewhere. She still thought that the brute next door had murdered his family and disposed of their remains.

"What is all this about?" she said, realizing that it was *her* room that was being searched and she hadn't seen a warrant.

"Madam, we are suspecting your husband is in cahoots with a known criminal," said the police officer. "A very dangerous man, Madam, by the name of Radhe Shyam. You may know him as Singh. Or Saeed. One day he wears turban. Next day he wears fez. Third day he shaves his head and becomes *sadhu*. Slippery fellow. You know this man, Madam?"

Naneeji shook her head, feeling her knees cave in below her.

"We have information that your husband is working as an accomplice."

"Doing what?" Naneeji asked faintly.

"*Bus*, all this terrorism *ka kaam*. *Goondagiri*, you know. Cutting telegraph lines, telephone lines, burning up godowns, destroying gorement property, derailing trains, looting post-offices . . ."

Naneeji's knees gave way. She sat down on the edge of the charpai and shook her head.

"There is some mistake. My husband . . . he is . . . he was . . . a civil servant."

The police officer nodded sympathetically. "Yes, Madam, so is this Radhe Shyam Sharma. Can you believe? He is university professor!"

"No, you don't understand," said Naneeji. "My husband is not a man of action." Her voice rose sharply. "He cannot even change a light bulb."

"*Sir!*"

They turned at the urgency in the voice. The second officer was dusting off flour from a brown packet. She had seen it before, that packet.

"This item was concealed in the *barni*, sir."

The police officer walked up and divested his junior of his find. He sniffed at it, ripped it open.

"See, Madam, what I am telling you. Gelignite sticks . . . detonator . . . switch . . . fuse . . . gunpowder . . . all chemicals, Madam, to make bomb. Madam, I must wait for your husband. I apologize for the inconvenience. Allow me to introduce myself. I am Sub Inspector Jagdish Kishore Kalra, Karol Bagh kotwali. If I can be of assistance, please do not hesitate."

Sub Inspector Kalra spoke formally and with the utmost politeness. He was beginning to encounter the pleasant prospects of a promotion.

Naneeji just sat there. "Are you going to arrest my husband?"

"I am afraid, Madam, there is no recourse. It is as good as being caught red-handed. Defense of India Rules 26, 129, 54, 124 . . ."

"How long?"

"Difficult to say, Madam, difficult to say. These are bad times."

Naneeji walked up to the trunk and started to pack. She would drop Neena off to school and take Indira directly to Babaji's house. Now with his precious son-in-law back in jail, he would have no choice but to take her back. Chotte could come and get the rest of her stuff during the day. She was done with this godforsaken place. She would write to the viceroy herself, recommending life imprisonment.

Naneeji woke the girls, telling them it was time for school.

"You can stay here and wait for my husband," she told the Sub Inspector. "I have things to do."

As Naneeji struggled down the steps of the chawl with her overfilled trunk, a gentle voice interrupted her: "*Beebiji, aap kahin ja raheen hain?*"

She looked at the miserable little girl from next door. Her hair was matted and filthy, and she had an ugly cut above her left eye. Yet she smiled sweetly as though unaware of her condition. Naneeji felt a sweep of remorse. Maybe she should have done something, all these months.

"Yes, we are leaving," she said stupidly.

She fumbled in her purse for a coin. Then she changed her mind and pulled out a new one-rupee note.

"*Jeeti raho beti*," she said, pushing the money into the girl's hands. "May you live long, may God grant you happiness."

She dragged the trunk down the stairs, followed by Neena and Indira.

THE LONG ARM OF DESTINY

Soldier was released in January 1943. The Kalras were invited to
a star-studded premiere at Novelty Cinema. Mrs. Kalra brimmed
with pride and jewelry. Inspector J.K. Kalra, who had recently
won a promotion for uncovering the workings of an insurgency
cell, wore a brand-new uniform tailored from his son's tax-free
earnings. Radhika wore the look of a hopeful starlet, her autograph book hungry in her hands. They hired a sleek tonga to take
them to the theater, and as they drove down the narrow length
of Tank Road, Inspector Kalra bestowed benedictory greetings
with a raised and kingly hand.

B.L. Ahuja, with his unerring instinct for the cash register,
had surpassed his own expectations this time. *Soldier* was one of
those rare films that won critical acclaim and was a resounding
hit at the box office. The film was praised for its courage and
foresight, for its unparalleled artistry and vision.

How did this transpire? We left B.L. Ahuja languishing upon
a hospital bed, certain that his deadly foe, Mohandas Karamchand
Gandhi, had driven the definitive nail into his coffin.

It was in that semi-drugged and despairing state that the

answer had come to him. A single word had whispered itself in his ear again and again: "Dubbing," "dubbing," "dubbing." Like a drowning man, Ahuja had clutched at this straw and pondered its implications in drug-induced sleep. His film had been shot and edited. It remained to be dubbed, there was no doubt about that. "Dubbing, dubbing, dubbing," he whispered. "Rub-a-Dub-Dub, three men in a . . . *Dub!*" He shot up in bed despite the obvious handicap of his weight and the tubes that restrained him. "*Dubbing! That is the answer!*" He jabbed at the bell that hung by his bed.

The nurse charged in. "Kandekar," he shouted urgently. "I must have Kandekar at once!"

"*Aap ko khane ka hai?*" she said, not understanding.

"Kandekar," said B.L. Ahuja.

"But sir, it is not lunch time yet."

"P.R. Kandekar, my P.A. Summon him at once. He is waiting in waiting room."

"But sir, it is not visitor time yet," began the nurse, but noting that her patient had clambered off his bed, changed her mind and rushed off to seek special permission.

On his arrival, Kandekar was prevailed upon to arrange B.L. Ahuja's immediate discharge, which he did with his customary handing out of large bills. Within three days, Ahuja was back in his office, locked in conference with his oily scriptwriter-nephew and the film's editor.

In less than a week, the film had been rewritten.

—∞—

To quote an influential Marxist critic of the time,

Not only is *Soldier* a most moving and powerful tale of love and heroic sacrifice, its young director, Vinayak Rao, stuns us with a most innovative technique: the use of sound as a tool for the depiction of inner character.

What a character says, and the manner of his acting, are not necessarily synchretic to his thought and emotion. Sometimes, in fact, they are in direct conflict leading to a most subtle tension on the screen.

We are all aware of the dissonance experienced in daily life between word and deed, a necessary condition of our human existence and the very nature of social intercourse. I might, for example, congratulate my boss for his enterprising leadership yet inwardly consider him a buffoon. *Soldier* formally introduces the dialectic of dissonance on the screen. The audience engages emotionally with the characters yet finds itself invited through a complex network of sound layering to question all motives and testaments.

We live in turbulent times, our emotions and intellect constantly wrung in different directions by a multitude of forces. *Soldier* addresses in essential Eisensteinian dialectic the contradictory fabric of our lives. Yet, its message is not abstruse or inaccessible. Rao's filmmaking, for all its sophistication, translates into a disarmingly simple, entertaining, and heartfelt tale, a rousing elixir for the masses. Vive la revolution! Soviet revolutionary cinema has come of age in India!

B.L. Ahuja threw down the review in disgust.

"What is he saying? Good or bad?" he asked Kandekar.

"Very good, sir," said Kandekar, scanning the page. "Except for Vinayak Rao, sir. He gets credit as usual."

B.L. Ahuja snorted. "Stupid critics. What do they know of movie production? Let him get credit, the duffer. As long as review is good, it is okay."

"It is good, sir. Very good."

—⟋⟍—

The dubbing of *Soldier* had been an intricate affair. It had been executed without consulting the film's director, whose contract was terminated the day the rough cut was complete. Needless to say, Vinayak Rao was as stunned as his audience during the film's premiere.

A dusty backdrop of desert studded with camels and a mighty pyramid: Allen, in medium close-up, addresses Suresh in his broken, accented Hindi:

"My friend! How fitting it is to find you by my side as in our childhood years. Here we are united by providence on distant shores. Together we fight a common enemy, to bring deliverance from the forces of cruelty and injustice . . ."

There Allen's fiery monologue fades on his lips. He continues to mouth words but we do not hear them. Suresh's voice rises instead, loud and clear.

"You are my friend. As a brother I have loved you. I will fight. I am a soldier and it is my duty. But the question is: who is the enemy? Is it possible for you and I to have a common enemy? Perhaps one day that will be possible but not until India is set free. One day, India, too, will be delivered from the forces of cruelty and injustice . . ."

Vinayak Rao rose to his feet and applauded along with the stamp and roar of the crowd. Then he checked himself and adopted the more serene and complacent countenance that behooves a film's director.

To quote, again, that influential critic:

How fascinating it is that such ennobling lines would *not* have been spoken full frontal! Here is an example of Director Vinayak Rao's astonishing inversion. Ashok Kumar actually has his back to the camera as he speaks. Why, we might ask. The answer is self-evident. The words are literally taken away from the Britisher's mouth, thus exposing their hollowness. Moreover, it is much more powerful to hear the emotion in Ashok Kumar's throbbing voice and be left to imagine his expression! *Soldier* teaches us an important lesson. Cinema is a rich and interactive experience, a dialogue between the audience and the screen. It is not merely substance, but form that carries the tale.

Suresh, the soldier, does his duty. He decodes the enemy's message and saves the British troops. However, Rao's technique of inversion lays bare the dilemma that is central to his soul, a dilemma, need I add, that is at the heart of our own struggle.

"Very good," Kandekar explained to Ahuja, "the review is simply very good. Except for Vinayak Rao, sir."

"The time has come for me to leave you forever. I have fulfilled my duty. Beloved friend, I leave in your charge my wife and minor son . . . promise me that you will take care of them, promise that you will not forsake me . . ."

Ahuja left Suresh's first line intact. He cut out the dying man's last request that his friend take care of his wife and son. This, he concluded, might prove offensive to the audience. Ahuja had some scraps of footage, unused heads and tails of reels. He ordered his cameraman to provide him with shots of a bird in flight. Directly from Suresh's anguished, blood-stained close-up:

"The time has come for me to leave you forever . . ."

Ahuja cut to a soaring bird and dubbed in the following lines:

"My beloved India, I carry you with me. My spirit will not rest until you are set free. All foreigners must be banished from this land. Promise me that you will leave, you will not forsake me . . ."

He then cut to Allen choking back his tears:

"I promise, I promise."

When Ashok Kumar was called in to dub the new version, he did not mind. Even though his screen time was reduced and several full frontal close-ups thrown out, his character had been greatly magnified by the alteration.

Victor Allen, however, had a fit.

"This doesn't make sense!" Allen said, clutching his head in disbelief. "He *has* to ask me to take care of his family. Suresh makes me *promise*. That's why I propose to his wife . . ."

"No," said B.L. Ahuja implacably.

"Yes," pleaded Victor Allen. "Why else would I propose to her, for God's sake?"

"You propose because you are a selfish, brutish, not to mention, illegitimate son of an Angrez pig," said B.L. Ahuja, counting off words on fat fingers.

—ɯ—

Master Bunty sniffs and puckers in close-up. We hear his mother's voice, off-screen.

"*Kabhi nahin!* Never! You traitor!
Is this the meaning of your friendship?"

There's the sound of spit ricocheting off the floor. Ahuja was particularly proud of this addition for which he had hired the services of a loud, belching dubbing artist and vast quantities of *paan*.

Cut to Mother Rajni standing tall and proud. She resolutely shakes her head.

"Never!"

Master Bunty chirrups on his mother's close-up,

"Mummy, do not worry.
I will take care of you.
I am the future soldier of free India."

Cut to Master Bunty. He wipes his tears and dons his father's cap. He turns his back to the camera. Over his shoulder, the camera zooms in slowly on a map of India. Ahuja had dubbed in a final song.

"Quit my hearth, O traitors.
Pick up your guns
and leave my soil.

The time has come
to break the fetters.
Our tears are spent.
Anger doth boil.
We pledge to live proud and free
with the fruits of our own toil."

Naturally, the applause was ear shattering. Vinayak Rao rose to his feet and clapped and clapped. Then, catching Kandekar's glare, he composed himself and regained his seat with a satisfied air.

—◊◊—

Ronu sat in the first row and watched his first movie. Whether it was the magic of the darkened auditorium, the whir of the projectors, or the captive rustling of the audience, Ronu Kalra was enthralled.

"Mummy, Mummy, why isn't Daddy coming home?
Mummy, why do you cry?"

"How totally idiotic!" whispered sister Radhika who sat next to him.

"Shhhh . . ." said her mother angrily.

"Beta, your father has been martyred . . ."

As Master Bunty released two large and carefully orchestrated teardrops from the forest of his lashes, Ronu Kalra wept in deference to his own image. Mohini Kalra sat at his side, digging her nails into his flesh, and sobbed uncontrollably.

"Wimp," hissed Radhika. But she had no ally, not even in her usually somber dad. Inspector Kalra tapped his stick in confusion and looked unfathomably moved. The image of his son wearing a soldier's cap and swearing allegiance to India left an indelible mark. For the first time, his own loyalties were in a state of tumult.

—⁂—

As they emptied into the lobby of Novelty Cinema, the famous actor Ashok Kumar sauntered up to Ronu and flung a casual arm on his shoulder.

"Well done, son," he said. "Wonderful job. It was nice being your daddy."

He shook hands with Inspector Kalra and bowed to Mrs. Kalra, who nearly fainted with delight. It isn't fair, thought Radhika. I am much smarter than he is, and much better looking, I am, I am.

Ashok Kumar smiled at her, too, and took the autograph book that was an extension of her hand. Ronu made no attempt to introduce Radhika. In all fairness, he was more than a little overwhelmed. After all, he had just seen his screen father suffer a nasty death, yet, here he was again, large as life.

"I'm Ronu's sister . . ." began Radhika.

"Good!" said Ashok Kumar.

"To Ronu's sister," he wrote. "Congratulations!"

"*Radhika*," she said. It was too late. It was there in her autograph book, committed to posterity unless she chose to tear the page out and she knew she never would.

—⁂—

With great astuteness, B.L. Ahuja made one print of the original version without the later dubbing. He used this to get his censor's certificate. Then in a veritable blitzkrieg, he opened the dubbed version simultaneously in as many theaters as he could. It was only a matter of days, he knew, before word got around and the government banned his film. His love affair with the British was over. But then, the days of the British Raj were over too, of that he was certain. Very soon his film would be heralded by a new leadership and would be shown in every theater through the length and breadth of the land. He was prepared to wait.

"My fillum will be the fillum of fillums," he said in an interview. "They are welcome to ban it. It has a long arm. It will reach out to destiny."

—⁓—

And so, Master Bunty, with his prophetic words, condemned himself at the tender age of five. No one would allow him to forget that he was the future soldier of independent India.

Vinayak Rao became India's hottest new director. He lectured internationally on his path-breaking sound innovations in *Soldier* and promised great visual feats in his upcoming *Cabinet of Dr. Kothari*.

Mohandas, Ahuja's oily and anxious scriptwriter-nephew, landed so many jobs that he started backcombing his hair and hired the services of a full-time stenographer with a secretarial degree from the Young Men's Christian Association to whom he dictated his rather salacious plots, actions, and dialogues.

Victor Allen retired from the cinema and returned to the stage. Pecuniary circumstances forced him to migrate to Australia in the '50s where he renounced acting forever and bred Afghan stallions instead.

Ahuja continued making fillums under the banner of Bombay Movietone. He received a lot of fan mail after the banning of *Soldier*. One letter, in particular, captured his interest.

Chi Ahuja, *(the letter went)*
    I am writing to commend you for your brave contribution to our struggle for independence. Unfortunately, I have not been able to see your movie as I am confined to Agra Fort Jail since August 9. Reliable sources tell me that it is very good.
                    With blessings for your endeavour,
                    Yours truly,
                    M. K. Gandhi

Ahuja had the letter framed and hung it in his office directly above his armchair.

THE END OF THE ROAD

Very little is known of Nanaji following the Quit India Movement. It is certain that he and Naneeji parted ways and lived apart for several years. Naneeji, along with Mummy and Auntie Indira, lived in her father's house on Curzon Road. According to Mummy those were the happiest years of her childhood. I'm not surprised. Like Naneeji, it wouldn't have suited Mummy to live in poverty for long.

Naneeji remained tight-lipped about Nanaji's missing years. When I asked her where Nanaji disappeared to, she simply shrugged as if it was of no consequence. Nanaji's diary too falls silent in the latter part of India's struggle for independence. Whatever it was that he was doing then, he did not have the time or the inclination to write.

Dadaji, my paternal grandfather, told me that Nanaji went in and out of jail several times and was finally rewarded for his patriotism when Jawaharlal Nehru's government came to power. "Your Nanaji had continued in the underground movement," he said. "That's why I do not know much about what he was up to. We were on opposite sides of the law, do not forget," he added, chuckling.

It seems that Nanaji and Naneeji's relationship improved only after India won her independence. "Pandit Nehru personally invited your Nanaji to accept a posting in the Ministry of Education. What a great honor for the family! He gave us our house in Diplomatic Enclave. As for Gandhi, did he get a posting? He was busy fasting with some Muslim illiterates. Tell me, who would rule the country if our leaders went and starved themselves to death?"

I hastily changed the subject. "So Nanaji got the job and he came back to fetch you, just like that?"

"Well, Babaji intervened. He reminded Nanaji that the tree of freedom must bear the fruits of responsibility. After independence, your Nanaji grew up. He got over his *khaddar-chappal* craze. We were very happy." I don't think I'm making this up but I can even recall Naneeji saying that theirs was a marriage made in heaven. She said this after Nanaji was dead, of course.

After *Soldier*, Master Bunty bagged the child star role in three upcoming features. Whatever reservations the Kalras may have had about Ronu's movie career, they were now unequivocal in their support. Fame is a heady thing and the money was flush. The sagging sofa in the living room had been disposed of and a new blue divan stood in its place. During World War II black money flooded the film industry and even child stars were loaded.

Inspector Kalra was fêted wherever he went. The Karol Bagh kotwali shed its dreariness every time the Inspector brought his son in on a visit. Business was suspended as the constables crowded around Master Bunty and Kalra looked on with benevolence. Yes, said Ronu, he did know Shehzaadi most intimately and would have no problem procuring an autograph. Yes, he could certainly manage a couple of extra invitations for the SP and his wife. Inspector and Mrs. Kalra had metamorphosed into eminent citizens of their community, their presence highly solicited at social gatherings. Much to Radhika's chagrin, invitations were addressed to "Master Bunty, Inspector and Mrs. Kalra" and sometimes simply to "Master Bunty and Family." "You are part of my family, of course," Ronu said charmingly to his sister. "You can come if you like."

A small smile of smugness etched its way onto Ronu's angelic face. He couldn't help noticing that people pointed him out on the street. They stopped him with scraps of paper and pulled out notebooks and asked him to write down his name for them. Teachers turned a blind eye when he didn't turn in his homework. They acted surprised when he did. When his marks fell, nobody scolded him. Instead, they changed the subject and inquired after his new film. He could stay away from school for weeks on end, traveling to exciting places like Bombay and Madras and Ootacamund and a hero's welcome always awaited him on his return. Nobody asked him for a medical certificate.

Mohini Kalra had begun to welcome these short and exceedingly comfortable stints in hotels and guesthouses around the country. Her erstwhile homesickness for her kitchen had been replaced by a new and gnawing hunger for a game called rummy. Rummy, Mrs. Kalra discovered, was a great leveler, inevitably drawing into its democratic vortex the company of stars and stagehands, vagabonds and vamps. Rummy made the waiting hours disappear in headiness and profit. Mrs. Kalra had become an excellent organizer of ad hoc rummy clubs, setting bets and building leagues. Inspector Kalra's one-income family had quickly escalated to three, as Mrs. Kalra's earnings at the rummy table often exceeded those of her husband and son put together. She now had the help of a full-time servant who washed and swept, fried the pakoras, and with whom Radhika was conveniently deposited whenever she traveled with Ronu on business. Life was sweet, indeed.

The shoots, too, were getting better and better all the time. The filming of *Rider Rani* in particular had been an exhilarating affair. On a dark and moonless night, dreaded dacoits ambush a peaceful hamlet where little Biku (played by Master Bunty) lives with his peasant father and mother. Daku Dhira bursts into their hut brandishing his sword and proceeds to loot and pillage their modest belongings. Biku's mother shrieks and grabs her boy while his faint-hearted father falls to the floor. Daku Dhira fills his coffers with pots and pans and the meager jewelry there is, and not finding much of interest, makes a rapacious grab for Biku's attractive mother. Lo, he beholds little Biku cowering behind her skirts. Like B.L. Ahuja before him, Daku Dhira stops in his tracks, mesmerized by those faultless eyes. Instead of making a grab for the mum, he grabs the boy and drags him out of the hut while she gives valiant chase.

Daku Dhira throws Biku onto his whinnying steed and leaps up behind him. He rides off into the night. He and his wife are childless, having produced one stillborn son after another. Sorrow has turned his *begum* mad and she drifts like Ophelia trilling from tree to tree while he indulges in a life of crime and dissolution. He is at heart a decent fellow, however, and abducting little Biku is really his way of making it up to the Mrs.

A masked figure on horseback bursts forth wielding her sword. Little Biku's savior is none other than Rider Rani herself, the incomparably Fearless Nadia. Ferocious battle ensues, complete with kicks, blows, and brandishments, and a near-decapitated head. Fearless Nadia lifts her sword to swipe off Daku Dhira's uncomely visage. The look of pleading in his eyes makes her hesitate and she lets him go instead with a vicious kick. Holding on desperately to the edge of a precipice, Daku Dhira relates the sad story of his life. Rider Rani is convinced that he is telling the truth and pulls him back to solid and moral ground. She turns out to be an herbalist of sorts and gives him a handful of potent weeds with instructions to feed them to his wife. The now reformed dacoit spends the rest of his days in useful labor, and Ophelia labors too, this time happily, and produces a male child who lives. All ends well, Biku is returned home to his rightful parents, and Rider Rani gallops off to new adventures.

Rider Rani was universally panned by the critics but it brought instant immortality in the hallways of Ramjas Boys School. The older boys, and they were the ones to watch out for, vied with one another in being nice to Ronu. They lured him away with the promise of treats in exchange for lurid behind-the-scenes stories.

Jasoos was a memorable shoot too, though for other reasons. The role of Master Bunty's mother, a Mata Hari–type prostitute/spy was played by none other than Shehzaadi, the nation's favorite vamp. Shehzaadi took a shine to Master Bunty and started taking him up to her green room. She gave him sweets and cold drinks and because he was such an angel didn't mind getting undressed in front of him. Shehzaadi carelessly threw off her shimmering *ghaghra-cholis* and walked about in bra and panties, smoking a cigarette. Master Bunty sat on her bed and watched her and doggedly sucked on the lollipop she had given him. He was rapturously in love and very confused. The vision of Shehzaadi's enormous breasts gave him a not unpleasant buzz in his underpants. He started coming to the sets even on the days he was not needed in the hope that Shehzaadi might spot him and invite him up to the big, green room, empty except for the promise.

Back in school, amply provided with rounds of *alu tikki* and ice-lollies, Ronu blushingly allowed the details to be wrested out of him. He stripped away layer upon layer of Shehzaadi's clothing until he was equally convinced that he'd seen the nation's heartthrob stark naked.

For three undisputed years, Master Bunty reigned child star supreme in Bombay's movies. Then he got bit roles in three films that came and went faster than the newly imported steam locomotives from America. Then nothing. Nothing at all came his way. The post-war slump had crippled the industry. A Master Chintoo had arrived on the scene who was getting the few roles there were. Ronu simply couldn't understand it. His acting had become better and better and he seldom needed more than three takes to deliver a winning performance. Yet his earnings had plummeted, his rate dropping from a whopping 100 rupees to a mere 26 rupees per film. Radhika's interest in her brother's career grew in inverse proportion to his earnings. She insisted on buying a ticket to see one of his later films since she had apparently nodded off for a few seconds during the premiere and missed his appearance entirely.

Inspector Kalra decided that it was time to pay B.L. Ahuja a visit. After the controversial success of *Soldier*, Ahuja had taken up permanent abode in Bombay. His attack of angina had forced unhappy changes upon his diet and his visits to Delhi no longer included the Kalra residence since fried foods were strictly forbidden. Ahuja's producer's license had been revoked by the British, but the Inspector rightly suspected that lurking behind the new producer, P.R. Kandekar at Bombay Movietone, there might well be an Ahuja.

None of Kalra's letters directed to Bombay Movietone were credited with a reply. Finally he wrote in the name of Master

Bunty and was granted an appointment. This in itself did not augur well for the Inspector's mood.

Ronu and his father arrived in Bombay without the convenience of a paid passage or hotel. They headed for the studio, where there appeared to be a strike in progress, red flags flying aplenty, and workers who shouted in unison, *"No daam, no kaam. Kandekar, Ahuja hai haraam!"*

Satisfied that he was in the right place, Inspector Kalra sent in Ronu's business card. "MASTER BUNTY," it said, *"Five Star Child Star"* and it immediately secured their admission to Ahuja's plush, air-conditioned office that seemed impervious to the threats outside. Posters from *Soldier* and Kandekar's blockbuster *Inaam* decorated the walls. *Inaam* did have a child star, Inspector Kalra noted with displeasure, but it was Master Chintoo who had nabbed the part.

B.L. Ahuja sat at the head of a large desk that resembled a racy red Cadillac. P.R. Kandekar rose to greet them from the sofa by his side. Apart from the goatee beard that he now sported, he looked more or less the same. Ahuja did not look up. His fat fingers were busy writing checks, presumably to quiet the infuriated mob outside.

"Namaskar ji. Long time, no see," began Inspector Kalra affably.

B.L. Ahuja looked up and appeared not to recognize them. He jabbed his fountain pen in their direction and looked inquiringly at Kandekar.

"Master Bunty, sir, and father," replied Kandekar.

"Yes," said Ahuja. "Please have seat." He waved them to the visitor's couch. "Kandekar, tea."

Kandekar rose, crossed over to Ahuja's desk and rang a bell.

"*Teen chai, ek* cold drink," he ordered the peon and returned to the sofa.

"*Acha, pharmaiye?*" said B.L. Ahuja, still writing checks. "What can I do for you?"

Inspector Kalra smarted. How many times had this man sat on his sofa and eaten his pakoras? He decided to remain unruffled despite the provocation.

"Ahuja saab, you got my son off to a flying start. *Soldier, Inquilab, Rider Rani, Jasoos.* But of late, his career is flagging. I should not bother you; after all you are no longer making films. It is these new producers . . ."

"What you mean I am not making fillums . . . ?" said Ahuja, looking up at last. "I have made four fillums after *Soldier,* two more blockbusters, *Chandni* and *Inaam.* What you mean I am not making fillums?" said Ahuja, pointing to the numerous posters that surrounded his Cadillac.

"I mean . . ." began Kalra looking meaningfully at Kandekar, who sat with eyes cast modestly upon the red carpet.

"Anyway, *mera matlab hai* . . . Ranjit . . . er . . . Master Bunty is not getting any roles. In *Inaam* there was a child star role . . ."

"Look at the boy. Take a look," invited Ahuja.

They all turned to look: Inspector Kalra, Ahuja, Kandekar. Ronu squirmed to get a better look at himself.

"He has grown," said Ahuja accusingly.

The fact was indisputable. Ronu had grown. He was ten years old now, tall and thin. His chubby, baby look was gone, replaced by a new and awkward angularity. His two front teeth protruded and the effect was hardly winsome.

"Child stars," said B.L. Ahuja in a placatory voice, "are between ages four and eight. He is over age and too tall."

Ronu squeezed himself further into the red settee in an effort to disappear.

"But Ahuja saab," began Inspector Kalra, "the five-year-olds have to become ten- and twelve-year-olds, no?"

"No," said Ahuja emphatically. "Not in fillums. The ladies have to cry. If the ladies do not cry, the fillum is a flop."

"But they do cry," said Ronu, thinking of his mummy weeping amply into her bosom in every one of his films.

Ahuja shook his head. "Look what happened in *Jasoos*." Ronu did not know what had happened in *Jasoos*.

"Trust me, I am not retiring you. Take a holiday. Concentrate on your studies. Get your teeth fixed. Play sports. Keep body in good shape. When you are eighteen or nineteen, we will stage comeback: 'MASTER BUNTY RETURNS TO SILVER SCREEN.' You will play Hero. We will use your good name: 'RAKESH'!"

"Ranjit," said Ronu.

The peon appeared, bringing the teas and cold drink.

"Ahuja saab, how can there be no role for a ten-year-old? That is not a very realistic portraiture of our society . . ."

But Ahuja was already on his feet. "Please, I have other appointment. This union, you know, always creating trouble."

He shook Inspector Kalra's hand. "And how is the Mrs?" he queried. "Very good," he added, without waiting for a reply. "Oho. You did not take tea. Never mind, next time."

Kandekar escorted them to the door. He gave Ronu a regretful smile and patted him on the shoulder.

They took the thirty-six-hour journey back to Delhi and Inspector Kalra sat scowling at Ronu the entire time. As soon as they reached home, he assembled the family into the living room and announced that Ronu's film career was over. "There is no need for any discussion of the matter," he said. Mrs. Kalra looked at Ronu, stricken.

"It's *you* who gives me Waterbury's Compound every single day," said Ronu choking back his tears, "and now they think I'm too big . . . !"

Inspector Kalra addressed the matter with finality. "Enough is enough. No more fillum shillum. No more *haraamzaada* tinsel *bakwaas*. Ranjit will study hard. He will join central service or armed force. Service to nation is service to God. Not this nonsense, *rona-dhona*, *jadu-tona*, *bevkoof-hona*, rubbish type of work. Good service, steady pay, rent allowance, medical benefit, rail pass, pension plan, that is proper job. He will bring honor to the family, honor to the nation." It was a long and impassioned speech.

"Go to your room," said Inspector Kalra. "And take that with you," he said, pointing an accusing finger at the coffee table, which housed for the prospective visitor, Ronu's photo album of movie memorabilia. "Get rid of it," he ordered as Mrs. Kalra hurried to rescue the offending article.

Ronu walked past Radhika's hateful I-Knew-Itness and into the bedroom. He slammed the door shut, threw himself down on the bed, and cried and cried. It was a speedy entry into adulthood.

"Long years ago we made a tryst with destiny and now the time comes to redeem our pledge, not wholly or in full measure but very substantially. At the stroke of the midnight hour, when the world sleeps, India will awake to life and freedom. . . ."

There is a photograph of Nanaji and Naneeji wearing garlands, vermilion *tikas* on their foreheads, and the largest of smiles. They stand with Babaji and his close Congress associates. Nanaji has been appointed undersecretary in the Ministry of Education and his perambulatory days are over. Naneeji has at last forgiven him for being a freedom fighter. She laments the fact that the Mountbattens are leaving the country forever but India's dashing new prime minister is recompense indeed.

One of Lord Mountbatten's last deeds is to lift the ban on *Soldier*, which runs to packed houses all over the country, keeping Ahuja's cash registers loud and ringing, and bringing renewed fame to all those associated with the film. Ronu is actually offered a few roles but Inspector Kalra turns them down. He is not one to forget a slight.

"If you want to serve the new India," he tells his son, "you will do it with your blood, not with Heinz tomato sauce."

TUTANKHAMEN

I make my way to the Colonel, who is examining the newspaper through a screen of cigar smoke. The Colonel has put on a lot of weight and uncharitably I tell him so.

"It's the fault of your mother's excellent cooking, my dear," he says, unperturbed. "You could do with some weight yourself. Why don't you come and spend some time with us this summer? Kaushani is splendid in the summertime."

He puffs on his cigar and takes me in, thinking, no doubt, how inappropriately I am dressed in a red jumper. It has been three weeks since they fished Nanaji's corpse out of the river but they continue to wear white in the house: Mummy, Naneeji, Bari Nanee, Ratna, Hari, the Colonel, even the brat is dressed in an all-white kurta-pajama. I have chosen flaming red. My ghosts are mine alone, I decide. Wearing white won't make me innocent.

"Thank you. I shall like that very much," I say, and smile levelly at him. We understand each other perfectly. He has extended the invitation with civility, and civilly he has been thanked. We both know that I have no intention of visiting Kaushani now or ever. Rajesh Khanna and Saira Banu have made way for Scarlett O'Hara this week and she inhabits me while I read *Gone with the Wind*. Scarlett is proud and poised and terribly selfish. I'm glad to have her inside me today.

I nod carelessly to the Colonel and move to the window to look upon the familiar garden, the dense mango tree, the riotous patch of dahlia. Naneeji has recovered sufficiently from her grief to begin with the inventory. She instructs Mummy to start look-ing around, list all the pieces that she would like to take back with her. Where I go now, Naneeji says dramatically, I will have no need for things. Bari Nanee, bless her soul, has fallen asleep, just sitting there on the sofa. Ratna comes to clear away the tea things; her eyes look red and haunted like she never stops crying. I stare curiously at her but she does not look up. I wonder what she thinks about my wearing red.

"Maybe we should wait till Indira gets here?" Mummy says hesitantly.

"Can I start with Nanaji's books?" I ask, and there is imme-diate admonishment in Mummy's eyes.

"He promised them to me, his books, papers, everything in the study."

"Yes, dear," says Mummy. "But let's wait, shall we? Once Auntie gets here, we can do everything together."

Auntie Indira has a way of slamming down on her accelera-tor whenever she suspects somebody is about to overtake her. That person is usually Mummy. Mummy knows this and keeps a safe distance. Naneeji knows it too but cannot help herself. Mummy has always been her favorite and she wants her to inherit the contents of the grand *almirah*, the one with the porcelain cups and saucers and cut glass pieces that Nanaji and Naneeji bought on their trip to China and never used.

"What do you want to take, dear?" Naneeji asks Mummy again.

I sigh with impatience. A long afternoon stretches ahead. I have no idea where I will store Nanaji's books and papers. My tiny hostel room at the university is already crammed full of things but I have made this trip determined to salvage Nanaji's lot, lest in the indifferent throng of *tempo wallas* and *kabari wallahs* they are sold for a song. Nobody will want them anyway, his jumble of papers and cuttings and letters tied up in laces.

"These are very expensive, my dear. You must have these." Naneeji holds up a dusty wine glass for my mother's perusal.

"We bought these . . ." but Naneeji is in tears again. Mummy is distracted by the brat who has attempted to climb the grandfather clock and has failed, tripping on his overlong pajamas. He delivers upon the clock a resounding kick. I look at him with distaste: Arun is the spitting image of his father and has none of Mummy's redeeming features. At any rate, Naneeji's sorrow is instantly diverted. She hastens to examine the clock's varnish while Mummy beseeches the brat to be a good boy. The Colonel rekindles his pipe and turns the page as though none of this has anything to do with him.

On a Sunday morning, perhaps a year before I moved into the hostel, Nanaji bundled me up in the Fiat and took me all over Delhi in a last-ditch attempt to acquaint me with my culture. History lives all around you, he said, somewhat plaintively, history as old as eight hundred years and you're unaware of it. I knew that he plain disliked my regular intake of English and French novels and considered them a waste of time. He had tried unsuccessfully to introduce me to some of the nonfiction in his study but I never went past a few pages. "It's so dull, Nanaji," I'd tell him. "Your books are so *dull!*"

I don't remember my grandparents taking me anywhere except to the annual *Ramlila*, which was at Naneeji's insistence. We didn't go out at all unless it was to run errands or to visit her relatives, especially Bari Nanee. That's why that Sunday stands out in my memory. Naneeji decided not to accompany us and I was glad. Nanaji, equipped with a map and a guidebook, drove me by turn to the Purana Qila, Jama Masjid, Lal Qila, Humayun's tomb, Qutub Minar. It was an exhausting day with names, dates, and battles merging inchoately by the end but Nanaji did transfer upon me his obsession for the ruins. He acted as if they were old friends and I had earned the right to an introduction. I remember his face then, calm and attentive, his white curls playful in the breeze. I never understood why he chose to acquaint me with the ruins that day or why he never repeated the expedition.

After Nanaji died, I sometimes went up to the Purana Qila to think about him. Though he had been cremated, I liked to think that this is where his bones rested, freed at last from asceticism and lust. I took his guidebook along and remembered his voice and the things he had told me. "This is where Humayun laid the foundations of this city. He called it 'Dinpanah,' which means the 'refuge of the faithful.' During the 1947 riots, literally hundreds of Muslim refugees holed themselves in here, awaiting deliverance. It was either death for them, or if they were lucky, transportation to Pakistan. Be careful," Nanaji had added. "Those steps are treacherous. I think this is where Humayun fell to his death, down those very steps."

—⁓—

Knock. Knock. Knockity. Knockity. Knock. On weekends Nanaji locked himself up in his study and sometimes I'd sidle surreptitiously up to the door and give out my Secret Seven's knock. Nanaji always played along. He'd wait a few seconds, open the door a crack, give a furtive look around, and then let me in. He'd bolt the door and we'd settle down to read in companionable silence until Naneeji called us for dinner. While the rest of the house was shrouded in darkness, there were always two beams of light in Nanaji's study, one lighting his desk, the other his armchair where I sat. Naneeji would have been furious if she had known that he kept both lights on whether or not I was in the room. He always remembered to put them out when we left for dinner. I think he liked my presence in that room, as constant as the armchair.

Knock. Knock. Knockity. Knockity. Knock. Silence. I turn the handle and let myself in. Nanaji's study is the way it has always been except that the lights are off. Perfectly tidy, the books placed neatly on the shelf and on his desk. The chair, half-turned, as if he has risen to let me in. A notepad turned to a new page on his desk, his favorite fountain pen by its side. The faint, musty smell of books and termite that he also wore on his clothes. Scarlett is beginning to give; I am hurting bad.

I turn on first one light and then the other and sit down in Nanaji's armchair. *Tutankhamen, Life and Death of a Pharaoh* stares me in the face. It rests on his desk bolstered by two wooden elephant supports. The book next to it is Galbraith's *The Affluent Society*, and next to it, a collection of poems by Emily Dickinson. Curiously, I reach for the book of poems. I had no idea that Nanaji read poetry. I have never come across any poetry in his study before. I flip through the pages and read the words "*death*," "*darkness*," and "*grief*," again and again, or perhaps those are just the words that hang outside the page and come up to greet me. I put away the book in my satchel, determined to read it afterwards in the privacy of my room. I wonder why *Tutankhamen* is lying on Nanaji's desk. It has been, without doubt, my favorite book in his collection but we haven't looked at it together in a very long time. It isn't the sort of book he would have picked up on his own.

Long before I learned to read, I stared at the glossy pictures of the golden king with the black, dead eyes. I begged Nanaji to tell me stories about his dog, Anubis, and the goddesses who stood guard over his coffin. When I began to read, I found the book as exciting as any fast-paced thriller. There were things in there that Nanaji judiciously omitted to tell me.

"What is viscera?" I asked him.

"Er . . . body parts, you know, internal organs."

I became a terrible interloper. I couldn't put the book down. It held the allure of death and decay, of unfinished bones, unfinished business, of lives unlived, forever unknown. I stared at the pictures until I could smell the smell of the king's perfume, feel the grit of his lapis lazuli, those beautiful sounding words: *"lapis lazuli."* Whatever they meant, they were fit for a king. I could smell the king's stomach as it sat preserved in a sacred urn.

"You can have that book, Sweta," Nanaji said one day when he saw me curled over it.

"In fact, you can have all my books, everything in this study. They probably won't mean much to you, but remember, you have the first choice." I thought nothing of it then. I wasn't interested in his books.

"Why don't you bury it all with you when you die?" I said thoughtlessly, my head deep inside *Tutankhamen.*

"Hmm, not a bad thought: to burn it all up when I go."

—〰—

I hold the loved book in my hands and open it. A folded note slides onto my lap. All at once I know why the book is there. It is a sheet from Nanaji's notepad, the one that lies open on his desk. I unfold the note as if in a trance. There are only a few lines written in his neat, careful hand.

My dear, do not blame yourself.
This has nothing to do with you.
Like Osiris, I seek to rise from the dead.
I have thought about it and I am not sorry.
You must not be sorry either.
One day, I hope you will understand.
Absence makes precious, what of that?
We cannot blame those we have for that which we
    have lost.
My single regret: I won't see you turn into a fine
    young lady.
But then again, we know so little. Maybe, I will.

I do not show the note to anyone. I let them think what they want to think. That Nanaji died of a weak heart.

Part Two

The Months have ends—the Years—a knot—
No Power can untie
To stretch a little further
A Skein of Misery—
The Earth lays back these tired lives
In her mysterious Drawers—
Too tenderly, that any doubt
An ultimate Repose—
The manner of the Children
Who weary of the Day—
Themself—the noisy Plaything
They cannot put away—

—EMILY DICKINSON

COMING OF AGE

While Ronu prepared for his end-of-school higher secondary exams, J.K. Kalra, now deputy superintendent of police (DSP), decided that his son should apply to the National Defense Academy for a career in the armed forces.

Equipped with pen and inkpot, DSP Kalra worked laboriously on the application forms. Ronu only realized that the forms had something to do with him, when, after demanding and procuring a measuring tape from his wife, the DSP ordered him to sit straight, turn around, stand up, extend one leg, extend the other. Ronu had a physics exam the next morning, which occupied him completely. He submitted unthinkingly to his father's exhortations. Besides, every one of the DSP's jottings-down produced from him such grunts of satisfaction that Ronu was glad to be doing something right after all.

"Very good," said Kalra. "Height within acceptable limit, leg length very good, thigh length very good, sitting height excellent."

It was then that Ronu spoke up.

"What's this for, sir?"

The rules of nomenclature had been laid down in a somewhat peremptory fashion in the Kalra household. Ronu, having reached puberty (a stage that coincided more or less with the demise of Master Bunty), was forbidden to address his father as "Daddy" or "Papa." No such restrictions were imposed on Radhika, who, Ronu was convinced, deliberately unfurled hidden lengths from her "Paapaas" the moment his lips had been sealed. This heightened Ronu's correspondence with the hired help, the only other inmates to refer to the DSP as "*Sar.*" Mrs. Kalra, as demanded by convention, addressed her husband variously as "*Suno ji*" or "*Aji suno,*" depending on proximity and the urgency of the matter at hand.

"What's this for, sir?" Ronu ventured to ask.

"Armed forces, son. NDA."

Kalra was pleased with the manner in which the forms were proceeding. In an unusual display of democracy, he asked, "Army, navy, or air force?"

Tanks, ships, or planes? Planes, of course.

"Air force," said Ronu, forgetting that the vroom vroom of a jet engine had got him into trouble before.

"Okay, son," Kalra said kindly. "We have to get your accurate weight. Let us walk over to the chemist."

"But sir! I have a physics exam tomorrow!"

"Okay," said the DSP, kindly as before. "We will proceed tomorrow, directly after your exam."

—⚬—

True to his word, DSP Kalra was waiting outside the examination hall to escort Ronu to Chowdhury Chemists. The weighing machine ingested their coin, chewed thoughtfully, clanked in triumph and spat out a small rectangular card. Ronu and his father both lunged for it, victory belonging to the longer-limbed Ronu, who meekly handed it over. His father looked at the card briefly, then committed it to his breast pocket.

"Can I see my fortune, sir?"

"You expect weighing machine to tell you what is going to happen in your life?" Kalra's voice had returned to gravel.

Ronu sighed. It had been a childhood pleasure, his and Radhika's, to have their fortunes told at Chowdhury Chemists. For all he knew, Radhika was still allowed that indulgence.

When DSP Kalra returned to his desk and reexamined the requirements of the application form, his initial optimism deserted him. There was no doubt about it: Ronu was underweight. For his height of 5'8¾", the minimum acceptable weight, according to the guidelines, was 123 pounds. Ronu weighed 119 pounds. Kalra stared glumly at the card. Could the machine be wrong? Unlikely. Chowdhury saab ran a meticulous store. He turned the card over.

> *Confucius says,* (said the card)
> *"Man who stand on hill with open mouth*
> *wait long time for roast duck to drop in."*

The DSP stared Ronu's fortune uncomprehendingly in its face. His jaw tightened with determination. Kalra summoned his wife, "*Arri, sunti ho?* Feed the boy! Nourishing food, cooked in pure *ghee*, *dalda*. Buffalo milk. *Kheer*. Spare no cost. He must gain two kilos in four months and that is an order."

Kalra's conscience had nosedived ever since he had masterminded the outbreak of a certain illness confining his son to bed. He did not think twice now of dipping pen to ink and adding five pounds to his son's weight.

NAME: Ranjit Kalra
AGE: 16 yrs
HEIGHT: 5'9"
WEIGHT: 124 lbs

Satisfied, he completed and signed the application form and sealed the envelope. He was not going to let his son stand around on any hilltop. He would trap the duck and feed the boy himself.

A few weeks later Ronu fell in love. It happened at Ronny's birthday party where the boys, though sixteen and older, had opted to play musical chairs because of the proximity the game afforded with the opposite sex. Ronny's younger sister, Ayesha, had openly been encouraged to invite all her friends. Ronny's parents had decamped for the occasion, leaving the gramophone in the capable hands of Ronny's young and exceedingly elegant Aunt Lily, who, Ronny promised, was "lenient," and wouldn't mind supervising a little flirtation on the side. As "Gotta Dance Tutti Frutti" came to a grinding halt, Ronu made a dash for the nearest chair and felt a soft, fragrant heap land on top of him. The chair was knocked over and they fell laughing to the floor.

"Ronu, you got the chair first. Sorry, Anu, you're out," Aunt Lily announced.

Ronu's heart had started to bang so hard he couldn't hear the music and was out in the next round. He headed in Anu's direction.

She was almost a foot shorter than he, slender and dark. The heavy drapes in the living room couldn't keep out the hot, stinging sunlight that reflected in her irises. She had a thick mane of curly hair and Ronu thought absurdly that she belonged to a forest, all eyes and hair and litheness. Seeing him approach, she smiled, and there was both shyness and boldness in her smile. Ronu felt there was nothing at all that was right with him then. He was too tall, too thin, too white, too wordless. It was love all right, the first-sight kind.

She extended her hand, "Hi, I'm Anu. I think we both got that chair." He nodded. "Are you also at Modern?"

"No, I'm finishing from Ramjas," said Ronu, nursing the inevitable shame that overcame him when encountering someone from one of the more anglicized schools.

"Didn't think I'd seen you around."

"Ronny and I play football together," said Ronu. "Inters," he added helpfully. Ronny winked at him from across the room. Ronu couldn't think of anything else to say.

"I'm in Ayesha's class," said Anu.

The interest in musical chairs had waned since the three remaining contestants were boys.

"So you're at Modern?" Ronu started again.

"Hmm. Class IX."

"We play football at a field near Barakhamba Road. Maybe we can meet sometime after school?" Ronu was horrified at his forthrightness. But Ronny was weaving his way in their direction, and it was now or never. "Can I call you?" he continued.

She looked taken aback, but said politely, "Okay." She fished around in her purse for a pencil.

"I'm good with numbers, I'll remember."

"To whom would I be speaking if you were to call?" Anu said, somewhat archly.

"You mean you haven't introduced yourselves all this time?" said Ronny, dropping his jaw and putting on his irritating I've-just-escaped-from-the-Ranchi-asylum look.

"Anu, allow me to present Ranjit Kalra, alias Master Bunty, world-famous movie star. No, I'm not kidding, yaar. The rest of us dream, but Ronu's gone and done it all. Give him your phone number, Anu. He might be a bit slow in the drawing room but he's a fast fullback on the field."

Anu looked embarrassed. They were saved by Ayesha, who dragged Ronny off to the dining table where Aunt Lily was lighting birthday candles. Anu looked inquiringly at Ronu.

"Sorry," said Ronu tersely. "Ronny talks rubbish. But I would like to call you. Can I?"

Later, Ronu caught hold of Ronny and called him a perfect good-for-nothing idiot. Ronny replied, *"Kya to taste hai, yaar.* Skinny and dark and no headlights to speak of. Now Simran, she's something else. If you wanted her number, you'd get no help from me. All's fair in love and war, right?"

—⁓—

Ronu waited three days before he made the call. He didn't want to seem too eager. Be casual, he told himself. I'm playing a match near your school. Do you want to meet for a cup of coffee, nice and casual, just like that.

A woman's voice answered the phone and Ronu hung up. He tried again the next day, later in the afternoon.

"Hi . . . Anu? It's er . . . Ranjit Kalra. I don't know if you remember . . . ?"

"Oh hi . . . listen, I can't talk now . . . can I call you back? What's your number?"

He sat unmoving next to the receiver for an hour, pretending to read the newspaper. It wouldn't do at all for his mother to answer the phone. And Radhika would be worse.

Seeing him captive, Mrs. Kalra deposited a bowl of kheer by his side. Ronu groaned.

"Mummy! *Abhi* to lunch *khaya hai* . . ."

"Doctor's orders," she said cheerfully and returned to the kitchen. With the family relying once again on the DSP's salary, the full-time servant had been released and Mrs. Kalra's rummy playing restricted to Wednesday afternoons.

"Mummy, every day you're feeding me *kheer* and *makhan*. Look at the state of my complexion . . ."

It was true. Ronu's face was splotchy, the pimples waiting abundantly to burst to the surface.

The phone rang. "Hullo! Er . . . yes. How are you? No . . . I was sitting right here. Nothing special. I called because I'm playing football tomorrow, near your school . . . remember we said we'd meet for coffee?"

She said she couldn't possibly, she was part of a car pool and had to get home straight away. But perhaps they could meet later in the evening at Firoz Shah Tughluq's tomb in Hauz Khas, did he know where that was?

South Delhi was the other end from where he lived but of course he said he would be there.

It took him almost an hour to get to Hauz Khas even though he had decided not to bus it and had borrowed his father's Enfield instead. He drove through the crowded lanes of Karol Bagh and Pahar Ganj, through Connaught Place and India Gate, until the urban landscape disappeared, and there were only scattered villages, dirt roads, and open forest land. He wondered whether he had taken a wrong turn. Did she really live this far out?

He had gone over the directions carefully with Encyclopedia Sardar, the school's security guard. True to Encyclopedia's word, the dirt road widened all of a sudden and led up to a rocky wall that was part of a rambling complex of ruins, vast, austere, and seemingly deserted. He heard shouts of laughter and children's voices. He parked the mobike and walked past the large water tank to a tall, domed structure. He saw her immediately, dressed in a knee-length frock with socks and sandals, her hair tied up in ponytails. She's just a kid, he thought ruefully. Somehow she had seemed older at the party.

"Have you been here before?" she asked shyly.

"No, never. I didn't know Delhi extended this far south."

"We used to live in Connaught Place. We moved here a few months ago."

They entered the tomb and sat awkwardly against the wall, far apart and silent. The wind slapped her hair into her face. He stared up at the dome. As his eyes adjusted to the darkness, he saw something shift and slip away from the blackness.

"Bees," she said, following his gaze. He looked at the enormous hive, undulating yet perfectly still, a living, vibrating extension of stone. He couldn't think of anything to say. Finally, she said, "It's very beautiful out here. Come, I'll show you around."

He followed her down the stone corridors, up a narrow, crumbling staircase to a sudden, surprising opening from where the land stretched out in unvarying flatness, spotted with cattle that grazed into the distance where the sky leaned over and touched the ground.

He was seized with a violent fit of jealousy. How easily she had brought him up here to this secluded spot!

"Isn't this pretty? Look, there's my house, that one." Anu pointed to a block of newly constructed bungalows in the distance.

"I love to come up here, to sketch and read. This place has been around for six hundred years, can you imagine?"

"Is it safe for you to come here alone? Looks deserted," he said, knowing he was disappointing her already.

"I don't come alone. Miriam or Jugnu . . . they work for us —they bring us here. My brothers go cycling down there by the *chattris*."

She pointed them out in the distance, a couple of boys chasing each other on bikes. A woman who was standing nearby waved up at them. Anu waved back. They sat on a stone bench where a latticed window overlooked the setting sun.

"Is it true you've acted in films? Master Chintoo or something?"

"Bunty. It was way in the past. I was a child."

"I've never met a movie star before!"

He sat there, dejected. Was that why she had agreed to see him?

"So, you're no longer interested in acting?"

"No."

She was surprised by the vehemence in his voice.

"What do you like to do?"

"Hobbies, you mean? Sports, mostly. Football, volleyball, hockey. What about you?"

"Well, I love drama. Nothing special, nothing like what you've done, but I do love to act in the school play. And I love to read and sketch. I love writing too. Prose. I'm not much of a poetry person. Today, though, we read a poem in class that was amazing. "The Highwayman." Do you know it?"

"Don't think so. I'm in the science stream."

"I remember the first verse." She cleared her throat and recited in a low, firm voice,

"The wind was a torrent of darkness among the gusty trees.
The moon was a ghostly galleon tossed upon stormy seas.

No. *'Cloudy'* seas.

The road was a ribbon of moonlight upon the purple moor
and the highwayman came riding, riding, riding,
the highwayman came riding up to the old inn door."

Ronu sat brilliant in his emotion. "That's beautiful," he said and felt drenched with inadequacy. He couldn't think of a single intelligent thing to say. It's still not too late, he told himself, but his mind drew a blank and he sat tongue-tied and miserable. The sun left streaky, dirty patches in the sky.

"I have to go now," Anu said, looking at her watch. She jumped to her feet and headed for the steps, then hesitated, looked back at him: "I'm here quite often in the evenings. Maybe I'll see you sometime?" In a flash she was gone.

His misery had turned to joy. He had been "totally idiotic" as Radhika would have wasted no time in pointing out, yet Anu wanted to see him again. He looked at the setting sun and, un-exceptional though it was, he thought he had never before seen it so crimson.

—⁂—

Ronu was convinced he'd botched up his math, but when the Union Public Service Commission published its roster of successful roll numbers for the NDA's entrance exams, DSP Kalra slapped the newspaper triumphantly down on his lap.

"Congratulations, son! Well done! You are called for inter-view to Allahabad, all expense paid: train, board, lodging. Let us take a walk to Chowdhury Chemist, see how your weight is progressing, hahn? Are you exercising daily? Remember, fifty push-ups at sunrise makes a boy healthy, wealthy, and wise."

—w—

"I have to go to Allahabad for an interview," Ronu told Anu. He couldn't stand the thought of leaving her, not for a day. I love this girl, he told himself with amazement. A yellow ribbon ties her hair that tumbles out in a hundred directions. Her eyes shine and her smile hesitates. What would she do if I kissed her lips?

He took his mind away from the baffling thought. There was a new awareness between them. They had met several times at the Hauz Khas ruins and the fact that they resorted to subterfuge to get there confirmed the notion of a romance. Anu pretended to go to Sheila's house to study. Miriam or Jugnu escorted her there and returned later in the evening to collect her. Sheila posed as her alibi while Anu slipped away to Firoz Shah's tomb where Ronu awaited her. Afterwards, he walked her back to Sheila's house, not all the way, for someone might spot them, but close enough and in time to be picked up. It was fortunate that Sheila's phone was yet to be installed and the parents found no occasion to speak to one another. Sometimes Ronu and Anu were afraid they would run into her brothers, but while the boys played near the chattris, they were careful to stay inside the tomb. Ronu spent his pocket money buying chocolates to keep Sheila quiet.

Ronu knew that Anu liked him and this made him confident. Anu knew that she liked Ronu and this made her shy. This changed the equilibrium between them, and they talked more easily now. Ronu told her that she reminded him of a little girl in a Grimm's fairy tale. Which one, she wanted to know. Gretel? No. Rapunzel? No, alas! Surely not Goldilocks? No, but Thumbelina perhaps. You mean, I'm ephemeral, she laughed. Yes, whatever, he said, shame-faced. He looked it up in the dictionary that night. It doesn't matter, he told himself. She may be smarter than I am but she does like me and finds me good-looking.

He told her about his father, his father's ambition to send him to the army. He confessed to her his love for acting. He told her there was a time when he thought he would be famous, really, really famous. But his career had ended in failure. He had let everybody down.

"How old were you?" she wanted to know.

"Ten," he said.

"*Ten!* How is anyone a failure at *ten!*? That's awfully hard," she said, reaching for his hand. He held her hand tightly, kissed it. She looked frightened but let her hand stay in his. After a while, Ronu said, "Dad wants me to join the NDA."

"What's that? I thought you wanted to go to university."

"National Defense Academy. It's like a university. I'll get a B.Sc. degree at the end of it."

"But won't you have to join the military afterwards?"

"I suppose so. I don't really know what I want to do. I wish I could be as certain as you. I thought I wanted to be an actor but that didn't work out. Dad won't hear of it now. I love planes. I think I'd love flying."

"You can fly planes and not join the military."

"Yes, I suppose so." He looked gratefully at her. Anu made things sound simple and entirely possible.

"It's only an application. It keeps Dad happy and off my back. Chances are I won't get in."

He held her fingers tightly.

—ɯ—

Wearing neatly pressed shirt and trousers, blazer and tie, a handsome Ranjit Kalra faced a panel of military experts at the final interview of the Services Selection Board.

"Why are you interested in a career with the armed forces?"

He couldn't help it. The question triggered off an automatic response. He'd seen it take after take. Ashok Kumar, his father, and the soldier in *Soldier* stepped forward and occupied his soul.

"What greater honor is there than to defend the nation in the hour of need?" Ronu stood tall and spoke with conviction. For a moment he had plummeted back into the welcoming arc of Arri lights, the comforting whir of the camera. The Board exchanged meaningful looks. The Air Force Commander, a well-built man with a luxurious crop of mustache, looked gravely into Ronu's eyes. He took over the next round of questioning.

"Son, you've opted for the air force. Why?"

Ronu hesitated. Ashok Kumar was whispering the answer into his ear but it sounded suspiciously like the first one. He decided to ignore the voice and responded as truthfully as he could.

"Sir, I've wanted to fly since I was four."

The Commander grunted. "Very well. Do you drive a car?"

"We don't own a car, sir. But my father lets me drive his Enfield."

"Splendid, my boy. The Bullet is the closest you can get to a jet plane on the ground. Do you know why?" Ronu did not. Ashok Kumar did not seem to offer any advice on the matter.

"Think about the turn, son. What happens when you negotiate a turn at high speed?"

"Oh yes, sir. You shift your weight to one side, sir, to maintain balance. A plane banks while it turns."

"Hmm. Now tell me about your activities. What sports do you play?"

"Football, cricket, hockey, sir. Volleyball and swimming. Ping-pong too, sir. I played for my school in both football and ping-pong, sir."

"Hmm. What about riding?"

"Riding, sir? You mean horses?"

"Of course I mean horses, boy."

"No sir, I have never ridden a horse, sir," said Ronu.

"But you have!" chirped the Major, who had been smiling benignly at him the entire time. All attention turned to the Major, who had an unusually thin voice for his large frame. "Don't you remember *Rider Rani*? In *Rider Rani* you galloped off on Fearless Nadia's horse!" Some of the panelists nodded in agreement. The Major addressed himself to the Air Force Commander.

"I do not know if you have seen *Rider Rani*, sir. Fantastic picture, sir. Master Bunty is a small boy, only six or seven, but not at all scared. Courage is in his blood, sir; after all he is a police officer's son. He gallops off sitting in front of Fearless Nadia. A band of *dakus* attacks them. Fearless Nadia . . ." (here the Major brandished the air feelingly with his pen) ". . . has to fight them off singlehandedly, sir, with her sword. She goes for them left and right, so it is Master Bunty, sir, . . ." he said, pointing decisively at Ronu, "who grabs control of the horse and says, 'giddyup,' sir, and expertly navigates the fleeing steed through the forest, sir. It is fantastic, sir, fantastic."

The Air Force Commander, who did not appear to be a movie buff, was evidently taken in by the account. The panelists nodded some more and Ronu looked bashful. He dared not add that while the events being described were perfectly true, they had little to do with him. It had been the handiwork of Sheru, a dwarf of great skill and indescribable ugliness, whose talent and torso had appeared in countless films, expertly disengaged from his countenance.

"He may not have ridden a horse since, but equitation is in his blood, sir," concluded the Major rousingly.

The Air Force Commander took down some notes. Then the Naval Commander spoke.

"In any case, this emphasis on equitation, sir, as I have always maintained, is largely inappropriate. Our poor Indian boys, how are they to acquaint themselves with riding unless they happen to be from the hills? It is all very well for our Chief of Air Staff. He was born on a horse's back in Surrey, but does that mean our boys are any the less for it? We'll match any Britisher, OLQ for OLQ, and that's a promise," intoned the Naval Commander, beating his fist into his palm while the panelists nodded in grim determination.

One by one they stood up and shook Ronu's hand. "Congratulations, son," said the Air Force Commander. His eyes had moistened inexplicably. "I don't see movies," he said gruffly. "But I did see *Soldier*. I showed it to my whole squadron. You were right even then, son. You *are* the soldier of free India. Welcome aboard! *Jai Hind*."

"Thank you, sir. *Jai Hind*, sir," said Ronu saluting back.

Maybe I'll fail the medical exam, thought Ronu. What do I know about the NDA? How will I live without Anu for six months? I'd rather die, he thought tearfully. Do I want to become a fighter pilot? I like sports, but do I want to spend the next five years crawling under barbed wire? Maybe I'll fail the medical.

He went through a battery of tests. He stood naked before the examining officer, genuflecting each limb upon command.

"Age 16½ years, height 5'9", excellent height, by the way, for your age. Weight is er . . . 116 pounds," said the medical officer, disappointed.

Ronu's hopes soared. His mother's prolonged feeding of kheer, malai, makhan-paratha, ghee-rice, and the unfailing pakoras had produced in him such severe indigestion that in the last weeks he had been forced to subsist on a diet of *Isabgol* and water.

"I am underweight?" asked Ronu hopefully.

"Yes, quite underweight. It appears to be a problem with your bones. But nothing that the NDA cannot fix," said the medical officer, giving Ronu a sly wink.

"Don't worry about your weight, young man. We won't let a few pounds here or there stand in the way of a bright future."

The officer grasped his hand in a hearty handshake.

"Master Bunty, we are proud that you have given up an acting career to join the force. May I ask one thing, since you have met Shehzaadi in person, is she so tall in real life, with such big . . . you know . . . ? Or does she use padding? Aah, they are real? Please, if you don't mind? My wife will love an autograph . . ."

Ronu struggled into his underpants and signed the proffered page.

Hormones

Anu's mother taught history at Delhi University. Her father was the managing director of the advertising firm, Lintas. "He's the funniest man in the world," said Anu, her voice rising enthusiastically. "You'll love him."

Her universe is large yet intimate, thinks Ronu. Mine is small and filled with dread. I know her parents without having met them. They are urbane, sophisticated; they charm without effort like Ronny's parents. How will I ever introduce her to mine?

As was often with them, Anu seemed to have read his thoughts.

"My parents are throwing a party on Saturday. They said we could invite some friends. Will you come?"

Anu's house was large and graciously furnished. Sofas and easy chairs littered the oval-shaped drawing room. There were plants and paintings, carelessly strewn rugs, beautifully draped women holding thin-stemmed cocktail glasses. Bearers in uniform wove silently amidst the guests, bringing scotch and soda and an astonishing array of snacks. Delicate pineapple figurines sported pickled onion hats. Crispy fish fingers stood like sentinels around bowls of tartar sauce. Ronu fought the impulse to turn around and leave. Anu spotted him in the crowd and dragged him off. All the kids are in the music room, she said. She introduced him to her brothers, Rahul, 10, and Sanjay, 8, who muttered "hi" without looking up from their squabbly game of carrom. Among the assorted visitors, Ronu recognized Sheila, and headed gratefully in her direction.

"Where's my chocolate for Tuesday?" asked Sheila shamelessly and burst into giggles.

A dark and beautiful woman wearing a maroon silk saree and a low-cut blouse peeked her head in the doorway. That's what Anu will look like when she's forty, thought Ronu, his heart thumping.

"Mummy, I want you to meet a new friend. This is Ranjit."

Anu's mother smiled at him. "I'll get you kids something to eat," she said, disappearing as quickly as she had come. Though she didn't have time for them, she acted as if her exit was designed for their comfort.

Soon after, a liveried bearer arrived with glasses of *nimbu pani* and tomato juice, a platter piled high with *shami kebabs*, fish fingers, finger chips, and the stand-up pineapple figurines.

Ronu looked at Anu in her ankle-length green dress, her hair tied back, forcibly tamed at the neck. He had never seen her so dressed up before, with kohl on her eyes, her breasts stretched tight beneath the velvet of her dress. He tried not to look at her. He reached instead for "Captain Marvel and the Ghost of the White Room."

Shirin, a plump girl in a white and black polka-dotted dress, entreated Anu to play "Blue Danube." It turned out to be the familiar melody to which their PE drills were conducted every Thursday morning during general assembly. While he hated it at school, he was grateful now for the familiar melody. Anu ran her lean, brown fingers against the white piano keys. Her hair was beginning to shoot out from around the edges of her ribbon. Ronu looked away, acutely aware of the contour of her breasts, the curl of her lips. She became lost in the music. A short and ruggedly handsome man came into the room and kissed her on the forehead. He collapsed onto the settee and pulled thirstily on a bottle of beer. Anu left the piano and settled on his lap. He kissed her hair. Ronu felt hate surge through him at the sight of a man who had the right to touch her in that way. When their father returned from a trip, they touched his feet. Even Radhika greeted him with formality though she still retained the right to call him "Papa."

"Daddy, this is Ranjit," said Anu, and Ronu felt himself keenly looked over. "Hullo Ranjit. Call me Sam." Anu's father was slurring. He's already plastered, thought Ronu, this most wonderful man in the world.

"So what're you up to, son?" Anu's father lit a cigarette and settled back for a chat. Unlike Anu's mother, he seemed to have all the time in the world.

"Sir, I've just given my higher secondary exams from Ramjas."

"Hmm," pondered Sam, ejecting a perfectly circular smoke ring. "How'd you meet my daughter?"

"Er . . . we're friends of Ronny and Ayesha De Mello."

"De Mellos! Yes. Delightful family. Absolutely first rate," Sam said, warming to the subject. "Do you know that Celia De Mello and I were at Oxford together for a year? Then she went and married that son of a bitch, Irwin. Gershwin she was then, yes, Celia Gershwin . . ."

Sam appraised his smoke ring. Satisfied by its perfection, he turned to Ronu, "What does your father do?"

"He's deputy superintendent of police, sir."

"I see."

He's summed me up already, thought Ronu. We're a notch below the De Mellos for sure. Second rate.

Anu was talking to Shirin but looked distracted.

Sam reached for the newspaper. Ronu thought he was dismissed and returned to Captain Marvel.

"So what are your plans, Rajiv? Which college are you applying to?"

"Ranjit, Daddy."

"I've applied to the NDA, sir."

"Call me Sam. You want to join the *army*?"

"The air force, sir, er . . . Sam."

Sam finished his beer with a noisy gulp.

"So that's the kind of life you're headed for, son. Can't fart unless it's in formation, ha!"

Anu's father seemed to have enjoyed that joke. "Now, don't you go and blow up the heads of our neighbors across the border, hmm? Be careful, young man, I have family living on the other side . . . brothers, uncles, aunts . . ."

Ronu had no idea what he was talking about. Sam stared at him across the rim of the *Business Times*, his expression inscrutable.

Anu looked worriedly in their direction.

"I've only just applied, sir. I may not get in."

Sam was no longer interested.

—⁓—

"You'll be gone for six months?"

They were sitting under the turret of Firoz Shah's tomb. He reached for her hand and felt the thrill race through him.

"It'll pass quickly. I'll write to you every single day."

Anu didn't reply. A tear rolled down her cheek.

"Oh, Anu!" He pulled her close and they clung together for the first time. They had started holding hands, awkward hands with hot, sticky fingers. Now, feeling her scent and the wetness on her cheek, he kissed her lips.

It was a cold, clammy, shut-mouth first kiss. Anu pushed him away. They sat without speaking until it was time to walk her home.

Ronu Kalra left for Clement Town, Dehradun, carrying the memory of his first kiss. He poured all his longing into it, making it something it was not.

After Ronu's departure, Mrs. Kalra made sure that Master Bunty's album of photographs, newspaper cuttings, and movie memorabilia found its way back on the coffee table next to the much-thumbed copy of the *National Geographic*. While entertaining his occasional guest, DSP Kalra never lost the opportunity to add, "My son gave up lucrative career in tinsel town for the sake of service to the nation. After all we are service family. Duty comes before booty, as I always say."

Darling Anu,

I miss you so much! I think of you every single waking minute of the day but there is no time to write. Our days are grueling. When it's lights out (10:30 p.m.) I am asleep before my head touches the pillow. It's a sleep of exhaustion. I don't even dream of you, sweetheart! I know nothing until the morning reveille (as they call it here) wakes me at 5:30. What a terrible hour that is! Pitch black outside. I don't think any-one should be forced to rise before the sun does but if I make that suggestion to the SC, he will turn my clock forward to 4:30! They are quick and easy with punishments here.

Yesterday, during equitation, I let out a yawn. Hell, I was tired! Before I knew it, the JCO had pulled me off the horse and for the next twenty minutes I had to wash, scrub, and groom the fellow! The horse I mean, not the JCO! Bloody hell! I'm sorry for the bad language but there's no polite way to say this. I now yawn with my mouth shut.

I hate the mornings the most. At 6 o'clock we are called to the drill field for the PT routine. Drills, pole vaults, horse jumps, cross country runs, you name it. By 9 I'm ready for bed but it's only time for class! We study the usual physics, chem, maths, along with military subjects. No flying at all. In fact, we won't be flying until our last year so I have to survive some-how without you and planes.

What allows me to go through the day (apart from the thought of you, that is!) is the food. The food is fantastic! Amazing variety—Indian and Western, eat as much as you like. A boy's stomach turns into a bottomless pit here in the boondocks or should I say Doon bogs! Guess what? The cadets have to hang up their hats and belts before they enter the dining room. The hats, I can understand, to show respect to the officers, but why the belts? Now I realize how essential that is! You have to loosen your belt several notches during the meal, might as well take it off!

I think of you all the time, I carry you inside me. I think of how you would react to this place.

We have different uniforms for different occasions: Fatigues, Backpacks, Number 8's, Marching Orders, Walking Outs. It's as if the uniforms are the personalities and we simply wear them.

There are rules for everything, for cleaning your bike, maintaining your cupboard, lacing your shoes. There are rules for eating as well. Remember, when I came to your house for dinner I was so embarrassed and you were embarrassed too, come on, admit it, because I couldn't handle a knife and a fork. Here, rest assured, darling, I am fast turning into a pukka Britisher. I handle meat knives and fish knives, soup spoons and dessert spoons, and forks for every occasion. At my first meal I counted no less than 10 pieces of cutlery around my place mat and thought I would have a heart attack! But thankfully, most of the other new cadets were equally at a loss, so we were taken aside and registered in a course on etiquette. I am pleased to say, I have graduated with honours. Now I can probably beat Sam at his own game. My only regret is I've lost the joy of eating with my hands. They do let us eat rotis with our fingers (how could they not?!) but it is a tricky business. You have to lift the roti with the tips of two fingers, break it with the tips of three, the last two fingers never come in contact with the food. I feel like Queen Victoria nibbling a crumpet.

I have made some good friends here, Arun Sondhi and Jaspal Singh. Arun is from Bombay and is also an air force cadet. He comes from a very poor family, six sisters to look after, and they're all counting on him to find them husbands and dowries. Jaspal is a landowning Serd from Ludhiana and is the most terrific mimic I've met. He does a brilliant impersonation of Regiment Sergeant Major Ayling who rides up on his horse every morning to inspect the drill. Jaspal swivels his nose, sniffs, sucks on his mustache and says in a perfectly clipped angrez voice, "there's an unwashed ARSE in the ranks. Line 2 Number 6, step forward, please. Unzip your pants, bend over, give us a sniff, thank you very much." Jaspal has us in stitches! It's hard to keep a straight face when we see Ayling in the mornings.

Arun and Jaspal are a real pain on Sundays when we go into town. They're always skirt chasing, a pointless exercise, since the military police always has an eye out for you. They've already been grounded a couple of times. They badger me for my lack of interest in girls so finally I let it out that I have a girlfriend. Anu, you are my girlfriend, aren't you? The thought thrills me. I keep your photograph under my pillow and kiss it every night, and well, the rest is censored. Can't you say you're going off with Sheila on a school trip and come to Dehradun for a weekend? I'm STARVING for you.

There's something I want to tell you. With all the food I eat here, and with all the exercise, my arms are becoming very muscular. I'm going to crush you in them when I get back, darling. I love you. Why haven't I said this to you before? Your beauty makes me tongue-tied. Send me some photos, Anu, please.

I kiss you again and again.

Yours,

Ronu

—⁓—

Ronu, my dearest,

I cannot explain my emotions when I received your letter. There had been no news from you for so long that I thought you had forgotten me. And then your long and wonderful letter arrived: I cried and I laughed! Ronu, you must not write all those things in a letter. You know what I mean by those things. They make me feel funny (and very shy!) but most of all, I worry that Mum or Dad might find the letter. Not that they would make it a point to snoop around, but accidentally, if they came across something, it would be very embarrassing. At the same time, the things you say make me feel very happy, and I want to keep hearing them. So, maybe we should invent a cipher code that nobody else will understand? Don't they teach you ciphers there at the military academy?

I will say it too. I love you. I can't wait for you to be back so you can . . . There, I've said it and haven't said it.

Your stories are funny! I laughed thinking about you grooming a horse! Poor Ronu! There is no real news to give you. Life goes on as usual except that I hardly go to Sheila's house anymore. Miriam is convinced I've had a fight with her and keeps asking me what's wrong. I no longer enjoy going up to the tomb. It has too many memories. I am bored with school—the same old rotten teachers, the same study by rote. I can't wait for these two years to pass so I can go to college and study what I want. I am thinking of going to Sophia's in Bombay. It will be nice to get away from Delhi, be independent. Mum's brother lives in Bombay so I am sure they will let me go there. And then I can steep myself in literature and read what I want. When you have your vacations you can come and meet me in Bombay and we can be by ourselves. As you see, I spend a lot of time daydreaming!

My only landmark since you left is a movie. Mum gets these passes from different embassies and I went with her to see *Children of Paradise* at the French Center. What a movie, Ronu! I have never seen anything like it in all my life. The story is nothing special. There's a woman of weak morals and great beauty who is loved and desired by no less than four men. Frankly, I did not find her at all beautiful and couldn't understand the fuss. But I am not a Frenchman! I suppose their tastes are a little different! One of the men is a saint and another is a sinner, and the other two are somewhere in between. Each of them, except Baptiste, the one I call the saint, has a physical relationship with the woman, but emotionally she is unattainable. Baptiste loves her with absolute purity, and he is the one she falls for, but by then it is too late as he is married already, and they are headed inevitably for tragedy. Oh dear, it sounds dreadful as I describe it! The story is nothing special, as I said. It's the way the film is made that is heartbreakingly beautiful. Baptiste is a pantomime artist, he's a wispy, ethereal, not-of-this-world character, more of an ideal than a person, if you know what I mean. There are sequences of mime that are so beautiful, Ronu, they made my hair stand on end. I don't think I have ever been so moved, not even by a piece of literature. Guess what? Baptiste reminded me of you. You have that same fragile look, as though you are always misunderstood. If you are now truly muscular, I am not sure the comparison fits!

I kept crying in the movie for all sorts of reasons. It raised the question of pure versus impure love and that confused me. My feelings for you are all mixed up. I would like to think I love you the way Baptiste loves Garance but I know my love is much more worldly. That fills me with guilt and makes me wonder if this love can last. Mum was crying as well, so I did not have to disguise my tears.

Anyway, I should not go on and on about a movie you may never have the chance to see though how I wish you could! I am now a French movie buff and have asked Ma to take me along whenever she gets an extra pass, though unfortunately, most of the movies are for adults only. Oh to be 18! I've started thinking much more about movies in general and what goes into them. I am filled with wonder when I think that you've acted in them! I know so little about your past, Ronu. I wish you would tell me about those times even if you have put them behind you. Write soon and tell me more.

With all my love to you, my very own Baptiste, Anu

—m—

Darling Anu,

Sorry, I wasn't able to write the last few days. I had a toss-up with that horse, the one I spent half an hour grooming, ungrateful wretch! I've been confined to the Sick Bay with my arm in a sling. Nothing serious, sweetheart, just a sprain, but my right hand's out of commission. At the Sick Bay, I met a guy called Dusty, a senior cadet, who, according to the nurse, is sick a lot and spends a great deal of time there. Well, Dusty turned out to be a most cheerful fellow with loads of great comic books. I've had quite a vacation hanging out with him! He isn't the "deep" sort—in fact, he backs off from serious talk—but this morning we had an interesting exchange. He told me that if it hadn't been for his dad, he would have become a musician! I felt sorry to hear that. I couldn't help telling him how much I had fancied acting when I was young and I too was joining the military because of my dad.

Anu, the only reason I haven't told you about the films I've acted in is because I'm not very proud of them. All of them were pretty stupid, except for one called *Soldier*, which was my very first and which everyone seemed to like, though to tell you the truth, that one's my least favorite! At any rate, those films were nothing at all like the French film you saw. For too long, I depended on my acting career for my popularity. I was happy when I met you because you knew nothing about me which meant you liked me for myself.

A part of me can't help feeling that I was a good actor even at that young age, and had I stuck to it, something good would have come of it. Dusty says he has no regrets now. He says he loves flying planes and that's all he wants to do in life. Maybe I'll get to feel that way too, if they let me handle a plane, that is. I've had about enough of handling horses! At least I've been formally excused from exercising all of next week . . .

I must have read your letter a hundred times. It confused me too. You say you love me: that sends me over the moon. I have known it and felt it, but to hear you say it makes me the happiest guy on earth! But what's all this about pure and impure love and guilt? Darling, I don't know what those words mean. My thoughts for you are very impure, I admit it. Yet, my love is completely pure. I want to marry you the moment I can, the moment I am allowed to, which according to my calculation will be in 3.9 years. By then you will be 18 too, and we'll be married, and we can go to all the French movies you want. When I'm back in Delhi, I'll get down on my knees and propose to you, and you'll have no doubt as to the honorableness (is that a word?) of my intentions. But don't turn me into Saint Baptiste. My thoughts for you are not saintly.

Please forgive this scrawl. My hand hurts and is pretty unsteady. I'll write a long one in a few days when I'm better.

Postman, postman,
don't be slow.
Go like a Vampire,
go man go.

Yours until-death-do-us-part,
Ronu

P.S. I'm working hard on a cipher so I can send you my most objectionable thoughts. Here's a sample:

Dohbc
Cj
Xdkk
Qja
gngmqoigmg

The key is "forever" in this letter.

If you find this too maddening, I'll be happy to translate!

—⟋⟍—

It was inevitable that when Ronu came home for the summer vacation their encounter would be strictly in the flesh. The absence had been too long, and too long fanned by fantasy. Now words were spent, left-behind carcasses.

Her parents were away during much of the day and Miriam was hard of hearing. Anu took Ronu up to her room and locked the door. They stared at each other, alone at last. No, she had been completely wrong about him. He was nothing at all like

Baptiste. He stood before her, tall and muscular, a handsome stranger. And yet she belonged to him; she had said as much in her letters. It was too late to turn back the clock, to say, Wait, who are you? He held out his arms and she went into them. She watched herself step into his arms, engulfed by his adoration.

They kept the radio on loud. Radio Ceylon's *Binaca Geet Mala*, news bulletins, talk shows, weather updates muffled their panting from outside ears.

Years later, Anu would catch the snatches of an old Hindi film song, replete with the most pastoral of emotions and find herself in the grips of an inexorable eroticism.

Apni kaho kuch apni suno
Kya dil ka lagaana bhool gaye
Kya bhool gaye . . .

Speak to me. Listen to me.
Have you forgotten
the call of the heart?

Her body would fill like a hot balloon and she'd smile a secret smile. A scent, a melody could set it off, bringing unexpected pleasure and hollow pain.

—⋙—

It was several months later during another of Ronu's home visits that Sushma Reza hauled her daughter off into her bedroom for a private chat.

"Now, what's going on with that boy?" Sushma said grimly. "He's here on a short vacation and spends all his time with you? What about his own family?" She did not want to think that her daughter was seriously mixed up with a boy, not at fifteen. She had to admit that she liked Ranjit well enough and found him handsome and personable. Even Sam, who thought Ranjit lacked sophistication and was certainly not good enough for his daughter, had reluctantly admitted that the tall, proud, and faintly remote young man who stood before him was nothing at all like the fellow who had stuttered and stammered at his table a year and a half ago. The NDA had done him a world of good. However, he wasn't Anu's type, Sam maintained, and besides, Ranjit did not like him, a compliment he felt obliged to return in full measure. Their meetings were polite and unmistakably lacking in warmth.

Sushma Reza's feelings were more complicated. She had been sixteen when she met Sam and fell in love for the first time. She had hurt no one but herself by eloping with her lover and having children early. It was only now in middle age that she was pulling together a professional life, an existence independent of her successful husband. She could see all the warning signs in her daughter: the pubescent blushing, the secrecy, the unexplained highs and lows, the reluctance to accompany them anywhere. Anu must not repeat her mistake, she decided, and felt immediately chastened. No, if she had to live her life all over again, her choices would be the same. So who was she to reprimand her daughter?

"I know we are a forward thinking family and pride ourselves as such but I do think you are much too young to be spending so much time with a boy." It hadn't come out right at all. It wasn't what she had intended to say.

Anu decided to come clean with her mother. Her mum might leave her alone but her father would tease and prod her defenseless. He had been eyeing her strangely over the last few days as if considering a confrontation. Anu was relieved that it was her mother, and not Sam, who accosted her now.

"We're in love with each other, Ma," she said quietly.

"Love! You're only fifteen, Anu!"

"I'm almost sixteen."

"You have all your life to fall in love. Where's the hurry?"

"You know you can't choose the moment, Ma. It happens."

"You're . . . not sleeping with him, are you?"

The thought had assailed her and Sushma blurted it out before it could be couched in propriety. Miriam had confirmed that the boy always came over when they were out and they remained in Anu's room the entire time. With the door open or shut, Sushma had agitated to know, but Miriam was such a nice Christian lady, it wouldn't do at all to put such thoughts into her head.

"Of course not, Ma!" Anu said, horrified, and watched her mother visibly relax.

"His intentions are perfectly honorable. He has another year and a half at the NDA. Then he goes to the Air Force Academy. We'll get married as soon as he's commissioned."

"Listen, miss," said Sushma Reza firmly, "I like Ranjit well enough, but you are both too young to be thinking of marriage. I want all such ideas out of your head. You are going to college. Who would think *my* daughter would want to marry at fifteen! Are we in the dark ages or what?"

"Ma, obviously I'm going to college. I don't see why I can't go to college and be married at the same time. You're one to talk! You finished college long after you were married to Dad. And you've done just fine with your life, haven't you?"

Sushma hesitated. It was something she hardly admitted to herself. She let the moment go.

"We were in the same city, Anu. It's different when you're married to someone in the forces. It's a hell of a tough life. He'll be posted to some godforsaken place—Ambala, Jaunpur, Pathankot, Begumpet. God knows where these places are on the map. Will you go to some third-rate college there? Or will you live alone in Bombay and meet your husband a couple of times a year? What's the point of being married in that case? Be practical, Anu. Remember Akhila auntie? Think of her life. She's always alone with the kids, and the Major is off to some front or the other . . ."

Anu had had depressing thoughts of a similar nature but when she discussed them with Ronu, they tended to disappear.

"We'll cross the hurdle when we come to it, Ma. Right now we're in love and want to be together. That's all there is to it."

Sushma Reza sighed. That's exactly what she had said to her own mother so many years ago.

—〰—

Her parents were away to one of their dinner parties and were not expected before midnight. They lay on her bed. Her skirt was hitched up to her hips. Raising himself on one arm, he gently caressed her inner thigh, there, where her skin was smooth as polished stone. Her thin cotton panties dampened at his touch. He rested his face against her thigh and inhaled the strange scent of her moistness.

Anu pulled him to her, her tongue curling between his teeth. He sensed violence stringing her like a bead and it both thrilled and shocked him. Anu had been so shy. He slid his hand under her blouse and her nipples tightened between his fingers. She started to moan and he turned up the dial on the radio. They strained against each other. Soon, too soon it would be over. She pushed him away to keep alive the screaming in her body.

"Guess what? Ma asked if we were sleeping together."

"*What?*" Ronu took his fingers away.

"She asked me if we were sleeping together. I said we were not." Anu smiled at him. "I didn't lie, did I? Does this count?"

He was agitated. Now that the moment was gone, she wanted it back. She took his hand and pressed it to her groin. He moved his fingers slightly and they slid inside her, pushing aside her soaked panties. He felt her smooth wet walls and an unbearable ecstasy overcame him. She held him tightly through his trousers and the madness seized them again. It was like this, day after day after day, whenever they were together. At night, far apart and silent, they felt the shyness and the shame that there hadn't been the space for during the day. Yet, all their fingers could do at night was retrace on the body the memory of the day.

"I never felt that way again," she said simply. "It was . . . it was so pure, you know. Because we were young. There were no rules. I mean, no rules other than those we created. There was no instruction . . . no baggage, no history, no context. How can you feel like that again? You don't allow yourself to feel that way ever again. And yet," she said, after a pause, "we never did make love. Not the way it's known."

I looked at her, not understanding.

"Yes. He refused. I wanted to, but he said no, not until our wedding day. What if he went and got killed. That's what he said."

What Ronu had felt for Anu was the very excavation of desire. Clean, irrefutable as death. It left no room.

After Anu left him, he slept with dozens of women. He had saved himself for her. Now he spent himself on women he could not love. He was relieved when his marriage was arranged. At last, the love dance could end. He would love his wife and be faithful till the end, he vowed.

It took a month before he learned to kiss his wife on the lips, when finally she asked him through her tears if her mouth smelled bad.

—⚭—

"It was his fault," Anu said. "I wouldn't have left him. I'd have followed him to every godforsaken posting, that's how strongly I felt. He let me down. He wouldn't stand up to his parents. Ronu was a coward when it came to his family."

I didn't believe her. I didn't want to. It's her I wanted to blame, even though I would have liked it all to have been different. I would have liked her to have stayed and to have married him, and for this, perhaps, never to have been written.

—⚭—

For two years Ronu did not take her home. It made no sense, he argued, bringing up the subject of marriage with his parents before he became a commissioned officer. Anu could not understand his reluctance.

"Why can't I meet them? I know they're different. I'm prepared for that."

"Anu, they're conservative as hell. They'll never accept you as my girlfriend. That concept doesn't exist for them. So they'll want to know what we're doing together since we can't get married. They'll make it impossible for me to see you. All the freedom we have now will be gone."

"Surely, you're exaggerating, Ronu? After all, it's my parents who should be getting all worked up. I mean I'm the one who could get pregnant if we were up to anything."

"I know. Your parents are wonderful, your dad, especially, since he doesn't even like me."

"That's not true!"

"My parents are from another planet, Anu."

"Well, I think it's time I visited Mars. I'm serious. Dad and Mum keep asking me why I haven't met your family. I have nothing to say. Dad said yesterday that you can't trust a boy's intentions until he brings a girl home . . ."

"I told you he doesn't like me."

"Can you blame him for being protective? Put yourself in his place . . . ."

"I wouldn't let anyone come near you."

"No, seriously, Ronu. Things can't go on like this much longer. If your parents don't like the situation, we'll get engaged."

"You know why I don't want to get engaged, Anu. For the same reason that . . ."

". . . you might die and I'll be left all alone? Okay, let's agree on something. If we get engaged, I promise, *one*, I won't seduce you. My hymen will remain intact for a host of other suitors. In any case, you have shown yourself to be quite unseduceable. *Two*, if anything, God forbid, should happen to you, our engagement is written off, and I, pure as the driven snow, or almost, will be free to marry the next guy who comes along."

Anu put her arms around him. "So let's go meet the Martians, shall we? From what you tell me, I'll live to regret the day."

—w—

There was nothing at all that was right with Anu. She was short, she was dark, and she thought no end of herself. She had refused the pakoras that had especially been prepared for her, saying fried foods did not agree with her. She had not tried a single one.

Ronu had brought her home without warning. Even though he had a key, he didn't let himself in as usual, but rang the doorbell instead. Mohini Kalra, seeing her son in the company of a young girl (who was not a cousin), had experienced the most palpable anxiety. Ronu had never brought anyone home, not even a male friend. This was as good as an announcement of marriage. Mohini Kalra examined the girl with alarm. She returned Anu's *namaste* without registering Ronu's introduction. Flustered, she rushed into the kitchen to do what she knew best. Ronu and Anu sat down at the coffee table. Anu picked up the photo album.

"Is this it?" she asked excitedly.

When Mrs. Kalra returned with a plate of pakoras, she saw their heads huddled close together over the album. She looks Madrasi, she thought fretfully.

Then Anu made the fatal mistake of saying no to the pakoras. "Auntie, I'm sorry, I don't eat fried things. Why don't you sit down with us? Please don't take so much trouble."

"Who is she to tell me to sit in my own house? I will sit if I want, I will not sit if I don't want," Mrs. Kalra fumed later to the DSP.

"These pictures of Ronu are so sweet! You must be so proud of him!"

"*Bilkul tameez nahin hai.* No manners. Chitchat, chitchat, no respect for elders."

"Auntie, are you knitting that for Ronu? Such a nice color! It will really suit him."

"Already she is commenting on his wardrobe, I tell you!"

"I have to confess I know nothing about knitting. I actually failed in my needlework class. . . !"

"*Nahin pata to nahin pata.* It is one thing not to know, it is another thing to be *proud* of your ignorance. She acted as if I am from some servant class and she some *memsahib.* . . . What is more, she is loose," Mrs. Kalra had whispered in the DSP's ear. "*Mera matlab hai*, look how she is going around with our Ronu. *Suno ji*, do something."

DSP Kalra made some inquiries and returned with the disquieting news that everything was indeed wrong with the girl. She was not Madrasi. It was much worse than that. Her father was Muslim. That's why she had a mixed-up name like Anamika Reza.

Mrs. Kalra covered up her ears. "Stupid boy. I don't think he even *knows. Aji*, do something."

Her ancestry firmly established in the negative, Mrs. Kalra made no further attempt to be nice to the girl. Forget pakoras, she was not offered a glass of water when she came to the house.

"Why can't you be nice to her?" Ronu pleaded with Anu.

"Why can't *I* be nice? Can't you see I've tried? How about telling *her* that? She plain dislikes me."

"Anu, she's a simple, uneducated woman. Don't hold that against her."

"I don't expect her to quote Proust at me, okay? But I can't talk to her about anything. It's as if she's judged me, her mind's made up."

"It's because of our situation. In her time, with her background, I mean, girls and boys didn't go out together before marriage."

"I know that. You don't have to explain our social mores to me. I'm talking about basic human feelings, Ronu. You're going out with me. Doesn't she want to get to know me, try to understand what makes you happy?"

He had nothing to say.

"My parents do that with you. They're not happy that you're joining the air force and that my life will be in constant jeopardy. But they go along with it because that's what *I* want."

"It'll take time. She'll come around."

"Your dad's no better. He taps his stick and quickly makes his escape as if standing near me he'll catch some infectious disease."

"He's socially awkward, that's all," Ronu said dully.

"As for your sister, gosh, does she think she's heir to the throne of England!? Why's she always tossing her head at me? Anyway. I don't want to talk about it. They disapprove of me and that's that."

"I told you it wasn't a good idea to meet them just yet."

"Have you told them about us?"

"Of course they know! I've never introduced them to a girl before."

"Well, spell it out. Tell them we're planning to marry as soon as you're able to. I'd rather we have a showdown and get it over with. Instead of this constant unpleasantness."

He tried to kiss her but she wouldn't let him. "I mean it, Ronu. If you're really serious about us, you'll tell them now, before you return to the Academy."

There were ten days to go before the beginning of his final term. This wasn't the time to bring up the subject of marriage, Ronu decided. He felt certain that the quiet, circuitous route would work best with his parents. Once he was a commissioned officer he would convey to them the seriousness of his intent. In the meantime, they would get to know Anu better. They would realize that beneath her sophistication, she was at heart a simple, loving girl.

BREAKUP

Ronu had begun his training at the Air Force Flying College in Jodhpur when the letter arrived. It wasn't entirely unexpected. Things had not been going well with Anu for quite some time. On his last visit to Delhi, following a glorious passing out parade at the NDA, they had shared nothing but recriminations. He tried telling her about J.B.S. Haldane, the guest speaker, and his experiments under water, but Anu had not been interested. It was so unlike her that he stared at her in disbelief. It was almost as if she had made up her mind that she would no longer be interested in anything he had to say.

"What is it, Anu? I'm through! We're almost there."

"My parents invited yours over for dinner. They didn't come. I suspect they were rude because Mum and Dad have been very upset ever since. They refuse to talk to me about it. It's a clear signal, isn't it?"

"My parents aren't the partying sort, Anu. They did the best thing by not coming. They couldn't have been rude. They're just awkward about these things. They would never fit in with your parents' crowd. It would have been embarrassing if they'd come!"

"How's this going to work, Ronu?"

"We're the ones who'll make it work, not our parents."

"I care what my parents think. I want them to be happy with the choices I make. I want to be where I'm wanted, where I belong."

"You are wanted, Anu, desperately, desperately wanted," he said, pulling her towards him. In the past, all disputes between them had been settled with kisses. Anu pushed him away.

"No, Ronu. We've gone along too long on the strength of that. That's too easy." She moved away from him to the other end of the bed.

"Dad's right," she added. "If you really cared about me, you'd have it out with your folks. You would tell them to treat me with respect. Or lay off."

"Who the hell is your dad to . . . ?"

"Dad's been through it, Ronu, that's why he can talk. He's been beaten blue in the face by his brothers and uncles for wanting to marry a Hindu. He walked out on them, all of them. He left everything, his property, inheritance, the joint family, just to marry Ma. Mum and Dad made it on their own with no one to support them. Now it's the same story all over again. Your parents treat me like dirt because I'm a Reza. That's what it comes down to. Except that you don't have the balls . . ."

"That's not fair, Anu. I haven't had it out with them because there's been no reason to. You have to trust my judgment. When we *can* get married, I will talk to them. I think they'll understand, and if they don't, I *will* say to hell with them. But right now, as far as they're concerned, I'm a kid, I just got out of the Academy, I'm in no position to marry. It's your fault for insisting on meeting them. I told you we should wait until the time was right . . ."

"The time, Ronu, will never be right."

—ɯ—

He recognized her handwriting on the envelope, and a feeling of dread overcame him. *Dear Ronu,* the letter began. She had never called him that before. Even her first letter to him, the very first sent to the NDA, had begun with the words, *"My dearest."* He had savored the words then, *my dearest, rest, est, est . . .*

Dear Ronu,

I am sorry for not returning your calls all of last week. I felt I needed time to think. I was afraid that if we met or if I spoke to you, I would be confused all over again and would not be able to see this through.

The writing is on the wall and I have to face it. I love you very much, yes, this is true, but it has become clear to me that we are mismatched. I see it clearly now. I can no longer deny it.

If there is one thing my parents have taught me, it is to be unafraid. To live my life with conviction. That is the quality I need to take for granted in my partner, whoever he may be. There was a time when I tried to model myself desperately on Dad. I'd put on his irreverent, slightly mocking tone even though it did not suit me. One day, he said, Anu, don't try to live my life, live your own. Go, find it, live it, do what you have to do. They both believe that. And that's why they've never interfered with our relationship even though they feel I'm way too young, and yes, that you're not the right man.

I feel like shaking you and repeating Dad's words. Go, get a life, live it. There's a whole world out there, we can make of it what we want. This is not just about me and your parents, Ronu. Daughter-in-law problems are common enough, why should I shirk marrying you for that? It's you, Ronu. You're happy to go along with what others have laid down for you. You adapt. You accept. You grow into the NDA, you learn to cope, you don't question. But that's not good enough, Ronu. At least, it's not for me.

This will sound like the typical last paragraph but it's meant from the bottom of my heart. You are a sensitive and wonderful man and I am sure you will make some girl very happy. I had thought I was that girl but now it is clear that it can never work between us. Forgive me for ending it this way, for not meeting you one last time. That would be very difficult for me, and I am being selfish as always. Do not write to me again or try to see me. I have given this a lot of thought and it is very painful for me but I do believe it is for the best.

> With all my love for the last time,
> Anu

A sick, giddy feeling overtook him. There was a vacuum in his chest, a weeping that wouldn't reach his eyes. He couldn't stop his hands from shaking. Rattle-rattle went the crinkly white, kitten-motif letter paper he held in his hands, the paper on which she always wrote to him, a hundred, love-lust-filled letters that had helped him survive three years at the NDA. The sheer want of seeing her again had kept him going. Every night, fugitive-like, he had knocked off yet another line on the crude, pencil-drawn calendar on the wall. One day less before I go home to her. He sat there holding the letter, feeling his life had ended. He knew she wouldn't look back this time. His misery was complete and overwhelming. The next day it gave way to anger.

He sat down and wrote her a letter. Before he could change his mind, he enclosed all the letters she had ever sent him and mailed off the package.

Dear Anu,

The problem is you're in love with your dad. I'm not sure you've got yourself a life either, you look for him everywhere. No, I'm not like Sam, and that's why you're probably right, it would never have worked between us. I lack his sophistication, his charm. I don't have his slightly irreverent, mocking tone, thank God!

I would have worked things out with my parents in my own way. They're old fashioned and conservative, they're not trained in social niceties like your folks. But they're well-meaning, honest, and they love their children and want the best for them.

But yes, you are right, we are completely mismatched. The way I see it, there are two kinds of people in this world. There's the kind that walks into a restaurant and says, chicken sweet corn soup, that's what I'll have today. You, Anu, are that person. You know what you want, so it's easy for you. But there's another kind of person too, one who says, well, maybe I'll have tomato soup today, or how about the shark's fin, that might be nice. Or maybe no soup at all, am I in a soup sort of mood? I'm this other kind of person, Anu. I wasn't born knowing what I wanted. I'm trying to find my way.

There was one thing I thought I was pretty sure of. To tell you the truth, it was the only thing I cared about and it was all of life to me, but hell, I was wrong about that very thing too, wasn't I? We are so entirely mismatched.

So good luck, Anu, and good-bye. I hope you'll find your dad in the next guy you date.

With all my love too for the very last time,
Yours,
Ronu

P.S. Your letters are enclosed. All the "always" and "forevers" whatever they meant. It was nice knowing you.

—␣—

I was so angry, she said, I had to do everything I could to stop myself from replying. But it would have gone on that way, back and forth, all that anger. So I swallowed my pride and put away the letters in an old shoebox. I did not read them again, not until 1965, when it was all over and I simply couldn't help myself. I brought down the shoebox then, and I read every single letter many, many times.

—␣—

His anger fortified him for a couple of months and he drifted into a brief affair with an older woman, an affair in which he lost his virginity. As he emptied himself into the unknown and unloved form, a devastating sadness enveloped him: Anu, Anu, my darling, my love, forgive me.

She was never discussed at the Kalra residence. It was as if she had never existed. His parents introduced him to several eligible girls and he went out with a few of them before he was asked to make up his mind. By then there had been so many officers' wives and so many whores that the absence of love was a foregone conclusion. Ranjit gratefully accepted the idea of an arranged marriage. They came up with a favored list of three: all fair, good-looking, convent-educated Hindu girls from respectable families. DSP Kalra tapped pen on paper and, not unlike an earlier application, asked his son, "Sunaina, Preeti, or Neena?"

"Neena," Ronu replied.

Ranjit Kalra and Neena Mehta were married in February 1957. I was born the next year.

Part Three

A *Lazzi* Involving a Secondary but Pivotal Character

Dastur Karanjia, who happened to share Ranjit Kalra's room at the Sick Bay on one occasion, was two years his senior at the National Defense Academy. As a cadet in the air force, Dusty's tactical maneuvers were designed to keep him firmly in bed. He successfully kept to his bed while the other cadets were up and running at the crack of dawn, subjecting their bodies to every form of physical abuse known to the ingenious minds of NDA's drill inspectors. Dusty simply would *not* participate in bodily exertion. He remained indisposed, clinically creditably indisposed.

Anyone quite so sickly would have been dismissed from the NDA long ago. But Dastur Karanjia happened to be the son of Flag Officer Commanding in Chief (FOC-in-C) of Western Naval Command, Bairam Karanjia, who was a force to be reckoned with. So Dusty's will, or rather the FOC-in-C's, prevailed, and he continued at the Academy. He was miraculously well for the classes that interested him, anything to do with aeronautics and engineering, but absent for the back crawls, rock climbs, and rope walks that the other cadets ingested as part of their daily diet. Dusty professed (privately, of course) that it did not suit him to slither, strain, and strive, and since he had no intention of being shot down in enemy territory, did not see why the practice should apply to him. Later, it was said, with predictable hindsight, that it was precisely this lack of team spirit that resulted in Dusty's downfall and that of his ill-fated formation on the morning of the seventh of September, 1965. He had somehow escaped one of the NDA's primary precepts that life is a struggle and to value life, you have to value the struggle. Dusty had always taken it easy.

Under his bed at the NDA, Dusty kept Grandmamma's large steel floral trunk with a few well-concealed secrets: three poorly bound, cheaply printed, heavily lined publications: *Doctor Vaidya's Guide to Good Heeling*, *Adventures in Homopathy*, and *Secretes of Ayurveda*. In addition there were several boxes of little white pills and powders, an assortment of vials, potions, unguents, emollients, and a large assemblage of weeds. Every night Dusty worked, arguably as hard as the other cadets, scribbling and concocting the course and conduct of various ailments that would assail him over the course of that term. During the day he scrounged around the garbage dump behind the mess rescuing a rotting array of vegetable peelings and scrapings. Back in his room he ground and mixed, stewed and fixed. Then came the moment of truth. Dusty placed little white powders under his tongue, drank noxious liquids, rubbed stinking pastes onto carefully chosen areas of skin, and drifted peacefully to sleep.

Nine times out of ten he scored. He awoke with a raging fever or acute diarrhea or fits of uncontrollable vomiting, which successfully dispatched him to the Sick Bay where he stayed in luxurious confinement on a bed that could be raised or lowered with the touch of a button. He stayed for hours or for days as it suited his purpose. Gentle Nurse nourished him back to health with bigger white pills and generous servings of soups and stews and drinks of hot chocolate. Sometimes, when his illness was particularly grotesque, he was sent away to the army hospital, and on occasion, was even sent home. The time, for instance, when Dusty awoke to find his body covered with an unidentifiable rash, the requisite tests had produced the disquieting results that this was not measles or roseola, not scarlet fever or syphilis, not small pox or adenovirus, not parvovirus. This was a new and virulent something unassailed by human intervention. Dusty was returned home to Bombay for the safety of the entire military establishment in Dehradun. While the FOC-in-C kept Bombay's doctors rich, Dusty always made a quick and remarkable recovery, fed on the love and incomparable *dhansak* of his mother, Dilshad Karanjia. He returned to the NDA in the pink of health, ready to contract his next ailment.

While Dusty concealed his scriptures, pills, and potions inside Grandmamma's trunk, he fumigated his room regularly with generous doses of Old Spice, stolen from the FOC-in-C's cupboard during home visits. Malodorous fumes, however, often escaped from under the door of Number 12 Echo House, forcing Dusty to forge a contract with his immediate neighbors, Arif and Ramesh. It was useful, moreover, to divide and distribute the incriminating evidence during inspection time. Ramesh and Arif provided loyal service for the small fee of one ailment each per term and occasional help with their homework.

Gentle Nurse gently exhorted Ramesh and Arif to file applications for a change of room. Living in close proximity with that sickly Parsi boy (all that inbreeding, you know) was sure to damage their systems. The boys seemed happy enough, however, to stay where they were, united with Dusty in sickness and strength. Echo House was renamed during Dusty's brief reign. The dorms were called Able, Baker, Charlie, Dog, Epidemia instead of Echo . . .

Two months before the annual passing out parade, an incident took place that returned Ramesh and Arif to a state of punctilious health, and there they were to stay all the way up to graduation.

"Poor boys," said Gentle Nurse feelingly. "Finally they have developed immunity."

"We'll keep your secret," Arif told Dusty, "but you must not pay us back."

"Let's forget our little debt," added Ramesh.

The reason for the change of heart was understandable. It wasn't easy to reconstruct an illness from its antidotes, working backward from the ass, as Dusty put it. Once in a while his efforts misfired. One morning, he was awakened by the reveille to discover that he couldn't open his eyes. They seemed to be weighted down by large, unwieldy objects. He staggered to the mirror in his room. He pried open his eyes, then shut them again.

"Dear God," murmured the agnostic Dusty. He managed to let himself out into the corridor. Ramesh, who was making a run for the bathroom, let out a high-pitched scream.

"You look like shit," said Ramesh hitting a sharp C in excitement.

"They were supposed to be boils in the armpits," said Dusty gloomily.

"Ha," said Ramesh unhelpfully. "Well, come along. Hurry up, yaar, I have the shits."

"I can't *see*," said Dusty, smarting under the disrespect with which the vision-endowed treat the blind.

"Ha," said Ramesh again. "Think you're too smart, hahn? Always fiddling around. Serves you jolly well right. Well come along. I'm late, man. I have the runs, I'm telling you."

Gentle Nurse almost fainted. "In all my years . . . ," she said again and again as Ramesh led Dusty into Sick Bay. "It's solitary confinement for you, oh dear . . ."

"You have to smuggle in my medical kit," Dusty entreated Ramesh when the nurse left to make the necessary arrangements.

"Stupid or what?" said Ramesh.

"Please, yaar," said Dusty.

"That BVR assignment? Can't get the calculation right."

"No problem, you can copy mine. Please Ramu."

"Okay. I'll bring your stuff in the break. GN is sure to notice though. Want *all* the little white packets?"

Dusty nodded.

"Where you going to hide them, man? You're in solitary."

Dusty reconsidered. He made a list and handed it to Ramesh. Kali Muraticum. Kali Biochromicum. Silicea. Belladonna. Naturum Muratica. Ferrum Phosphorica. Apis Mellifica. Carbo Animalis. Mercury. Rubbing alcohol. Sulphur. Arnica. Cantharsis. Dried radish leaves. Eel oil. Menthol.

"Shit. I need more than the BVR assignment for this."

"Get me a lime too, please."

"You've really done it this time." Ramesh looked at him with disgust and left.

Over the next few days, white powdery substances and reeking oils left the sanctity of Grandmamma's trunk and wound their way into Dusty's underpants. Sick Bay's solitary afforded no other hiding place. With the exception of the boys' nether regions, Gentle Nurse made it her business to prod all nooks and crannies with gentle fingers. If Private Parts occasioned to be the source of the trouble, they were relegated to the less-pleasing hands of DoctorSir. Dusty's pajamas had let out such a stench and a mighty protuberance, packed as they were with his pills and potions, that Gentle Nurse decided that Private Parts it was and summoned the doctor. Fortunately for Dusty, Arif dropped in to see him first, and he was able to divest himself of his holdings.

Eventually, after several ferryings back and forth by Arif and Ramesh and promises extracted of completed homework, cigarettes, brandy, and pin-up girls, but no more ailments, no, not ever again, the sties did subside, and Dusty recovered his eyesight. However, his left eye never did regain its full size and remained a little closed for the rest of his life. It gave him a permanently sleepy leer. Fortunately for him, and at the FOC-in-C's insistence, the disability did not impair his career as a fighter pilot. It did ruin his chances with the girls, however, but girls were a commodity that Dusty was willing to do without. In fact, he would have much preferred to have kept his half-shut eye if Shernaz could have been persuaded to stay away. Shernaz was Dusty's childhood betrothed. At least, that's how she saw herself.

The FOC-in-C had decided that as soon as Dastur became a permanent officer of the air force, he would be married.

"Waste no time," he warned his wife. "No females and the chaps turn homo. Dastur, in any case, is a peculiar fellow," said the FOC-in-C, pointing to his head. "Always bloody sick." He looked accusingly at Dilshad, convinced she had made the boy soft.

"We have a Steinway sitting in the house and the fool plays a bloody *dumroo.*"

This was true. There was a Steinway from 1925 ensconced in the alcove under the stairs. Grandmamma had performed on this very instrument to rapt audiences in London's Symphony Hall. To her great sorrow, none of her seven children had turned out to be musically inclined, a verdict she was forced to reach after submitting them to several years of exceedingly painful piano lessons. When Dastur was born, she finally divined a grandchild with the musical gift and willed the Steinway to Bairam's family. Unfortunately for Grandmamma, Dastur came to prefer the raga to the cantata. He was a consummate tabla player, who at the age of sixteen, had accompanied the great Shaukat Ali Khan when the maestro's own *tabalchi* was indisposed. Flying and music were Dusty's two loves and he could have gone in either direction except that the FOC-in-C decreed all Hindusthani music to be worthless: "No bloody harmony, no bloody chords, even." Eventually, the sheer headiness of barrel rolls, loops, and wingovers got the better of Dusty, and the air force it was, with *Raga Bhairav* relegated to weekends.

The FOC-in-C had a cousin named Dina Wadia who had a wide-hipped, big-boned daughter named Shernaz. The FOC-in-C decided one day that Shernaz would make Dastur an admirable wife. She had the frame to give birth to several strapping boys. He eyed Shernaz appreciatively whenever she walked her slow, swinging walk around his capacious flat on Napean Sea Road. Dilshad, however, was wary of her husband's niece. "Too cunning for my Dastur," she thought privately but knew better than to express her views. The FOC-in-C did not tolerate discord among the ranks.

What the FOC-in-C did not know is that once when Shernaz was sixteen and Dusty fourteen, he had accosted her behind the grandfather clock, kissed her full on the mouth and felt her up. Just then the grandfather clock had struck two in rich baritone. Shernaz, who was superstitious, had acknowledged the deeply felt destiny of that moment. Dusty was two inches shorter than she, two years younger, and had two inches too many on his waistline. They would marry, she decided, on the second day of the second month of her twentieth year and two children would be born of their wedlock.

The grandfather clock, if indeed it had spoken, had murmured differently in Dusty's ears. He had kissed Shernaz and sprung back, never to touch her again. The little fondle behind the clock had told Dusty all he needed to know about himself. "No, no," the clock had chimed. "Girls don't do it for you."

The passing years had turned Shernaz into an exceptionally well-endowed young woman who made heads turn wherever she went. Boys practically did headstands for the opportunity to look up her skirts. But Shernaz was committed to Dusty. To supplement the prophecy of the grandfather clock was the rather thin availability of Parsi boys in the community. There was Percy, the good-looking half-wit with his obsession for tops. There was Cawas, the miser, who wouldn't let his own mother eat an egg at home unless she had extracted it without cost from the *Parsi Panchayat*. There was Nausher, the incredible hulk, who couldn't button his own shirt and had his mommy do it for him every morning. And there was Cyrus, who seemed all right from the outside, but, rumor had it, he couldn't get it up. All the rest were over forty and married. In such company, Dastur stood out. Dastur was sexy, Dastur had brains, Dastur came deliciously packaged in uniform. And Dastur had lineage too and a flat on Napean Sea Road. So what if Dastur was interested in planes and not in Shernaz? She was prepared to wait.

Like any healthy girl her age, Shernaz loved a challenge. Her mother, Dina Wadia, a dressmaker by profession, had tailored especially low-cut blouses that showed off her daughter's bounty to advantage.

When the news came around that Dusty was home from the NDA, this time with some terrible eye disease, Dina pulled out one of *those* dresses for Shernaz and the two drove across to her cousin's flat in their battered Buick. Shernaz's attire unfailingly evoked a gleam in the FOC-in-C's eyes. He proceeded to embrace her broadly and stared down her cleavage from his great height.

"The great hills of Mandasor!" said the FOC-in-C approvingly while Shernaz blushed and her mother whispered in her ear, don't mind these military types, they speak in code, it's not what you think.

Dastur mumbled, "Hullo auntie, hiya Shernaz" and bolted into his room. His mother noted the proceedings with satisfaction. What did the Wadias think, dropping in only when her boy was at home, dressed like two-bit tarts? Her Dastur had better taste than that. Besides, the cup of Parsi girls brimmed fuller, and Dilshad Karanjia (whose Dastur was her only solace) was in no hurry to find him a bride.

When Shernaz, goaded by her mother, wedged her way into Dusty's room, she noticed his half-shut eyes. She sighed and resigned herself to her fate. He had not noticed her before with his eyes wide open. How would he look at her now? What was it with the Parsi boys, she thought. Those blessed with good looks and brains were intent upon joining the rest of the circus.

Shernaz pulled a chair close to Dusty's bed and stooped low to allow him a good view of the Mandasors.

"What happened to your eyes, ya?"

"Umm. Infection."

"That NDA. Unhealthy place, ya. Always falling sick."

"Umm."

"Not to worry, Dastur. I'll take care of you, ya," said Shernaz, laughing a little too loudly. She leaned across Dusty to reach for a magazine and the Mandasors grazed his chest. She paused there a moment, chest heaving, smelling the pleasant aroma of Old

Spice on his shirt. Dusty handed her the magazines and pushed her away as he did.

Shernaz idly flipped through the pile. She still had Dusty's smell in her nostrils. She looked at him from the corner of her eye. His shirt was open at the collar and she could see the beginnings of his black, thickly curling hair. Shernaz felt dizzy with excitement. She looked at his hands, broad hands, clean fingernails, hair curling richly on the knuckles. She wanted those hands to reach out and grip her breasts—just like that, no preliminaries, no thank you please, just short and brutal, the way he had touched her once behind the grandfather clock, a hand up her blouse, another down her skirt, filling four long years with fantasy. Only Shernaz could look beyond the golf balls of his eyes and find him attractive. She did.

"I'm reading this James Hadley Chase, ya, . . ." she began after recovering her voice. But Dusty was off the bed and into the bathroom. For a second Shernaz thought he wanted her to follow him inside. Then she heard the door shut and the decisive sound of a latch.

She moved over to the bed and sat strategically on the spot where Dusty would be at touching range. She flipped through the boring boys' magazines. She found an airplane almanac and, opening it, started mugging up some facts.

Dusty flushed and came into the room, his hand still buttoning his fly. Shernaz felt herself ooze into her panties. She clutched the airplane almanac. Dusty picked up his comic book and sat down on the chair that Shernaz had vacated.

"So the Vampire de Havilland carries four 20 mm canon and can fly at er . . . 530 miles an hour?" she said breathlessly.

Dusty stopped and stared at Shernaz over the rim of a *Mad* comic book. His half-closed eyes bore a meditative hole through her. This was the first time Dusty had *looked* at Shernaz. Had she been wearing a collar, she would certainly have been hot under it, but dressed as she was, a generous and unencumbered view of the Hills met Dusty's unblinking gaze and confused him completely.

"You interested in planes?" he said doubtfully.

"Yes, very," breathed Shernaz, thinking she was getting somewhere at last.

"Oh," said Dusty and returned to Shermlock Shomes.

Later Shernaz sobbed on her mother's shoulder and said that she hated Dastur Karanjia with all her heart and would not marry him if he were the last man on earth.

"Well he practically is, isn't he?" said Dina Wadia. "Even that Cawas has been taken and Cyrus has gone and got himself a third wife. How desperate can girls get . . . ?"

"There, there," she said comfortingly, as her daughter responded with a wail. "Let him grow up a little. Girls mature faster than boys. He will come around."

"Grow up? He's eighteen, isn't he? Mummy, I'm telling you, Dastur has to marry me this year. It's this year or never! I've received a sign, I'm telling you."

The second day of the second month came and went. Shernaz realized that she had misinterpreted the grandfather clock. What the clock had meant was the second day of the second month of *Dastur's* twentieth birthday, her twenty-second. She had two more years to wait.

So Dastur Karanjia returned to the NDA with his half-shut eyes and the calendar flipped its pages. Shernaz reached the formidable age of thirty without extracting a marriage proposal from him. While she remained committed to the idea of marrying Dastur, having imputed to the grandfather clock several multiples of two, she decided (wisely) that it did not augur well to reserve her now diminishing beauty for a man who paid her scant attention. In the passing years she had allowed three Hindu boys, a Christian boy, and an older, married Parsi man to visit the Mandasors from time to time. Of late, she had even taken up with the good-looking half-wit, Percy, who liked nothing better than to spend his afternoons spinning her tops. Not entirely unpleasant, decided Shernaz Wadia, as she leaned back on Percy's couch and closed her eyes and dreamed of Dastur Karanjia's broad and manly hands.

The rumors had been reaching Dina Wadia for quite some time. But it was only in March 1965, during Percy's son's *Navjot*, that she witnessed the enormity of the problem on her hands. Percy had been following Shernaz about with his eyes, and while his wife may have been too busy with the celebration to pay much notice, nothing escaped Dina's sharp scrutiny. When Shernaz headed for the bathroom and Percy bounded after her, Dina firmly followed. Just in time to see the half-wit lunge for her daughter's tits with outstretched hands.

"Please Shernu. Only once. Please."

"Not now, silly," said Shernaz giggling, slapping away his hands.

Dina Wadia had seen enough. She left the *Navjot* without a word and headed straight for Number 45 Napean Sea Road. Either Dastur Karanjia would have to be forced into marrying Shernaz or she had better accept one of the aging widower proposals that occasionally came her daughter's way. After all, there was the danger of the widowers dying off too.

Dina held a conference with the now ex–FOC-in-C, whom the intervening years and a stroke had rendered less than sensible.

"I don't think your Dastur likes my Shernaz," began Dina. "Is there someone else? If there is, you may as well tell me."

"Sir?" said the ex–FOC-in-C blankly.

Today was not one of his brighter days. The ex–FOC-in-C's mind often retreated into the past, making him a severe liability to the present. He had spent the morning shouting at the tear-stricken servant and demanding that she return to him at once the sum of nine rupees and fourteen annas, as one kilo of potatoes and half a kilo of onions could not possibly cost more than two annas. Dilshad had finally slapped the newspaper down on his knees. With vicious strokes of the pen, she circled the date *March 12, 1965* and scribbled next to it: *see ration prices.* The market prices were similarly encircled. "Please shut up," she said. The ex–FOC-in-C stared at the page in perfect bewilderment.

"Your son, my daughter," Dina continued, as if to a child. "Remember? They are supposed to marry."

"Yes sir," said the ex–FOC-in-C, his mind spiraling reluctantly to the present.

"Well, he doesn't seem to like her," said Dina.

"Nonsense," said the ex–FOC-in-C feelingly. "Such a beautiful girl. The boy is just busy with his career, that is all. I always had time, myself, for both," he said, chuckling.

"He earns a good salary. Surely it is time to start a family," said Dina.

"Yes, very good life in the service," the ex–FOC-in-C agreed. He counted on his fingertips: "Free house, free car, free phone, free uniform, free cap, free shoes, free socks, cheap booze, cheap cigarettes, cheap women, ha ha, ha." He was rapidly drifting into a happier past.

"Cousin Bairam," said Dina Wadia firmly, "don't you think it is time that your Dastur marry my Shernaz?"

"Definitely," affirmed the ex–FOC-in-C. He lowered his face to hers. "No females and the chaps turn homo," he said, winking.

Dina winced. "Well, maybe that's it then," she said. "At least he does not seem to like my Shernu, and you know how many men there are out there who would kill for her . . . ?"

"Who? What? What did you say?"

"You know," said Dina. "Dastur. Maybe he is . . . you know . . ."

"*No!*" roared the ex–FOC-in-C. "*No, never!* I will not allow it."

"He shows no interest in Shernaz," Dina repeated.

"Where's that boy? I will shoot him. Dilshaaad. Fetch my gun."

"Maybe marrying Shernaz will fix him," continued Dina.

"Of course Dastur will marry Shernaz," said the ex–FOC-in-C, smashing his fist on the glass table. "I will see to it myself. Tomorrow. When he comes home. Dilshaad," he shouted, as his wife came scurrying out of the bedroom where she hid herself whenever Dina Wadia made an appearance.

"Arrange for Dastur's marriage at once."

Dilshad glared at Dina. Dina glared back.

"*Now?*" she said. "Dastur is with his squadron in Halwara."

"Get him here. Bloody homo. I will shoot him like a dog."

Dilshad was used to her husband's eccentricities. "Dastur is in Halwara," she repeated. "When he comes home you can talk to him about it. And don't you call my son names. Shernaz Wadia is not the only girl in the world. Just because he's not interested in *her* (Dilshad sniffed loudly) does not mean . . . anything."

Dilshad picked up her dressing gown royally around her and returned to the bedroom. She was certain that the matter would be forgotten in the three weeks that intervened before her son's visit.

When Dusty came home he brought the news that he had been promoted to squadron leader.

"Well done, boy," said the ex–FOC-in-C, eyeing his son uneasily. He tried to square him out. Homos, in his experience, were thin, effeminate chaps. Dastur was short and stocky.

"Now is a good time to marry Shernaz."

"Sir?" said Dusty, dismayed. He looked at his mother for support. Dilshad looked mournfully at him but said nothing.

"Sir, if I may say so," began Dusty, "marriage is not for the likes of us military men. Here today, gone tomorrow. We are wed to duty."

Dusty knew that the ex–FOC-in-C had a soft spot for rhetoric. Over the last years, especially since his brain had addled, his eyes tended to moisten whenever he heard the national anthem. He probably thought India had won her independence yesterday.

The ex–FOC-in-C was not in a malleable mood. "What you mean?" he roared. His habit of shouting orders had never quite left him. When he shouted, the ex–FOC-in-C dispensed with unnecessary articles and came swiftly to the point. "I married, yes or no? You think I remained *brahmachari*?! Who is she, sir?" he said wagging a finger at his wife. "How do you think you got here? From homo buggery?"

"All I am saying, sir," said Dusty with equanimity, "let Shernaz marry someone she can count on for the rest of her days. Such a nice, beautiful, er . . . energetic girl," he added.

"You think World War III is coming just for you? You plan to be a bloody martyr?"

"It's Pakistan, sir," said Dusty, racking his brains. "All this infiltration. There will be war, sir."

"Pakistan!" snorted the ex–FOC-in-C dismissively. "Pakistan? How can Pakistan fight when it stops five times a day to rub its nose on the bloody earth? Besides," he said, cackling, "Pakistan has *two* fighter squadrons, ha, ha, ha, no match for India!"

"That was in '47, sir," said Dusty, realizing it was futile to pursue the point. "Anyway, sir, now is not the time to marry," he said firmly.

It was April 1965. Later, to Dusty's many credits was added the gift of prescience. Dusty had known. Dusty had seen it coming all along. What on earth would a beautiful girl like Shernaz Wadia have done nursing a posthumous Vir Chakra for the highest gallantry? After all, all the free travel on Indian Airlines and Indian Railways wouldn't bring a girl any closer to her dreams.

WAR

I had only lived with Nanaji and Naneeji for two years when increasing infiltration by Pakistani *mujahidin* across the Indian border escalated into a full-fledged war between the two countries. Almost overnight, Vietnam receded from the front pages of our newspapers, and the headlines became dominated by our own achievements:

INDIAN TROOPS CROSS INTO WEST PAKISTAN

ENEMY BID TO CROSS RIVER IN AKHNOOR FOILED BY INDIAN ARMY

LULL IN CHHAMB REGION AS IAF PLANES HUMBLE PAK SABRES

It was my grandmother's opinion that India had been too lenient in its dealings with Pakistan. The Congress's greatest mistake, she maintained, was to have allowed Lahore, our cultural capital, to be handed over to Pakistan during partition. "We should have attacked them first," she said. "Then they would have learned a lesson and wouldn't have set their sights on Kashmir." Nanaji sighed and said there was the matter of the promised referendum that had never taken place. I was too young then to understand their respective positions. I was simply grateful for the diversion that war afforded. Something of consequence was happening at last even if I didn't understand it. My dull existence was illuminated by a peculiar and heightened intensity. I felt the glow, the dread, of every passing moment.

We huddled over the morning papers, passing pages back and forth. I had a thousand questions for Nanaji. What is the cease-fire line? Who draws it? The man who draws the line, does he stand one foot on one side, one on the other? Why do Pakistanis always fire in a "desultory" fashion? Don't they want to win? And what are India's "mopping up" operations? I imagined a battalion of soldiers putting down their guns and picking up mops. They soaked up the spilled blood then killed some more.

What was Daddy's role in all this, I wanted to know. What "bids" had he "foiled"? Nanaji answered every question with his characteristic patience. Because of the evening curfew, he returned home early. We tuned into All India Radio's shortwave frequency and prepared for the evening's blackout.

Those days were full of a mysterious intent. I assisted Nanaji in measuring the windowpanes in our house. Naneeji, who was a talented seamstress, brought out a massive roll of brown paper and measured out squares and rectangles. She cut the pieces out, and Nanaji and I covered the paper with the sticky rice paste she had prepared and covered every window in sight.

The war outside had quieted the adversaries at home. Nanaji and Naneeji now conferred seriously about the political situation. She seemed resigned to allow him to make all the important decisions. Our house had always been gloomy and unlit as Naneeji was keen to save on electricity and only allowed the fluorescent to stay on. Now with the pasted-up windows it looked like a morgue. I was reading *Great Expectations* and felt that we were the rightful occupants of Miss Havisham's parlor.

It was a relief, actually, to keep the fluorescent off during the curfew and eat by candlelight. It was very quiet then, and we lived with a sense of waiting. We spoke in hushed tones; the candles set up their flickering dance, and all the night's shadows were let loose in our house.

Our refuge room, as it was called, was adjacent to the living room. In case of an air raid, we could be there in a matter of seconds. The room was bare except for a mattress and a small table. On this Naneeji had placed a jug of water, a packet of biscuits, some Band-Aids, cotton wool, a torch, a candle, and some matches. Every time we heard the air-raid warning, Nanaji grabbed me and rushed me off into the refuge room while Naneeji blew out the candles and followed. We threw ourselves down on the mattress. We plugged our ears with cotton wool and lay on our stomachs until the ghostly intermittent wail of the siren faded. My heart hammered away for those ten or fifteen or thirty minutes. I can die now, I told myself. If I am dead, I will feel nothing. I lay still and tried hard to feel nothing.

Nanaji lay between us, a protective arm across our shoulders. I had never witnessed any physical intimacy between Nanaji and Naneeji. Unlike Mummy and Daddy, they did not hug each other or even kiss perfunctorily on the cheek. To see them lying next to each other, his body almost on top of hers, was gross and unpalatable to me. It made the threat of the bomb a reality. Yes, we would surely die, all three of us, lying there just like that. I craved a just and fitting end. It doesn't matter, I told myself. If I am dead, I will feel nothing.

The first time I ever heard the air-raid siren I was at school. We had been warned that there would be a drill precisely at 11 a.m. Mrs. Mendez, our Grade 2 teacher, piped up, her voice, shrill and determined, "Girrrls, prepare for the drrrill."

Instead of quiet there was clatter as nervous fingers dropped pencil boxes, chairs were upturned, heads banged against desks. The siren began slowly, haltingly, then set itself off in ever-widening spirals. It had the lonely insistent howl of a mad-woman caught in a storm.

Nanaji had bought me a new scented nylon eraser. He gave me one at the start of every term because I loved them so, and at the end of term I carefully stashed away the remaining stub in a wooden pencil box. My box contained remnants of elephant, tiger, owl, gorilla, yak, antelope, all with the ubiquitous sickly sweet smell imported from Hong Kong. My latest acquisition was a pink flamingo that stood on one leg and inspected the other. I had used the eraser sparingly around the edges, trying to keep the bird intact as long as possible. When the air-raid warning sounded, I grabbed my flamingo and carried it into my protective enclosure under the desk. I held it to my nose and breathed deeply. War: the sound of the siren, the roar of the planes, became inextrica-bly linked with the overripe smell of pink flamingoes.

> Please God, don't let it happen.
> Please God, do let it happen.

It was hard to know what to wish for. This was a dreaded time but it was thrilling. I steeled myself for a terrible explosion, for the sky to part and a flaming ball to plummet through. Noth-ing happened. I knew so little about war that I imagined it to be beautiful, a cascading fountain of fireflies, while I lay safe under a desk, a flamingo held to my nose.

Please God, don't let it happen.
Please God, do let it happen.

Achla, whose desk was next to mine, also prayed. I watched her right index finger move from her forehead to her chin, forehead to chin, in rapid little movements. If I could have that time all over again, I would know what to pray for.

—m—

One day, on my way home, I found Mummy waiting to pick me up at the bus stop. I could hardly believe my eyes.

"Mummy!" I screamed, throwing myself into her arms. Nobody had told me Mummy was coming to Delhi!

"Where's Daddy?" I asked.

"He's been called to the front. I've come to spend some time with you and Nanaji and Naneeji."

"Oh goodie, goodie, goodie!"

We walked home holding hands, swinging arms.

No bombs fell over Delhi during the twenty-two day war. The closest we came to a real threat was on September 8 when a fighter jet flew overhead and was shot down. Next morning, the newspapers carried the lurid carcass of the mangled plane: "ENEMY'S BID FOILED," the headlines said. "DELHI IS SAFE."

Return

Anu shifted the bamboo chair until it directly hit the stream of light that poured onto the veranda. Later, as the arc of the sun would climb, the rest of the room would slowly irradiate with light and the specialness of her place, the chair in the sun, would be gone. In another twenty minutes, Miriam would wake up her parents with a tray of tea and Marie biscuits. Then, as the din of the morning's routine spread irrevocably through the house, in the scurry for bathrooms, her mother's instructions shouted across the length of corridor, the insistent clanging of the doorbell as vendors brought in the early morning wares: bread, eggs, fruit, vegetables, Toby rushing proprietorially to the door each time and barking his head off, she'd be driven once again to the quiet of her own room. Sanjay with his blaring stereo would be the last straw. She savored the peace while she could.

The indefatigable Miriam was already on her feet. She brought Anu a mug of whipped, frothy coffee, just the way she liked it, and a plate of Bourbon biscuits, then rushed off to answer the doorbell, the first of many.

"Parrots? How many times have I said we don't want parrots?! Aren't there enough outside, making a racket?"

"Maji, a parrot brings luck and prosperity. It will keep you company all day long."

"Ha!" retorted Miriam shutting the door on the smiling face.

"I don't have enough to do, right? All I need is to go about picking parrot droppings . . ."

Miriam was cantankerous and pushing sixty. She appraised, dismissed, and bargained with ruthlessness. The sellers tried to edge their way past her to the more forgiving Madam inside, but Miriam held her ground, bulldoglike.

"No, our knives do *not* need sharpening. You think we use cheap stuff like the kind you sell?"

Miriam adjusted her hearing aid as though she hadn't heard right. "Ear pierce, ear pierce, you want to pierce my ears?!" She waggled her ears at the terrified teenager, who leaned back on his bicycle in an effort to escape her wrath. Miriam's ear lobes were long and pendulous, with holes the size of grapes courting their middles.

"No Beebiji, but Baby has returned from foreign, no? Maybe she needs piercings . . . ?"

"You people know everything, right? You know all the comings and goings. Why not mind your own business, hahn? If Baby needs piercings, she will go to a proper shop, not to some fly-by-night who will give her gangrene and holes in the wrong places."

Really, Miriam had turned into a vicious old sod.

Where was the paper? It was coming later and later every morning. The nightly curfews had delayed the printing again.

One of Anu's earliest fights with Hans had been over Miriam. Sam and Sushma were patently feudal and aristocratic,

Hans maintained. For all their liberal proselytizing, they wouldn't last a day if it weren't for Miriam.

She had argued hotly in her parents' defense. "Yes, Miriam takes good care of us. But we look after her very well too."

"You call that well looked after? She's paid a pittance and slaves from morning to night."

"As usual you're converting everything to German marks. Miriam has everything she needs; she lives with us, eats with us. If she wants something, all she has to do is ask."

"So you expect her to fold her hands and say, 'Dear memsahib, I really want a cottage up in the hills with some time to myself.' How can she ask? She never gets a Sunday off unless there's a wedding or a funeral she absolutely has to attend!"

"When Miriam needs money, she asks for it. She's been with Ma's family since she was a little girl. My grandmother brought her up. She has no one else. What would she do with her own place?"

"That's for her to decide, no?"

She had snapped at him and changed the subject but the conversation left her feeling uneasy. Hans with his commie talk had a way of getting under her skin. He came from Duisburg, the son of steelworkers who had run down their tired little lives trying to get their son a passport out of poverty. "They gave everything to the factory. Little knowing that the steel they manufactured would be used by Hitler to destroy whole cities," Hans had told her the first time they met.

Every Sunday the Hopfenbergs had attended church and sat in the pew with little Hans between them, his future the only star in their firmament. He had not let them down. He had performed brilliantly at the village school and earned a place at Goethe University. He had specialized in Physics and finished with a degree in Electrical Engineering. When Anu met Hans, he was in Bombay representing Siemens on a special deputation.

Anu had always been in control in her relationships with men, but with Hans she felt lost and confused. Her knowledge, gleaned from books, seemed unworthy and insignificant next to the sureness of his experience. There was nothing Hans did not know, no subject on which he was unable to sustain a lively and polemical discussion. It seemed that he had done it all. He had started a working-class newspaper while still in school, and the Duisburg *Vox*, he told her, had run up quite a subscription and was the only surviving paper of its kind. After college, he had turned down several jobs to work for a year in the coal mines of Ruhr. He wanted to make sure, he said, that his communism was not just an intellectual conceit. Having tested his beliefs to his satisfaction, he had accepted a job at Siemens while continuing to be an active member of the Trotskyites. Almost a year into dating him, Anu discovered that Hans was also a published playwright whose plays had been performed by the Brechtian Forum in Hamburg. Hans made Anu feel as if she stood on the edge of a vast and mysterious universe. When he broke off with his girlfriend of six years and asked Anu to marry him, she could hardly refuse.

"Thieves and tricksters," Miriam mumbled to herself. Gyanchand Subziwallah had arrived, Miriam's favorite. A long time ago, he had slipped a molding tomato in the midst of her carefully handpicked ones. The slightly rotting vegetable had tipped the scales. Three years later, Gyanchand was far from forgiven. Not only did Miriam sniff, prod, and pinch before she made a single purchase but the very tools of the vegetable seller had become objects of her scrutiny. Miriam snatched his scales and held them up to her exacting eye, placing two- and five-gram weights as she pleased. Gyanchand muttered dark threats under his breath, and Miriam responded pertly with "thieves and tricksters." Yet he arrived unfailingly at her door every morning, and Miriam bought her vegetables from no one else.

How she had missed Miriam in her two years in Frankfurt! Miriam's acrimonious gentleness that mingled with the shrieking of parrots and the sudden bursts of Gulmohur. This is all she wanted: her home, the memories of days gone by, her music, books, her dear, aging parents who disguised their concern for her with bright, careless talk. She was fine, she assured them again and again. She was just happy to be home.

Had he been mean or neglectful, they wanted to know. Of course not, she replied. Hans was always the perfect gentleman. Had there been someone else? The old girlfriend? No, she laughed. It wouldn't *occur* to Hans to be unfaithful. What then? Hadn't she loved him? It had been a love marriage after all. She wasn't sure, she said. She wasn't sure she had loved him in the end.

Why had she left? Why? It wasn't Hans, she tried to explain. It was her in his world, the mismatch of her shape in the map of his world. It was Frankfurt, it was German gestalt, the nauseating presence of bratwurst, bockwurst, stadtwurst, knockwurst. It was the large people in their oversized coats, their pink faces, the smell of beer, and breaths that were ice cold. She laughed apologetically. She knew she was being unfair, she said. Everything had got to her—the bigness and fastness of the cars, the roar of the autobahns, the sickening surfeit of the supermarkets, the dreary whiteness of the winters.

She had stubbornly refused to learn the language. She hadn't liked its sound.

They said they understood, but she knew they did not. Her parents were in love with each other, and after all these years, one would still have followed the other anywhere.

"Honey, we visited Frankfurt once and thought it was a marvelous city," her mother said, then added quickly, "of course it's different when you live there."

Homesickness was not reason enough to break up a marriage, Sushma decided. There had to be something else. They concealed their worry as best as they could and welcomed their daughter home. When their friends wanted to know what had happened, they said, "it didn't work out between them," and knew from the nods elicited that the worst had been imagined. It had been scandal enough that the Reza girl had gone and married a foreigner, eight years her senior and of unknown lineage, but now she was back in less than two years without any acceptable explanation to offer.

The Hopfenbergs had not come to India for the wedding. Hans and Anu had decided to marry at short notice after Hans learned that he was required to return to the head office within the month. Nevertheless, the Rezas had organized a spectacular wedding for their only daughter. Hans said it would not be possible for his parents to attend, since their health was uncertain and they had never traveled by air before. India might prove too much for them. Surely he had a relative, an uncle perhaps, someone to represent the family, Sam and Sushma had wanted to know. No, Hans had said cheerfully, I'm all there is. They went ahead with the arrangements anyway, but the tongues had started wagging right then and there.

While Anu slipped easily and gratefully into the diurnal rhythms of her parents' home, she was reluctant to go out. For almost two years she had led a solitary life in Frankfurt. The initial excitement of being with Hans in a foreign country had dissipated after the first few months. When they first arrived, Hans had taken three weeks off, and they had spent that time going to museums and cafés. In those days they had worn their happiness on their faces in bright little newlywed signs. But with Hans back at work, Anu had begun to falter. Six visits to the Museum der Kunst, and she decided she'd seen all there was to see. Even the PalmenGarten, which she had declared to be the most beautiful in the world, had become commonplace. It was impossible to sustain a tourist identity, equally impossible to assimilate into a culture for which she felt no affinity. When she was alone, Anu realized, people stared at her. Perhaps they had always stared at her, but with Hans by her side, she hadn't noticed. Sometimes they spoke to her in their valiant English and asked her where she came from. When she said "India" they nodded their heads and responded immediately with "Gandhi" or "Nehru." Yes, that's me in a nutshell, thought Anu. Why didn't she wear a dot in the middle of the forehead, they wanted to know. Why did she wear trousers? Anu shrugged and they seemed disappointed. She felt like a picture walking about in its frame. It made her faintly derisive.

Two months after her arrival in Frankfurt, Hans took Anu to Duisberg to meet his parents. From the moment Anu entered the small, dark, and severe parlor that was home to Hans's parents, she was seized by a wave of claustrophobia. She took in the showcases dressed with lace and porcelain. Everywhere she looked, something small and fragile stared back at her, accusing her of being large and ungraceful. She allowed her backpack to slide silently to the floor, and there it sat, ugly and prominent on the hand-embroidered rug whose tufted edges seemed to spring back in horror. Hans towered like a giant in the tiny house, yet the glass figurines of cats and geese and ballerinas seemed to tolerate his presence as he did theirs.

Hans's parents did not speak a word of English, and Anu spoke no more than two salutary words in German. She said those words and they nodded at each other, and for the rest of the evening took one another in without affection. Hans's parents were both small and gray, and Anu wondered how they had produced such a large, blond child. Mrs. Hopfenberg seemed to have sized her up and reached a disappointing conclusion. It was clear that she did not consider her pretty. As for Hans's father, he seemed interested only in the newspaper, which he read with the aid of a magnifying glass. When Hans asked him a question he answered in monosyllables. They seemed so little interested in her that Anu wondered if Hans had even told them they were married.

Hans seemed to have grown larger since he entered the house. His voice was louder than usual and much more authoritative, and he spoke to his parents as if they were in his charge. His mother hung onto his every word. She never interrupted while he spoke, and when he fell silent, asked a few questions, listening attentively but without comment. Hans sometimes looked at Anu, and then she figured he was saying something about her. Hans's mother looked briefly at her, then turned away.

Anu counted eight cuckoo clocks in the room. There was nothing to do so she waited for the hour to strike to see what would happen. Six o'clock. One set off immediately, and soon they were all out, chirruping and chiming to different rhythms. The conversation ceased, and the parlor succumbed to an almost religious silence as brightly painted beaks fussed, fluttered, and flit. An image of her home in Delhi burst briefly upon her soul: the careless disarray of sprawling rugs and cushions, a Bach fugue filtering from her father's study, Toby splayed in disreputable abandon on the kitchen floor, her mother elaborately arranging an armful of flowers. She was doused with aching.

They had brought their bags with them with the intention of spending the weekend but Hans seemed to have reached the conclusion that the meeting was not going well. As the evening opened narrowly and without warmth through the only window, Hans said that they would have to head back to Frankfurt as he was working the next morning. His mother did not protest. She silently laid out a supper of cold chicken, potato salad, and sauerkraut, which they ate in the kitchen. They left soon after. They drove back to Frankfurt, and Hans was quiet and cool with her. All he said was, "You should start taking German lessons." Anu nodded.

She had intended to enroll in German classes as early as possible, but when the time came, she found herself searching for excuses. Her terrible migraines had returned, she said, the cold had never suited her. She told Hans she would wait for warmer weather and enroll in the spring. Spring turned to summer and before long it was winter again.

With Hans away at work, Anu was reluctant to go out. It was a lot simpler to stay at home, and very soon she stopped going out altogether. Once a week, however, she took the bus to Amerika Haus and brought home two or three books, which kept her occupied for the rest of the week.

Anu's survival in Frankfurt soon came to depend upon a careful regimen. She visited the library once a week on Mondays. She went on a Tuesday only if the library was closed that Monday. She began with the A stacks and worked her way down the alphabet. She decided that she would read an author whose name started with the letter A before she could read one with the letter B and would proceed in a strictly alphabetical fashion. She would allow herself to read up to three books from authors sharing the same letter but not a second book from the same author. She was not allowed to skip letters and was not allowed to abandon a book once she had started it. Once she reached Z she would be free to begin all over again and alter the rules if she pleased. This little game was fun and it involved both predetermination and randomness. The self-imposed rigidity introduced a tremendous vitality into her reading life. Unlike the ordinary reader, who, discovering a favored author, devours everything she has written, Anu was constantly changing writer, period, and genre.

The reading changed something in Anu. She found herself needing Hans less and less. Earlier she had waited impatiently for him to come home, for their life to begin. Now, hearing his car screech to a halt outside, she found herself putting down her book with reluctance. Hans's homecoming was fast becoming an intrusion.

In her second year in Frankfurt, Anu did nothing but drink coffee, smoke cigarettes, and read books. She read without pause and without discrimination. She maintained an alphabetical list and wrote down everything she had read in the order she had read it:

EDWARD ALBEE: *The Zoo Story*
SHERWOOD ANDERSON: *Kit Brandon*
DONALD BARTHELME: *Come Back, Dr. Caligari*
SAUL BELLOW: *Dangling Man*
PEARL BUCK: *The Good Earth*
TRUMAN CAPOTE: *Other Voices, Other Rooms*
JOHN CHEEVER: *The Wapshot Scandal*
STEPHEN CRANE: *The Red Badge of Courage*
JOHN DOS PASSOS: *The 42nd Parallel*

THEODORE DREISER: *Sister Carrie*

T.S. ELIOT: *Murder in the Cathedral*

RALPH ELLISON: *Shadow and Act*

She did not discuss what she read with Hans. They had less and less to say to each other these days. She had never enjoyed his friends, not even those who spoke English. All that Comintern talk that had stirred her imagination once now seemed pedantic and predictable. She was reluctant to go out with him and was no longer displeased when he stayed late at work.

WILLIAM FAULKNER: *Absalom, Absalom!*

F. SCOTT FITZGERALD: *The Great Gatsby*

ALLEN GINSBERG: *Reality Sandwiches*

DASHIELL HAMMETT: *The Thin Man*

NATHANIEL HAWTHORNE: *The Scarlet Letter*

ZORA NEALE HURSTON: *Their Eyes Were Watching God*

WASHINGTON IRVING: *The Legend of Sleepy Hollow and Other Stories*

HENRY JAMES: *The Portrait of a Lady*

JACK KEROUAC: *On the Road*

RING LARDNER: *The Young Immigrants*

HARPER LEE: *To Kill a Mockingbird*

SINCLAIR LEWIS: *World So Wide*

Anu was usually asleep by the time Hans got home. He would swallow the dinner she had left out, packaged beans and rice, or a ham and cheese sandwich. Neither of them was fond of cooking. He fell into bed, careful not to touch her. He would lie there sleepless, staring at the ceiling, wondering where it had gone, their passion, their curiosity, when he'd thought an entire continent was reflected in the laughing eyes of a girl. Now, more and more, he thought of Helke, good, strong, no-nonsense Helke and the ease and familiarity of their six years together. Tomorrow was Helke's birthday. Maybe he should give her a call, see how she was getting on.

NORMAN MAILER: *Advertisements for Myself*

HERMAN MELVILLE: *Billy Budd*

OGDEN NASH: *The Bad Parents' Garden of Verse*

CHARLES OLSON: *The Maximus Poems*

SYLVIA PLATH: *The Colossus and Other Poems*

ELLERY QUEEN: *The Chinese Orange Mystery*

ADRIENNE RICH: *The Diamond Cutters and Other Poems*

PHILIP ROTH: *Goodbye Columbus*

J.D. SALINGER: *Franny and Zooey*

JOHN STEINBECK: *Of Mice and Men*

HARRIET BEECHER STOWE: *Sam Lawson's Oldtown Fireside Stories*

ALLEN TATE: *Narcissus as Narcissus*

SARA TEASDALE: *Rivers to the Sea*

JOHN UPDIKE: *Cosmic Gall*

GORE VIDAL: *Julian*

KURT VONNEGUT: *Cat's Cradle*

WALT WHITMAN: *Leaves of Grass*

TENNESSEE WILLIAMS: *Cat on a Hot Tin Roof*

WILLIAM CARLOS WILLIAMS: *Journey to Love*

That's when Anu reached her crisis. She discovered that Amerika Haus did not represent a single author beginning with the letter X. She sank into a quagmire of her own making. Because of her self-imposed rule, she was unable to proceed. She held Richard Yates's *Eleven Kinds of Loneliness* briefly in her hands, then replaced it determinedly on the shelf.

—⟊—

"But why," I asked her. "What was the big deal anyway? I don't get it. Why couldn't you just move on?"

"Listen," she said. "It's very hard to understand, I know. But it was my Enterprise with a capital E. I depended on it, its order, its cleanness. I followed it devoutly. Without it, I felt derailed. I returned home without any books that day. I had nothing to read."

—⟊—

All of a sudden there was nothing to do, nothing to fill the hours. Anu made the bed. She pulled out the vacuum cleaner and cleaned the floors. Hans would be surprised. She never did any housework, none at all during the week. He was disgusted but left her alone. He returned home every evening at six, sputtering at the dank air, the stale smell of cigarettes, the still unmade bed. On weekends, Anu put aside her reading. That was also part of her enterprise. They did the cleaning and the laundry together, then went out perfunctorily in the evenings. Well, today was different. She would have it all done before he got home. There was nothing else to do. Maybe she would cook for a change too, some bratwurst, sauerkraut, potato salad, the usual. What she wouldn't do for some of Miriam's rice and dal!

In desperation she reached for the radio, searching the short wave for the BBC. Usually she tuned in only in the mornings, but today there was all this time.

"... as soon as the public accepts the fact that
the dark-skinned community consists largely of
criminals or people who are dirty ..."

She pulled out the antenna, moving closer to the window to steady the wavering voice.

> "... an example of how this imagery is mastered at the international level is the recent situation in the Congo. Here we have an example of planes dropping bombs on defenseless African villages ... That bomb is dropped on men, women, children, and babies. There is no outcry. There is no concern. There is no sympathy. There is no urge on the part of even the so-called progressive element to try and bring a halt to this mass murder. Why?"

She hadn't known there was anything going on in the Congo. She hadn't known much of what was going on anywhere in the world. She'd lived tucked away in her tower. *"Willows whiten, aspens quiver, little breezes dusk and shiver,"* she murmured, the words entering her from the hollows of her past. *"Four gray walls, and four gray towers, overlook a space of flowers ..."*

No flowers here though. Out on the street, a large Siberian husky left an ever-widening pit of yellow piddle in the deep white snow. The dog unhurriedly scraped his hind paws and splattered the air. Is this what she should weave into her tapestry?

> " ... so the American planes with American bombs being piloted by American-trained pilots dropping American bombs on black people, black babies, black children, destroying them completely goes absolutely unnoticed ..."

The voice continued. The husky lunged forward, and its owner, a deeply swaddled woman in mitts and muffs who blew puffs of cold breath, was swept off her feet. Ten paces later, the dog pulled abruptly to a standstill and lifted his leg to splay the lamppost. He had no piddle left but the white purity of the snow was disturbed by the confusion of footsteps.

> " . . . as soon as a few whites, the lives of a few whites were at stake, they began to speak of 'white hostages,' 'white missionaries,' as if a white life, one white life, was of such greater value than a black life, than a thousand black lives. They showed you their open contempt for the lives of the blacks and their deep concern for the lives of the whites . . ."

She was transfixed by the voice on the radio.

> " . . . you have had a generation of Africans who actually believed that they could negotiate, negotiate, negotiate and eventually get some kind of independence. But you're getting a new generation that is being born right now, and they are beginning to think with their own mind and see that you can't negotiate upon freedom nowadays. If something is yours by right, then you fight for it or shut up. If you can't fight for it then forget it."

The woman and the dog had passed out of her line of vision. It was empty again, and white, except for the circle of piss.

The applause rang loud in her ears and the white road was deserted. Why didn't I think of it before, she said to herself. It isn't too late. I can go home. I can go home now.

She went inside and sat down. It was almost 6 p.m. Hans would be home soon. She would tell him right away.

"Thank you, Mr. X," said the perfectly modulated British voice. *"That was Mr. Malcolm X addressing the Africa Society at the London School of Economics, February 11 . . ."*

Anu laughed.

"Why, thank you, Mister X," she repeated.

—~—

She hadn't noticed that Miriam had refilled her coffee. There was still no sign of that newspaper. In another twenty minutes the whole house would be up, and they'd be fighting over it. For two years she hadn't cared about what went on in the world. But now she had returned to it.

On the plane back to India, she had picked up a newspaper and read the brief notice,

> The controversial Black Islamist leader, Malcolm X, was assassinated in a public auditorium in New York City on February 21.

Her hands hadn't stopped shaking. It was incredible to think that ten days ago she hadn't heard of the man.

PAA-RAA TRUPPER

We never ventured out after dark. The government had issued strict orders that all travel had to be completed by 7 p.m. and any trafficking afterward could only be for reasons of emergency. I guess it was an emergency that made Nanaji bundle me up in the Fiat that night at 9 p.m. It was my bedtime, and Naneeji was very strict about making sure that I went to bed on time so I could awake at 6 a.m. and get ready for school. Mummy was away to Rohtak to pay her respects to Dadaji and Dadeeji. I had clamored to go with her on the trip but the adults had decided, predictably of course, that I was not to miss school.

Naneeji's sister lived by herself in her father's house on Curzon Road. Naneeji had tried for years to convince her aging sister to come and live with us, but Bari Nanee, being quite as obstinate and forceful, had refused. She was born in that house, she declared, and that is where she intended to die. I wondered whether she was planning to do so that night. We had received a phone call from a neighboring shop to say that she was most unwell, and could we please come over as soon as possible? I had never seen a dead person before, and I thought once again of Miss

Havisham, except that Bari Nanee did not own a wedding dress, and had never come close to owning one.

The plan was that if we found Bari Nanee well enough to travel, we would get her things and drive her back to our house. If her condition warranted it, we would take her straight to Safdarjang Hospital, and Naneeji would spend the night with her there. As there was no one to leave me with, I was dragged along on the mission.

"But she wants to die at home," I reminded them, thinking that Bari Nanee's last wishes ought to be respected.

"Shhhh . . ." said Nanaji, looking irritated, while Naneeji kissed the locket around her neck. Her locket had a wind-up mechanism, which, when pressed into service, called upon the entire pantheon of Hindu gods and goddesses. I wasn't sure which deity was being smothered by her kisses at the time.

We started off at a snail's pace. The streets were completely deserted, except for an occasional cyclist or pedestrian. Because of the curfew, none of the streetlights were on. Roadblocks had closed off several of the roads and all the houses had pasted-up windows, just like ours. The shops, too, were closed and shuttered. A dull, half-beam emanated from our headlights. Nanaji had cut half-circles of black parchment paper and covered the headlights at about the same time that we had pasted up the windows at home. I encountered the pleasure of seeing Orion distinct in the night sky.

"Go faster, faster," urged Naneeji while Nanaji patiently repeated that he couldn't see a thing.

"Jaswanti needs us. We have to hurry." There was reproach in her voice. Naneeji was a blind supporter of her own family, which by some curious illogic had turned Nanaji's sisters into her personal adversaries. Her family could do no wrong, not even

the youngest, Chotte, with whom she had always had a difficult relationship. Naneeji maintained that her father, Babaji, was
the only member of her family for whom Nanaji had had any
regard, and since his passing away, had become indifferent to
her kin. I don't believe this to be true but it was impossible to
argue with my grandmother. She treated Nanaji's sisters with
the greatest suspicion and the two families did not meet much.
As I understood it, by complaining that Nanaji was not driving
fast enough, she was implying that he didn't care enough about
Bari Nanee and was leaving her to die. I found myself deeply
absorbed by the games that Nanaji and Naneeji played with each
other.

"Hurry up. Can't you drive faster?"

"There are no lights. I can't see. They've blocked off half the
roads."

We entered the normally crowded marketplace that I knew
well. Naneeji came here to shop, and when I wasn't in school, I
accompanied her with our well-worn vegetable bag. Sarojini
Nagar market was always bursting with shoppers, sellers, stray
animals, and beggars screaming and vying with one another for
attention. It looked completely abandoned now. I could make out
scattered, huddled forms, men asleep under their shawls, a few
mangy dogs scavenging for scraps.

I don't know in what order they came: the loud thud, the
jolt that shook the insides of the car, the sudden screeching of
brakes, or the dogs that appeared simultaneously from nowhere
and set up their dreadful howling. All of a sudden there were men
there too, springing out of the bowels of the earth, milling around
the car.

"What have you done, what have you done?" murmured
Naneeji fretfully. Nanaji tried to open his door, but every time it

opened more than an inch, a pack of snarling dogs leaped up at him, forcing him back.

The car was quickly surrounded. The few sleeping men had metamorphosed into a rabid crowd. A self-appointed leader inspected the front of the car and set up a howl, *Maar daala!*

"Haraamzade ne Gou Maa ko maar daala!" (The bastard has killed a holy cow.)

A fearsome roar went through the crowd. Nanaji's door was flung open and he was pulled out of the car. The man who had set up the cry slammed his fist full into Nanaji's face.

War broke out right then and there. I had been waiting for it to happen and here it was, unlike anything I had imagined. This was quiet terror; there was no desk to hide under and no scented pink flamingo.

Naneeji's voice was hoarse. "I beg you. In God's name, let him go." Her window was rolled up so they probably didn't hear her. In any case the crowd was in no mood to be cajoled.

The snarling dogs retreated after receiving a few well-aimed kicks. The crowd didn't want to share its spoil with the dogs and lunged forward at Nanaji. I closed my eyes and prayed.

"Paa-Raa Trupper"

"Paa-Raa Trupper"

The mob chanted in unison.

"Saala Katwa!"

"Paki!"

The beating couldn't have lasted more than a few minutes or they would have done Nanaji in. There was the sound of a whistle above the crowd's roar, and a policeman broke into the front. He shouted for calm, and slowly, reluctantly, the crowd fell silent.

"Paa-raa trupper!" said the crowd leader, panting and jubilant, holding Nanaji up like a trophy.

The policeman opened the car door and pushed Nanaji inside. The left side of his face was completely bloodied. Naneeji was sobbing, loud racking sobs. She reached for his face, daubed at it with her handkerchief. Nanaji groaned and pushed her away. The cop began interrogating Nanaji in Hindi. Nanaji's voice trembled, and he was tight-lipped with anger.

"Of course I'm not a damn paratrooper. Do I look like a bloody paratrooper to you? I'm a government official."

"You have killed a cow."

"It was an *accident*. I don't make it my business to go around killing cows. It's impossible to see in the dark. The PWD is supposed to keep one in five street lights on. Do you see a single light on anywhere?"

"Why you driving at this time?"

The policeman switched to English and raised his voice back at Nanaji.

"Gorement officer, hahn, and you don't know there is curfew? Why you driving so fast?"

"Come with me to *thana*," he said when Nanaji did not reply. The cop tried to open the back door. I had locked it as instructed.

Nanaji motioned to Naneeji to get in at the back with me. She slid out of the car. The men leered at her. The cop got in at the front with Nanaji.

"Now drive. Slowly. You are not running horse race."

Nanaji fumbled with the ignition, then realized he couldn't see. His glasses were no longer on his face.

"My glasses," he said, defeated. "My spectacles, please. I cannot see without them."

I unlocked the door and jumped out. I had forgotten all about the dead cow. There it was, eerily white in the darkness, its head twisted back, its eyes frozen with surprise. Blood gushed out of its mouth. I stared at my first corpse, and it wasn't Bari Nanee.

Naneeji was out of the car in a flash. She pushed me inside and picked up the glasses, which were lying a few feet away. She handed them to Nanaji, and there was hostility in her movements. Now that Nanaji was safe, it was okay to shift the blame back to him, I figured.

Nanaji fumbled with his glasses. The frame was bent and both the lenses were smashed. Nevertheless, he put them on. Sometimes, when I look back on that incident, it's Gandhi's head I see transposed onto Nanaji's. Mahatma Gandhi, brutalized by his people, his broken spectacles on his face.

The policeman ordered the men standing around to remove the cow from under the car's wheel. "*Hum usko thane le jayenge*," he said reassuringly, and the crowd murmured its approval at the prospect of Nanaji being punished some more.

The self-appointed leader came across to his side and said conspiratorially, "Sir, *wo jo* reward *hai*?"

"*Koi* reward *nahin*. No reward."

"Five hundred rupees, sir?"

"*Bola na*, no reward," said the cop again, motioning Nanaji to get moving.

"I won't be surprised if I kill a few cows now," Nanaji muttered under his breath as he looked back and started to reverse. The policeman looked grim while Naneeji hissed at him to shut up.

"It's no use. I can't drive like this. Can't see a thing."

The policeman got out of the car and walked over to the driver's seat. Nanaji slid over to the passenger side. The policeman started up the ignition.

"We'll see if you really are gorement official," he said, reversing from the crowd. Nanaji rapped at the sticker on his window.

"Anyone can purchase gorement sticker for two rupees."

Slowly we drove out of Sarojini Nagar market. I had never seen Nanaji in the passenger seat before and he looked small and helpless with his bloodied face and ruined eye, his spectacles hanging from his nose. Nobody spoke. Nanaji occasionally gave directions. I kept seeing the cow's twisted face, the snarling fangs of the dogs, the equally snarling face of the man who hadn't got his reward.

As we entered Diplomatic Enclave the policeman began to shift uneasily in his seat. You should be more careful when you drive, he said. Nowadays, no one can kill a cow and get away with it. Nanaji told him curtly to stop in front of our house. They let us out; then Nanaji and the policeman drove off. Naneeji told me to go straight to bed, I had school the next day. She brought me a glass of hot milk and then locked herself up in the prayer room. A thin, quivering chant filled the air. Naneeji chanted every morning for about an hour but I had never heard her pray at this time.

I lay in bed listening to the thin icicles in her voice and waited for Nanaji to come home. His face stood before me exaggeratedly grotesque, his eye hanging open.

Finally, I heard the key turn in the front lock and rushed out of my room. Naneeji's singsong also subsided. Nanaji's face had been cleaned up and his bad eye had been bandaged. I hugged him tightly and couldn't stop crying.

"It's okay, darling. I'm okay. Everything is all right now," he said. But nothing was okay again. That night was a small measure of the things to come.

Naneeji appeared silently with a glass of milk. She gave it to Nanaji and said, "Go have a bath. Then come in and pray. After all, you have killed a cow. It will rest heavy on your karma. We will all have to pay for it." Naneeji kissed her locket fervently and returned to the prayer room.

The next morning I was in no condition to go to school. With great trepidation, Naneeji and I took the bus and went over to Bari Nanee's instead. Nanaji had said he would be unable to drive until his glasses were fixed. Naneeji looked terribly put out as though he had orchestrated the whole incident to cause inconvenience to her family.

"What if Jaswanti needs hospitalization?" she demanded.

"I will arrange an ambulance," he said.

As it turned out, there was absolutely nothing wrong with Bari Nanee! No, she had not asked any shopkeeper to call us, she said. What on earth was her sister talking about? We should know that all messages from her were relayed through Tinker Tailors. If some other shop had called us, we should have figured that it was a hoax. But who would play such a cruel hoax, asked Naneeji. All sorts of things happen during a war, Bari Nanee said. She chided her sister for her carelessness and sent us packing.

But the deed had been done, a cow had been killed, and as Naneeji had decreed, we would all have to pay for it.

CRUCIFIXION

Until that day I had had no dealings whatsoever with the Mother Superior. It was only the rowdy girls of the class whom the teachers could not control who were summoned to her presence. When my name was called, I was certain there was some mistake. With great trepidation I made my way to Mother Superior's office, expecting at last an encounter with the famed metallic ruler. Instead, I found myself looking at a pair of pale and watery eyes that swam with distress and love. She kissed her rosary and clasped my hands in hers.

"My dear, my dear, my dear."

On Mother Superior's desk stood a large porcelain bust of the Virgin Mary in blue and pink with liquid hands folded under her cheek and eyes staring heavenward. Two years at Mount Mary School and I had turned into a staunch Catholic. I was an avid chapelgoer. I loved the choir and the ritual of breaking bread and drinking sweetened water. I was a regular reader of the fortnightly editions of *Stories from the Bible*, which the school sold for ten *paise* per issue. Whenever I went home for the holidays, I spent my pocket money buying a little angel or a cupid as a present for

Mummy and Daddy. The Bible store offered a ten percent discount to Mount Mary students, and our home had quite an assortment of these celestial creatures. I would have bought them Jesuses and Marys too except that I thought they wouldn't quite appreciate them since they were Hindu by birth, though not the practicing kind. After receiving his fourth angel, Daddy laughed and said, "Now, don't you go and turn yourself into a nun." That confused me because until then I had every intention of doing so.

Seeing me stare longingly at the Virgin Mary, Mother Superior placed an arm around my shoulder and led me to a wooden cupboard in the corner of the room. "We will pray together," she said. She opened the cupboard, and I saw a lifesize figure of Jesus Christ nailed to the cross. There was something frightening about his face. It was not the one I had encountered in *Stories from the Bible*, and it was reassuring to think that it usually stayed locked up. Mother Superior flicked a switch and Christ's halo fizzed to life. Little lights flashed on and off above his gaunt cheeks, and I had the distinct impression that his eyes rolled backwards into their sockets.

"We must pray," said Mother Superior, "for your father, who has entered the Kingdom of Heaven."

I closed my eyes and placing my palms fervently together, recited the prayer that I said every night before going to bed:

"Dear God, please take care of my Daddy
and my Mummy and me, and Nanaji and Naneeji,
and Dadaji and Dadeeji, and Auntie Indira
and Auntie Radhika, and my cousins Shalini
and Deepika, and all my friends and loved ones."

I always added a few lines of immediate concern.

"Please forgive Nanaji for killing the cow.
As you know, it was not his fault. Thank you, God."

Mother Superior shut off the lights and Christ returned to anonymity. She locked up the cupboard.

"Dear God," sighed Mother Superior drying her eyes with a perfectly starched white handkerchief. She looked thoughtfully at me. "May your sight never wander, may your blessings never fail to fall upon this unfortunate family, amen," she said, and crossed herself.

"Dear child, now you must go home. There is a car waiting for you." I must have been obtuse or something for it was only then that I realized something was wrong.

Obituary

There came the newspaper now, its tightly rolled mass hurled through the air with perfect aim, hitting the glass door of the veranda, making her jump. Anu unlocked the door leading to the garden, retrieved the paper and returned inside, hugging her nightgown close to her. It had been an unusual September; it was already chilly in the mornings.

Anu scanned through the albums looking for Beethoven's piano concerto number 4. It must be on the turntable where she had left it yesterday. Dad would chastise her for not putting the records away. She made sure the volume was low, then lifted the stylus. She had spent hours with Hans, right here on this porch, listening to her father's classical collection. But in Germany she hadn't been able to listen to the same music. It had filled her with a raging nostalgia that had unsettled her for days. Odd that Beethoven, Bach, and Schubert should feel so much more at home here where the parrots were riotous, where a dung seller's cry lifted the allegro, and Toby yelped.

She settled back in the bamboo chair and lit her first ciga- rette of the morning. She went through thirty in a day but had promised her parents she'd cut it down to ten. The rubber band ate into the newsprint as it slid off.

INDIANS DESTROY 75 PAKISTANI TANKS IN 24 HOURS

She quickly scanned the page.

Indian forces created a glorious record when they destroyed 75 Pakistani tanks in 24 hours during their two new thrusts into Pakistan since yesterday. Till today 114 Pakistani tanks, most of them American-built Pattons and the rest Shermans have been knocked out. All Pakistani attacks were repulsed with heavy losses to the enemy.

U THANT CONDUCTS FIRST ROUND OF TALKS WITH AYUB

Anu folded the first page to find Sharmila Tagore smiling meaningful dimples at her.

MY COMPLEXION OWES ITS LOVELINESS TO LUX
"Nothing flatters a woman more than a flawless complexion," says lovely Sharmila. "That's why your complexion is as important as mine."

It was her father's advertising company, Lintas. Anu rolled her eyes and turned the page. War was man's work; women need worry only about their complexions. How much does she get paid for one of these, she wondered.

JAWANS MORALE MAGNIFICENT

IAF REAPS REWARDS OF SUPERB TRAINING

PAKISTANI PARATROOPERS SUSPECTED IN DELHI

She looked at a curious picture of villagers beating a paddy field with sticks and bats.

Civilians aid the police in their search for Pakistani paratroopers near Purana Qila. The government has offered a reward of Rs. 500 to anyone whose efforts lead to the arrest of a paratrooper.

Bored, she put down the paper. War didn't interest her at all, though recently she'd been reading up on the CIA-engineered coup in the Congo and the election of General Mobutu. She made a mental note to catch *My Fair Lady* before it left. It was already in its thirty-first bumper week. Bumper week, she repeated. Now, what's the etymology of that? She picked up the paper again. Dad hated it when he didn't find it folded down correctly. She started putting the pages together when she saw his picture staring at her.

A hand reached out, clutched her throat.

It was Ronu all right. Ronu in uniform. Ronu, whose awkward smile never reached his eyes. She had teased him about it. Too many cameras trained on him too early; they had stolen away his smile. Her heart pounded. She hadn't thought about Ronu in years. Not really.

She opened the paper, smoothing out the crease on his face.

There were a brief three paragraphs, and the words swam senselessly before her eyes.

The body of Flight Lieutenant Ranjit Kalra was flown to Delhi on Thursday night. Flight Lieutenant Kalra showed commendable courage in the line of duty where he was killed in action on the Western front.

The IAF handed over the body to the deceased's family. The deceased's father, Superintendent of Police Jagdish Kishore Kalra, thanked the IAF for its prompt service and said he was proud of his son for bringing glory to the family with his heroic death. Flight Lieutenant Kalra was cremated yesterday with full military honors.

Flight Lieutenant Kalra (28), a graduate of the National Defense Academy, was a Flying Instructor at Air Force School, Jodhpur. He had distinguished himself in his childhood as a child star in Hindi films. He went by the name of Master Bunty and was best known for his role in *Soldier.* A patriot since the age of five, Flight Lieutenant Kalra has sacrificed his life in service to the nation. He is survived by his wife and a six-year-old daughter.

She stared at the print as if somehow its meaning eluded her. He was dead. Ronu was dead. Dead at twenty-eight. He would have been twenty-nine on the fourteenth of December. A wave of anguish passed through her. She never could forget his birthday and the three birthdays they had spent together.

The sensations came and went, gripped her and left. Disbelief. Guilt. Remorse. She had scanned the papers without interest every morning, never stopping to think that the war meant anything more than a few headlines, never stopping to think that the war had anything to do with her. Because of a quirk of fate, she'd found her destinies much more closely entangled with those of sub-Saharan Africa.

She stared at Ronu's picture. He looked older, thinner, caught in a half-smile, still trying to decide which face to wear in front of the camera, smiling or serious. Ronu is dead, she told herself.

She sat there for a long time, the newspaper on her lap, the cigarette untouched in the ashtray, the LP revolving uselessly on the turntable. She should rise, lift the stylus, but she sat, unmoving. She could not cry but the bones ached inside her. He is dead, she repeated, dead. My love is dead, and it is only now that I realize how I loved him.

—m—

She read the obituary again and again as though there were a stone in there she'd left unturned.

The body of Flight Lieutenant Ranjit Kalra was flown to Delhi on Thursday night. Flight Lieutenant Kalra showed commendable courage in the line of duty where he was killed in action on the Western front.

The body was flown to Delhi on Thursday night. Thursday was the ninth. When had he died? Perhaps Thursday itself, more likely Wednesday. How had he died? What "commendable courage" had he shown? She wanted to know.

She looked at the first page again, searching for clues. No, of course not. It had happened on Wednesday or Thursday. She should look at Thursday's paper and Friday's.

She rose hurriedly, scattering the untouched plate of biscuits. In an instant Toby was there devouring them, and she let him have his way as she bent down over the magazine rack and pulled out the old papers.

Friday the tenth. Thursday the ninth. She scanned the headlines, her heart pounding. She had read these pages before, not realizing that perhaps she was reading an account of Ronu's death. There was nothing there.

TWO NEW THRUSTS BY JAWANS

FUTILE PAK BID TO INVADE AMRITSAR: PLANE DOWNED

She anxiously read the article. No, it was the army that had shot down a Pakistani C-130 transport plane that had come into Amritsar. That was all.

Nothing in Thursday's paper about aerial combat. In fact, India had not lost a single plane on those two days. So how did Ronu die?

In Friday's paper, she found a small paragraph.

The IAF carried out a number of sorties to strike at the Pakistani air base at Sargodha and other airfields. All Indian aircraft returned safely to base.

Perhaps it had happened even earlier. On Monday, Tuesday, or Wednesday. In the middle of a war it would take time to retrieve a body, especially from foreign soil. She ran back to the magazine rack and found the newspapers for the sixth, seventh, and eighth. She scanned them carefully, reading anything that mentioned the IAF. There was nothing there except tales of triumph. No losses at all. Could it have happened even earlier then, in the very first days of the war?

All of a sudden she was filled with urgency. Ronu had never appeared as vivid as he did to her then. She could smell his smell, a duskiness that was his alone; she could taste his mouth. She had stopped pining for him a few months after their breakup. Sometimes, though, the physical memory of him invaded her like an assault and she became, once again, the victim of an unexplainable eros. She laughed it off but remained surprised by its vehemence. First love, after all. Altogether inappropriate. Totally enslaving.

Desire burned in her, mixed with weeping. Ronu's physicality was palpable to her; it defied the announcement of his death.

"Good morning, *beta*," her mother's voice, frothy through toothpaste.

"Good morning, Ma," she said as levelly as she could.

She ran into the kitchen. "Miriam, where are the old papers?"

"In the magazine rack."

"No, I want last week's papers."

"I sell to the *kabariwala* every Sunday. Last week's are gone. Why do you need them?"

Anu didn't reply. Soon they would all know. They would all be saddened, Miriam especially, who had told her flatly that she didn't like that Hans, Anu should have married her first boyfriend, the tall and nice one, what was his name? They would all be glad, in retrospect, that she had not married him. Better a divorced daughter than a widowed one, Sam would say. Miriam would go to church and light a candle. Why was she thinking these futile thoughts? She went into her father's study, pulled out a pair of scissors, and carefully cut out Ronu's obituary. She needed time, a little time before she could go out and face the world. She would get dressed and go with her father to his office. They had all the newspapers there, from all over the country. She would read them carefully, find out what had happened.

Ronu, are you really dead? We talked so often about you dying and leaving me behind. I don't think either of us believed it for a moment. It could so easily have been me that's left behind now, bereaved, with a six-year-old daughter. Six-year-old daughter? Why Ronu, you didn't waste much time.

Captain Hook

Mummy looks beautiful in white. The color has always suited her. When she moved in with us, the atmosphere changed. Naneeji was more pleasant than usual. She started leaving Nanaji alone. Perhaps she was happier because she had her favorite daughter for company. Perhaps she was only trying to save Mummy further unhappiness and managed to control herself in front of her. She never had restrained herself with me! Anyway, I was glad for Nanaji. I knew he was troubled over Mummy's fate and mine but because Naneeji was behaving herself, a calm filled the house that I had not known before.

The only reason I had tolerated living with my grandparents (apart from the elementary fact that I had no choice) was that I always knew home to be someplace else. Home was with Mummy and Daddy, and even though it shifted around and was sometimes small and sometimes large, sometimes had a garden and sometimes didn't, there were things about home that were constant. There was always a peg behind the front door where Daddy hung his jacket and his hat when he came in. There was a rug on the floor where he did his stretches and where I clambered onto his back. There was a table where he and I did our jigsaw puzzles. Daddy and I had been doing jigsaws since I was three years old when somebody gave me my first twelve-piece puzzle. That summer of '65, Daddy brought home a thousand-piece jigsaw. On the cover, Captain Hook glinted evilly while ships warred, storms flashed, and hidden treasure remained undetected on the ocean floor. When we got down to it, however, the jigsaw was not as exciting as it looked. This will be very difficult, Daddy warned, but we'll finish it together, you and I, if you don't give up. I promised I wouldn't give up. He spent hours sorting out the pieces. When he found the ones that made up Captain Hook's face, he allowed me the pleasure of putting them together. I worked with him task by task. By the end of the summer holidays we were halfway done. He said, let's leave the puzzle on the table, just the way it is. When you come home in the winter, we'll finish it. Mummy promised us she wouldn't disturb the table.

When Mummy came to live with Nanaji and Naneeji, permanently that is, she tried to tell me that this was now our home, for there was nowhere else to go. We had lived in so many places (I could hardly remember their names) that I couldn't understand why all of a sudden there was nowhere to go. We lived in different places because of Daddy, she said. Now that Daddy is gone, we have to live here. But where has Daddy gone, I wanted to know. She sighed. Each of them had tried to explain it to me so many times, each in his or her own way. He has passed on, Nanaji had said. He has found eternal peace, Dadaji had said. He is united with God, Naneeji had said. He is dead, dead, dead, Mummy had said violently when I wouldn't stop asking.

I knew Daddy was dead. I knew all about death. I'd seen the dead cow, and I'd seen the frightening face of Jesus. I knew Daddy was dead but I still wanted to know when he'd come home so we could finish the jigsaw. He had told me not to give up. He was not allowed to give up either. I waited for the winter vacation when it would be time to go home, wherever home now was, behind the clouds perhaps, for according to Dadeeji, that is where Daddy had gone. I waited to go home and finish the jigsaw that waited on the table.

I did not cry when Daddy died. I forgave him for not being there on my seventh birthday. I just waited for the winter holidays. Mummy said we were not going anywhere except to Rohtak to visit Dadaji and Dadeeji. But we have to finish the puzzle, I said. Mummy took me to her cupboard in Naneeji's room. She showed me a large box. Yes, darling, she said. We will do the puzzle. Nanaji will help us. She brought down the box. It was Captain Hook and he glinted evilly. Inside, the pieces were carefully wrapped up in a bag, all of them. Mummy had taken it apart. I cried and cried. I hated her for breaking her promise. The winter came and went but I never forgave her.

Rani and Her Family

Nothing special happened in my life all the way until Rani came into it. I was ten then, and Rani must have been fifteen or sixteen. In a fundamental way Rani did not exist for anyone but me. Nanaji, I don't think, ever spoke to her. He didn't speak much in those days anyway. When he did, it was as if he'd made a decision to shake off the weariness that had settled on his soul. He only spoke to Naneeji when spoken to. It surprised me later to think that my grandfather had been a freedom fighter. It made me think that he must have been a very different person once, or perhaps he still transformed himself the moment he left the house. I never did meet the other revolutionary Nanaji except through his writings. Nanaji was always different with me, though. After Daddy died, he sought me out more and more, and even though we never talked about Daddy, it was as if the space we inhabited always had room for him.

Nanaji worked long days and was out of the house before I awoke. In the evenings, he would return in time to slide silently into his assigned place at the dinner table and await our dismal, fluorescent-lit meal. Immediately afterwards he retired to his study, offering no pretext, and none was expected of him. I followed him there to read my novels. Until Rani came along, Nanaji was my best friend.

I liked to think of myself as someone who preferred the company of ghosts. Nanaji lent himself easily to that fantasy. He seemed to belong to another time; he marched to a different tune. For some reason of his own or some indefinable purpose, he had emanated in our midst, but I, for one, wouldn't have been in the least surprised if one fine day he went poof, just like that, the way Daddy had done. Sometimes, I would turn to his chair and be surprised to find him sitting there, just as I'd left him.

Nanaji's ghost was gentle and considerate, and when I happened to be around, it made it a point to ask my opinion on some matter or another. But even Nanaji, for all his kindness, did not notice Rani as she carried a pail of water across to the outhouse or worked mud-encrusted in the vegetable patch. Rani was the servant girl whose family occupied our servants' quarters.

Naneeji, however, kept Rani in her cat-like gaze, watching her when her back was turned, making sure she hadn't slipped a little something into the folds of her white and blue *salwar-kameez*. Rani had the habit of clenching and unclenching her fists, and one day, Naneeji asked her to open them and show her what she was holding. There was nothing there. Naneeji felt compromised and made Rani empty out her whole sack. I ran across to take a look. There was a notebook, a pencil, and the deeply red ribbon that Rani wore when her hair was freshly washed and oiled. Rani turned redder than usual but said nothing. Later, when I felt I had acquired the moral right to know everything there was to know about Rani, I sneaked a look into that notebook. I was surprised to find that it was empty: clean and white, a notebook in waiting.

Rani had no authority so I too ordered her around.

"*Rani!*"

"*Hahnji.*"

Monosyllabic acquiescence, no matter who it was who addressed her, her parents, her brother, Naneeji, or I. Nanaji, I don't think, ever did.

"Rani, come play with me."

"*Ji hahn, babyji.*"

She hesitated, as though weighing the load of that request on a balance. Sometimes she'd stop whatever it was she was doing, peeling vegetables or sewing a button, and run aross to me for a game of catch-catch or hopscotch.

Sometimes she'd say, "Not now. I'll finish this and come."

I'd know then that she was engaged in one of Naneeji's tasks, something that could not be negotiated. Naneeji had fought her way to occupy top rung in the ladder of authority that supported our house. I was probably second in command. Nanaji was way down among Rani and the servants.

The first time Rani did not immediately jump to service, I became sullen and furious and knew from the look on her face that she was afraid I would complain about her. But I never complained, not once. When she was beaten or punished, it had nothing to do with me, except for that one time when I hid Naneeji's precious silver eye stick, the one that she always used to apply kohl to her eyes. I buried it in the garden because Naneeji was mean to Nanaji, and I could not stand it, but it was Rani who was blamed for making it disappear.

Naneeji did not approve of my friendship with Rani. Whenever she saw me with her, I was given a good talking to. I must not wander across to the servants' quarter; I must only mix with girls of my kind. But there were no other fat, pimply girls in my class, no one, in fact, who cared for my company. In the last few years I had literally eaten my way through sorrow, and as a consequence had lost the few friends I had. I could empathize with their concerns. There must be nothing more distasteful for a pubescent girl than the company of a fat and plain friend. But Rani was a servant girl, and her wishes in this regard did not matter.

Once, I saw Rani being beaten. I was playing in the bushes outside the servants' quarter when a loud and rhythmic thwacking drew me to their door. Looking in, I saw her father, Hari, wielding a stick to her knees. I must have screamed, for Rani's father froze. Rani turned to look at me, her face puffy with embarrassment. Her brother was standing there too, a still life in venom. I turned and ran back to the house.

From then on, I would anxiously scan Rani's face, arms, and legs for the telltale marks. When Rani and I became friends, I tried to talk to her about the beatings but she refused to discuss her family life with me. I could not begrudge her that as I hardly liked to discuss mine. That's what brought us together, our mutual unhappiness. We had each other, and that was all.

I spent all the pocket money that Mummy sent me (guilt money I called it), buying up the second-hand Enid Blyton books at Mohandeep and Sons, Bookseller and Lending Library, in Sarojini Nagar market. Mohandeep and Son, for there was only one son as far as I could tell, knew me by sight. Father and Son nudged each other whenever I walked in. I always insisted on buying the books from their lending library, which must have been extremely inconvenient for their inventory. "Read and return, ten *paise* only," Mohandeep or Son would plead every time, but I would shake my head and ask for the purchase price. I never could bear to return a book that I had loved. Father or Son would then click his tongue in irritation, open the book, hold it up against the light, examine the binding, the frequency of tear and stain, and name a price. Sometimes it was as little as four annas, sometimes a whole rupee, but I never doubted that the slight, be-spectacled man was being fair.

The stained and tattered pages transported me to the hallowed halls of St. Clare's and Mallory Towers. There I mingled with the crisply bright, blue and white English girls, pulling out pins from Mam'zelle's bun with the aid of a clever magnet. Our house was next to a gushing stream and my loving mother made me hot buttered scones while my father made me a tree house and took me fishing. I owned a Scottish terrier who followed me around with a look of happy devotion. And with that sort of nourishment, and despite the abundance of scones, I grew tall but remained slim and lovely with hazel eyes and auburn hair and wit that sparkled as brightly as the river. All the girls vied with each other to be my best friend. Among them was Rani: Rani, in her frayed *salwar-kameez*, her fingers clutching and unclutching the loose ends of her *dupatta*. Rani's presence assured me by its very incongruity that I had a fair chance of gaining admittance to this coveted English world, but not her, never Rani.

I remember the day Rani's family moved into our quarter. It was 1969, the year I'll never forget because Mummy got married and went away to live in Almora. I had been standing by the banana: tree watching Rani's family carry their frugal belong-ings into the quarter: a charpai, a stool, some pieces of bedding, a few pots and pans. While her mother set up inside, Rani was sent to sweep the courtyard. She emerged, doubled over the broom, her free hand neatly folded behind her back so it wouldn't get in the way.

Rani hadn't noticed me, so I could take her in. She was tall and ungainly, and there was nothing at all attractive about her round, moonlike face and her hair that was drawn submissively into a plait. She concentrated so hard on her sweeping that the tip of her tongue stuck out between her crooked teeth. I watched her for a while and she seemed slow and scared and that gave me the courage to walk up to her. I offered her one of my Parle toffees, the kind I hoarded and only produced on very special occasions.

For a moment she looked undecided. Then her free hand unfolded itself from behind her back and came forward to accept the gift. As if by afterthought, she smiled. That smile changed everything. Her eyes were alight, and her cheeks broke into laughing pools. Rani didn't smile often but when she did, it lurched in your heart like a gasp.

Naneeji used to say that Rani would do all right in life. Even though she was stupid and had no prospects, she would find a husband because she was fair of complexion. God only knows how she is fair, Naneeji muttered, when her parents are quite, quite dark. I hoped that Naneeji was right. I hoped Rani would find a husband and one that didn't beat her.

When Nanaji gave over our servants' quarter to Rani's family, it was one of the few times that I saw him put his foot down with Naneeji. They had one of their terrible rows and Naneeji's taunts went on for days. He had promised the quarter to the peon, Nanaji said, and couldn't go back on his word. How dare you make promises without consulting me, Naneeji shouted. The quarter is vacant, Nanaji replied, and the peon's family is on the street. Since when did we run a charity, said Naneeji. Why must I accommodate beggars on my property? It's not your property, Nanaji reminded her, it belongs to the government of India, and Hari is a government peon. In exchange for the quarter, Hari's wife would help Naneeji in the house. Mummy, after all, had remarried and left and was no longer there to help. They were getting on in age, Nanaji said, they could use some help around the place. Besides, Delhi was becoming increasingly unsafe; it would be reassuring to have a trusted family living on the premises.

Naneeji's grumbling finally subsided. I think, all along, she was weighing the advantages in that astute head of hers but felt it incumbent on herself not to give in without a fight. The quarter had been empty after all. She would be getting the place smartened up and four servants for no price (three actually, for even Naneeji hadn't bargained for the likes of Rani's brother, who wouldn't lift a finger unless it was to dig his nose).

Slowly but surely, Rani's family became entrenched in our household. Rani's father, Hari, went off early in the mornings to fetch our milk, eggs, and bread. He washed Nanaji's car, then drove him to work. In the evenings, there was always some lifting and carrying to do, man's work, as Naneeji put it, looking pointedly at Nanaji. On weekends, Hari worked in the garden, collecting and throwing out the dead leaves, mowing the lawn, sowing seeds, and tending to the vegetables and flowers. I don't think Nanaji noticed but Naneeji had sacked the car cleaner, the gardener, and the odd jobs man. If he noticed, he didn't say anything.

Rani's mother, Ratna, was a thin and lifeless woman who floated around the house in a specter-like fashion performing one silent task after another. She swept and mopped the floors, washed the dishes, cut the vegetables, polished the brassware. Naneeji kept finding additional tasks for her to perform but never delegated the cooking to her. Ratna was allowed to chop but not to stir, as though the act of cooking would somehow enable her to cross the caste barrier and pollute our food. A real pity because I loved Ratna's cooking and always waited for the opportunity when I'd get invited into their quarter for a sampling. Naneeji did not venture near the back of the house where the servants lived and fortunately did not find out.

Ratna never complained about all the work that Naneeji gave her. She seemed tireless. Something happened to her every time she washed our clothes though. Her thin, wiry frame became locked in a raging battle with demons. She whipped and pelted away at the clothes, letting out terrific gasps and snorts. I was both horrified and fascinated. Watching Ratna wash our clothes was like watching her lift up her saree and settle down for a good shit. Ratna didn't seem to care who saw her then. She became lost in herself. I used to wonder if she, too, was beaten by Rani's father every night when she returned home to the quarter. She had a prominent scar that cut into her left eyebrow. If I hadn't actually seen Hari beat Rani, I wouldn't have thought it possible. He was the mildest, most courteous of men with the rest of us.

—⁓—

Rani told me stories about the haunted *peepal* tree in her village. If you stand under the peepal tree on a moonless night, she said, you can hear dead spirits dance. How do you know they are spirits, I asked her. They never let themselves be seen, she said, but if you pass by and you are alone, they begin their dance, and you can hear their anklets tinkle and feel their hot breath on your cheek. How lucky you are to have escaped the village, I said. No, she answered. I miss it sorely. Those childhood years were free. We used to swing in the mango trees and steal the juicy fruit.

Please take me to your village some day, I said. I'd like to, she said, her face alight.

Then one day I went and spoiled it all. I came home from school and finished my bath. I gulped down the hot dal and rice, searing my throat in my eagerness. Rani wasn't waiting for me under the banana tree as usual so I knocked on their door and not getting an answer, pushed it open. There was no one inside. I decided to wait for her in the courtyard. I amused myself by stripping away the dried leaves from the banana tree until it ran virgin green and spurted sap. Mummy had told me many times not to do that as it hurt the tree so I did it all the more. When you were little and had a doll, she once told me, you liked to pull out its eyelashes, one by one. Though she didn't say it I could tell she thought there was something very wrong with me.

I heard the sound of splashing coming from the wooden outhouse that Hari had built in the corner of the courtyard. Rani had usually finished her bath before I got home from school so we could spend an uninterrupted two hours together. She must have run late this morning.

I crept up to the outhouse. I stood there listening to the sound of the *lota* hitting her brass pail, her slight indrawn breath as the cold water met her skin. I was about to call out to her, tell her to hurry up, but instead, I stood quietly and listened. The next instant I had pushed open the door and walked inside. There was just enough room in there for Rani and her pail of water. She stood in front of me like a large wounded animal. She dropped the lota and crossed her hands over her breasts, leaving bare her black, unruly thatch. Then her hands moved to her pubis and her breasts fell open. I stood there staring at her strange loveliness. Rani shut the door in my face.

I waited next to the banana tree, my heart beating wildly. The sound of bathing had ceased but Rani didn't come out. I wanted to call out and apologize but couldn't find the words. Rani refused to come out of the shed, and finally I left and went back to our end of the garden, where I spent the afternoon alone, wallowing in misery and shame. Rani was angry with me, there was no doubt. I concocted a story. The whole thing had been a mistake. I had had an urgent need to relieve myself and had not known that the outhouse was occupied. I rehearsed the story again and again.

It wasn't until a few days later that I saw Rani again. Naneeji told me she was ill and couldn't come out to play. There was nothing I could do but wait, and finally, when she couldn't avoid me anymore, I found her waiting at the end of the garden. I gave her my apology and she nodded. We both knew I was lying but that is how it was with Rani and me. She knew there was nothing she could do and I could do anything I wanted. So we continued to play in the afternoons, though something had changed forever between us.

Reporter

Anu sat facing Sarnath Dutt, the senior editor of the *Statesman*, who happened to be a close friend of her father's. She had initially approached him to access the newspaper's archives for certain military details but had ended up getting commissioned to write a series of investigative articles on the dead and missing of the war.

"With all due respect, but what you have published so far is a heap of lies. Whatever nonsense the government hands out, you accept at face value. I don't mean just your paper, it's every paper I've looked at. Doesn't anybody stop to think that if all those tales of triumph are true, how come so many died in the war?"

She held in her hand the first list of casualties released by the government of India. "Or did they die in their sleep? Doesn't anybody want to know what happened?"

"Dear Anu," said Sarnath Dutt, mildly reproving, "as you probably know, journalists were not allowed on the front. It was impossible to verify the facts."

"The fabrications, you mean," corrected Anu. "What about

the words 'allegedly' and 'reportedly' that journalists resort to, especially when they haven't checked out a story? How come those words weren't used? I don't recall reading a single article that questioned, that encouraged healthy skepticism. Actually there was *one* article, and it was in your paper, which mentioned in passing that if the Indian reports were to be believed, the entire Pakistani forces would have been destroyed several times over. Surely, that's a thought that must have passed through an intelligent reader's head! How come it doesn't strike more journalists? I'm no reporter, but I can do better than that."

Dutt sipped his coffee and examined her reflectively. "I'm not sure the intention is to do better than that. In times of war, the press's responsibility is not just to report but to foster er . . . national pride, optimism, patriotism, if you will, to tide the nation through difficult times . . ."

"So you're justifying your paper when it withholds information, or worse, gives false information?"

"It happens in every war."

"All the news that's fit to print. Not all the news there is."

"Anu, I don't have the time to enter into polemics now. You know you're very young . . ."

"And I'm a woman. What do I possibly understand about war?"

"I didn't say that. But you are young. You're in no position to appreciate the many pressures that operate on the press. I agree with you, the public had no information; worse, it had false information. We, the press, had no information either. We went by what we were told. Anyway, the war is over, there are no pressing security issues. I, personally, would be very interested in the article you suggest, if indeed you can pull it off. It has human interest. I'm not promising I'll publish it; that will depend on what you come up with. Remember, my editorial decisions are made within stipulated guidelines. But if the Ministry of Defense and the Services agree to talk to you, I doubt there'll be anything controversial in there, and we can go ahead and publish."

"Thank you. I can't imagine what could be controversial about what I want to do. It will be sobering, that's all. We know enough about the Keelors. They live to tell their tale and they've been justly rewarded. But what about those who didn't make it?"

"Occasionally, they've been justly rewarded too."

"You mean Squadron Leader Karanjia? Okay, if you think a posthumous decoration is a fair exchange for a life. But what about the others who died, and we don't so much as know the circumstances?"

Sarnath Dutt shrugged. "There are casualties in every war. You can't find out what happened to each and every soldier. And yes, I'll say it here, it doesn't help being a woman. It won't be easy to investigate."

Bright enough girl, he thought to himself. Bright, with a high degree of misplaced energy. At any rate, it couldn't be helped. He had to do this for Sam. "She's been through a bad marriage," Sam had told him. "She's holed up in our house, won't go out, won't meet friends. The death of this friend of hers is the jolt she's needed; it has shaken off her paralysis. She's doing this for the wrong reasons but at least she's doing something. Let her do the damn article. If you don't want to publish it, don't. We'll worry about that later. It will get her out, she'll get to meet some people, she'll regain some of her old confidence."

"Fine," Dutt had responded, "as long as we both understand the extent of my commitment."

Anu met the press attaché at Air Force Headquarters. He was singularly unhelpful.

"Can I access the files on the dead and the missing?"

"Certainly not. That's classified."

"What about the planes? Reports of damage and loss? Crash reports?"

"That's classified."

"So how is the public to know how the casualties were incurred?"

"From press releases and citations."

"The press releases carry stories of triumph. And only a handful of the dead ever receive citations."

"There are casualties in every war. Why should the public be interested in ordinary casualties? They are interested in heroic stories because they serve as an inspiration to future generations."

"But what about the victims' families? Surely the families have a right to know!"

"Of course. The families are given a full account. But it is counterproductive to burden a general public with unnecessary details. Casualties are minor setbacks. We have to look forward, plan ahead."

"If I want to trace the heroic sacrifices of some of our officers, will I be able to speak to members of their squadrons?"

"I don't see why not. You can approach the squadron commanders. They should have no objection. As long as there is no release of sensitive classified material, of course."

"Of course."

—⟋⟍—

REVISITING THE AERIAL WAR:
THE DEMISE OF TRUTH AND OTHER FATALITIES
By special correspondent Anamika Reza

If the Indian press reports are to be taken at face value, last year we lost a total of 6 aircraft in the 22-day war with Pakistan, a remarkably low attrition rate by any standards. A close examination of the daily press from this period provides the following tally: 4 aircraft (all Vampires) destroyed on the first day of war, a fifth aircraft (a Hunter) lost ten days later, and a Canberra reported missing on the 21st of September. Now let's take a look at the Pakistani reports. According to the Pakistani press, India lost 116 aircraft in the same war. There are, at the very least, two sides to this story. While claims and counterclaims continue to fly like missiles, horse sense suggests that

1) the truth must lie somewhere in the middle, and

2) war reporting has more to do with fiction than with fact.

According to an eminent reporter, who prefers not to be named, there was widespread censorship of the press in the recent war with Pakistan. Most importantly, it was **self-censorship** as the intention was not to explore a reality but to bolster national confidence and patriotism. I am being naïve if I believe that a journalist's job is to report. I am given to understand that in times of war, a journalist is, and ought to be, a **crusader**.

Looking back at the press reports, what strikes me as curious, in retrospect, is the admission made on September 1st (the first day of the aerial war) of the loss of 4 Vampire aircraft. There was a complete blackout of information in subsequent weeks and this stray report could only have been an error, a slip of the pen, as it were. The error would not be repeated for the entire duration of the war. The strategy of the war propagandists was straightforward enough in the subsequent weeks: make exaggerated claims and no admissions. This strategy has been justified as serving our best self-interests.

Unfortunately, once the war ends, something of the truth must leak out. After all, there remains the embarrassing matter of the dead and the missing. If the war was such a triumph, why did so many people die? In addition, there is the general detritus of the war machinery that must be accounted for. I have in front of me the Ministry of Defense's first and second lists of service personnel who lost their lives in the recent engagement. Let's examine the list of IAF casualties in the officer category: 16 IAF officers are listed as killed in action. This would suggest the destruction of 16 aircraft. In addition to the 16 killed, there are 6 officers known to be missing in action and 7 more are listed as Prisoners of War in Pakistan. Another 6 are known to have ejected safely in India from damaged/destroyed aircraft. This would bring the tally of destroyed or damaged aircraft to 35, without taking into account aircraft that were damaged or destroyed on the ground from Pakistani air raids, surely a far greater number. It would be realistic, therefore, to assume the loss, **at the very least**, of 70 aircraft in the recent air battle with Pakistan. Why this information was not readily made available to the public defies understanding.

It has been suggested that maintaining secrecy is essential for national security. I assume that the secrecy is intended to protect us from the enemy and is part of our military strategy. We do not want the enemy to know how many planes we have lost as this will make us appear weak in their estimation. Surely this is laughable, as those who have shot down our planes must have some idea of the damage inflicted! Moreover, the enemy, by the same curious logic, has multiplied those figures anyway, making themselves appear the stronger to their own public. War reporting is an infantile tussle between two belligerent boys: I'm bigger. I'm better. I'm stronger. I'm fitter. It is the public, and without doubt, the Services themselves, who get taken for a ride in this war of propaganda.

War is a sobering affair with the many concomitant pressures it places on our economy, our way of life, and the toll it takes on the lives of our civilians and Service personnel. Why pretend otherwise?

The second and apparently real reason for withholding the bad news and pumping up the good is that chest-thumping war reportage has the salubrious effect of raising the barometer of our national pride and of inducing more of our finest boys to join military service. In other words, we love our country more when we believe her to be invincible. The more we love our country, the readier we will be to sacrifice our lives for her and the more invincible she will become.

It is this correspondent's opinion that it is not only every citizen's right to know but his or her **national responsibility** to question, to seek out the truth, to remain vigilant against the official nexus of secrecy and propaganda. Patriotism is all very well, but a patriot is only worth his salt if he is well informed and has initiative. A well-informed and active patriot is the very foundation of a true democracy where a government is regulated by checks and balances and is honest and accountable to its people.

ENCOUNTER

Neena Kalra looks like the actress, Nargis, Anu decided. As different from me as apples from oats. She's tall and fair and graceful; her hair comes down to her hips. She looks kind. Ronu did well for himself; he must have made his parents happy. Anu knew she shouldn't be sitting here in this drawing room, holding Ronu's picture in her hands, accepting tea that Ronu's wife had made. She had questioned her motives squarely before allowing herself to dig around for Ronu's wife. Okay, I *am* curious, she had admitted to herself. Yes, I do want to get a good look at his wife and his child, at their life together. But once I've had that look, it'll be over. This desire to know, however, will remain. Of that I am certain.

"When did you last hear from your husband?" she asked Neena Kalra, replacing the photograph on the table. It was the same photograph of Ronu that had appeared in the papers. Mrs. Kalra poured her a second cup of tea.

"I did not hear from him once he left for the front."

"What day was that, do you remember?"

"The 1st of September. A Wednesday. We were living in

Jodhpur then. We were at a picnic with some friends when he got the call."

"How did . . . Flight Lieutenant Kalra react to the news that he had to return to his squadron?"

"There was no time to react. He had to leave right away. He was worried that I would be left alone. He told me to get a ticket to Delhi, to come here as soon as possible."

"Why Delhi?"

"My parents live here. This is their house. Our daughter goes to school here."

"How old is she?"

"Seven."

"Was she with you in Jodhpur then?"

"No, she was here. My husband didn't get a chance to say good-bye to her."

"I'm sorry. I know this is very painful for you. I hope that by investigating the officers' deaths, we can commemorate every one of them . . ."

Mrs. Kalra looked distracted.

"There's my daughter now," she said. They heard the front door open, then close.

"How was school today?"

"Fine. Naneeji told me to tell you she's gone shopping, she'll be back at six o'clock."

A thin girl with braids stepped into the living room dressed in a maroon and white school frock.

"We have a visitor, Sweta."

"Hullo," said Anu.

"Hullo," said Sweta. She sat down in the armchair and pulled out a book from her knapsack.

She's tall and gangly like her father but she has her mother's pretty features. Her mouth is Ronu's though, through and through, thought Anu. Neena Kalra appeared to have lost some of her ease. She doesn't want to speak near the child, Anu decided.

"Sweta, why don't you go to your room and finish your homework?"

"We had a free period today. I've done it already."

The silence lengthened. "Would you prefer that we talk some other time?" said Anu. "I'm sorry I was late."

"No, it's all right."

After a while, Anu started again, somewhat reluctantly. "Was your husband expecting to be called to the front?"

Sweta did not look up from her book.

"No," said Neena Kalra. "He was a flight instructor at Flying College. War was far from our minds."

"Do you know which forward base he was sent to?"

"No. I had no communication with him after that day."

"Which squadron was he with?"

"Seven Squadron," said Sweta. "Daddy flew Hunters. He said he would take me up with him one day."

She put down her Enid Blyton and looked squarely at Anu with large, round eyes.

"Sweta, why don't you go play outside?"

"I want to talk about Daddy too," the child said firmly.

Anu tried to look busy taking notes.

"Really, I can call some other time when it's more convenient."

Neena Kalra sighed. "Perhaps it's for the best that she's here. Things have been difficult lately. What else did you want to know?"

"Do you know any of the officers in his squadron? I'd like to get in touch with them."

"I know Flight Lieutenant Bhatia. And Flying Officer Shastri. They have been very nice to us. You can call them."

"When did you first learn . . . of the tragedy?" asked Anu, aware that Sweta's eyes were fixed on her. "It's okay if we talk about this?" she asked again.

Mrs. Kalra nodded.

"An officer came to our house in Jodhpur. Of course I was not there. I had already left for Delhi. Then they came to Rohtak to inform Ranjit's parents. It so happened that I was visiting them at the time. I was there when the news came. I could not believe it. I could not understand how they had found me there. I was sure it was a mistake."

"When was this?"

"It was the morning of September 9. We left immediately for Delhi. They brought him here later that day for the cremation."

"What did the IAF say had happened?"

"They didn't say anything to me. They told my father-in-law that Ranjit had been killed in action. He was cremated with full military honors. The air force took care of everything."

"What date did they give for his death?"

She hesitated. "The eighth I think. I'm not sure."

"Nanaji killed the cow on the sixth."

"Excuse me?"

"Don't mind her, she gets things mixed up."

The child scowled and put her face back in the book.

"What did the death certificate say?"

"My father-in-law has it. I haven't seen it."

"Did you ask your father-in-law about the circumstances of your husband's . . . demise?"

Anu chose her words carefully, acutely aware of the little girl's presence.

"That's all they said. That he died honorably, defending our country. Maybe you should speak to my father-in-law?"

Anu nodded. She had considered the option and decided against it. She had no particular desire to set eyes on Ronu's parents again, and besides, it was far from likely that they would want to talk to her.

"Do you mind if I take a look at his address book? Do you have his flying log book?"

"I know where Daddy's books are," Sweta said, and they both turned to look at her. She was staring fixedly at Anu.

"What do you want them for?"

An oddly intense child, thought Anu. Not very childlike, even though she reads *The Secret Seven*.

It was Sweta who had asked the question but Anu looked at her mother as she replied.

"Very little is known about the martyrs of this war and how they met their end. The fighters who live tell us stories of triumph. A few have been decorated but virtually nothing is known of the rest. I feel it is important to understand what happened in each and every case, if possible. Perhaps I'm being idealistic, but I think it might change the way we think about war. My effort will be to track down others in Flight Lieutenant Kalra's squadron, to speak to the Commander, speak to members of his formation, try to understand what happened that day. Of course I will share any information I have with you."

Sweta got up and left the room. A little later she was back with her father's books, which she placed on the table in front of Anu.

"May I?" asked Anu, looking at Neena Kalra.

"Go ahead."

"It's Daddy's log book and address book," said Sweta.

So, *she* is the keeper of the books and she has given me permission, thought Anu.

"Is it okay if I return these to you in a day or two?" Anu asked Neena, ignoring Sweta's fixed stare.

"Yes, of course." Mrs. Kalra looked pale.

Anu got up to leave.

"I will send these across. As soon as I have some information, I'll be in touch. It was very nice meeting you, Sweta."

She may have interviewed the mother, thought Anu, but she herself had been interviewed by a seven-year-old child.

Ronu, how did you produce such a spitfire of a girl?

It's as if she were my own.

—◊◊◊—

There's a very beautiful picture of Mummy and Daddy taken in Shimla before I was born. It has a windswept quality to it as though they are being blown away by happiness. The picture has always adorned our living room as we moved from Ambala to Begumpet to Pathankot to Jodhpur. When Daddy died, and Mummy moved in with Nanaji and Naneeji, she kept the photograph in what became our joint bedroom, and sometimes I caught her drying her eyes in front of it. After a few years, it disappeared. I asked Mummy about it, and she said she had kept it away carefully.

I didn't think much about it then.

After Daddy's death, Mummy convinced herself that she was earmarked for tragedy and ill would befall all those who came close to her. She never said this out loud so I was spared the irritation of having to convince her otherwise, but she wore the look in her white sarees, her trembling mouth, her throat where muscles rippled stoically. I was completely taken aback when she went and married the Colonel. It didn't fit in with my theory. Nanaji was deputed to break the news to me and for a while I went along with their suggestion that this was the best thing for all of us. I would have a home again, Mummy said, a permanent home.

I did try to live with Mummy in her new home. It was a large and beautiful house in the hills, and Mummy assured me that we would not have to move ever again. They said I could have my own room and do it up as I wished, so I put up all the pictures of Daddy that I had. However, the pictures started making Mummy uncomfortable, and she started staying out of my room. One day, she brought me an empty photo album and said, why don't you put the pictures in there and keep them close to your bed? That was when I asked her for that other photograph, the beautiful one of her and Daddy taken in Shimla. It was nowhere to be seen in this house. It had been replaced by a formal marriage portrait of Mummy and the Colonel taken at some studio. In it Mummy has discarded her white saree and wears a gold one with a brave and tragic smile. The Colonel, in full military attire, holds his young and beautiful bride like a trophy. I looked at Mummy's wedding photo and I said, "I want that other picture."

"Sweta, believe me, I will never forget him."

I stood there, unmoved, until she opened her almirah and brought down a large jewelry box. This was a new jewelry box, one I had never seen. She removed the top casing, and among the pearls and the brightly studded gold bracelets was a packet wrapped in a handkerchief. She handed it to me. In my room I unwrapped the photograph and buried my nose in the cloth. It carried Mummy's perfume, Daddy's tobacco, and the stale sweet smell of our short life together. I was glad I had rescued the photograph before it lost its smell in the brightly burnished gold.

CRUSH

Rani filled the void but it was Miss Reza who blazed it with light. The first time I met Miss Reza, or at least the first time I remember meeting her, it was August 1970 and I was the fattest, most pimply student of Class VIII C, Mount Mary School. Mrs. Naik, our English teacher, had fallen sick and Miss Reza had come in as the substitute teacher. Miss Reza couldn't have been more different than Mrs. Naik. Mrs. Naik was old and ugly and had a prominent harelip that provided endless ammunition to the more cruelly intentioned girls of our class. Even I, who bore the shamefulness of a disability, took secret delight when the onus was shifted from my weight to Mrs. Naik's harelip. With years of abuse behind her, Mrs. Naik had developed a moribund ear and eye. She entered the room, lisped, "Guth Mawning," and as the girls, especially the unruly elements at the back, began their extended chorus, "Guth Mawwwwning Mississs Naaa—YUCK," she resolutely turned her back on everyone and wiped off the latest Bugs Bunny rendition from the blackboard. She continued with the lesson with downcast eyes while rubber bands and pencil missiles pelted all around her. Mrs. Naik took refuge in the fact that she witnessed nothing.

Our class had divided itself into three sections. The "Goodie Goodie" girls occupied the first row, the middle rows belonged to "the Confused and the Uninitiated," while the last row was the undisputed domain of the "Truly Unrulies." If Mrs. Naik dared to look up at all from the written page, she made it a point to address herself doggedly to the first row. As a matter of course, one serious complaint a week about VIII C made its way all the way up to the Mother Superior. Eventually a note from her would wend its way down, summoning the Unrulies on a visitation. "The Mother Superior wishes to see the unruly elements at once." That is how the last row had delightedly named itself the "Unruly Elements," which over time had become "the Truly Unrulies."

Without waiting for their names to be called, the Truly Unrulies rose proudly to their feet and marched out, leaving the rest of us nursing a mixture of shame and awe. We didn't know what the Mother Superior did to the Unrulies. Rumor had it, as circulated by the Unrulies themselves, that each received ten stripes, one on each knuckle, from Mother Superior's sharp-edged metal ruler. The Unrulies claimed that the process was indescribably painful but cheerfully borne. They returned in such fine spirits, however, that I wondered sometimes whether they hadn't simply been called in for a round of tea and biscuits. Once, I summoned up enough courage to ask one of the Unrulies whether she had ever seen Christ on the Cross, which still assaulted me in an occasional nightmare, but she didn't know what I was talking about.

Before occupying row 3, seat number 4 from the left, I had given the matter much consideration. My natural impulse was to sit in the first row where caution and shortsightedness propelled me. But to be Fat *and* Goodie-Goodie would have left me with little chance of survival. So I chose row 3, which was at a fair proximity to row 1, and yet shared a respectable distance to row 5. This afforded me the opportunity to discern shimmering shapes on the blackboard when I screwed up my eyes. Clearly I was in need of vision correction but the prospect of furthering my ugliness with eyeglasses had prevented me from bringing up the matter with Nanaji and Naneeji.

Mrs. Naik gave us terribly boring essays to write but seemed not at all displeased with the results. The last assignment that she had given us before she came down with an attack of jaundice was a one-page essay entitled, "How I Spent my Summer Holidays." We had written our essays with Mrs. Naik in mind but found that a new teacher, a Miss Reza, would be reading them. Substitute teachers ("subs" as they were called) were particularly easy targets for the Truly Unrulies. Because of their lack of experience and standing in the school system, subs were easily reduced to tears and sent packing without lasting repercussions. Our sub periods were then taken over by class prefects, which meant we could pretty much do as we liked. When we heard that a new sub, a Miss Reza, would be taking our English class for the rest of the term, we naturally looked forward to a large dose of unwholesome entertainment.

All I can say is that when Miss Reza walked into our classroom that morning we were all completely taken by surprise. Every one of us stopped what she was doing and stared. For one thing, Miss Reza wore makeup! Nobody wore makeup in our convent school, except for the occasional *sindoor* and *bindi*. Miss Reza had darkly penciled eyes and a red slash of a mouth. She didn't wear a smocky frock like our Anglo-Indian teachers nor did she wear a saree like the Hindus. Miss Reza was dressed in a suit. Black flared trousers, short black jacket, and a frilly white blouse. She had a mass of curly black hair that was tied back in a ponytail but fell unrepentant onto her shoulders. Miss Reza looked as though she had gone out looking for the stables and had stepped into Mount Mary by mistake. Madhu, who was Truly the Unruliest of the Unrulies, let out a short, low whistle of surprise.

For a moment I felt I had seen her somewhere before. But I quickly dismissed the thought. I could only have met Miss Reza in a dream. My life with Nanaji and Naneeji left no room for the likes of her.

The last row was so taken off guard that it didn't have the wherewithal to orchestrate its usual foot shuffling, chair screeching, knuckle rapping routine, which got our teachers off to a highly flustered start. Instead, Miss Reza was allowed to walk around the classroom, smile pleasantly, and say, "Good morning girls. I'm Miss Reza. As you probably know I will be taking your English lesson until Mrs. Naik is well enough to return."

Eventually we did find our voices, and as we burst into a "Good Morrning Misss Ray Zaaaaaa," she arched a shapely eyebrow at us and smiled with amused detachment.

She picked up the register and stalked the room like a panther out on its morning kill. I noticed that Miss Reza didn't much like sitting. This gave her an unfair advantage over the rest of us, who had to be seated unless ordered to stand. All our teachers sat down while taking roll call so it was easy enough to alter your voice and give proxy for a missing girl who would return the favor at a later date. Miss Reza, however, asked each one of us to stand as her name was called and stared intently at her face as though permanently committing it to memory. It was disconcerting to say the least. Clearly she had no intention of leaving in a day!

"Forty-six names are a lot to remember," she said, "so it might take me a couple of classes before I get to know you all."

It was proceeding all too smoothly. I sneaked a look at the last row and noticed that some sort of conference was in progress, and a note was doing the rounds.

"Ratna Iyengar"

"Present, miss."

"Nalini Jaspal"

"Present, miss."

"Sunanda Joshi"

"Present, miss."

"Sweta Kalra. Er . . . Sweta *Kalra*," she said again, her voice lifting with surprise. I scraped my chair and stood up.

"Present, miss."

She scanned my face before moving on. I felt she had looked at me differently, as though expecting someone else.

"Sonia Kewalramani," she continued. There was a loud screech but it was Madhu from the back bench who was on her feet. I was filled with dread. Clearly the Mission had been deputed to the Unruliest. Miss Reza was already an attractive presence in our classroom. I desperately wanted her to stay.

"Miss . . . excuse me."

"Yes?"

Madhu was rocking back and forth, her face distraught.

"Miss, please. I . . . I . . . am bleeding. Miss, I'm scared. I don't know what's happening. Miss, Mummy said this . . . can happen. Please, miss, will I die?"

It was a known routine. We had witnessed it before: a different Unruly each time with a different teacher or nun. It was one of the nastier tricks in the big bad book of surprises, one that the Unrulies resorted to only sparingly when the teacher had withstood other onslaughts. It was a test that they all failed at Mount Mary School, as it involved the dreaded word "menses," and "menses" carried connotations that nuns do not like. They could shave their heads and pubic hair but they never could cut the flow. In every instance, the teacher was caught on the wrong foot, stuttering and stammering and making an utter fool of herself. One innocent voice after another would query: "What has happened, miss?" "Will she die, miss?" "Why, miss?" while a paint-soaked Unruly was dispatched to the sick room to get cleaned up. Miss Reza, on account of her formidable presence had been promoted right away to the acid test.

She put down the register. Kindly she said, "What is your name?"

"Madhu, miss. Madhu Mehra." Madhu had turned pale and looked like she was about to faint. That year, she had turned in a wonderful performance as Hamlet with a poignantly protracted death scene.

"Miss, my tummy hurts," moaned Madhu, doubling up with pain.

"Don't worry. It happens to all of us," said Miss Reza gently. Clearly she had fallen for the act, though unlike the other teachers, she showed no embarrassment. The giggles began to subside.

"Come up to the front, please."

Madhu waddled up clutching her stomach, her legs astride. Down her thigh dripped an unctuous blend of red. She kept looking down at herself, her face contorted with terror.

Miss Reza put her arm around Madhu and spoke to her with quiet assurance. We were too surprised to make a sound. All of a sudden, though, her face turned razor sharp. In a quick movement she turned Madhu around so her back faced the rest of us.

"I suppose your mummy told you not to get any blood on your frock, yes, Madhu?"

No one stirred.

"If you don't want to be in this class, please feel free to walk out. There's no need to waste a good tube of paint. All you have to do, any of you have to do, is inform me that you don't wish to participate. I prefer smaller classes anyway. As for you Madhu Mehra, you will stay out for this entire, or should I say *your* entire period. Please stand outside the door with your back facing the corridor, as in your present condition I am sure you will muster a lot of sympathy. You are *not* to clean yourself until the break . . ."

Madhu looked utterly dismayed.

"Very well acted though," Miss Reza added as Madhu backed out of the classroom.

"Anyone else menstruating today?" Miss Reza said brightly. "No? Well, shall we finish the roll call and begin the lesson?"

Class VIII C had never been so quiet.

Miss Reza asked us to read our essays aloud. There's no better way to get to know one another than through our writings, she said.

I think most of us read with extreme reluctance that morning, wishing dearly we were someplace else. I don't think there was a girl there who didn't want to impress Miss Reza, and yet we were particularly ill equipped to do so. After all, we had written our essays with harebrained, harelipped Mrs. Naik in mind.

"For this year's summer vacation our family visited Darjeeling. Darjeeling is a pretty and hilly resort set in the foothills of the Himalayas. It is cool there even in the hot summer. We had a nice time. We took pony rides in the day and stayed in a comfortable hotel at night."

"I did not go anywhere for my summer holidays. I stayed at home. I read two Classics, 'David Copperfield' written by Charles Dickens and 'Little Women' written by L.M. Alcott. They are both Classics and it is important to read them for one's education."

"This summer me and my brother visited my auntie and uncle and cousin sister in Assam. We had too much fun playing. We stayed in there house the whole time. They have a very big house and garden. They have two dogs. There names are Biscit and Toffee. I played everyday and I also studied for the exams."

"This summer I travelled with my parents to the verdant forest reserves of Almora district. The verisimilitude of flora and fauna and the clemency of the weather made for a salubrious sojourn. The plenitude of waterfalls, the invigorating air, the resplendent sunsets gave way in the nocturne to many a luminous moon . . ."

I faltered because a giggle had escaped Miss Reza's lips.

"The serendipitous recrudescence of cicadas . . ."

"That's enough, Sweta," Miss Reza said between peals of laughter. "You can sit down."

Shame-faced, I did. Was it possible that Miss Reza did not like my essay? I was the best in English in my class. I always came first. The readings continued, but I didn't hear another word.

Finally, Miss Reza looked around the classroom, part pity, part contempt on her face. "I feel sorry for you girls. You seem to have had the most boring summer vacations. You may have visited Darjeeling or the tea gardens or Almora or Puri beach but it seems that nothing at all happened to you. You don't have a single memorable moment to recount from two whole months of your lives! Others (and she looked pointedly at me) are so eager to impress that they have forgotten that the reason we use words is to communicate."

Never had I been pulled down in an English class before. I knew that this same essay would have scored highly with Mrs. Naik. I had become complacent seeing Mrs. Naik's "very goods" littering my notebooks. Nanaji had received a gift subscription to the *Reader's Digest*, and I mugged up new vocabulary with every issue, knowing full well that it paid to increase my word power. At least with Mrs. Naik.

"I couldn't leave Delhi this summer; I was here throughout," said Miss Reza, fishing out a piece of paper from her handbag and reading aloud.

"It was an exceptionally hot and muggy day. It oozed like sticky glue and clamped itself onto our faces. It was only morning and already we could not breathe. Barefoot, I ran into the garden, hoping it would be cooler outside. Not a leaf stirred, the wind was without whisper.

I turned to go inside, to position myself once again under the slow-winged ceiling fan. Something in the bare, brown earth caught my eye. It was red, a bright hibiscus, newly opened, and fallen from its branch. Its white piston looked blatantly impudent. Its mouth was covered with drops of dew that were large and trembled at my touch. The flower looked at me, inviting me in. I made myself as small as I could and slid inside her. Her walls were smooth, her scent naked. I could not bear the thought of returning to the hot afternoon. I spent the summer in the belly of the hibiscus."

We stared at Miss Reza in shock. Was she crazy? How could she write something like that and get away with it? Her reading, which was impassioned, had done something to me. It had started a churning in my throat that ended somewhere in my crotch. Miss Reza put away the piece of paper and I became aware of my ugliness. The cool hibiscus had made me feel ugly. I was fat, hugely fat. I would never fit inside the belly of a hibiscus. My eyes filled with tears.

"Nobody has asked you to be truthful. I have worked as a journalist, and when you report on real events, you are expected to endeavor for the truth. However, this is a class on comprehension and creative writing. You're being asked to *create*, to use words, spin stories. I want you all to rewrite your essays and bring them back next week. Maybe you'll remember something that happened, something that *meant* something to you. If nothing happened, make it up. Please don't bore me with trivial nonsense. Do you think I care if you stayed in a hotel and did your homework or not? If you write with feeling, there's truth in that. That's the only truth I care about. Don't try to impress me by saying the right things, or (she looked at me again), by using big words because that is *false*, far more false than Madhu's little act, which, to give her her due, was entertaining. Despite her obvious anatomical ignorance, she put up a fine performance. That's what I'm asking you for. Give me a fine performance."

—⟶⟵—

Miss Reza had successfully cast her net. We waited impatiently for her English classes every week. Madhu, the Un-ruliest, had been utterly uplifted by Miss Reza's backhand compliment, relayed to her by her fellow unrulies. She appeared all crushed out like me, staked in Miss Reza's presence, as if by lightning.

Miss Reza never did look as dramatic as she did on that first day. She stopped using makeup. She started wearing dresses that came down below the knees, like the Anglo-Indian teachers. The first time she came dressed like that, she winked at us, and said, "It's your nuns. They think you have to be a frump in order to be a good teacher. I'll be coming in disguise from now on."

Each of us started to write, to write "untruthfully" as Miss Reza had suggested, but I found to my surprise that I was being more truthful than ever. Miss Reza recommended that we maintain diaries and I spent every free hour filling the pages in mine. I secretly hoped that she would ask to read my diary but she never did.

I rewrote the summer assignment. I decided not to write about Mummy and her big new house and her big new life, which I had attempted to visit in Almora. Instead I wrote about Rani, my best friend Rani, the servant girl, who lived in our servants' quarter and was nothing at all like Darrell or Claudine or Elizabeth or any of the girls I wanted to be. I wrote about Rani and her parents, Ratna and Hari, and the beating that I had seen Rani get at the hands of her father, who was otherwise such a good man. It was a very simple essay. Nothing much happens in it really, but Miss Reza liked it so much she made me read it out loud to the whole class. Naturally, I did not mention the incident in the outhouse.

—⁂—

Miss Reza's notes to me were lengthy and encouraging. I'd pour over her indecipherable scrawl, my heart bursting with pleasure at her praise. It took me five minutes to figure out a line she once wrote, a line I will never forget, "I like the words you use. They shine like pebbles waiting to be picked."

Naneeji had never seen me work so hard, and with a rather bristling pride, she showed me the letter she was writing to Mummy.

Sweta no longer spends all day reading foolish novels. She now takes her studies seriously and works hard. You will be proud of her.

But proud of me Mummy was not. That term I came first in English with 80 but I got 52 in history, 48 in science, 43 in geography, and I failed in math and Hindi. It was the worst average I had had in years. I was elated that Miss Reza had given me an 80 even though with Mrs. Naik, I'd have gone as high as 98. I couldn't care about the rest.

—∞—

Then one day Miss Reza came into our classroom and said matter of factly that Mrs. Naik was well again and would be returning the following week. "I have to say I really enjoyed myself. You girls are wonderful. You've made me think seriously about teaching as a career." Her voice seemed to break a little though her smile was steady.

My world collapsed for a second time. It took everything I had to stop myself from weeping. I hung around after class waiting to talk to her, not knowing what I would say. I wasn't the only one. There were maybe seven or eight girls standing there with red eyes, Madhu included. Miss Reza made an appointment to see each one of us in the staff room. When it was my turn, she said the most unexpected thing, "Sweta, aren't you Ranjit Kalra's daughter?"

I stared at her, not believing my ears. "Yes," I managed to say. "How did you know?" My heart banged at any mention of Daddy and it did then, without relief. Bang, bang, bang.

"This is strange. But I came and met you once, you and your mother, at your grandparents' house."

"I don't remember."

"It was a long time ago. Five years, even longer. You were very little."

"I would have remembered you."

"I didn't recognize you myself. It's been so long."

I knew what she meant then. She must have met me when I was thin. I had been quite scrawny once. I was used to it, people who knew me when I was thin, refusing to know me now.

"I don't remember meeting you," I repeated.

"How's your mother?"

"Fine. She lives in Kaushani in Almora district."

If Miss Reza had asked to read my diary she would have known all about her. That year, there was a baby in Mummy's tummy, and Mummy no longer came into the sun with me. She liked to lie down instead in a dark, quiet room and care for the baby inside her.

"She's remarried?"

"Yes."

"Anyway," she said, looking intently at me, "that's not why I called you to the staff room. I wanted to make sure that you understood something important. You're lucky, Sweta. You have a special gift. You must always nourish it. You must never stop writing."

It was the first time in years that I had not felt fat and ugly and peripheral. A sob escaped my throat, and without thinking I put my arms around her neck. She returned the hug tightly, and holding me at arms' length, gave me her firm, bright smile. The other teachers stared at us with disapproval. Nobody behaved like that at Mount Mary School. Miss Reza smiled at them too, then gathered her things and walked out.

—∽—

That day I went on a diet. I went home and had a show-down with Naneeji. I announced that from now on I would be the one to decide what I ate and how much. I had a special gift. There wasn't a reason in the world why I should look like a frump.

Part Four

INVESTIGATION

Anu held her dead lover's address book in her hands. Automatically, she turned the pages to "R": there was no listing for Reza. She looked under "A": no, she was not there either. Ronu had struck her off his pages the moment she had left.

Anu's request to visit Seven Squadron and interview the Squadron Commander was turned down with a terse telegram:

REGRET THAT INTERVIEW IS NOT POSSIBLE
PLEASE CONTACT PRO IN AFHQ

Now she would have to proceed informally, write individually to the officers listed in Ronu's address book in the hope that one of them might know something about his mission, or in turn, might know someone who did.

She consulted N.K. Malhotra, the *Statesman*'s war correspondent. "It was a mistake to tell the squadron commander that you were investigating the deaths of air force officers. They've been through their courts of inquiry; they're up to their necks in all that. The last thing they want is a reporter nosing around.

You should have said you want to visit the squadron, see how the boys are doing after their victory, what lessons they've learned for the future, something innocuous like that. Once you're in there, you can always ask a few awkward questions and get away with it."

Stupid, stupid, Anu chided herself. I'll live and learn. I'll have to let a few months go by and get someone else to approach them, maybe Malhotra, who thinks I'm stupid and wonders why I've been given the job.

She went through Ronu's contacts and compiled a list of personnel who she figured were air force officers. To each she wrote a simple form letter explaining that she was researching a series of articles for the *Statesman* on incidents of triumph and tragedy in the air battle of 1965. She sought any information on the circumstances leading to the deaths of anyone in the officer category. She enclosed the list of casualties released by the Ministry of Defense. She included a copy of her "forthcoming" editorial. Sarnath Basu had commended her for it but had made no effort to publish it so far. He was awaiting clearance from the publishers, he said. She included her address and telephone number and expressed her willingness to travel for a good story. She urged the addressees to circulate her letter widely and wrote on the envelope, "Please redirect if necessary."

For a few weeks she heard nothing at all. Then the letters started pouring in.

Bagdogra, April 12, 1966

Dear Miss Reza,

    I commend you for the important task you have undertaken.

I knew three of the officers who were killed. Two were my classmates at the NDA, and one I met during my training in Hyderabad. However, as I am in Eastern Air Command, I was not called into action. I have a good friend, Flying Officer Harish Tripathi in Western Air Command, whose address I enclose. I have also sent him your letter. I hope he will be of help. I look forward to reading your articles in the "Statesman."

Yours truly,

Flying Officer Sandeep Sahai

Jammu, April 18, 1966

Dear Miss Reza,

Your letter was forwarded to me by Flight Lieutenant Phulnani as I, myself, was stationed in Halwara during the hostilities of September, last year. I thank God for sparing my life, for indeed, I had some close shaves and could have ended up on your list. I am grief-stricken as God almighty has taken away my dear friend, N. M. Suri, who was killed in action over Pakistani territory on September 21st. His body was not returned, so his wife continues to hope that he is alive. I have spoken at length to other officers in his squadron, and I regret to say that there is no reason to hope for such a miracle. I am attaching herewith the contact of two officers who flew with Suri on his final mission. You may contact them if you wish. After receiving your letter I penned some thoughts on Suri which I enclose.

I also have a photograph of Suri. Since it is my only copy I am not sending it to you but it can be made available upon request. If you would like to meet me, I will be happy to oblige.

> Good luck on your endeavour,
> Yours in service,
> Flight Lieutenant Naresh Jain

Ambala, April 12, 1966

Dear Miss Reza,

With all due respect, I fail to understand why you have sent me this list or how I can be of assistance. I have looked over your list carefully and there is only one gentleman who I know by name, if he is the same. An IAF officer by the name of Kalra, he may be the R.K. Kalra on your list, visited my auto shop here in Ambala some two years ago. He was interested in buying one second-hand Enfield motorcycle. He came quite a few times to inspect the vehicle and even took it for a test drive but finally we did not agree on the price. I feel I offered him a fair bargain. I did not know of his untimely death until I received your letter. Please convey my sad condolences to his family. As for your problem, I think it is best to approach the Government directly.

> Yours faithfully,
> Corporal Harbaksh Singh (Retd.)
> Ambala AutoWorks

Jodhpur, April 15, 1966

Dear Miss Reza,

I apologize for not replying earlier as I was out of station. I knew two of the officers killed extremely well: Flying Officer Bhatnagar, killed on September 1st and Flight Lieutenant Kalra, killed on September 7th. Bhatnagar and I were course-mates at the NDA. We were both inmates of Juliet Squadron and, as a consequence, became close friends. Flight Lieutenant Kalra had already finished from the NDA by then, but I did get to know him during my Jet Training at Air Force School, here in Jodhpur. Flight Lieutenant Kalra was an excellent flying instructor, and I was lucky to be under his tutelage. I was invited to his quarters for dinner on one occasion and often spent time with him in the Officers' mess. I do not know exactly how Flight Lieutenant Kalra met his end except that it was during the raid on Sargodha on the morning of September 7th. Theirs was a tragic mission as three of the four planes were completely destroyed and one was badly damaged. Posthumous Vir Chakra recipient, Squadron Leader Dastur Karanjia, was leader of the formation. Even though I never met Dusty (as he was called), I feel as though I knew him. The air force is full of stories about Dusty. He was an ace pilot, probably the best the IAF has produced, a daredevil fighter, and an inspiration to all of us. I must tell you that when I heard Dusty had been killed, I wept, even though I had never met him. I felt as though the force had lost ten men instead of one. The third plane destroyed in the mission was flown by Flight Lieutenant Pankaj Singh. It is believed that Singh managed to eject from the aircraft and was taken POW in Pakistan where he remains till today. Flying officer Basu, whose plane was also severely damaged, lives to tell the tale. I have made some inquiries and am sending you his address and contact information. You can write to him at his home address in Calcutta (enclosed) or care of 7 Squadron. You will be able to hear from him, firsthand, about the deaths of Squadron Leader Karanjia and Flight Lieutenant Kalra.

As for my poor friend, Bhatnagar, his entire formation was destroyed on the very first day of the war so there will be no eyewitness accounts! Arthur Koestler calls fighter pilots "the knight-errants of death," and that has never been more true than in this case. These officers, flying Vampires on India's first mission against Pakistan, were all killed. What an inglorious start! Madam, Vampires are obsolete, slow-moving aircraft. They do not stand a chance against Pakistani American-made F-86 Sabres and Starfighters! Why were these aircraft called into action when we had Gnats and Hunters? What indeed was WAC thinking? Did we completely underestimate the enemy? Were we so confident that we thought we could win the war with our worst aircraft? After this debacle, the Vampires were withdrawn from our fleet, but not before four brave men lost their lives.

Miss Reza, I am impressed by your editorial on press censorship. I completely agree with you that the public has a right to know, and that knowledge can only lead to a more responsible government. I urge you to write about this particular deployment of Vampires on the first day of the war but request that you do not identify me by name. I am not stating anything but the obvious. Any officer you speak to will share my view. I am eager to offer you all help and support. I think it is my duty to do whatever I can to perpetuate the memory of our colleagues. I do this on condition of anonymity, as I certainly do not wish to lose my job.

With best regards,

Flying Officer Kishore Shastri

Anu was beside herself with excitement. There were leads upon leads here. She thought back on where she had begun seven months ago. Like a bumbling fool, she'd looked at pictures of planes, trying to tell apart a Hunter from a Gnat, a fighter from a bomber. Now she was on the tail of at least three different stories and had the name and address of the last person to have seen Ronu alive. She picked up the telephone and booked a person-to-person call to Flying Officer Parikshit Basu in Calcutta.

SUMMER OF '71

Many things happened that summer of '71. Most importantly, I lost thirty pounds in three months and became thin again. I have to thank my cousin Deepika for this, who taught me to stick my index and forefingers deep in my throat and throw up whenever I wanted. Deepika also put me on a stringent diet of fruit and yogurt. I was allowed to eat rice, rotis, and dessert only on Sundays when Dadaji and Dadeeji sat down with us for their meals. The rest of the time Dadaji was away doing his policing work, and Dadeeji was busy with her kitty parties, and Auntie Radhika wasn't there to watch over us as she'd gone away to some ashram in Poona where no one spoke and everyone meditated, and alcohol was strictly forbidden. As Deepika told me quite nonchalantly, her mother was "a total dipso," so their dad had to send her off to get cleaned out while the children spent the summer holidays with their grandparents. It was only because there weren't any supervisory adults around in Dadaji and Dadeeji's huge and sprawling *haveli* that I was able to take the drastic dietary measures that I did. Staying with my maternal grandparents I'd been able to control my intake of rice and rotis only to a limited extent, as Naneeji had decreed that some carbohydrates were essential, and for once Nanaji had agreed with her.

But here in Rohtak, I did what I liked, or rather, what Deepika liked. She went through Dadeeji's *Femina* and *Eve's Weekly* magazines and came up with new remedies from the beauty page. "Listen to this: drink one liter of cucumber juice every day mixed with the juice of one lime and a pinch of black salt and white pepper for flavoring. One week of this, and you'll lose ten pounds, guaranteed. This is also the treatment for splotchy, oily complexions. Do you have a splotchy, oily complexion? Yes, I think so." Then, she'd stroll into the kitchen and instruct the cook to prepare a liter of cucumber juice, something I'd never dare do myself. "That's all you're having this week, apart from fruit," Deepika announced, while she and Manish ordered themselves thick *alu parathas* with butter and pickle, and sweet and creamy mango *lassis*.

It was Dadeeji's golden rule that, come what may, Sundays were to be spent at home with the family, and this was the only day that she "supervised" the preparation of special meals for us and spooned food onto our plates as we sat down all together to eat at the dining table. Above it on the wall was a portrait of Daddy taken when he was a chubby five-year-old on some movie set, and another of him in uniform taken in the last year of his life, and next to it, a portrait of Shirdi Sai Baba, who was Dadeeji's spiritual guru. On Sundays I ate fried potatoes and *puris* and *pakoras* and *kheer* and whatever else had been prepared, but I made sure I took it all out afterward in the bathroom. Deepika maintained stringent notes. She ran a detailed chart on me and knew exactly what I ate and drank. She checked my weight twice a week on Dadeeji's weighing scale, once on Wednesdays and again on Sunday evenings after I'd thrown up.

If Mummy thought I had a streak of cruelty in me, she should have seen Deepika! Deepika was beautiful, and so I thought it only natural that she should be completely manipulative. I was quite happy to have her trample all over me. She was mean about my weight but that only deepened my resolve. She tortured me with sixty squats a day and a hundred jumping jacks, and for all this I remained grateful. Deepika didn't have much to do that summer. She wasn't interested in hanging out with her brother, and she didn't particularly like reading, though she claimed she did. What she liked to do most of all was sketch tall, brooding models, dressed in billowing elephant pants, carrying long-tasseled sling bags on their shoulders, and while she did this, she liked to talk about boys. She told me she had a boyfriend but wasn't sure if he was tall enough for her. He was only an inch or so taller, which made it impossible for her to wear heels. Because of what I'd done to Rani, and because of what Miss Reza had done to me (without meaning to, of course), the lid had sort of lifted from my Pandora's box of desires. I asked her what it meant to have a boyfriend. Had they kissed and stuff? Deepika appraised her drawing critically and said, "Just a little." I waited but she didn't elaborate. Usually, Deepika liked to play the role of Big Sister out on a mission to destroy joy and innocence, but sometimes, when she figured that I was dying for information, she'd withhold completely and shut me out. But mostly, since she had nothing better to do, she talked and I listened. She said what boys did to girls was just "*chee*," and it was so much nicer what one could do to oneself. Without looking up from her sketchbook, she described to me at length what it was possible to do to oneself, so that night I tried it out, tentatively at first, then with growing confidence, and it turned out to be the most glorious thing in the world for which I will forever remain indebted to Deepika.

When I returned to Delhi in time for school's reopening, Naneeji stared at me shocked, and after she'd recovered her voice, declared that she had told Nanaji all along *not* to send me to Rohtak as it was obvious to her that my other grandmother was quite incapable of taking care of me. Nanaji, on the other hand, declared that I was looking "Quite lovely though a bit pale and tired," then added admiringly, "Sweta, you've proven you can do anything you want if you set your mind to it!"

I had set my mind on a few things that summer, though a nightly masturbation hadn't been part of the plan. Mummy had sent me a flood of baby pictures in March, and I'd torn them up. I'd stopped replying to her letters. I'd even stopped writing to thank her for the pocket money she sent. What I would have liked to have done is send the Colonel's money right back to him, and the first time that the money arrived after their marriage, good angel and bad angel had battled deep inside me for my soul, but I'd converted the currency into the number of second-hand novels I could buy, and bad angel had won. I told myself that at least I didn't ask Mummy for clothes or jewelry, which other girls my age who lived with their mothers probably did. And then, that summer of '71, I flatly told Nanaji that I was not going to Almora anymore. He took me into his study, which he did whenever he didn't want Naneeji intruding, and asked me why I begrudged my mother her new happiness. "I don't begrudge her anything," I said, "but there are things you can't force me to do." "You're being selfish," Nanaji said. "You're trying to hurt her. She now has two children, not one. You have to understand that the baby has not taken your place." Clearly, Mummy had set him up to talk to me. "I'm not jealous," I said. "But she has no time for me. She had no time for me last summer when the baby wasn't even born. How will she have time for me now?" Nanaji tried to tell me that Mummy hadn't been well last summer, that it was quite common in the early months, but I cut in and said, "I want to stop feeling bad. I don't want to feel bad all the time. I'm not going to do things that make me feel bad anymore." Then Nanaji opened his arms to me and I went into them. Even though I was twelve years old, I sat on his lap and I cried, and he didn't say a word, and he didn't ask me to do anything I didn't want to again.

That evening, Nanaji stood up to Naneeji and told her I wouldn't be going to Almora. I overheard him tell Mummy on the phone, "It's a passing phase, I'm sure. When she's ready, she'll seek you out."

Though Nanaji had supported my decision, he wasn't happy that I'd be spending my summer vacation with them. My grandparents' relationship was so bad at the time that it must have occurred to him how unhealthy it was for a child to witness. He was the first to broach the idea that when I was ready for college I should move out and stay at a hostel. I do have Rani, I tried to tell him, but even Nanaji didn't think she made a suitable friend.

Nanaji called my paternal grandparents to ask if I could visit them that summer. It was all most discreetly done, and Mummy was kept out of the picture, and Naneeji was quietly overruled because she hated Dadeeji, of course, and thought she lacked class. I heard Nanaji deliver the barefaced lie that I had been missing my other grandparents terribly, and Dadeeji, immeasurably softened at the other end, said how much she had been missing me too. So it was all set up, and the occasion turned out to be perfect because my cousins Deepika and Manish were also visiting Rohtak that summer so I would have company my age. Deepika was a couple of years older than me, Manish a couple of years younger, so Nanaji was confident I'd have a good time.

I packed very few clothes and a trunkful of books. I'd already decided that I wasn't going to like my cousins. I'd met Deepika once, at Daddy's funeral, and hadn't liked her one bit, and Manish I didn't remember at all. Boys, in my view, were best avoided. But I'd already given Nanaji so much trouble by refusing to visit Mummy that I knew I had to accede to this request.

Nanaji drove me to Rohtak, and Hari accompanied us just in case we had car trouble. We stopped at Lake Tilyar and ate the delicious *alu-puris* that Naneeji had packed for the journey. We sat down, all three of us, on a grassy knoll and ate together, something that we would never have been able to do if she were there. Hari would have been sent off to sit and eat at a distance, and he would certainly not have been sharing our food. I ate four alu-puris just as a way of saying farewell, as I had decided to begin my diet from the very next day.

Dadaji and Dadeeji were different in every way from my maternal grandparents. They were social and affable, and their haveli on Railway Road was always bustling with people, especially Dadeeji's friends who loved to play cards with high stakes and were always winning and losing what I considered to be shocking amounts of money. The house seemed to run on autopilot, though Dadeeji was forever telling everyone how she was always "supervising" in the kitchen, and "supervising" over the servants. If anyone ever praised Sarla, the cook, Dadeeji immediately responded that it had been *her* recipe and had been cooked under *her* "supervision." Dadaji wasn't in the least interested in Dadeeji's rummy playing but seemed happy enough to sit around in the evenings reading the newspapers and chatting with his associates, who would drop by to see him. Sometimes Dadaji and Dadeeji would lower their voices, and then I'd prick up my ears and hear them talk worriedly about Auntie Radhika's condition, and I'd feel sorry for her even though she had always acted as though she was sorry for me and Mummy and Daddy and anything to do with our lot. Deepika had inherited her mother's superior air but I think my cousin deserved it; she really was incredibly pretty. She was slim with thick hair that came down to her waist and very well-defined breasts that I couldn't take my eyes off. I had been wearing a brassiere too for some time now. On my eleventh birthday, Naneeji had gone off to Sarojini Nagar market and come back with a large, rough cotton fabric with pointy cups that she'd handed to me without a word, and I had turned red with embarrassment. Later, I'd examined the object closely in my room. It was a no-name bra, a size "S." I put it on, fumbling with the massive hooks that barely made it around my chest and stared at the sorry sight of two empty white cones pointing askance. I was too small even for the size "S," though too wide for its hooks.

Cousin Deepika owned two sets of imported bras and panties, which her father's family had sent her from Singapore. Auntie Radhika had married well, whatever good that did her now, and Deepika had gained from her foreign connections. She proudly showed off the "Maidenform" labels and her size 32 B lingerie. One set was silky white with a lace trim. The other was cream with tiny pink polka dots. She let me hold the fabric in my hands and smell it. One of the sets still had tags attached. "I'm saving these," she said, and the way she said it made me blush. Then she said, "Want to see?" I nodded, not knowing what she meant. She picked up the silky white set that had already been inaugurated and disappeared into the bathroom. Moments later she reappeared like a vamp in a Hindi movie, one hand folding her hair in a cascade down the side of her face, the other jauntily perched on her hip, all naked except for the perfectly fitting bra

and panties. She had the most gorgeous line of cleavage, a perfectly trim waist, and gently flaring hips. There was no full-length
mirror in the room, but she swayed her body snakelike, like we'd
seen Helen do so many times in her cabaret numbers, and pouted
her lips at the small dust-laden mirror on the wall. Then she
turned to me, her only spectator, and ran her hands sinuously
down her body, her fingers lightly grazing her nipples, a hand
running fleetingly over her cunt. A moment of recognition passed
between us then, which I have revisited many times. It was a
single, thrilling moment, but it wasn't as simple as us wanting
each other. No, she didn't want me at all. She wanted to be
wanted, and I'd given her that power in an instant. She giggled
and ran into the bathroom. I couldn't wait until the night. I went
and locked myself up in the guest room.

SURVIVOR

Anu decided to spend a substantial portion of the minuscule travel budget that the *Statesman* had given her on a first-class ticket to Calcutta on the Howrah-Kalka Mail departing that night. Her telephone conversation with Flying Officer Parikshit Basu had confirmed that he was the last person to have seen Ronu Kalra alive. Her father was categorical about her traveling second class. "No way," he said. "First class, ladies compartment, is how you'll go. If you're carrying my precious Revox, that is."

It lay between them now, its rotating spools recording Basu's voice amid the hum of ceiling fans and the clattering of coffee cups and cutlery at Flury's coffee shop on Park Street.

"Vir Chakra material, that's what we thought of Dusty. There lay the difference between Dusty and the rest of us. I don't think anyone was surprised that he got the award. When war broke out, it was the real thing after years of combat preparedness. Each one of us responded differently to the call. I would say that all of us were pretty competent but Dusty went beyond competence. Dusty was hungry, hungry for the kill. Even if he hadn't got that Sabre that day, and maybe he got both—we don't know who got that second Sabre—well, what I'm saying is, even if he hadn't got a single Sabre, he still deserved that Vir Chakra. Six days of battle, and he'd already destroyed three Pattons, six or seven armored vehicles, an oil tanker. The guy had unerring aim and just great guts. When we congratulated him on his ground kills, he said, that was nothing, just slow-moving targets, yaar, all he wanted was a Sabre in the sky."

"One of the officers who wrote to me said that losing Dusty was like losing ten men."

"Yeah, I second that. On September 1, the day that Air Chief Marshal called Western Air Command into action and we assembled in our squadron, do you know what Dusty did? I didn't see this for myself, but others did. He let out a whooping cry and sprinted around the air base. Now this won't mean a thing to you, but if you knew Dusty, there was a man who was bone lazy! He didn't lift a finger unless strapped to a cockpit. So for Dusty to run, it was like . . . who was that Greek guy who ran to his death to tell the Spartans or whoever that they'd won the war?"

"Pheidippides?"

"Yeah. It was as though Dusty had run the bloody Marathon. After that crazy sprint of his, we were confident as hell we'd win."

"Did you?"

(Silence)

"Did we win? You're joking, right? Surely, you know we won?"

"That's what the press says. That's what the government says too. But Pakistan says *they* won. It's all over their press."

"That's propaganda. Bullshit. They always say they've won. They said that in '48."

"Well, let's get back to that morning, the morning of the seventh of September."

"It was our first offensive in Pakistani territory. We had a clear mandate: knock Sargodha airfield out of commission. Dusty was excited as hell."

"Were you excited?"

"Yeah, I think so. I'm not sure about Kalra. He was a calm fellow. He told me that the difference between him and the rest of us was that he was married. It's true. Kalra was the only one in our formation who was married. Singh was engaged. Dusty was a confirmed bachelor. Are you married?"

"I was once. Are you saying because Kalra was married, he was more cautious?"

"That's what he said. He said marriage is a simple fact that changes everything. He said he wanted to live. He was crazy about his family, his daughter. I said, what the hell, married or not, I want to live too. We all wanted to live, of course, but someone like Dusty wouldn't lose sleep over it. Kalra would. Kalra wasn't a fighter, you know. He was a great instructor. He was my instructor at flying college. He was a relaxed chap; he gave his students a lot of confidence. If he had to pull you up, he would, but he never humiliated you like some of the other instructors. He was strict, but he made you feel you'd get it right in the end. When I was on my solo flight I felt he was there throughout, holding my hand. Whoever had him as an instructor was darned lucky. You can't imagine how fortunate I felt that morning to be included in that formation. Firebrand Dusty as formation leader, Singh as number 2, Kalra number 3, and I, my instructor's wing! What incredible luck, I thought.

"Personally, I'd be dead bored being an instructor. A lot of us want to be where the action is. A posting in Assam, now that's a pilot's dream. Not for Kalra though. He was happiest, I think, teaching. He loved the regularity of it, the interaction with pilot officers, the safety of it, you know. He must have clocked 500-odd hours in his two years at flying college. For someone who loves flying, that's a great life. I don't think he should have been called to the front. All we've gone and done is lost a great teacher."

(Silence)

"Were you ready for the attack?"

"We were tired. We had six sleepless nights behind us. Every passing day was knocking it out of us. The four or five daily sorties, the moving around from base to base, the poor communications, the lack of local organization, and basic facilities. Even the orders we were given were often in conflict; there were last-minute changes in tactics, now, don't quote me on that. You're recording this, right?"

"Yes. But I won't disclose your identity."

"You can't mention squadron numbers and you can't describe the specifics of a mission. Otherwise it's easy to figure out."

"I'll send you a copy before publication. Anything you disagree with, I'll delete. You have my word."

"Talk to enough officers, and they'll say the same thing. We had very poor tactics. It was our first war after all, for the IAF, that is. As you know, we weren't involved in '62. When you're under training, they give you the impression that they have everything under control. Air HQ has dotted all the i's, crossed all the t's: number of days of battle, quantities of armament, attrition rates, all figured out. Then you're faced with the real thing, and you're out for a duck. You don't know what the hell is going on. Is there a plan at all? Is anybody in control? After the first ground attack in defense of the army in Chamb, it seemed as if we were being shifted around from base to base solely in reaction to the attacks on Indian soil. It didn't inspire confidence, I'll tell you. That morning, September 7, was different. It marked a significant change in strategy. *It was our first offensive in Pak territory.*"

"They had attacked us the night before."

"That's right. On the night of September 6, we were attacked on all three front bases: Halwara, Pathankot, Adampur. Now it was our turn to retaliate. There was anger, the excitement was high. Naturally there was tension as well. The tension showed on all of us except Dusty, whose fingers ran amuck on any flat surface they could find. He just loved playing the *tabla*, you know. Maybe he was nervous, and that was his way of getting it out. I don't know. We were at a point when any of us could doze off, just like that, we were that tired. We hadn't slept for six nights. But that morning, there was a rush of adrenalin. We told ourselves we'd see this mission through and then we'd collapse."

Parikshit Basu drank the dregs of his coffee.

"I'll get some more."

"I didn't give it a thought then. But later it all came back to me. Three men lost in one mission. Who knows whether Singh will ever get back? A POW in Pakistan is as good as dead. How on earth did I survive? It could so easily have been me. I've gone over it, again and again. Every little detail. Each one of us, what he said, what he did, how he looked. The normalcy of every little thing, you know, when you have no idea that you're about to go. There was a strong smell of pheneol in the bunker. Clean, as if everything had been sanitized. I can smell it now. We had been waiting for take off. Then, at one point, Dusty yawned and said ours was a suicide mission. He said it matter-of-factly, just like that. I thought I hadn't heard right. Leads don't usually talk like that. One of them, I don't know who it was, Kalra perhaps, or Singh, there were other guys in the bunker too, one of them said,

'What do you mean?' He sounded frightened. 'Yeah,' Dusty repeated, 'this is one suicide mission. They're expecting us.'

"He was right, of course. You see, ours was not the first mission of the morning, it was the second. Six Mystères had already gone out at the very crack of dawn and done their damage. *Theirs* was the surprise attack. The Mystères had come back unscathed. Our sortie was sure to have a committee in waiting. Besides, there was a technical snag at Adampur. I don't know what it was, but our departure had been delayed. We had a TOT of 6:30. The intention was to come in soon after the Mystères while the enemy was still in shambles. But at 6:45 we were still in our bunker awaiting take off. That's when Dusty made that remark.

"You know the fellow has always been a bit of a legend. There are many stories about him. Some say he was prophetic, that he could tell the future. I don't know if they've always said that about him or whether his reputation grew after the fact. He was an unusual guy. He loved Indian classical music; Ayurveda; he was always dabbling in herbal remedies and homeopathy and stuff like that. He didn't smoke, he didn't drink, he kept far away from women. Never had a girlfriend, as far as anyone could tell. He was a real oddball in the force. Like he had no vices! So when Dusty called this a suicide mission, it was like the voice of God had spoken, you know? Now *he* didn't look worried himself! That was his way of saying, the Pakis will be waiting for us, we'll have ourselves a really good combat, a couple of sexy dog fights! But it jolted the rest of us. He was one strange, spiritualist warrior, yeah, like Arjuna . . .

"Kalra listened to him though, and became quiet. After a while I said, a rupee for your thoughts. He said, nothing much, just stupid thoughts filling an idle brain. Dusty was by then in tabla mode. Are you worrying about Dusty's remark, I asked. No, he said. I'm thinking about something irrelevant. This pheneol. It reminds me that I smelled a gas leak in my kitchen the evening we were called. We didn't even have the chance to discuss it. I hope my wife has seen to it.

"Funny, huh, what people worry about right before they die? I didn't give it a thought then. But when a man goes, someone you care about, everything comes back, every little thing, the way he looked, the things he said, everything has meaning. Are you all right?"

"Yes."

"Is it too hot for you here? Sure? Well, that's how it was that morning. Kalra was stuck on his gas leak. Dusty was stuck on one of his ragas. And Singh, poor Singh, was hell bent on cracking the filthiest jokes I've heard. No doubt that was his way of relieving tension. Well, sex was the last thing on anyone's mind, so we all told him to shut up. That's when we got the clearance to take off. Singh never got to deliver his punch line. 'What does a Sardarji do with three wives at one go?' Well, don't ask me for I'll never know!"

Parikshit Basu forced a laugh.

"And what were you thinking about?"

"I was upset by Dusty's remark too. I know he didn't mean anything by it. He was just sharpening his claws. But everybody's different, and a remark like that is irresponsible. It didn't scare him, but it did shake our confidence. I had a girlfriend then. I remember thinking I may not see her again. And Kalra. He was already on the edge. Something like that could tip a guy over."

"What do you mean he was on the edge?"

"God, you're worse than the Court of Inquiry!"

Anu stopped the recording. "There's something I haven't told you. I'm a friend of Ranjit's. No, I haven't lied. I'm a journalist too.

But my inquiry is motivated partly from friendship. I'd like to know as much about him as possible. Anything you can tell me, and naturally, it won't go into print. It won't interest anyone else."

After a silence, she continued, "Don't look at me like that. It's not what you think. I hadn't met Ranjit in years. We knew each other when we were very young, teenagers. I've spoken to his wife and daughter too . . . Can we continue?"

She turned the tape recorder back on.

"Why do you say he was on the edge?"

"The night before, we'd talked a bit. Kalra said he hoped this wouldn't turn into a sixty-day war; he wanted to get home in time for his daughter's birthday. October, I think, he said it was. He was wearing his exhaustion on his face. He was nauseous too, retched a few times. The food hadn't agreed with him, he said. I remember being a bit worried about him. Then he said something as though he had to get it off his chest. He said he'd been credited with a tank hit on an air support mission in the Chamb-Jaurian sector, very early on, on the second day of the war. Well, congratulations, I said. That's terrific, man. There was a guy in the Patton, he said. All I saw was a flash of light as if his head had exploded. 'You know how a light bulb explodes, that's how it was.' Those were his words exactly, and he couldn't stop trembling when he said it. God alone knows how many heads we've shot off in combat practice. But that's all it's been: combat practice. Kalra was distraught. I didn't tell anyone about this. A remark like that and the CO would have considered him unfit for mission. Kalra had lifted my spirits so many times in the past. It was my turn to comfort him now. I told him that the guy he had killed would have shot him down if he could. He had killed him in self-defense. Later, I regretted it. I should have had a word with the flight commander. I should have told someone. I should have had Kalra pulled out. Instead, I comforted him, made him go on. And now he's dead.

"When we were airborne, Kalra's voice was completely calm. It sounded calm on the RT all the way through. I don't think he cracked up after all."

There was a long silence, then Parikshit Basu said, "You know, I need a drink. Coffee isn't taking me very far. Will you join me for drinks and dinner somewhere?"

"That doesn't sound like an ordeal."

A Letter To My Daughter

Sweta, you were always a difficult child even in the womb. The sickness I felt, the nausea that threatened to spit out of my face—What words do I use to describe it? I had been beautiful once, but you took away my loveliness. I was estranged by my body. How could I love you who inhabited it? When you were born, you were not a pretty child. Your skin was shriveled and old and cracked. Your mouth attached itself to my burning nipples, and I was filled with ugliness.

They say that when an old soul revisits the world, there is nothing but trouble as nothing will satisfy it. That's what I thought about you then. I looked into your open, knowing eyes, and I thought you were a very old soul.

Later, I did learn to love you. When you were a little girl, I loved you completely. I cried my heart out when we sent you away to Delhi to live with your Nanaji and Naneeji.

I fought with your father. Let her stay with us, I said. I'll work with her, I'll teach her things, her education will not be compromised. But he was adamant. He had a notion of the kind of girl he wanted you to be and thought it impossible in a serviceman's life. Even though he was the one who sent you away, it was he you loved. As though you remembered that I had been indifferent to you once, and it was he who had stroked the swollen belly, who had whispered the stories, who had held your gnarled and grasping fingers. Sweta, you never did forgive.

We were happy enough, the three of us. I was the one who didn't belong when you came home for the holidays. Ranjit never was with me the way he was with you: playful, easy, open as a child. And you were prankish and adoring and already a woman with him. I turned instead to my xenias and foxgloves and sweetpeas. They needed me more than either of you. I didn't mind. We were happy enough.

Then, one day, everything changed. Your father came home dead, his body in a coffin, draped by the Indian flag. He didn't belong to us anymore. There were so many uniforms, so many faces; faces of strangers, curious, pitying, who said I must be strong, I must adjust. I must think only of you, a fatherless child.

I shielded you from it as much as I could. It wasn't I who took him away but you wouldn't forgive. As if you blamed me for being the one who had stayed behind. We are never given the choice, Sweta.

I didn't cry in front of you. The hardest thing was to sleep at night and not find his feet under the cover.

That is the only time I cried, silently every night, never in front of you.

We thought you were fine, you took it well. You seemed strong and calm and matter-of-fact. And then I realized there was something wrong. You hadn't got it at all, my poor little child. You did not know that death is forever and ever, death is what life can never be.

Yes, Sweta, I dismantled your jigsaw puzzle. I had to do it. Even though it made you hate me, I did it, for after that, you lost your sense of waiting.

ALL THANKS TO CHEIRO

Firpo's restaurant on Chowringhee Road was guarded by a set of double doors and a doorman named Montgomery, alias Mongesh Ghurman Dorji, who had stood his place for thirty-five years, dressed in the frayed uniform of the 39th Garhwal Rifles. His erstwhile employer, Richard Applethorpe, upon departing permanently for England, had left this article of clothing to his trusted servant, Montgomery, along with the abbreviated nomenclature. Applethorpe left instructions that his uniform be hung next to his portrait and both receive an adequate dusting from time to time. Montgomery, however, did no such thing. He carried Applethorpe's portrait to the local studio and received handsome compensation for its gilded frame. He donned the ill-fitting garb of the 39th Garhwal Rifles and walked smartly to Firpo's, where as luck would have it, the doorman had been fired only that morning. Montgomery presented himself as the new replacement and was readily accepted. Over the years, he gained a fair bit of weight until the uniform, now mended and darned, came to fit him perfectly. It irked Montgomery that the great Firpo's, once the unflinching bastion of the British Raj, had opened its doors to the general public. He did what he could to repair that error. Indeed, the combination of the doorman in military regalia and the set of double doors was enough to turn away all but the most determined customer.

A lumbering ambassador came to a halt outside. Anu paid the driver while Flying Officer Parikshit Basu, dressed in civilian clothes, exited and came across to hold the door open for her. Montgomery, working on the assumption that if he did not observe visitors, was likely to remain unobserved, examined the ground between his boots. Anu, however, walked straight up to him. Still he did not move. She faced him squarely and cleared her throat. Montgomery raised his eyes to hers, sighed, and relented. He pushed his weight against the door, bowed grimly, and muttered, "Madam." He may as well have said, "Tart." Anu stepped inside while Parikshit deftly reached past the doorman to open the second set of doors. Montgomery returned to his post outside. For thirty-five years he had opened and shut these doors, but with the Sahibs gone, the joy had crept out of his work. Indians did not believe in tipping doormen.

Inside, nostalgia peeled off the walls along with the wallpaper. The pristine chicken à la king reluctantly shared the menu with *murgh musallam*. The air conditioners hummed forth an aroma of dank fungi. A young couple sat intertwined in the darkness; otherwise, the restaurant, like an old, overused prostitute, was quite forlorn.

Anu headed toward a small table at the back. She liked this place, she decided. It was just the sort of colonial outpost that Hans wouldn't be seen dead in. Parikshit gave her a quick and appreciative lookover. She was wearing a cotswool jacket with a hugging, knee-length skirt and stockings, rather like a BOAC hostess, he thought. She'd given herself quite a lift with those platforms. Unlike an air hostess, however, her hair was loose and quite disheveled. She had told him she would be in Calcutta for three days, and he thanked his lucky stars for agreeing to meet her right away. The two hours spent at Flury's had been entirely effortless. She had done her homework, he thought approvingly. No time wasted on the ABC's of flying. And no wedding ring. She had told him she was married once. Well, she wasn't married now. Good he'd taken the trouble to go home and freshen up and change. You never know, he told himself cheerfully.

A black-cravated, red-jacketed waiter arrived, bearing menus.

"Good evening ma'am, good evening sir," the waiter grinned conspiratorially and left. Early evening, mid-week. A young couple meant clammy fingers under tablecloths. The days of the dignitaries were gone.

"I need a drink," said Anu.

"Yeah, me too. So tell me, how did you know Ranjit?"

Anu sighed.

"He was my first boyfriend. He was at the NDA at the time."

He was surprised by her forthrightness. She was so different from Mrs. Kalra, whom he had met on a couple of occasions. He couldn't imagine Ranjit with someone like her, someone that sophisticated, and yes, remarkable.

The waiter reappeared.

"A whisky and soda for me."

Anu ordered a martini.

"I recommend our famous balloon cocktail, Madam. It has vermouth also."

Anu nodded and lit a cigarette.

The waiter disappeared behind the bar to divulge the information that this was the drinking, smoking, high-class kind, probably with a hotel room lined up for the night. He was surprised, however, when she brought out a tape recorder and set it up.

"So you're doing this for him?"

"To tell you the truth, that's what started it. I happened to read his obituary in the paper. There had been no contact between us for years. I'd thought of him now and then, of course. I'd wondered what was up with him. Then one day I pick up the newspaper and find that he's dead."

She hadn't considered telling him. But she liked him, she decided. He was straightforward and somehow dependable. "I wanted to know what had happened to him, that's all. And then I realized that there is no way to find out. If you're the general public, I mean. The newspapers don't tell you a thing. So I started digging around on my own, finding out whatever I could about the war. I became sort of addicted to it. One thing led to another. It was then no longer about him. I really want to do this now. If there's another war, I want to be at the front, where the action is . . ."

"So you're going to be India's first woman war correspondent?" Parikshit said and grinned.

"Are you mocking me?"

"No," he said sincerely.

The waiter brought them their drinks, and in true diversity, a bread basket filled with hot cross buns, curls of butter, and *papadams*.

Anu handed Parikshit the microphone.

"Can we continue?"

"You're going to get me into trouble, lady."

"You have my word, Parikshit. Anything you want deleted, I will. I really appreciate your taking the time to do this."

"*Parikhit*. My name is pronounced *Parikhit* without the 's'."

In Class I, a diminutive boy with horn-rimmed spectacles, who hardly said a thing, had lifted his index finger, pointed it at Parikshit and said a single word: *Shitty*. And "Shitty" he had become all the way till high school. While filling out the NDA's application forms, hope flowered briefly in Parikshit's heart and he begged his father for permission to drop the 's' from his name.

"The 's' is useless," Parikshit said. "It makes no difference."

"Yes it does," Bimal Basu replied. "You may not be aware of it, but I have studied Cheiro's *Numerology*, and your success and good health are due in no small part to the letter 's', which is the nineteenth letter of the alphabet. One plus 9 equals 10, which is 1. Your destiny number is also 1. Add up your birth date, month, and year, and see what you get. Your name and your surname taken together add up to 1. As long as you keep the 's'. It is most auspicious. You see, my boy, your name is no coincidence. I have worked hard to give it to you. Bring me a piece of paper and I will show you," concluded Bimal Basu, warming to the task, while Parikshit resigned himself to being Shitty for the rest of his days.

According to Bimal Basu, Parikshit, thanks to the "s" in his name, lived to tell the tale of his miraculous escape on the morning of the seventh of September, 1965. Mr. Basu had leaped to his desk and scribbled out the numbers: 7+9+1+9+6+5 and yelled, "37! That is 10! See, it is *One*! Your badge number is 5203, 5+2+0+3=10! See, my boy, see! It is *One*!"

"Pari*khit*," Anu said, correcting herself.

"Cheers," Parikshit responded, clinking glasses. "Here's to survival."

"And new beginnings."

"And new beginnings." He smiled at her.

—◊—

"So tell me, in as much detail as you can, what happened on the morning of September 7?"

"Finally, we received clearance to take off. I told you we'd been delayed. Well we were close to an hour off from our planned TOT of 6:30 a.m. Dusty was real short, you know. He had to hoist himself onto someone's knee before he could lower himself into the cockpit. Well, that's what he did then, and I remember laughing at him. Singh stopped short of giving us the punch line to his Sardarji joke. Remind me to tell you later, he said.

"We had chosen Jupiter as our call sign. We checked our channels and the crystallization plan. 'Jupiter Formation Check in: 2, 3, Jupiter 4.' Everything was fine. Is this too much detail for you?"

"No, this is perfect. I'm not sure I understand the purpose of the call signs, but you can explain that to me afterward. Go on."

"In less than a minute we were airborne, flying northwest in perfect battle formation. It was a beautiful morning, very clear; there was this pale, pink light over the hills. We crossed the Chenab, and just short of Initial Point, Dusty switched frequencies and we checked in again.

"Ground Control broke in just then to warn us of the presence of five Sabres patrolling at some 15,000 feet to the northeast. We were flying low, around 200 feet, to avoid detection by Pakistani radar. We must have crossed under the enemy planes at some point, without knowing it.

"I chanted the SAFE mantra to steel myself. SAFE. SAFE. SAFE. It's a habit with me when I'm in danger. SAFE's an acronym for Sight, Armament, Fuel, Engine. You're damn busy in the fighter, you know. You have to keep track of fifty things at once. I chanted the words and went through the motions: gun Sight on and serviceable, live Armament circuit breakers and switches on, Fuel sufficient for attack and get away, Engine parameters within limits.

"We were almost onto Sargodha. We pulled up near target, and the whole airfield lay stretched before us. The Mystères had done their damage. There was burning wreckage on the ground, and black smoke billowed. We dived down onto the runway to drop our bombs in a single high-speed pass. Ack-ack was firing, and we could see scattered aircraft, fuel tanks, armored vehicles, all lit up. As number 4, I was the last to attack. I aligned my gunsight on a transport plane and saw Dusty's bombs score a direct hit on the air control tower. During his pullout, he strafed a Sabre that burst into flames. He'd got his first Sabre, even if it was a ground kill! With the PAF, you don't know which of their aircraft are dummies. They have a way of keeping their planes perfectly camouflaged. But we rained down on them anyway. Number 2 scored a hit on a hangar. My leader bombed a bunker that Intelligence had told us was a squadron crew room. I flew through the debris of that explosion. Fortunately, my aircraft didn't suck it in. The last thing I saw, as we exited southwest, was a row of Sabres scrambling on the tarmac.

"We flew home, a southeasterly course at about 480 knots. I'd say our mission was successful. We'd got one aircraft, and we'd hit the control tower, and a bunker, though it was hard to know the extent of the damage we'd inflicted. With luck we had created enough havoc to disable operations for a while.

"We left Sargodha behind, and the sky was calm once again, clean of smoke. Not for long though! We knew the scrambled Sabres were after us. We scanned the sky for bogies. I noticed two Sabres and reported them at eleven o'clock high. Dusty confirmed contact with two Sabres at Angels 3, that's 3,000 feet. He ordered us to clear wings, drop our loads. He then ordered a climbing hard turn at one hundred percent power. We dropped our external fuel tanks and swooped upward, picking up speed. We were probably no more than ten minutes from the border. We had enough fuel for twenty minutes of flying time, no more. Is this too much detail?"

"No. This is great."

"'Split!' Dusty called out. 'Jupiter 3 and 4, split. I'm going for them.' That was a tactic our squadron had practiced for engagement. While one section went in for attack, the other perched and watched their tails.

"The thought went through my head: Why on earth? We're low on fuel. We can easily outfly the Sabres, make a clean getaway. The enemy planes posed no threat at that point, there was no need to engage. But it was Dusty's call. He wanted his dogfight!"

"You're saying something serious here."

"Yes, and I'm saying it to you. You're not going to print this. Because Dusty's dead, and he's been decorated. You can't bring down a war hero."

"Go on."

"So, 1 and 2 went in after the enemy. Dusty fired at a Sabre, missed. The second Sabre had split from its leader and was diving down at him from above. It fired a GAR-8 Sidewinder missile. Fortunately, we were low enough in altitude; the Sidewinder isn't very effective at low altitudes, and it fell away. Moments later, there was a short burst from Dusty's 30 mm and he got the first Sabre in its tanks! Another short burst, and the Sabre was up in flames, flicking over, falling off. I saw it clearly.

"'Got him!' We heard Dusty stammer on the RT. I don't know what happened to Singh. I had lost sight of Singh completely.

When Dusty had called the split and they'd veered off left, I'd seen Singh for some seconds engaging one of the Sabres. I didn't see him get hit, but the next thing I knew, his plane had disappeared. Dusty was on his own now. Mind you, he was in no trouble then.

"But it didn't stop there. Yeah, from then on, it just rained on us. Ground Control warned us that five enemy aircraft had entered our area at a height of 1,000 feet! Those were the planes we'd missed while coming in.

"'Head back to Adampur,' was our instruction. 'Return immediately to Adampur base.'

"By this time, we'd lost all visual contact with Dusty and Singh. Kalra and I changed course and headed back home. We figured that Dusty had received the GC's communication; he'd lie low and fly back when the coast was clear. I wasn't particularly worried, for at that low level, the Hunter can outfly the Sabre. We were only about five minutes from the border.

"Kalra informed Ground Control we'd lost contact with 1 and 2. He gave them our coordinates. We sped on, relieved to know that our distance from the Sabres had widened. That's when it happened, just minutes from the border. Dusty's voice suddenly crackled live on the RT: 'Jupiter 3, Jupiter 4, do you read me? Jupiter 3, come in.'

"We came in. 'Jupiter 3, I need you to cover my tail. Singh's been shot. Acknowledge, Jupiter 3.' Kalra responded at once, 'Wilco.'

"That's how it happened. Out of the fucking blue, excuse the language. It made no sense, no sense at all. Flight Lieutenant Kalra told me to head back to base; he turned and went in after Dusty. His fuel tank was near empty, but he turned his back on the Indian border and went right back into enemy territory."

"What are you saying? You had instructions to return to Adampur."

"Yes, but our formation leader was in trouble. He needed cover."

"And what about you? You were Kalra's wing. Why didn't you go with him?"

"Save me the sarcasm. I did. Kalra told me to head home but when I saw him turn back, I changed course and headed back too. That's when it turned into a downright suicide mission. You would think Dusty wanted to die. But no, that doesn't make sense. He could have killed himself without killing everyone else. Quite the contrary. He thought he was invincible, and in his presence we'd be invincible too. According to my dad, I'm alive because of Cheiro, but that's another story. Ready for a second drink?"

E N D   O F   A N   E R A

*The 30th of January, 1948: It is almost half past five. I close the file
I am working on and prepare to leave the office when Saxena
bursts into my room. Tears stream down his face; his placid
countenance is gripped with hysteria. I cannot understand his
words. He pulls me out into the street, which is milling with people.
I hear the frightful words. They fill the air in a rush of whispers.
The Mahatma is dead. The Mahatma has been killed by a madman
with a gun. Mahatma Gandhi has been assassinated! It has
happened no more than ten minutes ago, but his death is instantly
communicated in the wind, as tens of people merge into hundreds,
then thousands, all walking together in the great silence of their
grief. A single thought repeats itself in my head. Let this madman
not be a Muslim. Please, dear God, let him not be a Muslim. A faint
hope: perhaps the Mahatma is not dead. He has survived so much
fasting, surely he will survive a bullet?*

*That is not to be. The 6 o'clock news carries a restrained
announcement:*

Mahatma Gandhi was assassinated in New Delhi at twenty
minutes past five this afternoon. His assassin was a Hindu.

One prayer, at least, has been answered.

At last, Delhi is quiet. For the past months we have witnessed nothing but horrors. We have witnessed the abject bestiality of the human soul as Hindus and Sikhs have turned on their Muslim neighbors and taken unspeakable revenge for the stories of brutality that refugees bring from across the border. The Mahatma's death is the terrible price we pay for such madness. At last, the violence is stilled. Even with his death, he spreads the message of peace. Hai Ram! This is no place for the soul of souls.

Nanaji's diary begins and ends with Mahatma Gandhi. After Gandhi's assassination, it's as though he had nothing left to say.

—⁊⁊⁊—

I remember discussing politics with Nanaji on a single occasion. It was probably the last meaningful conversation we had. It was the autumn of 1975. Mrs. Gandhi's Emergency Powers were in full force, and Nanaji's cynicism was complete. The newspapers depressed him inordinately, until finally, he had stopped subscribing to them altogether. He said that the only blessing of his career was that he had reached the age of retirement before Nehru's daughter went and became mad.

I had just started a bachelor of arts degree program at Delhi University, and in my first month at the hostel, we became completely caught up in the vortex of student politics. Though I considered myself distinctly apolitical, it was virtually impossible to stay outside the fray of competing groups and ideologies. The seniors were already plugged into their respective coalitions and viewed us freshers as new soil to plow. One morning, our college became rife with rumors that a student of Jawaharlal Nehru

University in South Delhi had been kidnapped from within the grounds of the campus and was being held indefinitely under Mrs. Gandhi's notorious Maintenance of Internal Security Act. As to the nature of the student's crime, there were several stories in circulation, all attesting to his essential innocence. He had protested against the Emergency, we were told, and that was cause enough for indefinite arrest without bail. He had organized a strike and disrupted classes, and such behavior was not tolerated under the present regime. A more likely story went that he had insulted the prime minister's daughter-in-law, also a student at JNU, and she had complained to her husband, Sanjay Gandhi, who had had the miscreant disposed of. In fact, the police, in its haste to please the prime minister's son, had picked up the wrong student but was not about to let him go. Let this be a warning to students in general appeared to be the message of the arrest. Our Student's Union had proposed a university-wide protest and we were alternatively entreated by our seniors to participate in it and to exercise caution and stay away. The secretary of the union sought me out, saying she had heard that someone in my family was a high-up bureaucrat and could I try to get an investigation started on the missing student? As a matter of fact, Nanaji had retired from his post a couple of years ago, but I assured her that I would speak to him and see what could be done.

Nanaji did not know anything about the kidnapping. "It won't be in the papers anyway," he said, "whether or not I read them. Now with the censorship, the only news that the papers carry is how the trains are up and running on time, and the number of public engagements that Sanjay Gandhi attends in a day." He wasn't surprised, he said. Anything was possible under the rogue regime.

As instructed, I asked him whether he could contact some of his colleagues in the Home Ministry and instigate an inquiry into the case.

"The ministries are all stooges. The country is run by the prime minister's office and the lieutenant governor of Delhi. There's no other rule of law."

I was secretly relieved that I was absolved of the burden of taking this further. Nanaji sat in his chair, quiet and despondent.

"We do not value our freedom. Those who have power abuse the freedom of others; those without power are slavish and throw away their freedom for personal gain." He looked utterly dejected. "It was all for nothing. All, all, for nothing."

A Thursday Afternoon

The hostel soon became my home, and I moved from being a freshman to a senior. Nanaji and Naneeji paid the fees since I refused to accept any money from the Colonel. I only came to see my grandparents on the occasional weekend. Most hostelers went home to their local guardians every week, to have their clothes washed and to stock up on home cooking, but I preferred to put up with the execrable food of the hostel mess. I spent most weekends in my room, reading voraciously, watched over by the two men in my life: Mick Jagger, whose whooping mouth and infinitely sexy crotch stretched tight on the wall across, and Daddy, who smiled intimately at me from under his hat on my bedside table.

On weekend evenings, the few of us who remained at the hostel went for walks along the beautiful ridge that circled the university, and listened to rock music, shared illicit drinks, and smoked hashish. For the first time in years, I was completely happy. Nanaji and Naneeji said they missed me very much and I was often consumed with guilt for having abandoned them when it suited my convenience. I lied to them that I simply had too much to do. The commute to visit them took several hours (which was true), I had all these extra-curricular activities (sometimes true), and there were so many papers due (not entirely true). Every time I did go over and see them though, they were obviously overjoyed, and we ended up having a good time together. It was quite different from the years when I had lived with them. Naneeji would send me back with a tuckbox filled with *alu-puris*, *mathris*, and *mithai*. Anything your heart desires, she'd say, and I'd feel terrible and resolve to go again the following weekend, but usually ended up changing my mind.

Since I saw so little of them, it was virtually impossible to slip into Nanaji's study and spend time with him alone. I knew Naneeji would be hurt if we shut her out, so we always spent the little time we had together, though Nanaji was never entirely at ease in her presence. They no longer squabbled in front of me. Clearly, they made a huge effort to appear normal for my sake, though I could always sense their underlying tension.

Then on Thursday, the ninth of March, everything changed. I cannot forget the date. A labor dispute that had been brewing for weeks at the university escalated into violence, and all hostels were shut down until further notice. My best friend, Anjana, invited me over to her aunt's house, but since it was a Thursday, I decided to go and spend some quiet time with Nanaji. I knew that on Thursdays, Naneeji went over to Bari Nanee's house and spent the day with her. Bari Nanee, who was keeping far from well, had staunchly refused the services of a full-time *ayah*, and had also refused to move in with her sister. So on Thursdays, after finishing her own housework, Naneeji took the bus to Bari Nanee's and spent the day helping her with her laundry and grocery shopping. She cooked enough food to last her sister a week, and the two then spent the rest of the day watching television.

Just about a year or so ago, Nanaji had bought Naneeji a black-and-white television set that had revolutionized her life completely. After Bari Nanee became incapacitated, Naneeji insisted on shifting the television to her house on the grounds that her sister's need was greater. Naneeji had been completely addicted to that television set, and I realized then how unselfish she could be. Thursday evenings was "Chitrahaar," the sisters' favorite program. They watched the Hindi film songs together and then Nanaji drove up to collect Naneeji around 8:30 when the program ended. As it was only early in the afternoon, I thought Nanaji and I would get several hours to spend together and then we would drive across and collect Naneeji. I'd also get a chance to visit Bari Nanee, who threatened every time I saw her, that this would be the last time.

The university had organized "student specials," buses that would transport hostelers to different parts of the city. It was around 3:30 in the afternoon that I alighted at our bus stop in Chanakya Puri. I had a key and let myself into the house. I walked straight to Nanaji's study, sure to find him there. I knocked, and getting no answer, pushed the door open. Both the lamps were lit as usual, and a book lay open on the table: J.K. Galbraith's *The Affluent Society*. "Hullo! Nana!" I cried out. No answer.

I went out into the garden to see if he was taking a stroll. But it was a hot afternoon, and Nanaji didn't care for the sun. He only sat in the garden in the early mornings while it was still cool to have his tea and read a book.

Too bad he's out, I thought. I should have told him I was coming, but I do have the house to myself, and that's not a bad thing. I went up to my room and started unpacking the stuff I had brought. My room had been meticulously cleaned since my last visit. I felt a jab of regret. Poor Nanee, she tried so hard. I felt like an impostor, sneaking in while she was out. I pulled out my bag of dirty clothes and went downstairs toward the back of the house where Ratna washed our clothes and did the ironing. I dropped the clothes into the laundry basket, and as I turned to leave, I heard a sound in the spare room. This was a small, dark room with just a divan and a table, and a few odds and ends that Naneeji kept there for storage. It was rarely used, though I had slept in it once or twice when Mummy and Arun had come on a visit and I had had to give my room to them.

Ratna might be working in there, I thought. I would ask her if she knew where Nanaji had gone. I heard a muffled cry and thought she was in trouble. I turned the handle and opened the door. The sun just burst in on them. I don't know if Ratna screamed, but I remember her mouth frozen with terror, her eyes dazed by the light that I had let in. I watched him fumble for his glasses. I watched her roll off the bed.

I slammed the door, and I ran. I raced to my room, picked up my satchel and ran out of the house. I did not remember to lock the door. I did not remember that I had left behind a bag of dirty laundry.

It caused a lot of trouble. When Naneeji found my clothes, she kept trying to call the hostel, but it was closed, and the phone went unanswered. I went straight to Anjana's house. I was shaking and incoherent, and even though we were very close, I wouldn't tell her what had happened. I had no clothes with me and had to borrow some of her things over the next few days. It took four days for the union trouble to get sorted out before the hostel reopened.

I got Naneeji's call the very day I returned to my room. She was frantic with worry. She had been trying me for days, she said, and there was no answer. The hostel was closed, I said. She screamed at me then. How could I leave a bag of dirty clothes and just disappear? What on earth was I thinking? Since you were not home, I said, I thought I would go to Anjana's local guardians. But Nanaji was there! I did not see him, I said. He must have stepped out, she said. You could have waited. I did intend to return by the evening, I said, but Anjana was so sick, I didn't want to leave her. And what were we supposed to think, she cried. Didn't I stop to think that they would be worried to death? Couldn't I have called? Just a telephone call? I'm so sorry, I said. How irresponsible of you, Sweta, she shouted. She started to cry, and I cried too. What's wrong with you, she asked; are you all right? It's Anjana, I lied. She's very sick, and I'm afraid she'll die. She won't, said Naneeji. Don't be silly. If this happens again, you must leave us a note. Next time you're here and I'm not, and Nanaji has stepped out, you must leave us a note. I will, I said, I will the next time.

But next time it was Nanaji who left the note.

There are some stories that cannot be told.

There are some stories that turn you inside out and shake you senseless. There are stories that kill, even when you keep them inside, safe.

I didn't go over for two months. I cried myself to sleep, night after night, as the same nightmare bared its nails.

He tried to call me one day. Somebody picked up the hostel phone and shouted my name. When I heard his voice on the phone, tentative, urgent, I banged it down. After that I always asked them to check first, make sure who it was. They thought I was weird anyway. While all their fights were with their boy-friends, mine was with an old grandfather.

I will never see Nanaji again. Sometimes the regret runs so deep, it is hard to breathe.

STORY WITHOUT A SONG

It was like the time, many years ago, when I was invited to view Christ on the Cross. I did not understand it then, but this time I was prepared. The hostel warden summoned me to her house at night. Your grandmother called, she said. She needs you home first thing in the morning. Can I go now, I asked. Not now, she said; we don't want you traveling alone at night. But first thing in the morning, you must go.

The house was sprawling with cops. Dadaji, in his capacity as retired superintendent of police, had set the wheels in motion. Nanaji's photograph had been dispatched to police stations and hospitals all over the country. Dadaji maintained that if a man disappears at this age, and no foul play is suspected, he is likely to show up at some ashram seeking enlightenment. Naneeji scoffed at the idea. There was nothing at all spiritual about Nanaji, she said. I tended to agree.

It was strange to have Dadaji in Nanaji's house and to have Nanaji missing. Then Mummy arrived with the Colonel, and my half-brother, Arun, and Dadaji promptly took his leave, leaving the case in the hands of Delhi's chief commissioner of police. Ever since Mummy had married the Colonel, Dadaji and Dadeeji had distanced themselves from her. The Colonel was only a few years younger than my paternal grandparents, and just as it was impossible for me to look upon him as a father, they refused to regard him as a son.

Finding Nanaji was clearly Priority Number One as the phone never stopped ringing and important looking officials came and went all day. Finally, the call came, late on the second day. A corpse vaguely fitting Nanaji's description had been fished out from the river and was awaiting identification at the morgue. The Colonel, who was the only adult male member of the family present, went off to do the needful, but insisted on taking Hari with him. He had only met Nanaji half a dozen times, he said, and he might have difficulty identifying a body so disfigured by drowning. We all prayed that it would turn out to be somebody else. I know I prayed like I never have in all my life, but when they returned some hours later, Hari's eyes were red with weeping, and that said it all. All of them: Naneeji, Mummy, Ratna, even Bari Nanee, who was always stoic, started wailing and beating their breasts. The moment was half-real, half-ritual, but it pronounced Nanaji's end with finality, like the drum roll had at Daddy's funeral.

Then Auntie Indira arrived with my cousins, and I, being the oldest, was told to take care of them. I shepherded away Shalini and Ankur and the brat, and we watched the proceedings from behind half-closed curtains. Nobody told us anything directly. What we heard was secondhand, an intricate game of Chinese whispers.

"It was a heart attack," the Colonel said soothingly. "I've spoken to the Coroner, and that's what they'll put down on the death certificate."

"Shark attack!" whispered Ankur excitedly. "Shut up," said Shalini.

Nanaji's body wasn't brought back into the house. They took him straight from the morgue to the cremation grounds. Naneeji said that if a body comes home, the soul might reattach itself to things. I felt like reminding her that Nanaji had hardly been attached to anything while still alive, just a few musty old books. Hari assisted in all the exhumation rituals. Naneeji had been horrified when it was first suggested that the low-caste Hari be Nanaji's pallbearer, but she had little choice. Both Nanaji's sisters had died childless. The pallbearers ended up being the Colonel; Uncle Monty, who flew in from Bombay for the occasion; Naneeji's youngest brother, Chotte; and Hari, the peon. Naneeji made such a fuss about Hari that finally I snapped at her and said that he was the only man among the four who had ever cared for Nanaji. Mummy looked at me with wounded eyes and comforted Naneeji by saying that Hari would be properly instructed in the bathing rituals both before and after the cremation so there would be no pollution.

During the *Sradh* ceremony many people came to our house to offer condolences. There was a regular stream of visitors from the Ministry even though Nanaji had retired some years ago. Some of the visitors introduced themselves as associates of Nanaji from the days of the national struggle and spoke of his integrity and fearlessness. One person said that Nanaji had not only been a great man but a good man. I stared coolly at the unfolding hypocrisy around me. Nanaji's words echoed hollowly: *"We do not value our freedom. Those who have power abuse the freedom of others; those without power are slavish and throw away their freedom for personal gain."* The ultimate irony, I thought, to have your indictment used against yourself. I said nothing.

Ratna kept herself busy bringing water and tea and distributing *prasad*, her eyes bloodshot from crying. My gaze followed her everywhere, but she never looked back at me. Rani, who was married and lived in Darbhanga, had come all the way to Delhi to pray for Nanaji's soul. I asked Rani if she was happy in her marriage. She smiled and her plain face became alight in the way I knew well. She pointed to her belly and smiled some more. I put my arms around her and hugged her tight. Good girl, I said stupidly, good girl. I saw Ratna glance at us, then quickly avert her eyes. I looked at her with hate. Your secret is safe with me, my eyes said, but she wouldn't look up to meet them.

A couple of weeks after the *Sradh*, Hari and Ratna packed their things and left the quarter. I made sure I wasn't around. Naneeji would also move out soon. The government would reclaim this house, and my grandmother would live with her sister in their ancestral home on Curzon Road, which had now been renamed Kasturba Gandhi Marg.

All the Way

The land of freedom, which became my adopted home, gave me the license to go all the way with whomever I chose. In some sense it took away something as well, something precious that I'd hoarded for a long, long time. Going all the way had loomed large over our heads while we were college students in India. There were girls at the hostel who had gone all the way with their boyfriends and were proud of it. Some had even done it for money. But there were others like me who didn't have regular boyfriends or were too uptight, and for whom going all the way was like the last and highest hurdle in an obstacle race where you have to stop and evaluate the dangers and decide whether you'll be able to take it in a flying leap or end up in a heap with a twisted ankle. Both Anjana and I lost that race, and when we went on to win scholarships to study in the United States, she for a master of arts in political science, and I in English literature, we decided (having recently read Erica Jong) that it was in the new world that we'd overcome our fear of flying. Mother India, her finger raised in admonition, her head shaking sorrowfully at our moral torpitude, would be left far behind, unable to exert an influence.

So it was at the University of Illinois at Urbana-Champaign that I went all the way with a Paul someone or other who worked as a counselor at a boys' high school and was a follower of the Soto sect of Zen Buddhism. Paul was only twenty-six but he had plans to give it all up and move to California and join a Zen monastery. In America, I realized, all things are possible. You can be a monk of whatever calling, without ever having visited Japan or Tibet, and without having laid eyes on the Dalai Lama. I had joined a film club on campus that met on Wednesdays and that's where I met Paul, who came to the films after sitting in on a class on the philosophy of religion. Paul said he loved Fellini, and that, coupled with the fact that Zen was completely new to me, seemed reason enough to go all the way with him. He was pleasant enough to look at in a soft, forgettable sort of way, but I wasn't remotely attracted to him. In Delhi I'd been attracted to at least two boys at the university but hadn't done it with either (not all the way, anyway) because "love" had stood in the way, and I hadn't fancied myself "in love." Here in America, people were always "seeing" each other, and it seemed okay not to worry about love. Paul and I saw an Ozu film together that had an elaborate tea ceremony, and he suggested that I come along to one of his *zazen* meetings and stay on for the tea ceremony that would follow. We drove to a town called Rantoul in his Toyota, and out in the middle of nowhere, he parked the car on one side of the road, and that's where I went all the way with him, and it was just not very memorable.

The Soto Zen "temple" turned out to be a bare, airless room in the basement of a brownstone. There were maybe seven or eight people there, and we sat cross-legged in a circle with eyes closed, our backs facing the center of the room. I knew we were supposed to meditate but I assumed Paul's "Master" would be there telling us what to do: follow your breath/become aware of passing thoughts/banish all passing thoughts/concentrate on the second toe of your right foot, that kind of thing. However, there was no instruction. The Master (and there was one; I soon became aware of him through half-closed lids) was doing the rounds behind our backs. After several minutes of just sitting there, I abandoned all hope of receiving instruction, and with great effort, concentrated my mindfulness on the itch that was beginning to devour my back. I willed it to go away: go, go, go, but all the while the confounded area demanded more attention, gathering the force of a cavalcade of itches. Then, I have to say, I jumped out of my skin. A loud "thwack" made me spin around, and I caught sight of the Master's equanimous stare and the flash of a bamboo stick retreating behind his back. For a moment I thought it was Paul who had been struck for his unmonkish act along Route 45 but the victim turned out to be a much older man. No one else had stirred, and the Master resumed his pacing. I turned back to position, closed my eyes, and became cognizant that my itch had been successfully willed into oblivion. I sat petrified in the knowledge that a fully grown Caucasian male had been whacked for I don't know what crime, and I might well be next in line. My spine stiffened, my mind was in turmoil, and all the while the seconds took their time in passing. Finally, the zazen concluded with the ringing of a bell. Pairs of frozen limbs uncoiled, and we filed out into a small backyard where the tea ceremony, for which I had supposedly come all this way, was disposed of with very little tea and not much ceremony. The Master slurped the contents of his bowl in a single gulp, bowed wordlessly, and departed, leaving his assistant to pass around the hat, in this case, a folded velvet cloth, on which everyone left five- and ten-dollar bills. The man who'd received a beating left a crisp ten-dollar note.

I noticed that Paul, with the egalitarianism so noteworthy in his countrymen, made no attempt to pay for his date, so I delved into my purse and parted with two dollars of a brutally earned teaching assistantship.

Paul and I "discussed" the tea ceremony on the drive back to campus. We didn't know each other well enough to have an argument. Why hadn't he *warned* me, I wanted to know, a bit testily. "Oh, he would never have hit *you*," he explained. "You have to raise your hand and ask to be hit. It's the wandering consciousness that requests the Master's attention." "Weird," I said with finality.

From then on, Paul and I said hullo politely to each other at the film club but made no further attempt to "see" each other. He left for California a few weeks later, leaving me the address of the monastery where he'd booked himself as a resident and where he said he could receive mail. Of course I never wrote to him. It was just one of those things. I had been in America for all of three months and had needed someone to go with all the way, and Paul, after being here so long, had probably needed someone too, to go with for the last time. After that incident, I decided that Fellini or no Fellini, I wasn't going to just throw it away.

The other thing I learned in America, outside of my degree program, that is, is that it's perfectly okay to devote a lot of energy to finding yourself, defining yourself, and giving yourself an identity you're comfortable with. I guess that's what Paul had been doing too. Most of my friends had very definite notions of themselves. Nicole was a "socialist feminist," Brad was a "queer theorist," Joline was an "Afro-Caribbean dissident poet," and Allison described herself as an "experimental multi-media conceptual artist." I marveled at their confidence at such a young age. If anyone asked me what I did, I'd say, "I'm studying English literature," or at best, "I want to write." And it wasn't just the good stuff that folks were proud of either. I once met someone at a party who introduced himself as "a survivor of substance abuse," and in all my years in my own country, I had never met such a person, though indeed they must have been in existence. I suppose, in fact, my aunt Radhika was one such survivor, though she would have been completely mortified if she knew that the cat was out of the bag, and someone had described her as such.

Growing up in India, we were strongly discouraged from thinking about ourselves, from giving ourselves the slightest importance. Mahatma Gandhi's legacy still held the fabric of our nation in a tight stranglehold. Frugality and self-denial were upheld as guiding principles, and extravagance and self-seeking (except the spiritual kind) were frowned upon. Moreover, central to our thinking was the belief that life's journey is about the search and not about the finding. We grew up with plangent songs of misbegotten love and turbulent waters and the eternal boatman, all pretty depressing stuff, where it is only after death that the seeker can rightfully aspire to be escorted to the opposite shore. I mean, we had nothing at all along the lines of "Material Girl."

In America I learned to be selfish. I learned not to feel guilty all the time about other people and what I had done to them, or what I had failed to do. Mummy might think I've always been selfish, but in reality, I've spent too much time feeling regret for all sorts of things, for her and my stepbrother, for Rani, for Nanaji most of all, and for Naneeji too, for abandoning her when Bari Nanee died and she was all alone. America taught me to look closely at myself, my needs and desires. For one, I decided it was perfectly okay to change my mind. I still loved literature, but I didn't have to love literary criticism. While my dissertation (yet one more) on *A Passage to India* may have been a labor of fine scholarship, as my advisors said it was, it had not been a labor of love. I told myself that I had repaid my debt to Empire for granting me the Queen's language. I had fulfilled my degree requirements. I wasn't letting the university down, and E.M. Forster didn't care one way or another whether I devoted a lifetime to his cause. I could move on. I decided to think very hard about what I wanted to do next. It's amazing what you *can* do in America. My friend Nicole laid it out for me. You can do anything you want, she said, as long as you are totally confident and you *never ever* apologize.

—⁓—

Gaylord Restaurant, New Delhi, December 12, 1989. I am back on one of my NRI visits, the same time every year, always in the winter, because having lived away all these years, I can no longer take the heat. It is half past one in the afternoon, and I am convinced I've been stood up. I nurse a second cup of coffee and give myself another five minutes. When I am about to ask for the check, I see her, a skinny, upright woman, no longer young, look searchingly at the tables. There is something familiar about her, even from this distance. I raise my hand as if in a dream. She nods and approaches.

My past, present, and future are interlocked in that moment, taut like an instrument waiting to be plucked. I stand at the brink of knowing something, something important, but I don't know what it is. It is a moment fearful of destiny, and yet,

I do not believe in fate. It is a moment filled with wonder at the orchestrated accidents of life, and grief too, if accident is all it is.

We shake hands; her voice sounds far away. "I am sorry to have kept you waiting. There was an emergency at home."

I look at her face, and it is different from the way I know it.

"Miss Reza?" I say, though of course it is she.

"Anamika," she replies.

"I had no idea," I manage to say. I had no idea that Dr. Anamika Reza of the Department of History, Jawaharlal Nehru University would turn out to be Miss Reza.

"Miss Reza," I stammer again.

"Anamika," she says and smiles.

"Miss Reza, I don't know if you remember . . ."

"Of course, I do. But I'm no longer your schoolteacher, and I figure you must be around thirty yourself, so please stop calling me Miss Reza . . ."

Her face is sharp and filled with amusement. She has not changed much except for the lines that crisscross her face (too much sun) and her hair (still wild), which is lightly brushed with white. She has turned ethnic, no Western suit or skirt anymore. She wears a cream-colored *churidar* and *kurta*, and a red *bandini* mirrorwork shawl (Gurjari, of course) glistens on her shoulders, setting off sparks against Gaylord's peeling walls.

She offers me a cigarette, and when I refuse, lights it herself.

"Well," she says. "This *is* a coincidence." She blows away the smoke and looks inquiringly after it. "Didn't think I'd see you again."

I am once again a speechless schoolgirl, ensconced in the fulsomeness of a first crush. I speak incoherently, or so I think. I am so delighted that she remembers me that I can hardly attend to my thoughts. I ramble on about my post-doctoral work on the functions and modalities of warfare in the formation of national identities. I describe the series of happy accidents that led to my discovery of her unpublished dissertation, which has been so fundamental in my own research. "I had no idea . . . when I read your work, when I wrote to you, that it was *you*."

"I thought it might be you. I remembered the name. And I figured you would be about the right age. But I couldn't be sure, of course. There could be more than one Sweta Kalra."

After a pause, she exclaims, "I'm afraid though, I can't be of further help to you. You've read everything I've written on the subject."

That's when I make my request. Would she grant me access to her primary materials? "It's a personal quest," I explain. "You see, my father was a fighter pilot. He was killed in the '65 war. I hardly knew him. The reason I started studying wars was because of him." I think Miss Reza is about to say something so I wait. She looks away, and I continue, "Your manuscript had more information on the aerial war between India and Pakistan than anything I have encountered elsewhere. But naturally, you had to change names, anonymize missions; you had to protect your sources. That's why I need to look at the original materials. He's probably in there somewhere."

She appears to have lost her ease. I assure her that I have no intention of free riding off her research. "It's about him and me," I say. "That's all."

Still she looks troubled. "Do you remember," she says, "do you remember that I told you I had come to your grandparents' home and interviewed your mother after the war?"

"Yes," I reply, as slowly it comes back to me. "You told me you had met me before but I couldn't remember." It has all happened before. She and I in this coffeeshop where she tells me this. I feel I have known Miss Reza all my life.

"Is this what you were working on then?"

"Yes, this is what I was working on. I actually have a lot of material on your father." She will need a few days, she says, to put her papers and tapes together before she can let me have them.

Jupiter 3

As it turned out, I ended up listening to Miss Reza's war tapes in her *barsati* in Nizamuddin East. She had them on old reel-to-reels and had to borrow a player from her father. "I'm sorry I can't lend them to you," she said, "but Dad won't let his antique out of my sight." I thought she would leave me with the material and go off and do her own work, but she preferred to stay around and pretended to keep busy and watched me intently from time to time. I felt awkward as there were things about Daddy that I was learning for the very first time. I said to her once, "You know, your tapes are safe with me," and realized from the look on her face that I'd misunderstood. Her concern was for me, not the tapes.

The ashtray was piled high with cigarette butts. The ash fell onto the pale *chattais* that lined her terrace. She smoked without a break, and I could only stand it because we were under the open sky. There was a time, she said, when you could see the planets clearly from up here. But now, there's only this haze. Really, she said, it's silly of you to worry about my cigarettes. If you're going to get lung cancer, it's more likely to be from the wood fires and dung smoke. Not to mention exhaust fumes. She looked nervous. She'd been nervous ever since she'd spooled on the tape marked "Sargodha, September 7."

Soon we'll run out of batteries, she said; we'll have to move indoors. If you would only stop smoking, I'd be happy to move inside. Slowly I was overcoming my awe of her and its residual claim on my memory.

"What is it with all of you who end up in America?" she smiled. "You return filled with good health and intolerance. I'm sure you're into organic this and organic that."

"Yes," I admitted.

—❧—

"'Jupiter 3, Jupiter 4, do you read me? Jupiter 3, come in. Jupiter 3, I need you to cover my tail. Singh's been shot. Acknowledge, Jupiter 3.' 'Wilco,' responded Kalra.

"That's how it happened. Out of the fucking blue, excuse the language. It made no sense, no sense at all. Flight Lieutenant Kalra told me to head back to base; he turned and went in after Dusty. . . .

"So there we were, headed *back* into Pakistani soil, if you please. I wondered if Kalra believed in God. It sure would have helped if he did. I didn't particularly, and I felt alone. You have to remember we were flying on reserves, our tanks were near empty, I mean e-m-p-t-y.

"In the distance I saw a plume of smoke. Another plane had pranged. Couldn't tell if it was one of ours or the enemy's. Later, we learned they'd lost at least two Sabres that morning apart from the one on the ground. I saw Dusty get one. I'm pretty sure he got that other one too, the one I saw fall off.

"We tried to establish contact with the lead on the combat channel. No response. Dead silence. So there we were flying back into enemy territory, no sign of our leader whom we were supposed to cover, fatally low on fuel, with four, maybe five enemy aircraft on the lookout for us. Not very comfortable, as you can imagine.

"It wasn't quiet for long. We spotted them at treetop level. Dusty had lured them down, and there's really nothing to beat Dusty when he's dogfighting that low. Except that there were four of them and he was alone. Crazy.

"We went in after them. Two of the Sabres left Dusty and turned in on us. We'd created enough of a distraction now. Dusty had two planes to deal with instead of four, and we had two tailing us. We couldn't do more than that. So following Kalra's orders, I dived and accelerated. All we had to count on was speed until the fuel ran out. It was a chase once again back to India. We couldn't tell anymore if we were following the correct course back to base. One thing was for sure. We would almost surely run out of fuel. I mentally geared up for an ejection or a crash landing. We raced on for what seemed like minutes. That's when I was hit in my left wing. My engine flamed out. I knew he'd get me in the tanks next. I pulled my seat's ejection handle and was thrust out of the cockpit. I'll never forget that rush of cold air, that feeling of plummeting while strapped to my chair.

"It's only seconds, but you're out of your body then. You're seeing your own body riddled with bullets, crashing to the ground. Luckily, the damn thing worked, and the parachute opened like a flower. I drifted to the ground gently. I didn't know where the hell I was. I was sure as hell I'd be on the wrong side of the border, and I'd heard enough stories of Pakistani mobs and how they loved to lynch Indians alive. I prayed. I hadn't prayed in years so

I prayed without hope. I landed in wilderness, my legs all tangled up in shrub and bramble. I stayed still for a long time, certain somebody had seen me fall. It was quiet. I extricated myself from the bramble and the gear and started moving eastward, toward the sun. I was crawling on all fours because I couldn't take the risk of standing. I'd injured my leg in the fall . . ."

It was a disembodied voice. It could just as well be Daddy's voice, which I no longer remembered, Daddy telling me that he was safe, he had made it.

" . . . I knew I had to go on. To stop would be certain death. I told myself I could still cross the border on foot. I crawled along for almost two hours. The shrub gave way to open fields, and I had to be careful. I heard voices in the distance. I stopped and listened carefully. They were male voices speaking Punjabi. I stayed hidden and watched for signs. Sikh farmers! Everything was telling me this was a miracle. I was alive, and I was in India, somewhere in the vicinity of Amritsar, I figured . . ."

"What happened to Ranjit?"

"I wish I knew. That's when they must have got him too. All I knew was that he was ahead of me and he was fine. I had hoped he might have ejected or crash-landed somewhere, somehow made it back. We didn't know it, but we were practically at the Indian border."

"Didn't they pick up any communication from him?"

"Apparently not. We heard later that Singh was alive, taken POW in Pakistan. Dusty was listed as missing in action, taken for dead. They never recovered his body. Kalra was cremated with full military honors. They thought I was dead too. That's the news they were preparing to give my parents when I showed up two days later."

(Silence)

"Maybe I did die, and this is heaven because I get to meet you."

(Laughter)

"I'm glad I met you too."

"Want another drink?"

"No, thank you. I've been watching that doorman who looks like he's straight out of *The Charge of the Light Brigade*. A *firang* just walked in, and he practically rolled himself into a carpet and waited to be stepped on."

"Yeah. I've changed my mind about tipping him. Let's go someplace else."

The tape had ended. Life, it seemed, had carried on.

A Letter to My Daughter (continued)

You give me the impression, Sweta, that I am not
worthy of you. What right does a daughter have to
treat her mother this way? Nothing pleases you.
Even the fact that I am regarded as beautiful is a
curse. I stand in front of the mirror and run a comb
through my hair and catch your reflection and read
its contempt. Yes, I have married again, but you
despised me long before that. As though with your
father gone, you felt you could do without me
as well. As if you had only put up with me on his
account.

What else could I have done, Sweta? A widow at
twenty-eight? White, for the rest of her days, living
again with Amma and Abba? Oh, Sweta, that would
have been an unbearable fate! You are young, you are
romantic. You think marriage is about love and love is
an undying thing. Yet you have lived with your Nanaji
and Naneeji and have seen firsthand what it can be like.
I wanted to believe that things had changed between

them. How else could I justify leaving you with them in an unhappy home?

I have childhood memories that haunt me too. I never told you about them, but that doesn't take them away. Like the time that Amma and Abba bought their first car, a brand-new Fiat, and we took it out for a test drive. Indu and I were so excited; it was the first time we were traveling by car. I think I was about ten and Indu was eight. It was soon after Independence and we had started living in a nice new house, and I thought our troubles were over. We drove off, but soon they started arguing, about money as usual, how much Abba had gone and spent on the car. They had both agreed to buy the car, but something, I don't remember what, had ended up costing quite a bit more. Amma went on and on at Abba for what seemed like an eternity. Indu and I tried to shut our ears and enjoy the passing view. Abba said nothing, absolutely nothing. Amma wouldn't stop. It went on like that, unbearable, until finally Abba screeched to a halt. He braked so hard our heads hit against the front seat. Abba lifted both his arms into the air, and I thought he would bring his fists down on Amma's face. Oh God, it was terrible! I had never seen him hit Amma. He waited like that an instant, his head thrown back. Then he let out a terrible cry and smashed his fists down on the steering wheel. He set off the horn. It got stuck. It blared and blared, it wouldn't stop screaming. I have never been so scared! Then Abba put his head down on the wheel and cried like a child. I fiddled with the car door, unlocked it, and stepped out, right in the middle of the road where the cars zipped by. Abba hadn't given it a thought; he had stopped in the middle of the road. I thought of running out between the cars and ending it all. But Indu had crawled out after me too. I held her hand. It started to rain. We stood there, our tears hidden by the rain. The cars just flew past. Nobody stopped for us. Finally, I suppose, the battery ran out and the horn fell silent. Abba got out of the car and walked away to find a mechanic.

I couldn't have gone on living with them for the rest of my life, Sweta.

When I married your father, I was terrified. It was an arranged marriage, after all. We did not know each other. But I was relieved too, to be getting away. And I think we were happy. I think neither of us had any expectations; that's why we were happy. Perhaps you need a lifetime to get to know another person. There was a side to Ranjit that he kept locked up. You held the key, Sweta. Only you could open him up. I would watch him play with you on the floor, the laughter that came out of him then, from deep inside, and I would feel, not jealous, no, but something, an odd presentiment . . .

I do regret that I did not try harder. I thought we had more time.

That's why I'm writing to you, Sweta; that's why I'm telling you these things. Maybe I'll have the courage to post this letter. Maybe you will read it, and there will still be time.

REVISITATION

I can venture to say that Anamika and I became friends. I wrote her long and enthusiastic letters from New York where I now lived. Anamika wrote less frequently, but when she did, her tone was warm and affectionate. I regularly sent her copies of articles that I published. In response to one of my best quoted articles, she wrote,

. . . to be perfectly honest, I had a tough time wading through some of the jargon. The ideas were arresting, but I had to engage in a grave tussle with the suprastructural edifice of your language. I understand very little of these post-colonial, subaltern critiques and methodologies. Please don't take my comments to heart. As I see from the rest of the journal, you are in fine company. Thank you for thanking me. I'm not sure how I have helped your work but thank you for your graciousness.

I thought of a line that Miss Reza once wrote in an old notebook: *"I like the words you use. They shine like pebbles waiting to be picked.*" I felt that my entire education had been a waste. If Gayle hadn't been around, I might have chucked it all up and taken to poetry. But Gayle saw me falter and rebounded with her characteristic no-nonsense. She quickly disposed of Anamika's letter and its contents. She reminded me of my commitments to my students, the many upcoming deadlines and conference submissions. In the year that Gayle and I had lived together, we had quarreled over Anamika no less than three times. She had accused me of pandering to infantile obsessions. I had accused her of harboring unreasonable jealousies. Gayle said we were approaching our second anniversary. Wasn't it time we cemented our relationship and got ourselves a cat? I relented.

The house on Kasturba Gandhi Marg fell into ruin. After Bari Nanee passed on, the house was divided up and leased to tenants. Naneeji stayed on in a small section of the house that consisted of a bedroom, a bathroom, and an attached kitchenette. Every year when I visited Delhi, I forced myself to spend a few days with her. I stayed in the adjoining room that was really a storehouse. Auntie Indira lived in Bombay and rarely came to visit her mother. My cousins, Shalini and Ankur, were both in Delhi but remained preoccupied with their lives. Mummy came to visit about once a year, usually timing it with my arrival, and then we had an uncomfortable reunion of sorts.

Naneeji had grown hard of hearing. In order to communicate with her, you had to face her squarely and enunciate loudly with large, fishy, globular movements. The additional collaboration of hand movements was an occasional help. She stubbornly refused to wear a hearing aid. Even though I had buried our hatchet long ago, staring at her with such directness and shouting at her invariably evoked the texture of hostility. I finished one of these exchanges feeling anxious and frustrated.

Naneeji's paranoia had only worsened with age. She drove the tenants mad with her suspicions and stinginess, and Mummy was afraid that one day they would poison her and lay claim to the property. Mummy tried to convince Naneeji to sell the house but she refused. Like her sister before her, she insisted that this was where she was born and this is where she intended to die. The Colonel, I think, was secretly pleased with this arrangement. Even though he always told Naneeji that she was welcome to come and live with them in Kaushani, he could hardly have been serious.

Like Bari Nanee before her, Naneeji lived alone and refused the help of a servant or an *ayah*. With Nanaji's pension and the rent she received from her tenants, Naneeji could afford to live in some luxury, but she insisted that her needs were minimal and servants these days were not to be trusted. Her usual spot was Nanaji's old armchair from where she watched television all day long. With twenty-four hours of satellite television at her fingertips, Naneeji whiled away her final years in the throes of a frantic entertainment. Ridge was her favorite in *The Bold and the Beautiful*. She talked tirelessly about Ridge and the many unsuitable women in his life. It was impossible to engage her on practical matters relating to her health and daily care.

—m—

I could see upon entering her room that Naneeji's condition had worsened in the last year. She hadn't bothered to oil or comb her hair, which fell in thin and angry waves over her shoulders. She hadn't bathed yet, though it was the middle of the afternoon. Although Naneeji had hit eighty, she was usually particular about her appearance. This time I found her dressed in a torn blouse and petticoat.

I gave her a hug and handed her the box of liquor-laced Lindt chocolates that I'd picked up from Duty Free. Her eyes gleamed briefly, and she opened her almirah and stashed the chocolates away. Usually, she opened up the box and ate a couple right then and there.

She had already forgotten my presence. She moved abruptly about the room, lifting plastic bags and clothes, muttering to herself. I could see that she had stopped caring about her room, which was increasingly filled with junk.

"Are you looking for something?" I shouted.

She did not hear me so I took her by the shoulders and shouted again, "What are you looking for? Can I help?"

She smiled and hugged me. "When did you come?"

"Yesterday."

She knocked over a lamp in an effort to look under it.

I forcibly sat her down in the armchair.

"Calm down," I said. "What are you looking for?"

The television set blared at the highest volume. Ignoring her glare, I turned it off and waved my hands speculatively at her. *"What are you looking for?"*

She heard me this time. "My *surma* stick. The wicked girl stole it."

I realized then that she was talking about Rani. Some twenty-five years had passed since the incident to which she referred.

" . . . shameless girl," she muttered, and rose purposefully to her feet.

"It wasn't Rani. Rani didn't steal your surma stick, *I* did. *I'm* the shameless girl who stole it. Rather, I buried it in the garden to teach you a lesson. I tried to tell you, but you wouldn't listen."

I was shouting at the top of my voice. I couldn't tell from her expression if she had heard. Even if she had, she would never believe a word of my confession. She never had in the past.

"Let me help you find it."

She watched suspiciously as I headed toward her dressing table, piled high with empty bottles and plastic bags. I tried to open the drawers, but they were jammed shut, crammed with pencils and hair pins and empty pill boxes. I looked under the dresser, which was opaque with filth. Finally, I pulled the dresser away from the wall, and a smattering of odds and ends met the floor. Naneeji started to shout and flail her arms. I ignored her and picked up the broom that I found propped against the wall. I used it to sweep out the contents from under the dresser. Out came bits of newspaper, cottonwool, peanut shells, a giant dead cockroach, more empty pill boxes, and her silver surma stick, wrapped in a wad of hair. I grabbed the edge of her petticoat and wiped it clean.

"There you are," I shouted. "Your surma stick."

It was the same heavily engraved silver stick that had remained buried for three days until Rani had been beaten by her father, and consumed with guilt and shame, I had dug it up and returned it to my grandmother. Even when I'd handed it to her, she'd remained convinced that Rani had been the culprit and I had been covering for her.

"Look," I said. "Here it is. Nobody stole it."

A blissful smile crossed Naneeji's face. She turned the television back on.

"This can't go on," I shouted. "You can't live alone. You need help."

Of course she did not hear me.

"When did you come?" She smiled at me, her fingers clutching the stick of silver.

"Yesterday."

The clock on the wall had stopped, but she pointed to it and said, "Just in time. Ridge will propose to Brooke today."

And she turned up the volume.

—◊◊◊—

I called Anamika and invited myself over for dinner. As you know, my dinner invitations never include home-cooked meals, she said. Sure your foreign-returned intestines can withstand the true test of Nizamuddin? Try me, I responded.

When I saw her later that night, she was dressed in one of her splendid ethnic numbers, a large bindi smack in the middle of her forehead. In my role as the U.S.-returned academic, I was appropriately and scruffily dressed, though for the occasion I had on some ill-applied lipstick. She hugged me warmly, and I handed her the expensive bottle of cabernet sauvignon I'd picked up at Duty Free. I had actually considered getting her a carton of cigarettes as well but had resolutely replaced it on the shelf. I wasn't about to hasten her demise, I told myself. In any event, she was most proprietary about her Classics.

I suggested that she save the cabernet for an important occasion and we open the Golconda instead.

"This *is* an important occasion," she said, smiling.

That evening was different from all the other times that I had spent with her. Perhaps it was the bottle of wine that we downed together, remarking on its smooth and lustrous finish. Perhaps it was her regret over the contents of her last letter, to which, finally heeding Gayle's exhortations, I had not replied. Perhaps it was just Naneeji who had depressed me inordinately and loosened my tongue. I told her about Naneeji and how I feared she was at her end. I told her about Nanaji and Naneeji and the sheer waste of their life together. I revealed to her that Nanaji had killed himself, though I didn't tell her the real reason why. I told her that I too was sharing my life with someone, knowing that it felt wrong. She smoked a lot and told me about her German husband and her years in Frankfurt and how she almost hadn't got away. I asked her if she was seeing anyone, and she said offhandedly, "On and off, nothing serious. I never want to live with anyone again." And then she added, somewhat ruefully, "I've only ever enjoyed living with my parents, you know, because nothing was expected of me." I was emboldened by her confidence and told her that I lived with a woman. I watched her face carefully, and it revealed nothing, not a single, passing flicker, and I felt I had come home.

I ended up spending the night in Anamika's study. I had intended to go back to Naneeji's, but past midnight I didn't want to leave, and I knew that my grandmother would neither remember nor care whether I turned up or not. In the morning Anamika made coffee and *Ekuri* on toast, "The only thing I rustle up that's never a disaster," she said. We sat around her kitchen table. I nursed my coffee, readying myself for the chaos that would greet me at Naneeji's. "I think it's going to happen again. She's going to die after I leave, and I won't be around for her last rites. I'm beginning to feel that today's that last good-bye."

We sat companionably across from each other, not speaking very much. Gayle was always so energetic in the mornings that after she left for work I would crawl back into bed to recover from her optimism. Talking to Anamika was like talking to myself.

"I've always had this need to look a dead person straight in the face. I'm not being prurient, really, but because Dad was in a coffin, I never got to see him. I never got to say good-bye. I wanted to see my grandfather one last time, but they wouldn't let me go to the morgue or to the crematorium. I wasn't around when my grandmother's sister went. If you don't see them dead, a part of you refuses to believe it. Death's such an abstraction, anyway. Dad's death is just a piece of mythology now. All I remember is that splendid gun salute, the bugle's call, and I see of all things, Tutankhamen's face in that coffin with his eyes wide open. It's all a bit unbelievable. Sometimes, I can't help thinking, what if Daddy's coffin was empty? What if he really wasn't there?"

She looked strangely at me. "What do you mean?"

"I mean he *shouldn't* have been there, should he? There never should have been a corpse. It's so unusual that he was found. I thought, listening to your interviews, I might find the answer somewhere, but no. It's the missing piece in a jigsaw."

She didn't respond, so I continued, thinking I hadn't made myself clear. "I find it very strange that they recovered his body so quickly. Daddy died on the seventh of September, and he was cremated on the ninth. Isn't that unusual in times of war? You'd think it would be difficult to retrieve a body from enemy territory. The enemy wouldn't be particularly cooperative."

"Yes."

"In most cases there isn't even a body."

"Yes, that's true," she said.

"So I can't help thinking, what if the coffin was empty? Or what if there was someone else in there? What if Daddy's alive today, and a prisoner of war in Pakistan, and I've been searching for him in the wrong places?"

"Oh, no, no, no," she said emphatically. "You *can't* think that. It's very dangerous to think that way. That's not what's going on."

"I tell myself it's ridiculous. But I can't seem to come to grips with the logistics of the thing. How does someone who gets killed in action in Pakistan get cremated in Delhi two days later?"

"There is an explanation," she said quietly. "I never wanted to tell you this. There are things that are best left alone. But I can't let you think what you *are* thinking. Your father *is* dead, Sweta. He *was* in that coffin, even if you didn't get to see him."

"How do you know? How *can* you know?"

"The question that you raised, I thought about it a lot. I discovered that all the bodies that were recovered were in fact casualties that occurred on the Indian side from Pakistani attacks."

She looked meaningfully at me. "All the bodies recovered were from *our* side of the border. Our fighters killed on the other side were listed as 'missing in action, believed to be killed.' So how come Ronu . . . your father's body was recovered so quickly? It bothered me. Then I told myself that he had crashed right along the border, and that's why his body was found. You remember Flying Officer Basu's testimony? They were practically at the Indian border, and your father was ahead of him. So that's how I justified the recovery of his body."

"Yes . . . that's what I've told myself too. But I'm not convinced. I keep thinking, did anyone see him dead? My mother did not see the body; neither did Dadaji . . ."

"I was convinced. But then, years later, I changed my mind. I changed my mind completely."

"What about?"

"About how your father was killed. Some new piece of evidence came to the forefront that I couldn't ignore."

"What are you talking about, Anamika?"

"It's a long story. I happened to be in Islamabad for a cousin's wedding. I have family there, from my father's side. I went to a party where there happened to be this guy from the Pakistani Air Force. We got talking about my work, and he said, why don't I do some interviews on the Pakistani side, see what they have to say about the wars, that way I'll have a more balanced picture. To tell you the truth, I wasn't particularly interested, because by then I was done with that work. I'd finished with '65. I'd written about the '71 war too, and I'd moved on to other stuff. Besides, I was on holiday. But this chap got really excited and gave me the number of a good friend of his, a fighter pilot, who, he said, had fought in '65. Well, the next day I got a call from this pilot, so I went ahead and met him. One contact led to another, and by the end of the week, I had actually tracked down two of the fighters who had flown that fateful mission in defense of Sargodha. Can you imagine? Once I was there, I couldn't stop. I mean, what are the chances of being able to follow through on a piece of research all the way to the end?"

"Yes," I said, trying hard to keep up with her.

"I was hurled into the past. I actually ended up interviewing one of the fighters who engaged your father's formation in the final encounter. Remember, when he went back in with Basu and there were four Sabres after Dusty? Well, Flight Lieutenant Nurul Aslam flew one of those Sabres."

"Why didn't you tell me this? I came all the way to meet you. You let me hear your tapes, but you didn't tell me you had anything new."

She shrugged. "There was no point, Sweta. I shouldn't be telling you now."

"What shouldn't you be telling me?"

"Honestly, if you hadn't said what you did about your father, I would never have told you. Flight Lieutenant Aslam described the whole encounter to me. It pretty much corroborated what Parikshit said. I'll fish out my notes if you like. I don't remember the details anymore. One thing he said didn't make sense though. He said one of the planes got away."

"So?"

"When they had their inquiries afterwards in Pakistan, there was consensus on the numbers. I don't remember the sequence of events, but what is crucial is that the two Pak formations of the morning were credited with three kills in all. They shot down three Hunters that morning. One got away."

I failed to react, so she continued.

"Now you know the level of propaganda that operates on both sides of the border. They would be only too happy to claim another hit if they could. However, they all maintained that one plane got away unscathed. Flight Lieutenant Aslam was emphatic on this point."

"But we know that . . . ," I said impatiently. "We know that Parikshit Basu got away, the guy you went and had an affair with . . ."

"No," she said, ignoring my undisguisedly peevish tone. "Don't you see? They hit Parikshit! *He was one of their hits!* They severely damaged his plane. He was just lucky to get away alive. They got Singh. He's still a POW in Pakistan, if he's alive, that is. And they got Dusty Karanjia. 'Missing in action, believed to be killed, Vir Chakra.' Those were the three planes they shot down that morning over Sargodha. It was your father who got away."

My head reeled. What was she telling me? Was she saying Daddy was still alive?

"Naturally, I was completely confused. I didn't know what the heck to think. As soon as I got back to India, I started digging around. I delved right back into the old stuff. Look. I have something to show you."

She went into her study, and I followed. My nerves were so much on edge that I just sat there and waited while she moved her boxes around, making no attempt to help her. Finally, she found the box she was looking for and pulled out a thick file with newspaper clippings from 1965.

"Look at this," she said, handing me a photocopy.

FUTILE PAK BID TO INVADE AMRITSAR: PLANE DOWNED

September 8: A lone Pakistani C-130 that strayed into Indian territory was shot down outside Amritsar at 8:25 a.m. yesterday. Meanwhile dusk to dawn curfew has been imposed at a number of places in Punjab including Chandigarh, Amritsar, Pathankot, and Ambala. The Government warns the public of the possible danger of Pakistani paratroopers who may have been dropped by the C-130 prior to its dispersal and urges vigilance.

I was left holding the paper and it didn't make sense. "I'm sorry. I've completely lost you. I don't see the connection."

"It wasn't a C-130 they shot down. It was your dad's plane. Don't you see? *They shot down one of their own planes!* The whole thing was a cover-up."

"I don't see how you can jump to that conclusion. It's quite far-fetched."

"Sometimes it's best not to know too much. But I realize now that you have to know. I can't prove anything. But look at the facts, Sweta. The Pakis swear that one plane got away without a scratch. They would love to claim another kill, but they don't. So where the hell did that plane go? It went toward Amritsar at around that time. We know that from Parikshit's testimony."

"So what? Just because it headed toward Amritsar at around the same time doesn't mean the Indians shot it down . . . besides, Dad flew a Hunter, and this is a C-130. Really, Anamika . . ."

"Okay. Let me tell you something else. *There was no C-130!* I checked out that C-130 story. It drew a blank. The Indian side was completely tight-lipped about it. They had no photographs of the wreckage, no reports other than this brief announcement. You know, Sweta, how we love to display captured planes and POWs and pieces of debris but when it came to this mysterious C-130, there was nothing to show for it! I was told the wreckage was not found! Can you believe that? A wreckage, right outside Amritsar, that could not be traced!" She paused, took a long pull on her cigarette.

"I know it's hard to believe, but it all adds up: why they never published any of my articles, why the squadron commander refused to speak to me, why I always came up against a wall. Quite inadvertently, I'd hit upon something, and it was ugly."

"Please, Anamika, how can they shoot down one of their own planes? Will you please stop smoking? I have a headache."

She stubbed out her cigarette.

"Surely, there are all sorts of checks and balances?"

"Sure there are," she said, "but mistakes happen. Remember what Parikshit said? The last time he saw him, Ranjit was ahead of him, and he was fine. Clearly, they had strayed off course. In that crazy, second fray of the morning, they'd headed for Amritsar instead of Adampur. It's an easy enough error to make. They were too far away from base to establish communication. And look at it from the Indian side: a lone aircraft roars into Indian air space at the outskirts of an army camp. You haven't been told to expect one of your planes, so naturally, you think it's the enemy. You can't afford to take chances so you shoot at it, reflex action.

Perhaps the plane's too far up to see the markings, and even if you see Indian markings, you may not believe them. After all, there are stories circulating about Pak planes with false Indian markings. So you open fire and bring the plane down. All very glorious until you discover that a terrible mistake's been made. And then, what's the army going to do about it? Admit it to the press? Hey, sorry, we shot down one of our own planes, killed one of our boys!? Hell, when they don't admit that the enemy's got one of their planes, are they going to tell the public that they've shot it down themselves?! They cover up. Somebody's sure to have seen the Hunter wreckage. So they make up a story about a C-130 and paratroopers. Keep the nation sufficiently alarmed and gung ho about the war. Let everyone know that we're doing just great. I wouldn't be surprised if there's been a stink between the army and the air force over this, but we'll never know."

She couldn't help it, she'd lit up again. I wish I smoked for I would have loved to control the shaking in my hands.

"That's why your father's body was recovered so quickly, and they tried to make amends with tip-top service, full military honors, and all that crap. He's dead, Sweta. He was in that coffin."

"Why didn't you tell me this before?"

"How could I? And take away the glory? How could I tell you it was a stupid accident that never should have happened? In the final analysis, I suppose it doesn't matter. He's gone. How does it matter who got him in the end?"

I didn't speak for the longest time. When I did, I thought my voice was steady. "I'd like to preserve my heroes."

"He was one. Not because he went and got killed but because he did his duty and went back. He didn't get any thanks for it. Neither did Parikshit. It's the guys who score the hits who get the decorations. That's how it goes, Sweta. In your father's case, I'd say that even if the Indians hadn't shot him down, he would have been killed by his own people. They got him at the age of five."

I didn't think of asking her what she meant. Anamika is the deep sea of secrets. If I let myself go, I will drown.

An End and a Beginning

Mummy looks beautiful in white. She still does. Her skin is soft to the touch because of the Oil of Olay that she uses nightly and has tried to gift me on more than one occasion. I refuse to surrender to my mother's beauty secrets. She does not dye her hair, and she has not put on an extra ounce. That's the way I'd like to age, I think. Though I could never be as beautiful. Or as feminine.

The Colonel, on the other hand, is not a pretty sight. His cheeks are waxen and green and his mouth is open as if in mid-snore. Not much else is visible through the stacks of marigolds and tube roses and gladioli that press down on him. Mummy's done much of the decoration herself, picking flowers from the profusion in her garden. The flowers frame his face, then rise in a formidable mound around his waist before leveling out at his feet. It's been years since I laid eyes on the Colonel.

He'll be a tough one to carry on a stretcher. I seem to have read my half-brother's thoughts. Why don't they dispense with that formality, Arun suggests, and use a station wagon instead? He is easily dismissed by the Colonel's firstborns, a pair of large, thug-like twins who I am meeting for the first time. Auntie Indira whispers in my ear that in grasping for their newborn lives, they took it away from their frail mother. The twins inform Arun that their father will be carried in a grand procession all the way to the *ghat*, which is two miles away. Poor Arun! I ponder over the logistics. The thugs are a good six inches taller than my half-brother, and the cousin who is the fourth pallbearer is somewhere in between. The firstborns are entitled to the head, so the Colonel's journey to meet his maker will be, at the very least, tilted. Arun is at a severe disadvantage.

He is unrecognizable today in a white kurta-pajama, a hand-kerchief wrapped around his head. Usually he's in his skin-tight denim jeans and terylene shirts that he leaves open to the waist. Arun is determinedly good-looking with clean-cut features, a protruding jaw, and lacquered hair. He spends half the day work-ing out at the gym and the other half waiting for that call from Bollywood. He is frequently mistaken for Hrithik Roshan, and that makes him optimistic. When we met earlier that morning, he announced that he'd been promised a role in an upcoming feature starring Twinkle Khanna. Isn't that Rajesh Khanna's daughter, I asked, impressed.

Naneeji always had high hopes for Arun. Toward the end of her life she consoled me by saying that even though I was get-ting into middle age, I could still marry an old, rich man, like my mother had done, and produce a handsome and talented boy like Arun. I'd have to hurry though.

When Mummy called me with the news of her bereavement, she said that they would hold the Colonel's body until I came home. But why, I asked, nonplussed. They were holding the body anyway, she corrected, for one of the Colonel's sons who lived in America, so I would be in time if I came. I had no intention of coming to India that summer, but I heard the need in her voice, and I did. It's been births and deaths that have held Mummy and me together over the years. I call her on her birthday every year, no matter where I am. I called her when I heard there was a severe earthquake in her region. She calls me on my birthday every October, and on 9/11, she managed to get through to New York to see if I was okay. I had visited Arun only last year in Mumbai when his son was born, armed with a stroller, a car seat, and stuffed Disney toys that the baby ignored. But here I am again, sooner than I'd thought.

I wonder why they don't close the Colonel's mouth. Perhaps dentures don't burn well, and they'd opened his mouth to remove them and couldn't get it shut again. Then I have my answer: the priest pauses with his chanting and summons my mother. She reluctantly releases my hand and goes to him. He offers her a plateful of puffed rice and instructs her to place some in the Colonel's mouth. Mummy shivers but does as she is told. With Daddy, it had been easier, as there had been nothing to look at except the tricolor. The priest tells my mother to remove her wedding pendant and to place it around the Colonel's neck. Mummy hesitates, but the thugs are standing guard, and she removes her necklace and places it clumsily among the flowers.

The reading of the scriptures has come to an end. The priest rises to his feet and announces that it is time for the Colonel's journey. The thugs lift the stretcher at the head. Arun is a little late in following; the Colonel lurches, and for a second I fear the worst. Then they are up and out of the house. The mourners sing the Lord's name, and Mummy and I stand in the doorway and watch them go. Still she does not cry.

A little later, when we are alone, she turns to me and says, "Sweta, I have written you a letter. Actually," she laughs her nervous laugh, "I have been writing it for a very long time. It has been my way of speaking to you." She is quite calm. "Now that this is all over, I can give it to you."

A LETTER TO MY DAUGHTER (CONCLUDED)

I will tell you a story. There was a time when we were poor, very poor. I was four years old and your aunt was only two. We were so poor that we lived in a slum. We didn't even have the whole room to ourselves. The room was partitioned and on the other side was a family of six. A drunkard father, a mother who screamed all day, and four small children—two as big as myself, and Indu, a girl who was a few years older, maybe ten, and a newborn baby. The girl always wanted to play with us, take care of us, but Amma would never let her. She was dirty and ragged, and we were different, of superior stock, Amma said. Well, it seems that Abba used to help this family out whenever he could. When he bought sweets for us, he bought those poor, miserable children some sweets too. When their father drank up all the money and they had no food, Abba gave the family some of our rice. Of course Amma did not know this. She would not have allowed it.

Sweta, I do not remember any of this. I was too little then, and if that ten-year-old-girl hadn't told me the story herself, I would not have known. But you see, she came around to see me a few years ago when your Nanee died. Of course, she is a grown woman now. She had heard of Amma's death and felt she could see me now and tell me everything. She is someone you know well.

There were so many things that I understood only after she came to see me. You have carried the dark secret all these years, my darling, and in protecting us from it, how deeply you have hurt yourself. And you have hated your Nanaji, whom you have protected the most. I have written and torn up maybe ten pages in trying to understand how to write this to you. I have to tell you that you are no longer alone. I have to tell you that I know what you know, and now, between us, we can put it to rest.

You judge harshly, Sweta. That is probably your biggest fault. You have always judged me, and you have judged your Nana. You must know better than anyone else how unhappy he was. Well, she told me all this when she came to see me. She was in a terrible state. She told me that he had killed himself because of what you had seen. At first I thought she was mad. I refused to hear anything she said. I was so ashamed! I told her to get out of my house. But she kept talking and crying, talking and crying. She told me so many sad, terrible things about Amma and Abba and their life together. Sweta, I never would listen when you tried to tell me. I am sorry. There are many things for which I am deeply sorry. Ratna told me she had brought him only happiness. She told me he was her destiny. He had saved her when she was a child; he had saved her whole family when they lived on the other side of the partition. She told me how Abba had always helped them out, and how even Amma, before she left, had given her a whole rupee. She bought a doll with it, she said, the only toy she ever owned. She used to hide her face in that doll when things happened in the room that she didn't want to see. When her father sold off her mother, and she was forced to sleep with different men in that room, a little girl hid her face in a doll. Oh Sweta, life can be very cruel. We cannot judge what we don't know.

I have written so many pages and have torn them up, one by one. But she wants you to know this. Tell Babyji to forgive Ratna, she said. Tell her to forgive her Nanaji for he never did anything wrong. That's why she came all the way to see me, distraught and crazy as she was. She had come looking for you too, long ago, but Amma had told her you were gone to America. She said that until you knew, his soul would not rest in the wind or the waves. Those were her words, my dear. She has given me the courage to write to you.

It seems they go back a long way, Sweta. Abba stayed in touch with that destitute family even after we moved out of the chawl. He tried to save the girl from sharing her mother's fate as her father would surely have sold her off as well. He arranged her marriage and got her husband a government job. Then he gave them the quarter. They were good people, and with the little they had, they helped out the rest of her family, her younger sisters and brother.

She said that one day she found Baba weeping in his study. It seems that Amma had locked him up and left the house and she is the one who found him. She could not bear it, she said, and she went to him. She sought him out and she gave him some happiness. He was her destiny, she said.

Sweta, who are we to judge? I didn't want to hear it, any of it. But now I cannot forget her words. I have struggled with it for many many months. I have learned to accept. I cannot forget that woman. I think only of her courage. To tell me such a thing to clear his name! It must be love, Sweta. That is all it can be. We have to understand the power of love.

It is she who has given me the courage to write to you. Last year, when you came to see Arun's child, I tried to speak to you, but you are so forbidding, my dear.

There is much to be done with the funeral arrangements. Yet, in the middle of the night, these words tumble out of me. I am free at last. And for the first time I am no longer scared to be free. Tomorrow I will see you and I will give you this. I will give you years and years of letters, thirty long pages after thirty years of silence. It has been my way of speaking to you. Maybe you will read these pages, and there will still be time.

—〰—

The curtains are drawn. They have covered up the room to save it from the light. The room has always been dark and dank. It is the forgotten room that nobody uses. On Thursday afternoons, the room changes. I do not know how long it has been changing in this way. Their clothes are folded neatly and lie on the empty chair. This is not an act of violation or of unbridled passion. Each has undressed fully, and his clothes and hers are neatly folded. She is the one who has folded them, she who washes them, who whips and thrashes them spotless, who soothes them gently on the ironing board. She has placed his on the chair and then placed hers next to his. He has handed her his glasses, and she has placed them next to his clothes on the chair.

She lies on top of him. That is why I almost do not see him at first. It is not he who pins her down, but she. Her dark, sinewy arm lifts his head and feeds it firmly to her breast. Her hair is long and it falls over them both. It lifts with terror when I enter. For a second I do not recognize her because of the hair which she has always worn tied up, which I have never known to be beautiful.

I stand there and rip the image apart. He blinks into the light and fumbles for his glasses. She screams and covers herself with her hair. I turn and run.

When that image has refused to go away, I have looked it directly in the face. I too have learned not to be afraid anymore. I have looked at it so deeply that it has become familiar, like a friend.

—〰—

I've bought my ticket for Kathgodam. This is the first summer that I will be spending in India in twenty-five years, apart from the brief visit last year when the Colonel died. Mummy, who has been taking driving lessons, will come and receive me at the railway station and we'll drive back to Kaushani together. She is both excited and nervous. She asks me on the phone if I would prefer that she bring a driver. Driving in the hills can be very dangerous, she adds. No, Mum, I assure her. I want to drive back with you, alone. I want to spend the summer with you, alone. And then, perhaps, you can teach me to drive too. Nobody has succeeded thus far.

I've read and reread Mummy's letters and have wept over them without shame. Thirty long pages, she called them, after thirty years of silence. A little girl trips and falls, and her prisoners fall out of her. There is literature and music in the world, and inside her, the girl finds her very own voice. It is not the borrowed voice she has been carrying inside for so long. This is the story that I will tell Arun's son.

I've paid a little more attention to my appearance tonight. I've bought Anamika a bunch of tuberoses. In the past, I've always brought her wine or books, never flowers.

She hugs me tightly, tells me she absolutely adores the scent of Rajnigandha and goes off to arrange them in a vase. She pours out glasses of Old Monk and coke and we go out onto her terrace. It's a warm and lovely night, and if you look long enough, there's almost the hint of a star. "Rained last night just for you," she says. "I thought you'd never spend a summer in India."

"Well, it's cooler up in the hills. I leave for Kaushani in two days. Maybe you can come and visit us there? I've told Mum so much about my old schoolteacher. She wants to meet you."

"Oh no, I don't think so," she says, and my heart sinks. "What I mean is," she quickly adds, "I don't think this is the right time. You need to spend some time together." She lights a cigarette.

"Don't tell me you've started again. I thought you'd given up."

"Lasted all of five days. How is she?"

"Mum? Oh, she's great. She's never been better. She's even got herself an Internet connection and is already on e-mail! She picks up stuff so quickly. We write to each other almost every day now."

But I'm not here to talk about Mummy. I tell her that Gayle and I have finally broken up. "I'm sorry," she says.

"Well, I'm not. It never did work between us, but I couldn't get out of it. I suffer from this guilt thing and get paralyzed. She's always been so good to me."

She nods and looks uneasy.

"Does your mother know . . . ? About you, I mean?"

"No. But I'm going to tell her this time. Mum . . . she can handle it." My laugh sounds strange to my ears.

"So what made you do it at last?" she says with calm deliberation.

Here is the moment I've been waiting for.

"I don't know. Everything changed. Mum wrote me a letter after her husband died. It seems she has been writing it for years, but never had the courage to mail it to me. When I read it, I felt like a curse had lifted. I'd lost so much time, I couldn't bear to lose more."

She waits, but I've lost the courage to continue. We talk some more about Mummy. An awkwardness grows unrepentant and she goes back into the kitchen to warm up the *biryani* and kebabs she's picked up from some neighboring joint.

We eat on her terrace. She tells me about her upcoming re-tirement and how she is looking forward to all the free time when she can study Urdu and enroll in pottery classes. I tell her I'm up for a sabbatical next year and am thinking of spending it in India. She says nothing. The distance between us has widened and taken the shape of something unsaid. She says she needs an early night, she has to teach the next day. So while she is asking me to leave, and I'm still staring up at the sky, and the timing is completely wrong, I miserably blurt it out. The way I feel about her, the way I have always felt about her from the moment she walked into the classroom. I tell her why it cannot work with Gayle or any-one else. I cannot bear to look at her, but I tell her that for the very first time I've started to believe in destiny.

When finally she speaks, her voicc is sad. "I haven't been very honest with you, I'm afraid. There is something you should know about your father. And me."

I turn to look at her, and she looks very old. It ends up being a long night.

Anamika sees me off at the platform. She hasn't intended to, but she does, anyway. Anamika. I hear my father's voice, bid-ding farewell. No, she corrects me. He always called me Anu, never Anamika. This is different.

I've told her about that moment between Daddy and me. He throws me in the air and catches me as I fall. There's a rush of laughter, of sunlight, a fear of falling, a delicious knowing that he will not let me fall. The first time I had that memory, I looked everywhere for the corresponding photograph. You see, every memory I have of him comes from a photograph. So I looked through all the albums, all the old shoe boxes, but I couldn't find it anywhere, that photograph. It didn't exist! At first I cried. Had it happened at all, or had I made it up? And then I realized it was mine alone, that moment. It was mine and Daddy's, it had no witnesses. Whatever she tells me now, she cannot take that moment away.

My anger is intense, my jealousy, insane. She refuses to show me his letters. Then she reads parts out loud but refuses to read the rest. She considers my curiosity morbid. These are things no daughter should know of her father, she says. You are being unnatural, she says. Unnatural? What's natural about any of this? When my father does not visit me on birthdays, when he does not smell bad in the mornings, when he does not become fat or old or wrinkled, when his hair does not gray, when he does not break his ankle in a fall, when he does not have difficulty urinating at night because of an enlarged prostate, what's natural about that, then? Daddy is young and tall, and oh, so handsome. Daddy is a uniform, a smile, a wave of the hand. Daddy is younger than I am, is that not strange? I go searching for Daddy and I find you. I come searching for you, and I find him. How can this be? I have erotic fantasies of you and me. I have had them for a long time, and now, they are fantasies of you and him. There is nothing natural about this.

Perhaps, she says, we should not see each other again. Perhaps, I shrug. But she sees me off at the station, nevertheless. The train pulls out toward the pinpoint in the distance where my future glimmers with possibility.

AFTERWORD

While the characters in this novel are entirely fictitious, I have attempted to be true to the history of the time in spirit and incident. Several historical sources were consulted in the writing of this book. Among published works, I am particularly indebted to:

The Collected Works of Mahatma Gandhi. Publications Division, Ministry of Information and Broadcasting, Government of India (1958);

Francis G. Hutchins, *India's Revolution: Gandhi and the Quit India Movement.* Cambridge: Harvard University Press (1973);

John Fricker, *Battle for Pakistan.* Shepperton, Surrey: Ian Allen Limited (1979);

Christiane Desroches-Noblecourt, *Tutankhamen: Life and Death of a Pharaoh.* The New York Graphic Society (1963).

I am grateful to the collections of the British Library, the National Archives of India, the New York Public Library, and the libraries of Columbia and New York Universities where I conducted my research. For details of aerial combat, I am indebted to Fricker's excellent book and my conversations with Retired Air

Commodore Pritam Singh. Pat painstakingly explained combat maneuvers to me, until I (who have little head for such matters) "got" it. Thanks go to Retired Captain Sailesh Ranjan Debgupta for taking me on a virtual journey of the National Defense Academy of the fifties.

I am deeply indebted to my friends who took the trouble of reading the first draft and have contributed significantly to the novel in its present form. I thank Freny Khodaiji, Srirupa Roy, Anjali Singh, and Thom Powers. I thank Joe Sacco for his inspiration and his incredibly sensitive and careful reading. I thank my brother, Lalit Vachani, for all his nitpicking, which has made this so much a better book. I thank Siddharth Dube, for giving me home and hearth, and the heart to write. I thank my parents, Nand and Mira Vachani, for their unstinting support at all times; Dad, for spotting the odd error when all others had failed. I thank Corinna Barsan, my editor at Other Press, for her insightful comments that have made working with her such a pleasure. I thank my agent Sarah (Stalwart) Chalfant for refusing to give up, and my remarkable publisher, Judith Gurewich, who stakes out fiercely for what she believes. And there are no words, indeed, to thank Debraj Ray, my partner in life, and staunchest and most unflinching critic. I owe him the title of the book, I owe him the audacity to write, I owe him the highs and the lows of the last so many years. This book is as much his as mine.

A HISTORICAL APPENDIX TO HOMESPUN

"My Aruna, my Kasturba, my Sarojini" (page 8): The young and idealistic Nanaji, in his quest for the perfect bride, valorizes "Aruna, Kasturba, Sarojini." The reference is to Aruna Asaf Ali (1908–1996), Kasturba Gandhi (1869–1944), and Sarojini Naidu (1879–1949), prominent women leaders in India's struggle for independence against British rule. **Aruna Asaf Ali** was an active participant in Mohandas Karamchand Gandhi's salt march of 1930 and was imprisoned on several occasions for her public speeches and protests. Her anti-war speech of 1941 (page 36) becomes the immediate impetus for Nanaji taking that bold step himself. Ms. Asaf Ali continued to be active during the Quit India Movement, presiding over the hoisting of the Indian flag in Gowalia Tank Maidan in Bombay. This was on August 8, 1942, when Gandhi made his famous "do or die" speech (page 49) and officially launched the movement that demanded the end of British rule in India.

Kasturba Gandhi was an unusual freedom fighter, as in many instances she did not endorse her famous husband's views. On the contrary, she suffered greatly under the severe injunctions he imposed upon her. Yet Kasturba never left Mahatma Gandhi's side, remaining committed to his cause and frequently going to jail with him. She is reported to have kept her spirits alive during incarceration by playing rounds of carrom, in which she was indisputably a master, an activity in which one is hard pressed to imagine her husband's participation. In his memoirs, Gandhi writes with characteristic honesty about his often turbulent relationship with his wife, her distress at his forcible confiscation of the gifts and ornaments she received from an adoring public, and his insistence that she give them away. Gandhi's wife was forced to clean the public toilets at the ashram at Wardha, a task reserved for "untouchables" by the rules of Hindu casteism. Gandhi replaced the opprobrious word "untouchable" with "*harijan*" or the son of God, and instructed Kasturba to clean toilets like everyone else in order to give respectability to the task (page 49).

Sarojini Naidu, the poetess, who was affectionately called "the nightingale of India," was a feminist and a social reformer, a close friend and associate of Mahatma Gandhi. She was the first woman to become president of the Indian National Congress, in 1925. She marched alongside Gandhi in the Dandi salt march, and was imprisoned five times by the British, including a period of twenty-one months during the Quit India Movement. After India won independence, she was the first woman to be appointed governor of a state, the state of Uttar Pradesh.

Naneeji's name, "Kaushalya," means "one who is skillful." In the Hindu epic, the *Ramayana*, King Dashratha's first wife, the serene and steadfast queen mother, is also named Kaushalya.

Satyagraha (page 33): Gandhi's method of revolt was entirely novel. His *satyagraha* or "adherence to truth" method was based on the principle of nonviolence and passive resistance. In Gandhi's view, satyagraha was "the only road" to achieve *swaraj* or total independence. While *ahimsa* or nonviolence was its driving force, noncooperation was the principal action. In Gandhi's view,

> *the Government cannot exercise control over us without our cooperation.*

His method, therefore, was one of polite refusal. Do not cooperate. Do not join the police force or the army. Do not pay taxes. Do not wear western clothes. Do not retaliate violently. If they beat you or take away your land and assets, bear the punishment cheerfully.

> *Real suffering bravely borne melts even a heart of stone . . . there lies the key to Satyagraha.*

"Our Weapons are different, Mr. Gandhi, but one of us must finally win."

"Battle of Textile" (page 10): The tussle over clothing between Nanaji and Naneeji is symbolic of the struggle at the national level. The export of fine Indian muslin and silk in the seventeenth and early eighteenth centuries had seriously threatened European textile industries. The East India Company, acting on behalf of the Crown, imposed tariffs and trade restrictions on Indian cloth that eventually crippled textile production in India. The vacuum that was created was conveniently filled by the export of textile goods from England and elsewhere. Instead of the lucrative supplier it had once been, India now served as a market for Manchester cloth. Raw materials were exported from India at very low prices, and were manufactured in England and returned to India for resale. The fictional B.L. Ahuja, as a franchise-holder of British mill cloth in India, prospers sufficiently to diversify into movie production (page 17).

Swadeshi (page 10): Nanaji, modeling himself on Gandhi in every way, attempts to make Naneeji part with her silks but with disastrous consequences. Finally, he pleads with her that if she must wear silk, she should ensure it is *swadeshi* silk. Swadeshi (homegrown) or khadi silk as it was called, was hand woven and hand spun using indigenous silk yarn available in very few places in India and was therefore exorbitantly priced. In addition, Gandhi's belief in nonviolence had to be taken into account when it came to sericulture. Manufacturing silk resulted in the destruction of the silkworm, and less violent methods had to be considered in the production of swadeshi silk, all adding to its expense. Nanaji's impracticality is a reflection of the deeper irony inherent in Gandhi's textile war with England. As Sarojini Naidu is said to have remarked, it cost a great deal of money to keep Gandhi in poverty. (For more on the subject, see Emma Tarlo, *Clothing Matters*, University of Chicago Press, 1996.)

Dhanush takli (page 28): Gandhi's famous spinning wheel was the iconic representation of his philosophy of satyagraha and India's struggle against British rule. With the ideal of creating an economically self-sufficient, egalitarian, craft-based society, Gandhi adopted *khadi*, or homespun, as his vehicle of rebellion. Until 1915 khadi cotton was hand woven in India from machine-spun yarn. Gandhi insisted on "pure" khadi where the cotton was both hand spun and hand woven. Ironically, the coarse and uncomfortable material that resulted was labor intensive, required substantially more time to produce, and was economically far less viable than imported mill-made fabrics. It was hardly a solution for India's poor. Intended as it was to obliterate all outward distinctions between rich and poor and offer a commonality of ideology and purpose, the discourse surrounding homespun was rife with irony. Though considered poor man's clothing, it was only afforded by the rich. Besides, there were many variations in the homespun available in the country. Finely spun and woven khadi was considered a luxury item, no less than the finest muslin from Dacca.

THE SHIRTED AND THE SHIRTLESS

Nanga fakir (page 13): Naneeji refers to Winston Churchill's famous comment made in Epping on February 23, 1931.

It is alarming and also nauseating to see Mr. Gandhi, a seditious middle temple lawyer, now posing as a fakir of a type well known in the East, striding half-naked up the steps of the viceregal palace, while he is still organizing and conducting a defiant campaign of civil disobedience, to parley on equal terms with the representative of the king-emperor.

Churchill and Gandhi finally met in London during the Round Table Conference later that year. Gandhi, obdurate as ever, and undaunted by the cold, refused to wear anything but his loincloth, wearing it even to his meeting with King George V in Buckingham Palace. The king had initially been reluctant to meet the "little man (with) no proper clothes on and bare knees," but did eventually send Gandhi an invitation that made no specific requirements of dress. In the meeting that followed, according to Viscount Templwood, Gandhi was beautifully polite, though the king looked "resentfully" at his knees the entire time. (Templewood, *Nine Troubled Years*, London: Collins, 1954.) Later, when pointedly asked by the press if he had been adequately dressed for the occasion, Gandhi is said to have quipped,

"The king had enough on for both of us."

"One day, while going through Nanaji's pockets, she came across a piece of uneven cloth, one-and-a-half feet by two feet, loosely woven, edges undone." (page 12): Interestingly enough, another of Gandhi's random homespuns was gifted to none less than the Queen of England.

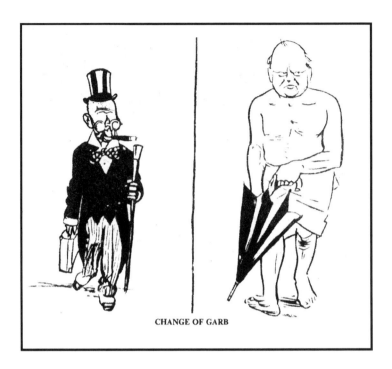

CHANGE OF GARB

Queen Elizabeth II's sixtieth wedding anniversary in 2007 coincides with India's sixtieth year of independence. In a public exhibition, the couple's wedding gifts received in 1947 are on display in Buckingham Palace. Among them is a piece of coarse cloth, frayed and yellowed, about 12" x 24", and of no apparent use, that is reputed to have been spun and woven by Mahatma Gandhi himself. The dowager Queen Mary had found the gift "rather vulgar" and had tucked it away from public view. It is displayed for the first time alongside other and more predictable gifts from India: a nineteenth-century ivory table of exquisite workmanship from the Maharaja of Patiala and a platinum and diamond necklace from the *nizam* of Hyderabad (reported in the *Times of India*, July 28, 2007).

"They flogged me publicly, twenty-four times on the bare buttocks." (page 32): Nanaji recalls that the greatest "discourtesy" he suffered was the whipping he received while serving a prison sentence. Political prisoners were frequently flogged in Indian prisons by order of the British Jailor. In response to parliamentary questions raised in England on the alleged whipping of 22,400 civilians in India, including women and children, in the years 1941–42, the Secretary of State for India, L.S. Amery, gave the following reply:

> *Whipping is a penalty long used in India and the enactments regarding it were consolidated in the Whipping Act of 1909 which applied throughout the whole of India and authorised whipping as an optional punishment for certain offences— theft and housebreaking, rape or unnatural offences, robbery with violence and dacoity.*

Apparently no distinction was made between ordinary criminals and political prisoners. The whipping prescribed was as follows:

> *. . . The Bombay Jail Manual (which may be taken as typical of Indian practice) provides for infliction with a light rattan cane of half inch diameter on the bare buttocks covered with a thin cloth soaked in antiseptic solution. The drawing stroke is forbidden and whipping is not to be executed in installments. The Super or Medical officer or medical subordinate must be present. The maximum punishment is 30 stripes for adults, 15 for juveniles. The punishment is sparingly used and is not applicable to the non-violent protestor. Only 1200 or so have been whipped and we have no information on the numbers of women and children. In such severe situations, the use of this method is perfectly justified, and the lives of many have been preserved as a consequence.*

(For more on the widespread practice of whipping in the years 1939–1941, see India Office Library's Public and Judicial department records.)

"Among the first luminaries selected to offer satyagraha was Vinoba Bhave and Naneeji's favorite, Jawaharlal Nehru." (page 33): Because of the value Gandhi placed on spinning, it was dedicated spinners alone who were selected to offer *satyagraha* or "truthful struggle." The provincial congress committees compiled lists of satyagraha volunteers, then sent them on to Gandhi, who made the decisions himself, based on their spinning records and other charitable works. Nanaji increases his daily spinning and maintains a log of his other good deeds in the hope that he will be selected, and this does indeed happen in April 1941, six months after individual civil disobedience first began. **Vinoba Bhave**, the great spiritualist and Gandhian, was unknown nationally until Gandhi selected him to be the first satyagrahi on October 17, 1940. Bhave had been corresponding with Gandhi for several years prior to this event. He was so influenced by Gandhi's ideals that he supported himself by spinning alone in a village just outside the Gandhi ashram at Wardha. Later he was to mastermind the Bhoodan movement of land redistribution in independent India where he traversed the country on foot, appealing to landlords to accept him as a son and donate land, which he then passed on to the landless poor.

Jawaharlal Nehru (1889–1964), who was to become free India's first prime minister, was selected by Gandhi to follow Vinoba Bhave on November 7, 1940, as the second satyagrahi. However, he was arrested on October 31 and sentenced to four years' imprisonment for his anti-war speeches made earlier that month. Hutchins, in his book, *India's Revolution: Gandhi and the Quit India Movement*, mentions a third satyagrahi, an "ordinary villager" by the name of Brahma Dutt Sharma. This unknown villager is a source of great inspiration to the fictional Nanaji, giving him the necessary impetus to resign from his government job and dedicate himself to peaceful protest (page 33).

Gandhi's assassination (page 278): Mahatma Gandhi was assassinated by Nathuram Godse, a member of the Hindu Mahasabha, a fundamentalist organization that believed Gandhi had made far too many concessions to the country's Muslim population and had only spearheaded the demand for Pakistan. On January 30, 1948, while Gandhi approached the rostrum to address a public gathering at Birla House, Delhi, he was shot three times by Godse at point-blank range. There had been five previous attempts on his life, but Prime Minister Nehru's government had been unable to convince him to accept armed escorts. Gandhi was well aware of the danger to his life. Two days before the assassination he said,

> *If I am to die by the bullet of a mad man, I must do so smiling.*
> *There must be no anger within me. God must be in my heart*
> *and on my lips.*

Producer B.L. Ahuja unwittingly echoes the words that will be Gandhi's last, *"Hai Ram"* or "Dear God" (page 50).

Jai Prakash (page 50): A disciple of Mahatma Gandhi, Jai Prakash Narain (1902–1979) disagreed with him eventually on the role of nonviolence and advocated armed revolt as the only effective method of expelling the British from India. Jai Prakash, or JP as the charismatic leader was called, was frustrated by the restrictions that Gandhi imposed on India's struggle for freedom. Gandhi never allowed satyagraha to turn into a mass movement, always choosing specific individuals, venues, and slogans that remained on the whole extremely considerate of British rule and were designed only to attack India's participation in World War II, which he disagreed with on account of his long-standing belief in nonviolence. According to the rules Gandhi had laid down, the satyagrahi or protestor had to inform the district magistrate in advance of the date, time, and venue of the protest (page 35), leading, in most cases, to arrest and rigorous imprisonment under the Defense of India Rules. Apart from arresting the protester, the government levied fines and, if payment was not forthcoming, confiscated land and assets. In this way the war fund was increased rather than decreased. Jai Prakash questioned the wisdom of this approach and espoused a mass upsurgence that did not rule out violence. JP's radical views, written and circulated as the "Jai Prakash papers," made a deep impression on Indian revolutionaries, and Nanaji, in *HomeSpun*, is so fired up by them that his allegiance temporarily shifts away from Gandhi. Gandhi's famous "Quit India" speech made on August 8, 1942, twenty-two months after the individual satyagraha movement first began, was considered a bold departure from his earlier reticence and was hailed as such by Nanaji and other revolutionaries.

"Swaraj (Independence) *is my birthright and I will have it."* (page 50): Now famous words, spoken by Bal Gangadhar Tilak (1856–1920). Prior to Gandhi's arrival from South Africa, Tilak was India's foremost revolutionary. Unlike Gandhi, Tilak's approach was hard-core militant. Following a split in the Congress in 1906, *Lokmanya* (or "Beloved of the People") Tilak headed its extremist faction. He was the first to demand complete self-rule and formed the Home Rule League in 1916 with Anne Besant and Muhammad Ali Jinnah. A Hindu nationalist at core, he evoked Hindu scripture as a way of justifying military violence against the British.

Radhe Shyam Sharma (page 58): Hutchins has a fascinating account of Radhe Shyam Sharma, the chemistry professor of Benares Hindu University who was prominent in the underground movement of Quit India. After staging a revolt on campus on August 9, 1942, Professor Sharma escaped with a bounty of 5,000 rupees on his head, walking seventy miles to Allahabad "with the shaven head and saffron robes of a *sadhu.*" From Allahabad he moved to Gwalior and then to Delhi, where he became a specialist in the manufacture of explosives. He was finally arrested on December 31, 1942, after having escaped detection over a period of months with rapid identity transformations "from *sadhu* to *maulana,*" and "by shifting daily between twenty-five separate residences." (Francis G. Hutchins, *India's Revolution: Gandhi and the Quit India Movement,* Cambridge: Harvard University Press, 1973.) Nanaji is one of his accomplices in Delhi.

Muslim League, the demand for Pakistan and the Partition of India (page 54): Muslims constituted about twenty-three percent of British India's population in the colonial era. After its formation in 1885, the Indian National Congress had remained largely unsuccessful in involving the Muslim community in the struggle for independence. Muslims viewed the Congress as a Hindu-dominated party that would never represent its interests. The All India Muslim League was founded in 1906 to specifically address the religious, cultural, and educational needs of India's Muslims. At that point it had no other political agenda. The demand for a separate Muslim state in India was first made in 1930. Known as the "two-nation theory," the contention was that Hindus and Muslims had irreconcilable differences, and the minority community would never be allowed to live in peace and prosperity alongside the majority. This view, fed by Britain's "divide and rule" policy, was fully exploited for political leverage and ultimately led to the partition of the country and the creation of Pakistan in 1947.

The two-state solution had consistently been rejected by Congress leaders who favored a united, secular, and democratic

India. The Congress had offered the Muslim electorate a one-fourth representation in the proposed legislature of a free India, but this was rejected by Jinnah and the League, who insisted on a one-third representation. By 1946, with its disastrous war debt, the British had neither the political will nor the financial and military power to maintain India in subjugation. Unable to reach any agreement between the Congress and the Muslim League, the last British viceroy, Lord Mountbatten, presided over the partition of India. A bloodbath ensued in territories where populations were mixed, and large-scale migrations of people divested of homes and belongings, and cultural and kinship ties, were inevitable. The unmitigated violence that was a consequence of India's partition is the "madness" of which Nanaji speaks in his final entry in his diary (page 278).

"Long years ago we made a tryst with destiny ..."
(page 81): This was the historic address made by Jawaharlal Nehru to the Constituent Assembly of India "at the stroke of the midnight hour" that heralded Indian independence on the fifteenth of August, 1947. Nehru was acknowledged to be a great orator, and this is considered to be his finest speech:

Long years ago we made a tryst with destiny and now the time comes when we shall redeem our pledge, not wholly or in full measure, but very substantially. At the stroke of the midnight hour, when the world sleeps, India will awake to life and freedom. A moment comes, which comes but rarely in history, when we step out from the old to the new, when an age ends, and when the soul of a nation, long suppressed, finds utterance. It is fitting that at this solemn moment we take the pledge of dedication to the service of India and her people and to the still larger cause of humanity.

"Even with his death, he spreads the message of peace." (page 279): The riots that followed the partition of India left close to one million dead and eleven million homeless. When India gained independence, Gandhi did not rejoice. In the last two years of his life, he distanced himself from Congress leaders and governance and attempted instead to quell the wave of violence that had overtaken the country. He walked from village to village in riot-torn Noakhali (in present-day Bangladesh, where Hindus were being killed in retaliation for the killing of Muslims in Bihar) to spread his message of peace. In Calcutta, where fighting between Hindus and Muslims was ferocious, he became, in Mountbatten's words, a "one-man boundary force" between the warring communities.

Nanaji refers to the Hindu and Sikh refugees from Pakistan, whose tales of horror had resulted in reprisals and violence against Muslims in Delhi. In an attempt to put an end to the killings in Delhi, Gandhi began his last fast unto death on January 13, 1948. He lifted the fast only when representatives of all three religious communities signed a pledge promising peace. It was the shock of Gandhi's assassination that finally, in effect, put an end to the rioting.

Ashok Kumar (1911–2001) (page 26): A legendary actor of Indian cinema, Ashok Kumar's career spanned sixty years, beginning in 1936 with *Jeevan Naiya* (*Life Boat*) and *Achut Kanya* (*The "Untouchable" Maiden*). By the early 1940s, Ashok Kumar was already an established name, having played the lead opposite heroines like Devika Rani and Leela Chitnis. His blockbuster *Kismet* (*Fate*), like his fictitious *Soldier* of the same year, was the biggest box office success of the '40s. By the time of his death at the age of ninety, Ashok Kumar had acted in close to 300 films, with every character role to his credit.

Fearless Nadia (page 75): Born Mary Evans in Perth, Australia, she moved to India in 1913 at the age of five and changed her name to Nadia on the advice of a fortune teller. Trained in a circus as a child, with skills as diverse as riding, ballet, and archery, Nadia had a long and successful career in the cinema where the "adventure" or "stunt film" became her hallmark. With her blonde hair, blue eyes, and tight-fitting clothes, and the ability to electrify the screen with nerve-racking stunts that she pulled off on her own, Nadia provided edge-of-the-seat entertainment in the '30s, '40s, and early '50s. She carved herself a special niche as a heroine, neither chaste and submissive, nor sexually objectified vamp. Nadia's scintillating film presence is evident in films like *Hunterwali* (1935)*, Miss Frontier Mail* (1936), *Hurricane Hunsa* (1937), and *Diamond Queen* (1940). Master Bunty costars with her in the fictitious *Rider Rani* which, had it been made, would have done Fearless Nadia proud!

The spirit of the early studios and the nationalism that had begun to pervade the aesthetic imagination is depicted in Master Bunty's films, particularly the great and accidental success, *Soldier*. Director Vinayak Rao's *The Cabinet of Dr. Kothari* (page 70) is an ode both to Fritz Lang and V. Shantaram.

"He was born on a horse's back in Surrey" (page 107): The reference is to the last Royal Air Force chief of air staff in India, Air Marshal Sir Gerald Ernest Gibbs. He handed over charge in 1954 to Subroto Mukherjee, who became the first Indian Air Force chief of air staff.

Kashmir referendum (page 159): At the time of Britain's transfer of power to India and Pakistan, respectively, there were 565 princely states and colonial provinces that had to opt to join either country or choose independence. Sardar Vallabhbhai Patel, India's first home minister and deputy prime minister, was given the mammoth task of convincing the states and provinces to join a united India under a federal form of government. Using negotiations, diplomacy, and threat, when required, Patel enabled the accession of every state with a majority Hindu population into the Union of India. The three "problem" states were Junagadh, with an eighty percent Hindu majority but a Muslim ruler; Hyderabad, with a Muslim majority and a Muslim nizam but too geographically distant from Pakistan to unite with it (the nizam of Hyderabad therefore preferred independence); and Kashmir, where the situation was the reverse of Junagadh: a majority Muslim population but a Hindu Maharaja who preferred independence. Patel resorted to military force in these states. The nizam of Junagadh was overruled and a plebiscite was held that established the population's preference to merge with India. The nizam of Hyderabad was dissuaded from seeking independence and was made to sign the Act of Accession to India. The Hindu maharaja of Kashmir was also persuaded to join the Indian union under circumstances that are shrouded in controversy. Following the widespread unrest in Kashmir after its accession to India, Jawaharlal Nehru said on November 2, 1947,

> We have declared that the fate of Kashmir is ultimately to be decided by the people. That pledge we have given, and the Maharaja has supported it, not only to the people of Kashmir but the world, we will not, and cannot back out of it. We are prepared when peace and law and order have been established to have a referendum held under international auspices like the United Nations. We want it to be a fair and just reference to the people, and we shall accept their verdict. I can imagine no fairer and juster offer.

The referendum, despite being backed by a U.N. Security Council resolution, has never been held, on the grounds that the conditions for a plebiscite, namely "peace and law and order," were vitiated by Pakistan on account of its infiltration into Kashmir, and the new conditions thus created in the state do not allow for the possibility of a fair and just referendum.

Newspaper reports of the 1965 Indo-Pakistan war (pages 159, 163, 191–193, 195, 320): All newspaper headlines and reports quoted in *HomeSpun* are authentic except for Flight Lieutenant Kalra's obituary and Special Correspondent Anamika Reza's unpublished editorial.

A close comparison was undertaken of the daily reports covering the twenty-two-day war of 1965 in the *Times of India* published from Delhi and Calcutta, and the Pakistani newspaper *Dawn* published from Karachi. Jingoism and propaganda were evident in the reporting from both countries, but *Dawn* was inflammatory to the extreme. On its first page, *Dawn* ran a column entitled "Word of God" with quotations from the Quran. The following are examples of front-page quotes during the course of the war:

On September 10, 1965:

The Believers fight in the way of Allah and the Disbelievers fight in the way of the Devil. So fight against the friends of the Devil, certainly the struggle of the Devil is ever weak. (Al-Quran Part IV:76:7)

On September 12, 1965:

And kill them wherever you find them, and drive them out from where they drove you out, and persecution is worse than slaughter . . . such is the recumbence of the disbeliever. (Al-Quran, Part II 24:190–191)

Nilita Vachani

On September 14, 1965:

*Fight them: Allah will chastise them at your hands and bring
them to disgrace, and assist you against them, and relieve the
hearts of a believing people.*

(Al-Quran 9:14 Suratul Tauba, Rukoo 2, Ayat 14)

Dawn also ran a daily column entitled "The Price of Treachery,"
which ran Pakistan's "official" version of India's war losses. The
language in this column was anything but restrained. The following is from September 17, 1965:

> *The heavy price that India pays in men and material for
> its wanton aggression against Pakistan is vividly evident
> from the following figures released officially yesterday in
> Rawalpindi: Soldiers killed: 6889; Tanks destroyed: 387; Air-
> craft destroyed: 93.*

And here is a *Dawn* editorial from September 20:

> *By her perfidy and shameless resort to brute force, India,
> whose leaders had been dreaming about their country as-
> suming the leadership of the Afro-Asian world, today stands
> completely exposed and isolated as their cowardly aggres-
> sion against this country has clearly shown.*

**"Actually there was *one* article, and it was in your
paper . . ."** (page 212): The only honest piece of reporting, according to Anu, appeared in the *Statesman* on September 17,
1965. Written by "the military observer," it read,

> *If the claims hitherto made in successive communiqués were
> added up, it would be found that the tank and air forces of
> both India and Pakistan have been destroyed twice over:
> which of course they have not.*

The Keelors (page 213): The brothers Denzil and Trevor Keelor were both credited with destroying Pakistani Sabre aircraft in separate incidents during the '65 war and were awarded the Vir Chakra, making it the first time in aeronautical history in India that brothers were awarded for identical feats.

Sargodha attack, September 7, 1965 (pages 245, 260–261): India's first attack on Pakistani soil resulted in significant losses to its fleet, sufficient for the Pakistanis to honor the day ever since as "Air Force Day." The IAF planned and executed six strikes against Sargodha at different times that day involving a total of thirty-one aircraft. The PAF claimed a downing of ten aircraft, including five shot down by Squadron Leader Mohammad Alam (see John Fricker, *Battle for Pakistan*, Shepperton, Surrey: Ian Allen Ltd, 1979). Later, revisionist theories by Pushpinder Singh Chopra and Rakesh Koshy in India refuted this view and established the losses on the Indian side to be five aircraft. My fictional account of the events of that morning is a composite of two squadron attacks involving Hunters. While there is no similarity in the characterizations of the players involved or the events described, many details are derived from combat records of that morning. Of particular inspiration were the stories of Squadron Leader Ajjamada Boppayya Devayya, recipient of the Maha Vir Chakra, awarded posthumously twenty-three years after the event, and the untold story of Flight Lieutenant Tapan Kumar Chaudhuri, who was a child actor in the '40s and was killed in action on September 7, 1965. Flight Lieutenant T.K. Chaudhuri's obituary read, *"Tapan Kumar in his childhood had distinguished himself as a stage and cinema actor. He was then known as Master Minoo."* (*Statesman*, September 17, 1965)

"Vampires are obsolete, slow-moving aircraft." (page 246): The utilization of Vampires by Western Air Command on the first day of aerial warfare and the destruction of all four planes came into serious criticism, and Vampire aircraft were subsequently withdrawn.

"Thank you, Mr. X" (page 179): The Black Nationalist Islamic leader Malcolm X (1925–1965) made this speech at the London School of Economics on February 11, 1965, ten days before his assassination. A central theme of Malcolm X's talk was the U.S. intervention against the liberation forces in the Congo. The Congo had declared its independence from Belgium on June 30, 1960, and Patrice Lumumba who led the liberation struggle against Belgian colonialism, was elected the first Prime Minister of that country. The U.S. and its allies moved swiftly to destabilize the new government, backing a breakaway regime established by Moise Tshombe in the south. By late 1960 Lumumba had been deposed, and in early 1961 he was assassinated by Tshombe's U.S.-backed forces. In 1964 Tshombe was installed as prime minister. For several years Lumumba's followers waged a struggle against the imperialist forces but a combination of Belgian troops, paid mercenaries, and U.S. war planes contracted to the Tshombe regime crushed the popular uprising. Malcolm X said at the gathering called by LSE's Africa Society:

Imagine a murderer—not an ordinary murderer, a murderer of a prime minister, the murderer of the rightful prime minister of the Congo . . . the United States, the country that I come from, pays his salary. They openly admit that they pay his salary. And in saying this, I don't want you to think that I come here to make an anti-American speech. I wouldn't come here for that. I come here to make a speech, to tell you the truth. And if the truth is anti-American, then blame the truth, don't blame me.

Helen (page 255): The "cabaret queen" of Hindi cinema, born of a Burmese mother and Anglo-Indian father, played the sinuous and sexy "bad girl" roles of the '60s and early '70s that heroines refused to accept. Helen, the proverbial "guest star," provided scintillating dances, a tradition that continues in today's Bollywood as "item" numbers. She wore revealing clothes, drank alcohol and smoked cigarettes, and in the image of the thoroughly fallen "Western" vamp, was usually the unwedded consort of the film's villain.

Indira Gandhi and Emergency Powers (page 279): Indira Gandhi (1917–1984), the daughter of Jawaharlal Nehru, became India's first woman prime minister, serving for three consecutive terms from 1966 to 1977, and a fourth term from 1980 until her assassination by Sikh bodyguards in October 1984. In 1971 Indira Gandhi had won the electorate with her *Garibi Hatao* (Abolish Poverty) campaign, which, however, remained far from implemented. She had shown autocratic tendencies by using her parliamentary majority to amend the constitution twice and by imposing President's Rule on federal states on the grounds that their rule was lawless.

On June 12, 1975, Justice Sinha of the Allahbad High Court, in response to a petition filed by an opposition candidate, delivered the judgment that Indira Gandhi's election had been won by fraudulent means and was invalid. She was not to seek reelection or hold office for six years. Instead of resigning, Indira Gandhi appealed to the Supreme Court. The opposition parties called for her immediate resignation and dismissal. On June 25, Jaya Prakash Narayan (JP) called for a weeklong nationwide campaign of civil disobedience to remove Mrs. Gandhi from power. Without waiting for the Supreme Court's verdict, Indira Gandhi retaliated the next day by getting the president of India to declare a state of Internal Emergency under Article 352 of the constitution. The constitution had a provision for a national emergency "caused by war, external aggression or armed rebellion." Such an emergency had been declared in 1962 during the Indo-China war, and in 1965 and 1971 during the Indo-Pakistan wars. In 1975 Indira Gandhi invoked a National Emergency on the grounds that the country was "threatened by internal aggression." This unconstitutional act gave her the right to reserve extraordinary powers for herself and the Prime Minister's Council. All prominent members of the opposition who had opposed her rule, including JP, were imprisoned. President's Rule was imposed on the two non–Congress-ruled states of Gujrat and Tamil Nadu, bringing the entire country under her control. Police were granted powers to impose curfews and indefinitely detain citizens. All publications, including newspapers, were subject to substantial censorship by the Ministry of Information and Broadcasting. A campaign to stamp out dissent led to the widespread arrest and torture of political activists. The ruthless clearing of slums around Delhi left hundreds of thousands of people homeless or dead. The family planning program of compulsory sterilization was blatantly misused against India's rural poor. Fortunately for Nanaji, he had already retired from government "when Nehru's daughter went and became mad." (page 279)

"... a student of Jawaharlal Nehru University in South Delhi had been kidnapped from within the grounds of the campus ..."** (page 279–280): The Shah Commission, a commission of inquiry appointed by the Janata Party in 1977 to inquire into the excesses committed during the Emergency, discussed, among other cases, the kidnapping of JNU student Prabir

Purkayastha from outside the School of Languages on September 25, 1975. The intended recipient of the victimization was D.P. Tripathi, president of the Students' Union, who had instigated a boycott of classes as a means of protesting against the Emergency. Earlier that day he had apparently prevented Maneka Gandhi, Sanjay Gandhi's wife and Indira Gandhi's daughter-in-law, from attending classes. Despite this being a case of mistaken identity, Purkayastha was not released, and remained in jail for over a year. This was one among hundreds of cases of the government's violations of civil liberties during Emergency rule.